hit the ground

JULIA WOLF

More Books By Julia

MILE HIGH BILLIONAIRES

In The Details

By The Letter

To The Chase

The Kelly Ranch (small town romance)

See It Through

Hold The Line

Hit The Ground

The Harder They Fall (Billionaire office romance)

Dear Grumpy Boss

Sincerely, Your Inconvenient Wife

P.S. You're Intolerable
Not So Truly Yours

The Seasons Change (Rock star romance)
Falling In Reverse
Stone Cold Notes
Faded in Bloom
Where Waves Break

Savage U (college romance)
Soft Like Thunder
Bright Like Midnight
Sweet Like Poison
Real Like Daydreams

Savage Academy (academy romance)
Save One Thing
These Two Wrongs

Jump On Three

Blue is the Color (Rock star romance)
Times Like These
Watch Me Unravel
Such Great Heights
Under the Bridge

Unrequited (Rock star romance)
Unrequited
Misconception
Dissonance

Never Blue Duet (Angsty rock star romance)
Never Lasting
Never Again

Playlist

"Not With Haste" Mumford & Sons

"Falling" Florence & The Machine

"God Needs The Devil" Jonah Kagen

"Yellow Light" Of Monsters And Men

"Southern Star" Gregory Alan Isakov

"Asshole" The Lumineers

"I Will Wait" Mumford & Sons

"Hello My Old Heart" The Oh Hellos

"You Found Me" Waxahatchee

"In Dreams" Sierra Ferrell

"Years" Sierra Ferrell

"She Lit a Fire" Lord Huron

"Another Story" The Head and the Heart

"watch" Billie Eilish

"Deep End" Birdy

"Washing Machine Heart" Mitski

"Atlantis" Seafret

https://open.spotify.com/playlist/5eQxyFOPoS6OgX2CIog4Fg?si=16afd56e4dbe476b

Author's Note

Dear Lovely Reader,

Hit The Ground is a sweet and spicy romance, filled with small town, found family goodness. However, I would be remiss if I didn't tell you about the sensitive topics that are touched on within the story.

Some of the topics include:

-Past medical trauma

-Death of a sibling

-Attempted assault

-Mention of past sexual assault (side character)

Please treat yourself kindly when deciding whether to read this book.

xoxo,

Julia

Chapter One
Caleb

MIDMORNING, AND THE SUN was already high, beating down on the back of my neck like it was trying to teach me a lesson. Taking the bandanna out of my back pocket, I swiped my forehead and scraped back the loose strands that had escaped my hair tie, reminding me it was past time for a haircut.

I'd get to it eventually.

I scanned the horizon for my crew. A few were scattered close enough, making repairs on a section of fence in the distance. I swiveled my head, surveying the cattle nearby. A gust of icy wind struck my face, blasting the last of the sun's sweat clean off.

Spring came late to this corner of Wyoming, and it never came soft. The last patches of melting snow left soggy ground and slick rock, and the wind hadn't stopped blowing since February. After a lifetime here, the change in seasons didn't slow me down. Rain, snow, or shine, my responsibilities on the ranch were here, so I was too. Being put off by temperature was a waste of time. It was what it was, and we rolled with it.

I was out on the western ridge checking fences. This part of the ranch went on as far as the eye could see, made up of raw, open country scarred with granite and sage, the land more bone than skin. More cattle moved like shadows in the distance, dark specks grazing between patches of cheatgrass and sagebrush. A hawk circled overhead, across the wide blue sky.

The radio on my hip crackled to life, and Bill's voice came through.

"Caleb, think you'd better come back to the stables. Shelby's here. Says she needs to talk to you."

I frowned. Bill Eddings had been a hand on the ranch longer than I'd been alive. Not only did he know every corner of this land, he knew *me*—including my history with Shelby.

"What's she need?"

"Won't say. Seems real antsy," he replied.

"Ask her if it's about Jesse."

"Hang on."

My heart worked its way up my throat as I beelined to my vehicle.

The UTV started on the second try, engine reluctantly sputtering like it didn't want to make the trip either. I turned toward the heart of the ranch, tires grinding over loose stone and tufts of golden grass stubborn enough to grow in this unforgiving dirt.

Shelby showing up at the ranch couldn't have spelled anything good. As far as I remembered, it wasn't something she'd ever done. Hell, we might've shared a kid, but now that Jesse was thirteen, his mom and I only really saw each other in passing. Not much to discuss about a self-sufficient kid smarter than the both of us combined.

Just last week, he'd shown me a math problem with the same excitement I'd once gotten when I'd land a touchdown. The kid was teaching himself calculus from a book he'd checked out at the library. I didn't understand a word of it, yet I hung on every syllable. He never failed to fascinate me with the way his mind worked.

Bill's voice came through again. "Caleb, she says it's about Jesse, but it's not an emergency. She just needs to talk."

In the background, I heard Shelby say, "Tell him it's urgent."

I chuffed, annoyed at the interruption to my day, but relieved it wasn't an emergency. "I'm on my way."

"Got it."

I gripped the wheel tighter. The vehicle jolted over a rut, jarring my spine, but I didn't slow down. I had a lot to get done today. This would set me back who knew how long, so I intended to get it over with as quickly as possible.

Ten minutes later, the stables came into view. Long and low against the base of a hill, sunlight flared off the metal roof. Bill appeared first, coming toward me as I killed the engine and stepped out into the swirling dust.

He tipped his hat. "Sorry, Cay. I tried to tell her to call you, but she wouldn't hear it."

I shoved more of my hair back from my face. "Not your fault, Bill. You're not my social secretary, and she knows damn well she can call." I clapped his shoulder. "Don't worry about it. I appreciate you trying to run interference, but I'll take care of it."

He tipped his chin toward a row of SUVs and trucks. "She's waiting by her car. You shoulda seen her face when she walked into the stables. Girl acted like she's never been around a horse."

Laughing, I shook my head and moved toward Shelby's dusty silver SUV. As I approached, she climbed out and leaned against the door. Sunglasses on, she crossed her arms and tapped her foot like she had to display her impatience.

At least I knew what I was about to deal with.

"What's going on, Shel?" I asked as soon as I was within shouting distance.

Of course, she waited for me to be right in front of her to reply. "We need to talk about Jesse."

I stood three feet from her, lowering my chin to look her over. We'd had a casual thing off and on when we were teens and into our early twenties. One of those "on" times had resulted in Jesse.

We'd been co-parents all these years, and it'd been all right. Never too many conflicts or fights. Shelby was easygoing for the most part and a good mom to our boy. She was also a fine-looking woman, with her thick blonde hair, curves that looked good in a tight pair of jeans and, when she took those sunglasses off, bright-blue eyes that were nice to look into.

There'd been hope—and not just from her—we'd end up together. The pretty homecoming queen and heir to the Kelly ranch. There'd been a time she would've jumped if I'd said I wanted to do the whole family thing with her, but we weren't a real match, and we'd both moved on from each other.

"We need to talk...in the middle of my workday?" I groused.

"Yeah, Caleb. You're either working or busy. Not much time to sneak in a conversation that needs to be had."

"You could have called."

"I could have, but I didn't." She dropped her arms, sighing. "Sorry if I alarmed you by showing up here unannounced. Jesse's fine, all right? But I do need to talk about him—and you and me."

I frowned. "You and me? There's no you and me, Shel."

Her mouth puckered like that had tasted sour to her. But if she was trying to imply there was something between us, I'd missed a chapter or two. That was news to me.

"Cay…"

I canted my head. "Shel, I've got a list a mile long I need to get done. If Jesse's fine, I can't think of anything else we need to talk about. Clearly, you've got something on your mind, though, so how 'bout we get on with it?"

She took her time huffing, showing me how displeased she was with me. "I'm thinking about moving."

"Okay." I couldn't see what that had to do with me. Shel had lived in a couple different places over the years. As long as I had the address, it was none of my concern. "Why's that urgent?"

"Because I'm thinking about moving to Denver."

I did not hesitate. "Not with Jesse."

She flicked her hand out like this was a casual topic. "I'm not leaving my kid behind. Of course Jesse would come too. It's only a three-hour drive, so—"

"No." My hands balled into fists, and that wouldn't do, so I rested them on my hips. Getting mad over something that wasn't going to happen wasn't in my wheelhouse. "I'm shutting this down. You move to Denver, I'll work with you on making sure you see him, but you're not taking my boy."

She shoved her glasses to the top of her head, giving me those sky-blue eyes, and batted her lashes at me, like that'd have any effect.

"Nothing's set in stone. But I'd like you to really think about it before you fight me. I—"

I shook my head. "Not fighting you, Shel. It's not gonna happen. There's nothing to fight about."

She blew out a heavy, exasperated breath. "There's better opportunity in the city. I don't think I have to tell you Jesse is outgrowing the schools here. He needs—"

"Nope." My hands were balling again, so I tucked them into my pockets. "This conversation is finished."

I started to turn, and she scrambled toward me, her hand landing on my bicep. "It's not only Jesse who needs a bigger pond. There are a lot more jobs in Denver, and Kent has a lead there."

I stopped dead in my tracks. "So this is about your boyfriend, and not our son, right?" My jaw worked back and forth to keep my voice steady. "You've been dating this guy...what? A few months? And you wanna uproot your life and Jesse's for him? I thought you were smarter than that."

Her cheeks reddened, and not with embarrassment. No, I'd set her off, and I was about to get it.

"Six months," she hissed. "Kent and I are very serious, if you must know. And not everyone has been handed a cushy life on their family's ranch. He's had to work for everything he has."

I almost laughed. Sure, this land had belonged to my family for generations, and I was lucky as hell for what I had, but Shelby implying I didn't work my ass off had to be a joke. But I wasn't feeling particularly humorous, and she kept right on going.

"The job market in Sugar Brush is tiny. Kent has friends in Denver who'll put good words in for him at their companies if we move down there. And the schools are really good. Jesse will have access to—"

I put my hand up. "No. You and Kent want to move; have at it. Jesse isn't going, and I'm done with this line of conversation."

Her mouth flattened into a hard line. "Don't make this difficult, Caleb."

"It isn't difficult at all. Open and shut. It's done."

Groaning, she tossed her arms out to the side. "I'll have to talk to my lawyer then."

"You need to take a step back and realize what a bad idea this is."

"And you need to stop being so damn stubborn," she clipped.

It'd been said before, and maybe there was some truth to it. But when it came to my son, I wouldn't compromise. I already had to miss him on the weeks he lived with his mom. No way was I missing a single other second.

I tipped the bill of my hat. "Have a good day, Shelby."

She could linger in her anger all she wanted. I walked back to my vehicle, my mind already on the tasks I had to get through.

Chapter Two

Alice

I WAS DEEPLY FAMILIAR with paper. I spent my days in a world filled with it. Rows and rows, stacks and stacks. The scent of old books—made of dust and ink and paintings formed with words—was as close to home as I had found. I could tell the difference between a vintage encyclopedia and the soft weight of a new novel with the brush of my fingers. And when I rubbed them together just right, my nerve endings sparked with memory, like I could summon my favorite page of a book from thin air.

Paper had never been just paper to me. It was comfort. An escape. The one thing in my life that made the most sense.

Which was why the envelope felt so wrong.

It was heavier than paper had any right to be. Not the cardstock or thickness of what was inside, the ink itself. Like it had its own gravity. Like the words typed across the front had mass, giving it a foreign weight in my hands. As I pushed into Joy's Elbow Room for my shift, I clutched it close, holding it like it might slip free and cause a scene. Knowing my luck, that was exactly what would happen.

The door banged shut behind me. I ducked on instinct, but didn't drop the envelope. A few heads turned to look at me, but I was a familiar sight around here, so no one's stare lingered.

It was only five, and the bar was already half-full. Friday nights were always busy, and since Joy's drew in ranch hands whose days started with the rise of the sun, their drinking started early too.

A familiar country song played on the vintage jukebox, and the smell of beer, fried onions, and old wood hit me square in the face.

I never would have guessed I'd find comfort in this scent too, but the last four years I'd waitressed here as a second job, it had become as familiar as the library where I spent my days. My home away from home, in a weird, unexpected way.

Joy looked up from behind the bar, where she'd been wiping a sticky patch with the ferocity of someone personally offended by other people's fingerprints. But she always kind of looked like that.

When we first met, she'd scared the dickens out of me. But I quickly learned behind Joy's gruff, no-nonsense nature was a heart of gold.

"'Bout time you got here." She narrowed her dark eyes at me as I rounded the bar. "Why do you look like that?"

Alarmed, my feet stopped moving. "Like what?"

"Like you either committed a crime or you're trying to sneak a stray kitten in under your coat."

If I hadn't been holding on to the envelope for dear life, I would have patted my face to check my expression.

"No kitten here." I wished that was what I was holding. Then again, I already had the look and lifestyle of a spinster cat lady; actually having a cat might've been a bridge too far.

Her brows rose, crinkling her forehead. "What crime did you commit?"

I shook my head, my lips twitching toward a smile. "No crime either, I swear."

She jabbed her rag at me. "What've you got there?"

"Oh, nothing. Just mail." I skirted around her, heading toward the back so I could drop my things and grab an apron.

Joy was a dog with a bone, nipping at my heels. "I'm not buying it. Mail doesn't make you look like you're going to faint. What's going on, Alice?"

She herded me into her office, and I sank down on the lone stool, accepting my defeat, while she perched on the edge of her cluttered desk.

Joy wasn't the kind of woman anyone messed with. She was capable of making a grown man cry with a single hard look. But she'd been nothing but kind to me from day one. Even in the early days when I screwed up more orders than I got right, she never lost her patience.

She was old enough to be my mother, but she wasn't exactly maternal. Though I could say, without a doubt, she was much more than a boss. Joy had become the closest thing to a best friend I'd ever had. We'd never braid each other's hair or gossip about boys, but if I ever needed to lean, she'd be there to prop me up.

I set the envelope in my lap and smoothed my fingers over the stark black ink. "It's from a lawyer."

That made her raise one brow. "A lawyer, huh?"

"Yes. My sister passed away," I said quietly. "Three weeks ago."

Joy's face softened, which didn't happen often. "Didn't know you had a sister."

"I guess I never told you about her. We weren't close." I hesitated, then added, "At all."

She didn't say anything, waiting for me to fill in the rest. That was her way with me. She didn't push, and more often than not, I came to her with my thoughts. This time, though? I didn't know what to think or how to feel, so I gave her the facts.

"She left me everything," I said finally. "The letter says I'm the sole beneficiary of her estate."

Joy let out a slow whistle. "Everything? That a lot?"

I wasn't exactly an open book. Not because I was especially private, I just assumed no one would be interested in the ins and outs of my family matters. But I'd spent a lot of time around Joy. Sometimes when the bar was slow, she'd ask questions, and I'd answer.

She knew my parents had died within two years of each other. My mother first, after a short battle with cancer, then my father followed twenty-two months later from a heart attack. I hadn't seen them for years, and we'd never been particularly close, but I'd been sorry they'd passed too young.

Now...my sister. This one was trickier. I didn't know what to feel.

I nodded. "Our parents left everything to Silla. I guess she didn't have anyone else to put in her will, so she listed me."

She looked me over like she was seeing me anew. "Were they rich?"

"Yes, they were well off." I shuddered. "They were both in banking, and my mother had family money."

That earned me a grunt. "Guess you're rolling in it now too."

I let out a weak laugh. "Technically? Yes, I guess so."

"Good for you. I'd understand if you wanted to quit, though I'd miss the hell out of you now that you finally stopped breaking all my glasses."

I gasped at her teasing dig. In my early days, I had broken quite a few glasses, but I was as steady as they came now. "I haven't broken a glass in at least two years."

She shrugged and shot me a grin before getting serious. "My point is, if I have to lose you working here, I'll understand. Just don't go running off to Cancun or something stupid like that. You're too pale for all that sunshine."

"I haven't even considered quitting...or what this money will be used for. It'll probably sit in my account," I admitted, as terribly embarrassing as it was. I *should have* been able to think of one thing I wanted.

She huffed. "That's why I worry about you. You should have an idea of something you want to spend some of that money on to make your life easier. Or something fun, just for you."

As soon as she said it, it came to me. "Books. If I spend it, it'll be on books."

She clucked her tongue. "You're surrounded by free books day in, day out."

"But those books live in the library. I want them to come home and live with me."

I'd disappointed her, I could tell. I wondered what she would have bought if she had piles of money to spend. I would have given her mine to find out, but she would have given me a swift kick in the butt for even trying.

Elbows on her knees, she contemplated me. "You doin' okay with this news?"

"We weren't close," I repeated, hoping she'd let me off the hook.

She didn't. "That's not what I asked."

I pulled in a deep breath and slowly let it out. "I'm not sure. Silla was sick for a long time. My whole life revolved around getting her well. Her being gone now...I don't know. It's sad. I know it's sad. But—"

"You're not feelin' it yet." She nodded like that made sense. I wished it did to me. I was still somewhere between numbness and riding the cusp of overwhelm.

"Not yet," I almost whispered.

She gave my knee a rough pat. "If you need the night off, take it. I don't want you crying in anyone's beer."

I shook my head. "No, I'd rather be here working. I won't cry, I promise."

She climbed to her feet, giving me one last wary look. "All right. That's my final offer. I have to get back out there before the guys start helping themselves to drinks."

I laughed. "They know better." As she passed, I brushed my fingers over hers. "Thanks, Joy. I'll be out in a minute. All pulled together."

She looked like she might've wanted to say something else, but she squeezed my hand then hurried out of the room.

I didn't linger either. After tucking the envelope away, I tied my apron around my waist and put my hair up in a ponytail. I probably should have swiped on some lip gloss—more than a few guys had mentioned if I made some effort, my tips would be higher—but I'd never really mastered makeup. I wasn't sure it was me.

And I guess I no longer needed to worry about how high my tips were.

A wave of sadness lapped at my shores. Overfilled coffers were all that was left of the family who had turned away from me when I'd stopped being useful to them. It was...such a waste.

I didn't have time to dwell on it, though. As soon as I emerged from the back, one of the regulars called out to me.

"Allie-bo-bally. Fancy seeing you here."

I stopped by Bryan Thomas, who was seventy if he was a day, perched on the stool he'd long ago claimed as his, offering him a smile. "What are the chances?"

He slapped his weather-worn hand on the lacquered bar. "Don't know, but it feels like my lucky day. How are ya?"

"I'm all right." I touched my shoulder to his arm. "Is Joy taking care of you?"

"Always." When he smiled, his face looked like a field of clay in summer, all craggy lines and cracks along sunbaked skin. "Your guy's here. Looking cranky. You might wanna go cheer him up."

I stiffened, and my ears burned. I didn't have to ask who he meant. Bryan might have been half in the bag most of the time, but he knew.

Joy knew.

I didn't want to think about how many other people knew.

I didn't turn right away. Didn't let my eyes scan the bar. I didn't have to. I knew exactly where Caleb Kelly would be. He was a creature of habit, always sitting at the same table near the back. Sometimes alone, sometimes with members of his family. I also knew what I'd feel when I finally looked—like someone had knocked all the air from my lungs.

It was silly. Twenty-nine years old, and I was no better than a teenager with hearts in my eyes. I tried to hide it and thought I'd done a good job, but four years was a long time to pine for one man.

At this point, I suspected at least half the town was aware of my feelings.

I squared my shoulders, smoothed my apron, and took a breath so deep it tickled the base of my ribs, steeling myself the way I always had to.

When I thought I was ready, I turned, homing in on him immediately.

Sitting at his usual table near the back, hat tipped low, arms crossed, his lips and chin lost in his thick beard. I traced the path his hand took as he reached up and scratched behind his ear—a habit I'd learned he did when his mind was somewhere else. I wondered what he was thinking about. If he was worried. I hoped Jesse was okay.

That was an unnecessary concern. Caleb wouldn't be here if his son wasn't okay. That was the man he was.

His brothers-in-law, Remi Town and Deke Slater, were with him. They were married to his sisters, Hannah and Phoebe, and were probably just as handsome as Caleb, but I couldn't say. When he was around, everyone else became a blur.

He didn't look up as I started my approach, but that was better.

If he didn't look at me, he wouldn't see what everyone else did: my big, enduring, unrequited crush on Caleb Kelly.

I cleared my throat, hoping to get through this without my voice cracking. "Hey, guys."

Remington Town offered me an eye-crinkling smile and a friendly greeting. He was always kind. That was his way. Remi enjoyed being around people, talking to them and asking questions.

His wife, Hannah, was just as kind, but where he was the calm, she was the storm. And from what I'd heard, their little boy, Silas, was just like his mom.

Deacon Slater was more reticent. He lifted his chin, offering a quiet, "Hello," but he too, was unfailingly kind and always polite. Deke was Joy's nephew, and though she'd never say it, it was clear to anyone who observed them Deke was the apple of her eye.

Deke had become part of the Kelly family when he married Phoebe last year. If I were to choose the Kelly I thought I'd get along with most, it would have been her. She was quiet and soft but not shy. She paid attention to people and truly cared. Phoebe owned Sugar Rush, a cute little bakery café on the opposite end of Main Street.

Then there was Caleb. He finally looked up, but I didn't quite meet his eyes—I couldn't. Every time his warm, chocolaty gaze landed on me, I became a butterfly pinned to velvet, exposed and unmovable.

"Hey, Alice," he said. Just my name. Nothing fancy. Nothing flirty. But it still landed somewhere deep in my chest like a stone dropping into a smooth, calm lake.

"Hey." I gripped my notepad and clicked my pen, trying to keep things professional. "What can I get for you?"

They ordered beers to start, and I scurried away from their table as fast as I could. I wished I didn't scurry. I wished I was a smooth strider. But that wasn't me. Not when he was around. Probably not ever.

When I came back with their drinks, the three of them were speaking quietly.

"You look ready to spit nails," Remi remarked.

Caleb shrugged his massive shoulder. By rights, it should have caused the air to tremble, but the only thing trembling was me.

Internally.

Hopefully.

"Shel dropped by the ranch. Pissed me off," Caleb grumbled as I slid his beer in front of him. "Not worth getting into."

Deke nodded toward his glass. "Drink up. Get your mind off it."

Caleb picked up his glass, and it looked miniature in his grip. "I intend to." Then he raised his brows, his gaze landing square on me. "Are you ready to take our orders?"

"Yes." I rubbed my lips together and scrambled for my notepad. "If you're ready to give them."

I didn't need the notepad, not even for my largest parties. Our menu was small, and my memory was rock solid. But it was easier to focus on the paper in my hand than the faces of the people placing their orders.

Especially *his* face.

The first time I saw him, I drank him in in hulking, greedy gulps. It was all I could do to pull my eyes away from the stunning breadth of his shoulders. His overgrown hair. Thick beard. Legs so long they barely fit under the table. The span of his hands. The freckles dusting the bridge of his nose...Caleb Kelly was unlike any man I'd ever seen. And for a short time, I gorged on everything about him.

And like most overindulgences, I'd hurt myself by taking in too much, too fast, too often. My stomach ached when he barely looked at me. When his smiles were friendly and polite for me, but his laughter was raucous and untethered for his friends. When, on rare occasions, he gave his attention to one of the many women vying for it. That never lasted long, but it stung the most.

Yet, in all these years, I hadn't been able to kick the crushing pressure he caused in my chest every time he walked into Joy's. I'd gotten better at handling it, though.

I only allowed myself sips.

A glance at his brow.

A quick peek to make sure his eyes were the same shade of chocolate I remembered—they always were.

A short wander down the slope of his chest to his center, where his strength and vastness gave way to the one part that convinced me he was human: a soft stomach beneath impenetrable granite that only made him more attractive.

Remi's voice brought me back to the task at hand. He ordered a cheeseburger, extra pickles. Deke went next, asking for the chicken-fried steak and onion rings.

I peered up from my pad, picking a spot near Caleb's ear to focus on. "Burger with tomato, lettuce, mayo, and grilled onions, right?"

His chuckle was so low, it rattled my bones. "Damn, am I that predictable?"

My lips twitched. "A creature of habit, I guess. There's nothing wrong with that."

I felt him studying me more than I saw it. Since it was impolite not to look at him, I swept my eyes past his, pausing for a moment. Long enough to steal my breath, not so long it was dangerous.

"Thank you, Alice. Appreciate the vote of confidence," he rumbled.

Remi patted his shoulder. "Think she's too polite to tell you you're boring."

Caleb cocked his head, still pinning me with his gaze. "Am I boring?"

I dug the tip of my pen into my pad, willing my heart not to fly out of my chest. Joy wouldn't appreciate the mess that was sure to make.

I flung my gaze at him like a plate of spaghetti, hoping it would stick. And it did, for a long, sliding moment. His grin slowly fell, and something passed over his expression...something I didn't recognize but really wanted to.

"I doubt it, Caleb," I whispered, using his name for the first time.

My belly ached. I'd overindulged. It was time to get the hell out of here.

"I'll get those orders in."

I didn't scurry away this time, but it was close.

Chapter Three

Alice

I HAD TO RETURN to their table eventually, but I'd calmed myself enough I wasn't in danger of imploding. The three of them were deep in conversation about a trip Phoebe and Deke were taking soon, so I wasn't the center of attention when I slid their plates in front of them.

I saved Caleb's for last.

He looked at the food then up at me. Just a flash of his eyes. A beat. Then he gave me the smallest nod. Like he approved of me.

"Thanks, Alice."

My heart beat too fast when my name formed on his lips. It was a problem to be sure.

I stepped back. "Let me know if you need anything else."

I turned and took a deep breath, getting a handle on myself. There were other tables to see to. Keeling over because Caleb Kelly said my name would be incredibly inconvenient for everyone.

Nearing the hi-tops and two-seaters in the back by the pool tables, I slowed, dreading checking in on my last customer. Bart Miller was soused. There was no two ways about it. I didn't know what it was about him that rubbed me the wrong way. Plenty of rough men got drunk around here, and their antics and insinuations slid off my back. Bart wasn't always hard to deal with, but he got meaner with each passing year—divorced, bitter, and twice as loud when he drank.

But I had a job to do, and since he'd been watching me cross the room, I couldn't exactly avoid him any longer. I approached, my pen and notepad poised in front of me.

"Damn, Alice," he gruffed, his voice thick with beer and bad intentions. "You ever get tired of playing waitress and want a real man to take care of you, you let me know. I got a feeling there's a fine-looking woman under all that baggy shit you wear."

This wasn't anything new. Ignoring him, I steamed right ahead. "Would you like me to get you a glass of water or something to eat?"

Faster than he should have been able to, he moved, his fingers wrapping around my wrist like a steel cuff. Before I could process what was happening, he yanked me forward. My hips collided painfully with the edge of his table.

"Sounds like you think you can cut me off." His eyes narrowed into slits. "I got rid of my bitch of a wife for tryin' to tell me what to do. Not gonna stand for that shit from you, girl."

I tugged my hand, but it didn't budge. "Let go of me, Bart. This isn't how you get what you want."

"Maybe I don't need another drink. Not if you keep me company." He leaned back in his chair, spread his legs, and pointed to his crotch. "How 'bout you park that sweet ass right here, Allie?"

"You're hurting me." I pulled harder, but he was stronger than he looked and determined to keep me here. "Let go, Bart. You don't want Joy to step in."

He gave my arm a jiggle and laughed. "Don't get all offended. We're just talking, girl. I'm a friendly guy."

He gave me a sudden tug, throwing me off balance. My free arm pinwheeled, trying to grab something to hold on to so I didn't land on my face, but I only succeeded in knocking two glasses onto the ground. Their crash was muffled by the alarm bells ringing in my skull, but even in my panic, I still thought of how smug Joy was going to be about me breaking her glasses. I'd never hear the end of it.

I had those thoughts on my way down—to Bart's lap or the ground—wherever gravity decided to take me.

I didn't make it to either.

One second, I was falling, and the next, I was upright, wrapped in two strong arms, the warmth of a solid wall of muscle and the cushion of a soft stomach fitting just right in the arch of my back. I didn't have to turn around to know I'd ended up in Caleb's arms. He was exactly how I'd imagined him, and at the same time, nothing at all. He smelled good—like sunshine, a hint of sweat, leather, and the wind. His hold was careful but not tentative. Like I was delicate but not fragile.

I let myself melt against him. Knowing it was fleeting and would end soon enough, I soaked it up, forgetting where I was and what had just happened.

Caleb hadn't forgotten.

"That's enough." His voice didn't rise. He didn't snarl. He didn't puff his chest. But it worked better than any shout or act of violence.

Bart chuckled, trying to play it off. "Hey now, I was only kidding around—"

"You weren't," Caleb ground out. "You put your hands on her."

Then the worst happened.

Caleb let go of me to lean over Bart, speaking to him face to face. "You're drunk, and you're running your mouth. Apologize to Alice and see yourself home."

The tension in the air was thick enough to chew on. The music had gone fuzzy. A few heads turned, but no one interrupted. Bart seemed like he had more to say, but he took a long look at Caleb and decided against it.

My fingers curved into my wet palm. I must have gotten Bart's drink on my hand when I knocked it over. I'd take care of it...later.

Bart's jaw worked, like he still had some fight in him, then he grunted. "Jesus. Fine. Sorry."

"Try again." Caleb's voice was crushed gravel.

"Sorry, Alice," Bart muttered louder, though he didn't bother looking in my direction.

I nodded, forcing my voice past the tight knot in my throat. "It's fine."

I clenched my hand tighter. Something dripped. I'd definitely have to take care of that.

"Nothing's fine about this." Caleb moved beside me. We were two soldiers facing down our common enemy. "Get outta here, Bart. And don't forget to leave a generous tip. Think she deserves it, don't you?"

He grumbled more, my hand dripped, and Caleb glared. Finally, Joy showed up, shooing us both away.

I hurried toward the bar, hoping for a moment to compose myself. No such luck. Caleb had followed. Composing myself in his presence had always been difficult. Now that he'd saved me and I knew exactly what it felt like to have his arms around me...? Well, it was going to simply be impossible.

"You okay, Alice?" He was so close I could feel his body heat.

It would have been rude if I didn't turn around to face him and thank him for taking care of Bart. I just wasn't sure if I could make myself do it.

Before I could make up my mind, Caleb put his hands on me again.

"You're bleeding." He cupped my elbow and spun me around, his fingers curling around my wrist the way Bart's had.

But it wasn't the same at all.

Caleb's grip was firm, but he wasn't hurting me or trying to hold me captive. "You must've sliced yourself on the broken glass."

"Oh." I looked down at my hand, surprised to see the drips were blood and not vodka. That made a lot more sense. "Oh no. I should clean this off. Joy has a first-aid kit in her office."

"All right." Twin lines carved between his eyebrows. "Let's go."

My pulse took flight. "No. I'm fine. I can take care of it."

"I know you can," he said gently. "Thing is...I'm feeling all kinds of guilty for not stepping in the moment Bart put his hands on you. For me to sleep well tonight, you're going to have to let me fix you up and make sure you're okay."

I pulled in a shuddering breath and almost smiled. "That was pretty manipulative."

"It's the truth." The corner of his mouth quirked a little bit. "Did it work?"

"Yes. I guess it did."

He followed me into the back, and I let him. If I'd said no and meant it, I was certain he would have taken that as my answer. That was who he was. But he was also a man who needed to make sure I was all right, so I let him have it.

I let myself have it too.

It had been a rough, strange day. Giving myself these minutes of good wasn't the wisest move, but I wanted it more than almost anything. For once, I wasn't going to deny myself.

My palm stung as Caleb held it under cold water in Joy's bathroom sink. I looked up at the mirror, watching him with reckless abandon. Brow furrowed, he concentrated on cleaning my wound, his mouth flat in a line of displeasure.

"Hurt?" he rumbled.

"It's not so bad."

My reply was so unmistakably breathless, his eyes darted up to find mine in the mirror. I'd been caught, and this time, I did not look away.

"Sorry," he gruffed. "Won't take much longer."

"I'm not in a rush."

He turned off the tap and reached for a paper towel. First he turned me to face him, then carefully, gently, he dabbed at my skin, inspecting the gash.

"I don't think it needs stitches," he murmured. "But you're gonna be sore."

"I don't even feel it."

His eyes cut to mine. "You will tomorrow. You need to take it easy, or you'll open it back up."

I didn't know how to respond, so I didn't. I stared at him as he tended to me, taking him in from a proximity I'd never experienced.

There was a tiny cut above his knuckle, a scar at the edge of his brow, a worry line between his eyes. He was so big, he barely fit in this narrow bathroom. The space felt smaller and smaller the longer we stood in it together.

He wrapped gauze around my hand and secured it with tape. My fingers twitched when his thumb grazed my skin, and our gazes collided again.

"This feel okay?" he asked.

It felt great—like a slice of heaven.

But it also hurt. My hand was in his, but he wasn't holding it. He was being a good Samaritan to the little waitress who served him a couple times a week. This wasn't about me. He didn't see *me*. Just a woman who'd needed rescuing.

Suddenly, I was so very tired of not being seen; I couldn't stand it for another second.

Maybe I'd lost more blood than I'd thought. Instead of cowering or scurrying, I stepped closer. His brows lifted—just a little—but he didn't move back.

He said my name softly. "Alice..."

And I yanked him down.

Grabbed the collar of his flannel and pulled him low enough to reach me.

He bent automatically—because he was polite, because he was Caleb, and I kissed him.

Firm and fast.

One breath worth.

My lips on his, pressing like it would only ever be this once. Maybe that was all I thought I'd get.

He didn't return my kiss. Not at first.

He froze. Every inch locked like he'd stepped on a live wire.

I felt it and nearly expired on the spot.

Except...

Except, except, *except*.

His mouth moved.

Caleb Kelly was kissing me back.

Chapter Four
Caleb

I wasn't thinking, just reaching for something good.

Warm, sweet lips opened beneath mine, and a soft little body melted against me. My hands moved, gliding over her hips, surprised by the flare of them. I liked the feel of her. The taste. The feathery, floaty whimper she made as our tongues touched.

Everything about her hit me sideways. Kissing this woman was like biting into the first ripe peach of the season—not expecting much but ending up standing still for a second, taking it in.

She tilted her head, kissing me deeper, and something about the way she clutched at the front of my shirt made my mind go blank. White noise. The world had narrowed to this one bright, unexpected moment where Alice had her mouth on mine.

Then she pulled back.

And I stood there like a damn fence post, blinking at her.

Alice.

Alice had kissed me.

I'd never noticed the exact shade of Alice's eyes. They were the color of the cottonwoods down by the south fence line. Lively and bright, and when the wind hit just right, they shimmered. The kind of green that meant life was holding on.

I stared at her, probably looking like I'd taken a shovel to the head. She'd stunned me. This woman, who'd been nothing but polite in all the years she'd waited on me, had planted her lips on mine without warning. For no reason I could think of.

And I wasn't sure what to make of it.

But I couldn't say I minded. Not even a little bit.

She was flushed, eyes shining, chest rising with shallow little breaths. "Will you go on a date with me?" she asked. "One. Just to see."

A date?

I wasn't the dating kind. Didn't see the point. Never had the time, and sure as hell didn't have the energy to sit across from someone, pretending I was better company than I was.

But Alice wasn't just someone, and I didn't think she'd expect me to be anything other than myself.

And really, what was the harm in taking her out for a meal? One night. One dinner. I could do that much.

"Yeah," I said hoarsely. "Okay. One."

The smile that spread along her kiss-bitten lips was brighter than sunshine. I felt it all the way to my gut. I wasn't sure what she thought she saw in me, but the feel of her lips on mine had made me curious enough to want to find out.

Things looked different in the cold light of day—when last night's kiss had faded, and I was walking through the Grocery Barn, looking at flowers, feeling out of my depth.

The only women I bought flowers for were my mom, grandmother and on occasion, my sisters. Scanning the small selection for a bouquet for Alice, I stopped and rubbed my jaw. Alice what? Hell, I didn't know her last name and I was in the midst of trying to decide if she'd prefer daisies or carnations. What had I gotten myself into?

"She'll like anything you bring her."

I turned my head, lifting a brow. Joy had sidled up beside me without me noticing. "Who?"

She narrowed her eyes, leveling me with an assessing look. Joy wasn't a big woman, but life hadn't been easy on her. All the years she'd had to get by with nothing but vim and vigor were worn right on her face. If she wanted to cut a man down, all she had to do was glare and he'd feel it in his bones.

I knew this through experience. When I was eighteen, I'd tried to use a fake ID to buy beer at her bar. She hadn't said a word to me. All she'd done was look, and look hard, and I'd walked myself right out, not going back once until I was twenty-two.

"Don't play coy with me, Caleb Kelly. I know exactly who you're looking to buy flowers for. I have to say, I approve." She reached for a bouquet of mixed flowers. "Alice likes color. She'll appreciate these."

I took the bouquet, trusting she knew what she was talking about. "Thanks."

She wagged a finger at me. "I don't think I have to tell you to treat her right. She's the sweetest woman I know, but she went through some serious shit before she got to town. Going out with you..." Her chest rose as she took a deep breath. "Yeah, going out with you'll do her some good. It's been a long time coming."

A long time coming? What the hell did that mean? She'd only asked me for this date last night.

"You don't have to worry about me treating her right, Joy." I waved the flowers. "Thanks for the help with these."

I'd said the words without thinking, and they echoed in my head after I walked away. Treat her right. Of course I would. That wasn't where my doubts came in.

Truth was, I didn't know much about dating. Or Alice. But something told me if I screwed this up, it'd stick with me, and I didn't know how to feel about that.

Once I was clear of the grocery store, I had time and questions, so I stopped by Sugar Rush to check in on my sister, Phoebe.

Her café was all pink and sugar, just like her. She was behind the counter, smiling at her customers, spreading her special brand of sweetness around like confetti.

If she didn't have the Kelly eyes and my mother's face, I'd have suspected she'd been switched at birth. Our parents were good, solid people, but Phoebe was like a fairy, sprinkling pixie dust everywhere she went. She was the best of all of us, and my siblings and I were extra protective of her. In the last couple years, since Deke had come into the picture, we'd eased up, but that was because he'd lay down his life for her without a moment's hesitation.

When she was free, she rounded the bakery case to throw her arms around me. "Hey, you."

I gave her a squeeze. "Hey, Phe-Phe. How's your day been?"

She took a step back, nodding toward her nearly empty case. "Busy, as you can tell. It flew by, though, so that's always good." She smiled at me. "How about you? What's up?"

"Does Alice come in here? You know Alice, the waitress at Joy's."

A tinkling laugh burst out of her. "I know who Alice is, Cay. She comes in once or twice a week."

I rubbed the back of my neck, uncomfortable with this entire situation. "What's she usually get?"

"You want to bring her something?"

I went with the easiest explanation—the one that didn't involve me mentioning our one-and-done date.

"Mmhmm. Some idiot gave her a hard time at the bar last night, and she ended up cutting her hand. Thought I'd take her a treat to cheer her up."

Pink rose on Phoebe's cheeks as she pressed her lips together. It was a strange expression I couldn't decipher. Almost like she was about to burst.

"Okay," she squeaked. "That's so nice of you. I'll box up some of her favorites."

She rushed behind the counter, pulled out a large pink box, and set about filling it to the brim. Alice wasn't a big woman, and while her appetite might've been healthy, I couldn't see her eating all this before it went stale. But my sister was determined, so I wasn't going to stand in her way.

I leaned my elbow on the top of the case. "What's Alice's last name?"

Phoebe's head shot up, and she sent me a puzzled look. "You don't know?"

"Wouldn't have asked if I did."

"It's Clark." She slapped the lid of the box closed. "Sometimes you amaze me, Cay. You help run one of the largest ranches in the state, but I'm not sure you see what's right in front of your face."

"Should I have known Alice's last name?"

She shoved the box at me. "Yes. It's not like this town is big, and she—" She shook her head. "Just be nice to her, all right?"

Straightening, I tucked the box under my arm, wariness stirring in my gut. It couldn't be good this was the second warning I was getting about treating this woman right. I didn't have any kind of reputation for doing women dirty, so I wondered if it had more to do with Alice than me.

"Is there a reason you think I wouldn't?"

She patted my chest. "I know you're a good man. That's not in question. Like I said, it's taken you all this time to notice her, while she—" Phoebe cut herself off again, biting down hard on her lip.

"She what? Fill me in so I don't screw this up."

After a beat, she sighed, tucking her hands in the pockets of her frilly apron. "I don't know anything for sure, but I think she's been into you for ages. And if you're just noticing now, well…"

"Into me?" That couldn't be right. Sure, there'd been the kiss, but Alice and I had barely exchanged words.

Phoebe poked the spot she'd just patted. "See? That's what I mean. Everyone knows, but it's brand-new information to you. At least you finally opened your eyes. You have no idea how happy that makes me."

I shook my head. "Nothing to get happy about. Like I said, I thought I'd be nice and take her something sweet after a crappy night. Don't read into it."

She nodded, trying to control her flighty smile. "Sure, Cay. I'm not reading into anything. Have fun and tell her I say hey, all right?"

After leaving Sugar Rush, I sat in my truck with the box of treats and a bouquet of flowers, wondering what the hell I was doing. This wasn't me. I wasn't this guy.

So...why was I doing it?

That kiss...

In those minutes after she'd kissed me, I would have agreed to a hell of a lot. I remembered exactly what her lips had felt like, but now that I was clearheaded, agreeing to tonight was looking like it'd been a really unwise decision.

Everyone knows.

Phoebe had said that. Joy too, in her own way.

Like Alice had been waiting for tonight longer than I could wrap my head around. She'd asked for one date, but what if that wasn't all she wanted?

This wasn't feeling simple.

No.

I wasn't equipped for this. I hadn't been in a long time. The more I thought about it, the more it felt like the right thing—the *fair* thing—would be to back out before anything else happened.

I stared at the flowers, the pink box, my hands gripping the steering wheel too tight...

Hurting Alice was the last thing I wanted. I had to figure out what to say to let her down easy.

It was the right move, but I was dreading every second of it.

Chapter Five

Alice

I SHOULD HAVE WAITED and let him come to my door, but I was too antsy to stay inside, and so nervous I needed fresh air so I could actually breathe.

It had been twenty hours since I'd kissed Caleb Kelly, and I still couldn't believe I'd done it. I didn't know exactly what had come over me. It had been a strange night. The letter from Silla's lawyer had unsettled me, then Caleb and I were close—so close, I could see the blond and red whiskers peppering his unruly beard.

I simply couldn't *not* kiss him.

That kiss...wow. It had been pulled straight from my favorite books. The reckless thrill of Romeo and Juliet's first kiss without the shadow of tragedy, I hoped at least. It was Gatsby finally kissing Daisy again when, for one fleeting moment, everything had been golden.

Fireworks and a revelation, like Elizabeth seeing Darcy for who he truly was.

Caleb had finally seen me too.

I couldn't say what had gotten into me. How I'd made the decision to be bold. Probably something to do with being so very close to him for the first time. And even more to do with the news about Silla. My sister, who had never let me be close to her, wouldn't have the chance to kiss the man she liked or ask him to take her out.

I was still here.

I had taken that chance.

My toes curled inside my shoes, which were more sensible than I would have liked for the occasion, but I hadn't had any time to go shopping, so I'd done the best with what I had.

My hair was in soft waves—which were already falling flat since it was too long and heavy for its own good—and I swiped on lip gloss I'd picked up at the five and dime. I was wearing my favorite red dress. It skimmed my curves and ended mid-calf. Nothing fancy or sexy, and it was still cold enough I had to wear a sweater over it, but I felt pretty, if understated.

I hoped Caleb liked it.

I hoped he didn't mind if I talked about books and asked him a hundred questions about his family's ranch.

I hoped we kissed again. At least once, but I would take as many as he wanted to give.

The rumble of his truck reached me before the headlights came around the corner. My stomach swooped. I'd seen his truck parked in front of Joy's or along Main Street a hundred times, but it was here for *me*.

Pulling up to the curb, he killed the engine and stepped out. Tall and broad in a dark flannel and jeans, his hair scraped back in a messy bun, casual and unassuming, I couldn't look away.

He walked around the front of the truck, something in his hands. Two somethings.

A small bouquet of wildflowers wrapped in brown paper and tied with twine, and a pink pastry box with *Sugar Rush* printed on the side.

I started to get even more excited...until I looked at his face. He didn't have the expression of a man eager to pick up his date. His jaw was set too tight, and his eyes were on everything but me.

"Hey," I said, moving forward, trying not to let my voice wobble. "You came."

"Yeah." He stopped a few feet from me. Too far. "You look really nice, Alice."

"You do too." And he did. I didn't need him to make a great big effort. He always looked nice, even after a long, hard day on the ranch, and this evening was no different.

"Appreciate it." He scuffed his boot on the walk. "There's something I need to talk to you about."

The bakery box and flowers shifted in his hands like he wasn't sure what to do with them anymore.

I looked at them, then back at him, trying to piece together what was happening. "Is everything okay?"

He hesitated. Then nodded stiffly. "Everything's fine."

He rubbed the back of his neck, his discomfort like a neon sign. This wasn't going to go the way I wanted. I braced myself, and still, when he finally spoke, I wasn't ready.

"I've been thinking about the right thing to do. As much as I'd enjoy taking you to dinner, Alice, I'm not going to. It's not right for either of us."

This.

This, this, *this*.

I should have known this was coming. This was exactly why I kept to myself. *This.*

"Oh," I said quietly.

"You didn't do anything wrong," he rushed out, stepping forward like he could soften the blow with proximity. "Last night was unexpected. You took me by surprise. It was good. Real good. And I guess...I got swept up in it."

I nodded, my mouth dry. "And you aren't swept up anymore."

His lips pressed into a grim line. "It's not that I don't want to. It's just—I've got Jesse, the ranch, and...well, this isn't something I do..." He glanced down at the flowers, like maybe they'd speak for him.

"This isn't something you do?"

"It's not." He exhaled, and when he spoke again, he was more decisive. "If this was only one date, I'd go through with it. But I have the feeling that's not all you're looking for, and I am not the one who can give you more."

"You'd go through with it," I intoned. Like in other circumstances, a date with me would be a test or challenge he'd be willing to see through.

"It wouldn't be a hardship." He looked me right in the eye, like he needed to make sure I understood him. "The thing is, I grew up seeing my parents in a good, strong marriage. That kind of example could have gone one of two ways for me. I could've seen what they had and sought it out for myself. If I didn't have Jesse, I might've been more inclined. But I've got my boy, a tight family, a job that takes a hell of a lot of my time, and I'm content. I'm not looking to settle down with someone. I'm settled as I am. And you...you deserve a man who'll give you that. As much as I'd like to take you to dinner, I think it'll be better for us both to leave it here."

My ears were ringing, and my face was so hot, sweat prickled at my hairline. Everything he'd said was rational. It made sense. This wasn't personal. Caleb wasn't a relationship guy, and he thought I was a relationship girl.

Was I? I didn't even know.

Probably.

He was most likely right. One date with him wouldn't have been enough. Now that I looked at it that way, I was almost relieved he was canceling on me.

There was a long beat where neither of us spoke. The wind stirred the hem of my dress, tugged at my sweater, reminding me how cold it still was.

I nodded sharply. "Thank you for explaining. I understand. And you're right, I don't know if I would have proposed marriage, but if I went out with you once, I'm sure I would have wanted a repeat, so I'm glad I don't know what I'm missing."

"Alice..." he groaned. "Look, I—"

I held up my hand, desperately needing this to be finished. "I don't think there's anything more to say. Have a great night."

He shifted between his feet, conflicted. "All right. You too." Then he offered me the flowers. "Wait. These are for you."

I backed up. "No, thank you."

He shook them lightly. "I want you to have them. It's the least I can do after dragging you through all this."

I took another step away from him. "Really, thank you, but no. I've never been given flowers before, and I'd rather not start with a pity bouquet."

He chuffed. "That's not what this is."

"It's fine. Truly, I'd rather not."

I looked down at the pretty pink box in his other hand and decided I could use a lot of whatever was inside it. A cookie, a muffin—*anything* sweet to cover up this bitterness in my mouth. Being bold one more time, I dashed forward, slipped it from his hold, and danced back.

"I'll never turn down Phoebe's baking." I cradled the box close. "Thanks, Caleb. I guess I'll see you at Joy's."

Then I walked into my house, closing the door behind me. When I peeked through the sidelight, Caleb was standing exactly where I'd left him, one hand clutching the flowers, the other on the back of his head, staring at my door.

I sighed. At least I knew the answer to the question that had been poised at the tip of my tongue the last four years. Caleb and I were never going to be.

Now...

I could get over him.

Chapter Six

Alice

I DIDN'T GET SAD. Not like I'd expected. Disappointed. Embarrassed. And for a moment, the rejection stung, and it stung badly.

But over cookies and a mug of tea, I thought about what had happened and decided I wasn't going to take it personally. Yes, Caleb didn't want to date me, but his only reason was that he didn't date. Period. It wasn't specific to me. How could it be? He didn't know me.

I'd never even tried to let him know me.

If he'd turned me down because he thought I had crappy taste in books or didn't like the way my face looked, I probably would have been crying into my chamomile. But that wasn't it. He just didn't date.

Still, I couldn't shake the gnawing thought that maybe part of the problem was me. Not as in who I was, but as in how I moved through the world. For as long as I could remember, I'd been firmly on the sidelines, watching the world go by.

I lived in this town. At night, I served a good portion of the population at Joy's. During the day, I checked out books to the rest of them. I was as much a part of the fabric of Sugar Brush as everyone else, but how many of them *knew* me? How many knew my last name, what music I liked, or that I was writing my own novel?

I sipped my tea, the steam curling up into my eyes. Maybe I'd gotten so used to being a pane of glass to my family, I expected everyone to look right through me. Maybe Caleb wasn't the only one who didn't see me. Maybe I'd never given anyone outside of a small handful of people a chance. No one knew me because I didn't let them.

That thought turned into resolve. For once, not being known didn't make me feel sad. I was motivated to end my ghostly existence.I liked my little house, mugs of tea, and quiet life, but I'd like it even more if I had someone to share it with. It wouldn't be Caleb, but there was someone out there for me. Except if I kept on how I was, I wouldn't find him.

Wrapping my hands around my mug, I made myself a promise. I wouldn't let this shut me down further. I'd let it be what cracked me open.

Joy looked like I'd punched her in the nose. "You want *what*?"

I picked up the end of my heavy ponytail. "A haircut. And some highlights too. I don't know where to start."

Tossing her cleaning cloth over her shoulder, she folded her arms across her chest. "This have anything to do with the date you don't want to talk about?"

I tucked my hands in my apron pockets, clicking the pen I kept in there. "I did talk about it. There isn't anything to say about a date that didn't happen."

"Yeah, you said that." She worked her jaw back and forth. "Yet, here you are a week later, looking for a makeover. I'm not stupid, Alice. I see the connection, and I don't like it."

I sighed, leaning my elbows on the bar. "Can't this be about me? I'm ready to make more of an effort. For me, not anyone else. For heaven's sake, I'm almost thirty, and I've never done a single thing with my hair and have no clue how to put on makeup."

Joy propped her arm on the opposite side of the bar, leveling me with a probing gaze. A few customers were seated nearby, but her focus was solely on me.

If I had faltered, even for a second, I didn't doubt she would have taken the shotgun from beneath the bar and hunted Caleb Kelly down. But I wasn't lying. I had changes to make, and I was starting on the outside and working my way in.

"I hear you," she gruffed. "But do I look like I'm the one to come to for beauty advice? I've been using the same black-box dye since my first gray showed up. I cut my ends with nail scissors. If you want that kind of treatment, I'm your gal. Anything else—"

"Excuse me, ladies."

We both turned to the woman who'd slid in beside us. In her forties or fifties, Margot was more glamorous than a patron at Joy's had any call to be, but this seemed to be her default setting. She was a regular, and from what I'd seen, had a penchant for rugged cowboys.

I smiled. "What can I get you?"

She slid closer. "I'd apologize for eavesdropping, but I'm not really sorry since I think I can help you."

Joy shook her finger at Margot. "That's right. You're exactly who this one needs. I'm useless in this department."

Margot's lips curved into a confident, bright smile. "I manage the salon at Sugar Brush River Ranch Resort. Why don't you come by tomorrow? I'll set you up with a full treatment. Cut, color, style, and maybe a brow cleanup if you're brave."

My mouth fell open. The Kelly ranch. Caleb's family. A long time ago, it had been partially turned into a luxury resort for billionaire tourists and company retreats. I'd never even thought to set foot on the property. It wasn't for me.

"Oh, I don't know…" I stammered, reaching for a valid reason to say no aside from the idea making me nervous. Of course, I couldn't find one.

Margot didn't allow me to say no anyway. "What don't you know? You said you wanted a makeover, didn't you? I'm so keen on the idea; if you turn me down, I'll be insulted forever."

Joy clapped her hands once. "That settles it. We're not offending our customers. You're going."

I felt like I'd been handled. But could I really complain when I was being given exactly what I'd said I wanted?

"Thank you. Really."

"Don't thank me yet," Margot teased with a wink. "Wait until you see what I can do."

The next morning, I walked into the salon at Sugar Brush River Ranch Resort feeling like an impostor. With pale wood, bronze fixtures, and big windows overlooking the cottonwood-lined river, everything gleamed. The lights were low in the waiting area, and soft, relaxing music emerged from hidden speakers.

Before I could take a seat in one of the plush armchairs in the reception area, Margot swept in to greet me.

"Alice, darling, welcome!" She wrapped me in a hug like we were old friends then held me at arm's length to assess me. "We're going to have so much fun. I love when I get to play with a blank canvas."

Ouch. That wasn't my favorite thing to be called, but it wasn't untrue. I presented exactly nothing to the world and was as close to a blank canvas as a person could get. But I wouldn't walk out of here as one, for better or worse.

Before I knew it, I was in a wide leather salon chair, draped in a sleek black cape. Another stylist brought me a cup of steaming herbal tea in a porcelain teacup while Margot gently undid my ponytail, letting my hair spill down my back.

"Oh, honey," she murmured, running her fingers through the thick strands. "This is some beautiful hair. We'll bring it to life, I promise."

"That's exactly what I want. Life." I looked at her reflection in the mirror. Her perfect blonde waves, flawless makcup, stylish clothes, and mentally handed myself over. "I trust you to do what you think will look good on me."

She squeezed my shoulders. "I love that for me. I'm going to take really good care of you."

She and another stylist consulted over swatches, pointing out caramel and honey tones. I sat there, my nerves frayed, as many, *many* foils were wrapped around pieces of my hair. It was nice, though, being the center of attention. To have my hair gently tugged and arranged. To be showered with compliments and asked questions about myself.

The process went on longer than I'd expected, but the library was closed today, so I had nowhere else to be. I let myself relax and savor the experience. Maybe I'd make it a regular thing. After all, I could afford it now.

Once the highlights were finished, and I'd been rinsed, toned, and conditioned, I was brought back to the chair for a haircut. Margot circled me while one of her stylists combed through my hair, listening to her instructions on how she wanted my hair to be cut.

"Elena!" Margot called out brightly. "You're early."

I tracked Elena Kelly in the mirrors as she strode through the salon. She wore slim black pants and a sage-green silk blouse, her icy-blonde hair pulled into a low ponytail. Everything about her was polished but relaxed, like someone who knew exactly who she was and had never once felt a shred of doubt.

Sometimes I had trouble wrapping my head around her being Caleb's mother. She didn't look old enough to have a son in his thirties, and while he was rough and a little unkempt, she was unfailingly put together.

"My last meeting wrapped up ahead of schedule," Elena said, draping herself on one of the empty salon chairs. "Thought I'd stop in and see if you had a minute to go over the new website banners. Plus, if I looked at another spreadsheet, I was going to scream."

Margot folded her arms. "I thought you were going to retire soon."

Elena flicked her manicured nails. "Oh, I've been saying that for years. But what would I do with myself all day? I'd be bored to death." She caught me watching her in the mirror and flashed a warm smile. "Well, hello."

I waved from beneath my cape. "Hello."

She canted forward, getting a better look at me. "Is that Alice?"

Margot nodded proudly. "She's my project. I overheard her telling Joy she wanted a change, and I brought her right in. She's never done anything to her hair. A virgin. Can you believe it?"

Elena hopped up from the swiveling chair and moved in front of me, propping her hip against the stylist's station. "Well, this is exciting. Is Margot giving you the works?"

"Yes. I think she is. After my hair's done, she's going to teach me how to do my makeup," I replied.

Her eyes narrowed. "Not too much. Your skin is already gorgeous. A little color and you'll be perfect. If you weren't so sweet, I'd hate you for how naturally pretty you are."

Margot hummed her agreement as chunks of hair rained down around me. With every lock that fell, a rush of relief came with it, like I was shedding a weight I'd carried far too long. Even if I ended up with a pixie, I wouldn't mind. My hair had been nothing but a curtain to hide behind, and suddenly, I couldn't understand why I'd clung to it for so many years.

"I don't need to be perfect. A little color would be nice, though," I said.

Elena tilted her head, considering me. "You'd look stunning in purple. It would really bring out your eyes."

"I'm not sure I own anything purple, but I'm planning on doing some shopping, so I'll be on the lookout."

Elena and Margot exchanged a look, then Elena smirked. "Oh, you are a *project*, indeed. We're taking you shopping. Now, if I had my druthers, we'd take a trip to Denver, but I suspect we should start a little smaller. We'll go to Cheyenne as soon as you have the time."

I barely stopped myself from gawking at her. I'd met Elena Kelly as her server at Joy's and helped her at the library, but that was it. We had never had more than a passing conversation. Plus, she was Caleb's mother. I didn't understand what was happening—or why.

"We will?" I asked.

"We will. Are you in, Margot?"

Margot rolled her eyes. "Obviously. An artist can't let her masterpiece go unfinished."

The two of them seemed more excited about my makeover than I was, but if they wanted to help me, I couldn't think of a reason to tell them no.

By the time Margot finished curling my hair into glossy waves and brushed the final sweep of peach blush across my cheeks, I hardly recognized the woman in the mirror.

My hair was no longer a long, dark sheet. Margot's team had brought it to life with golden-caramel and honey highlights, layered to frame my face and skim my shoulders. When I moved my head, it *bounced*. She gave me a tutorial on how to style it myself, and I was hopeful I could do it.

My brows had been shaped into clean arches for the first time in my life, opening up my eyes. My makeup was subtle, a hint of shimmery eyeshadow, a flick of brown liner, and a sheer pink gloss that made my lips look full and soft.

When it was all finished, Margot stepped back, hands on her hips. "Well," she said, her voice brimming with satisfaction. "I think you're my magnum opus."

Elena stood behind her, arms folded, appraising me with a discerning smile. "You look beautiful, Alice. You've always had fantastic hair, but it was so long and thick, it overwhelmed your frame. Now, I see you first then your hair."

I blinked at my reflection, feeling a sudden tightness in my throat. "Thank you," I managed. "I don't even know what to say. I...I've never looked like this before."

Margot squeezed my shoulder. "This is all you. I made a few minor adjustments."

Elena cocked her head, her silver earrings catching the light. "So, tell me, Alice. What made you want to make a change? Please don't say a man."

I let out a surprised little laugh. In a way, she was startlingly close to the truth. Not that I'd ever tell her about my disaster of a nondate with her son. And anyway, he wasn't the reason I was doing this. I was moving on from him.

"Not exactly. There was a man I liked...but it didn't work out. He doesn't feel the same." I drew in a deep breath. "I'm moving on now. I'm going to date."

Elena's brows rose. "Tell me more."

"I was thinking I'd try online dating." I rubbed my lips together, startled by the gloss on them. That would take some getting used to. "The pool here is small, and I'm not one to hang out in bars on my own. So...I guess that's what I'm going to do."

Margot wagged her finger. "You need good pictures for your profile."

"Probably," I agreed, though I hadn't gotten that far in my planning yet.

"Well, let's go." She held out her hand. "No time like the present. Give me your phone and let's give those men something to drool over."

Elena chuckled. "They will absolutely drool over you, sweetheart, and you deserve every drop." She scrunched her nose. "Oh, that was gross. Never mind the drool. You deserve a man who'll ignite for you."

I couldn't imagine a man ever burning for me, but I'd settle for a little drool. With my new hair and makeup, I felt good enough to think I might get a little of that if I put myself out there.

"All right." I smiled. "Let's do it."

Margot shook her head and whispered, "Magnum opus."

Elena rested her hand lightly on my shoulder. "Smile like that, and you'll make the app crash from all the guys trying to message you."

As Margot held up my phone and Elena angled the salon lights just right, I sat up straighter, lifted my chin, and smiled.

I wasn't quite ready to crash apps...but putting myself out there didn't seem so daunting anymore.

Chapter Seven

Caleb

I DIDN'T KNOW WHAT was up with me, but I'd been in a consistently foul mood the last couple weeks. It'd begun with Shelby's bullshit visit to the ranch, and I hadn't been able to kick it. Not even a week with my boy had done the job.

He was back with his mom, and I was at loose ends, so I took a trip into town to have dinner with my brother, Cormac. We both worked at the ranch, but he managed the resort side, so it was rare we got to spend solid time together during the day.

He was standing outside the entrance to Gray's Diner, tapping on his phone, dressed in one of his many suits. Seeing him in them always threw me off. Eight years my junior, it was hard for me not to think of him as a kid. He was supposed to be little Maccie, not Mr. Kelly.

Guess he'd always be Maccie to me, no matter how many sleek suits he owned.

I strode up to him and clapped him on the shoulder. "Hey, man. Lookin' good."

He grinned, slipped his phone in his pocket, and wrapped me in a one-armed hug. "You too. Bigger than the sun, as always."

I poked him in the ribs. "Skinnier than a fence post."

That'd once been true, but not so much anymore. Mac had outgrown his beanpole status years ago. He was as tall as me and lean but strong. Not that I'd ever concede that to him.

He smoothed his hand down his front. "That's right. You better feed me before I disappear."

Both of us laughing, we walked into the diner and waited to be seated. Cormac scanned the room before his gaze landed back on me.

"Surprised you suggested coming here. I thought Joy's was your spot."

"Most of the time, it is," I agreed. "But I was in the mood for something different."

"All right. I'm fine with that, but I'd be down for a round or two of darts after we eat."

I lifted a shoulder. Not about to tell him I hadn't been to Joy's in almost two weeks, for Alice's sake. Deep down, I knew I'd done the right thing, but that didn't mean it felt good, and I was damn sure it hadn't been anywhere near pleasant for her.

Eventually, I'd go back. Once she'd had time to lick her wounds. To do that, the least I could do was give her space. Then she'd see I'd done her a favor by cutting things off before they started.

Cormac and I were led through the diner by the hostess, stopping here and there to talk to people we knew, passing others with a wave. We were seated in a four-seater booth by a window near the back, menus slapped down on the table in front of us.

I scanned the menu, trying to decide between breakfast and dinner. From somewhere nearby, a laugh that sounded like leaves rustling in a cool breeze drew my attention. I raised my head, finding the source at a table kitty-corner from ours.

A man and a woman sat across from one another, his back facing us. The woman laughed again, and something about the lightness of it resonated in my chest.

I trailed my gaze over the flowing caramel waves resting on her delicate shoulders up to her face and jerked. Alice? That was what her laugh sounded like?

While I watched, her companion reached across the table to take her hand. Her laughter stopped, but she didn't take it away. She let him hold it.

He was talking, and she was smiling. Smaller now. No more breezy laughs.

"What are you looking at?" Cormac twisted around to check for himself. "Oh, that's Alice."

"Yeah," I muttered. "I'm not used to seeing her outside of Joy's."

"She looks good. Changed her hair up." Then, like the do-gooder puppy he was, he raised his hand and called out, "Hey, Alice."

She jumped in her seat, averting her eyes from the man to look at Cormac...and me. She was close enough I could see the flush rise in her cheeks as our gazes collided.

She slipped her hand free to wave back. "Hello."

Cormac nodded. "Have a good dinner."

She offered my brother—only my brother—a grin. "You too."

Her eyes slid away from me, and Cormac twisted back around. "She looks different, doesn't she?"

I shrugged. "Didn't notice."

Cormac snorted. "Didn't notice, my ass. She looks nice. I've always thought she was sweet."

I grunted, flicking open my menu again, staring hard at the words as they blurred together. All I could see was the way Alice had let that man hold her hand. Why was I fixating on that? We were barely more than strangers. What she did didn't matter.

Still, she'd kissed me two weeks ago and was already off on a date with another guy. It didn't sit right with me. Was I that easy to get over?

Hell, looked like I was.

"How are things going on the ranch?" Cormac asked, settling back in his seat. "Haven't heard you cuss out the irrigation system lately."

"Plenty of other things to cuss out, but that's all part of the fun." I forced my eyes down to the menu. "Everything's fine. Busy, like always."

"That's good." He flipped his menu shut without even looking at it. He always ordered the same damn thing anyway. "What's Jesse up to this week?"

"School, the library, his usual haunts. His robotics club has a competition coming up, so he's hyped about that." My jaw ticced. "Shelby's talking about moving him to Denver."

Cormac's eyebrows shot up. "What? Since when?"

"She brought it up a couple weeks ago then mentioned it again when I brought Jesse back to her. She wants to move there so her boyfriend can find work."

"That's...man. I don't even know what to say." He shook his head. "Is she serious about this guy?"

"Seems like it, but you know Shel. She's always serious about one guy or another," I muttered. "Jesse's pretty cagey about how he feels toward him."

Cormac went quiet for a minute, drumming his fingers on the table. "What are you gonna do?"

"Don't know yet." I rubbed a hand over my jaw. The stubble scratched against my palm. "I'm trying to keep the peace, but I'm not letting her move my kid three hours away. I shut that down fast, and I'll continue to shut it down every time she brings it up."

"Yeah." He nodded firmly. "What is she thinking? Jesse's family lives here. There's no way he'd want to move that far away for one of his mom's boyfriends of the moment."

I blew out a slow breath, trying to unclench my shoulders. "I'm mad I even have to expend a second of mental energy on this."

"I get that." He picked up his menu again. "If Shelby tries to push it, we'll figure something out."

"Yeah." My gaze drifted back to Alice before I could stop it. Her date was talking, and she was nodding along, her smile small and tucked away.

Cormac, oblivious, cleared his throat. "So, darts after this? Or you got an early morning tomorrow?"

I forced myself to look at him. "Early morning. Let's just eat."

"All right." He set his menu aside, grinning at the waitress as she approached. "Then I'm making you buy me pie before we leave."

"Fine," I agreed, but my mind wasn't on pie. It was on the woman sitting across the diner, laughing softly at something another man said.

Wondering why the hell I disliked it as much as I did.

A couple days later, I still hadn't outrun the dark clouds looming over my head. Instead of going home after work and sinking further, I took another drive into town to see Phoebe.

Sugar Rush was hopping with late-day caffeine seekers. Phoebe, Camille, and Hailey bustled behind the counter, making drinks and helping customers. Deacon had been put to work, busing tables and wiping them down. Though if I had to guess, he'd volunteered. If he had a choice, I was pretty sure he'd never let Phoebe's feet touch the ground; that was how gone for my sister he was.

It sure made it easy to see him like a brother.

I greeted him then planted myself at the end of the five-person line, letting my gaze wander around the place. It was mostly women chatting in small groups, a couple ranch hands looking scruffy after a hard day of working, and people tapping away on laptops. My eyes snagged on a table by the front window.

Alice.

She was sitting across from a man with an open laptop in front of him. He was older than the guy at the diner, with salt-and-pepper hair and a pressed dress shirt, the sleeves rolled up. He was talking, leaning forward slightly. She smiled as she listened. Small, interested, like she cared about what he had to say.

He wasn't making her laugh like the other guy had, but her attention was rapt.

"Next," Phoebe called, dragging my attention back to the counter.

I stepped forward, giving her my order of black coffee and one of her pecan sticky buns.

"Are you doing okay?" Phoebe asked as she punched my order into the register.

"Fine." I jerked my head to the side. "Who's that guy, the one with Alice?"

She peered over my shoulder. "Oh, that's Charlie. He's on year five of working on his novel. Sometimes, he and Alice brainstorm ideas. I think she's writing too."

I turned back, noticing the closed laptop in front of her. What was she writing? And what did Charlie have to say that was so fascinating?

"Why do you ask?"

I faced my sister and shrugged. "Just curious. I recognized him but didn't know his name."

She huffed a laugh. "Because you live in your own world. Charlie's here almost every time you come in. It wouldn't kill you to pay attention to something other than the ranch and Jesse."

I smirked. "That hasn't been proven."

She waved me away. "Go wait for your drink and get out of my face."

I reached over the counter to tug the end of her braid. "Only teasing you, Phe-Phe."

She swatted at my hand, but her eyes crinkled for a second before she gave her attention to the next customer. I moved down the counter to wait for my drink, checking my phone for messages to give me something to do.

I told myself not to look back at Alice. She was none of my concern. Of course, I looked anyway.

Charlie was typing now, his fingers sailing over his keyboard, while Alice sat back in her chair, holding her mug in both hands, her eyes on him but slightly unfocused, like she was thinking hard about something else. The light from the big front windows caught in her hair, making the caramel strands glow.

She must've gotten some kind of color added in. Last I remembered, it was so dark, it was almost black. She didn't need to change it. Her original color had been nice. Real nice. But this was good too. It suited her.

I frowned at my phone. Was there something going on with her and Charlie? He was a good bit older and didn't seem like he was her type.

Not that I knew what her type was. I barely knew anything about her, aside from the bits I'd picked up in the years I'd been going to Joy's. She was quiet. Polite. Always smiling at customers, even when they were rude.

She'd grown up in Colorado but had gone to college at Savage University in California, my parents' alma mater. Four years ago, she'd moved here from San Francisco and owned her little house. She always wore the same pair of silver hoops. Her voice was quiet, but her sneeze was loud enough to make people jump.

She liked to read. Her favorite book was *The Shadow of the Isle*. I'd overheard her mentioning it and looked it up. A fantasy story written over seventy years ago, and she'd read it at least twenty times.

I knew a few things about Alice Clark, but not her type. If I'd been asked after she kissed me, I would have said maybe it was me. Now, I wasn't so sure.

I really didn't like being unsure about anything.

Once I got my coffee, I grabbed one of the last available tables, and Deke joined me soon after. We shot the shit for a while, him telling me about his latest carpentry projects and the plan he had for building a deck on the back of his and Phoebe's house. Between family and friends, it'd get done in a weekend. Luckily for all of us, he'd finally accepted his place in the Kelly fold, so it was no longer a struggle to get him to accept we *wanted* to help.

We'd finished talking about lumber prices when Alice started packing up her things. She slipped her laptop into a worn canvas bag and tucked her mug onto the dirty dish tray at the end of the counter before heading for the door.

I didn't think. I just stood.

"You headed out?" Deke asked, his brow raised.

"Yeah," I muttered, grabbing my coffee and sticky bun. "Catch you later. Tell Phoebe bye for me."

He nodded, not pushing. One of the many reasons I liked the guy.

I made it to the exit a second before Alice did. Her eyes rounded at my sudden appearance.

"Evening, Alice." I pushed open the door and gestured for her to go ahead. She passed by me, giving me a whiff of cinnamon and other spices I couldn't name, murmuring, "Thank you."

I followed her out, calling her name again as she hurried down the sidewalk.

She paused midstep, turning around slowly. Her hair shifted over her shoulders, catching the fading light. "Yes?"

"You headed home?"

She nodded. "I am."

"Where's your car?"

She glanced away, her fingers tightening on her bag strap. "I walked today."

I frowned. Her house wasn't far, but it wasn't exactly close either. "Let me give you a lift."

"That's okay. I like walking," she said, then added, "It's nice in the evenings."

"It is nice, but it's getting late. It'll be close to dark by the time you make it to your place. I'll drive you." I nodded toward the street. "My truck's right there."

"There's plenty of light still. Really, it's not necessary."

I couldn't say why I was pressing this, just that I didn't like the idea of her walking the quiet streets alone. And I had a feeling she wouldn't have turned me down if I'd made the same offer a couple weeks ago—before I was a jackass to her.

"It's not necessary, but I want to do it anyway." I held my arm out toward my truck. "Come on. It'll only take a couple minutes."

She hesitated, looking up at me, her eyes shadowed in the low light. Finally, she gave a small nod. "Okay. Thanks."

I took her bag before she could argue, and she followed me to my truck. She didn't say anything as I opened the passenger door and set her bag on the floorboard. She climbed in, smoothing her sweater around her hips, her movements neat and quiet.

Once I was behind the wheel, I pulled out of the lot, the silence between us thick enough to chew.

After a minute, I cleared my throat. "You've been going on a lot of dates lately."

She glanced out the window. "Not really."

"I saw you with that guy at the diner. The one who kept making you laugh."

She huffed. "I saw you too. And yeah, he was kind of funny."

"And?"

"And nothing." Her hands were stacked neatly in her lap, and her body was as close to the door as she could get without falling out.

"Not going out again?"

"He asked, but I don't think so. We weren't a match."

I risked a glance at her. She was staring out the window, her reflection in the glass faint and unreadable. Guilt burrowed deep in my gut, but I didn't know what to do with it.

"How'd you meet him? Was he a customer too?"

"No. I don't make it a habit of asking my customers on dates. That was a one-time thing." She tucked her hair behind her ears then shook it back out to curtain her face. "I learned from my mistake."

Ignoring her comment, I charged on. "You didn't say how you met him."

"On a dating app," she replied.

My hands flexed around my steering wheel. "Is that safe?"

"As safe as any date." She leaned down and wrapped the strap of her bag around her hand. "I'll be fine."

"I wouldn't want my sisters using those apps. You never know who you're gonna meet."

"Well, your sisters are married, so you don't have to worry about it." She pulled her bag onto her lap. "You don't have to worry about me either."

I pulled up to the curb in front of her house and put the truck in park so I could twist around to look at her. "Because you're not going to be using the app anymore?"

She shook her head, her mouth curving into a smile that didn't look anywhere near happy. "No, I'll still be using it. You don't have to worry because I'm none of your concern."

She wasn't harsh, but her words were a punch to the gut anyway. I didn't understand it. She was right. Alice was just a waitress at Joy's. She wasn't my concern in the least.

But I didn't like the idea of her meeting strange men on an app—men who'd see a small, quiet woman like her and take advantage. I'd be concerned about any woman in that situation.

When the silence stretched too long, she unbuckled herself and pushed open her door. "Thanks for the ride, Caleb."

"Yeah," I rasped, my throat tight. "Anytime."

She paused, like she was going to say something else, but she only nodded and climbed out, shutting the door gently behind her. I watched her walk up the cracked path to her porch, the light above her front door flicking on as she approached. She didn't look back as she entered.

I sat there for another minute, staring at her closed door, my chest feeling too small for my lungs. Then I put the truck in drive and pulled away into the quiet night.

Chapter Eight

Caleb

I LOVED LIVING IN a small town. Wouldn't trade it. The shitty part, though? It was small, making the chances of running into people I didn't want to sky high.

The Grocery Barn was a veritable hotbed for such occurrences. I avoided it as much as I could, but I needed to eat, and my parents and grandparents would eventually get sick of me if I kept showing up at their door, begging for dinner.

I was pushing my cart down the dairy aisle when a cart bumped into mine. I looked up, frowning at the man.

"Hey, Caleb. Sorry. I didn't see you there."

Recognizing Kent, Shelby's boyfriend, my frown deepened. "No problem," I grunted, aiming to continue on my way without getting stuck in a conversation.

No such luck. He swiveled around, falling into step with me. "While we're in the same place, I thought I could talk to you. You know, man-to-man."

I threw a block of cheddar into my cart. "If it's about Denver, I've already spoken to Shelby. The subject's closed."

Kent was a little guy, the top of his curly brown hair barely reaching my shoulder, but he kept up with me. In his button-down tucked into belted khakis, he looked like he'd stepped out of a real estate ad. Something about his easy grin put me on edge. It rang false, calculating.

"Look, I get that. But I don't know if Shelby imparted how much we're willing to do to make this work. I'll personally drive Jesse up here to spend every weekend with you. You won't ever have to make the drive."

I stopped walking to look down at him, my chest gripped by something hot and clawing. "So you, a man whose last name I don't even know, who I've exchanged a few sentences with, get to spend all week with my son? Have him living in your house, and I should be thanking you for the scraps you're willing to throw me? No, Kent, that's not gonna happen. Jesse's not going."

He put his hand on my arm. "You really need to think about this, Caleb. I love Shelby, and Jesse's great—"

I shrugged him off, cognizant as ever we were in public and I couldn't toss him to the ground like I wanted. "I know my son is great. I don't need you telling me that."

"Of course you do." He held his hand up as if placating me. Like I was some wild bull and he was the levelheaded one, talking me down. "I didn't mean to imply anything. My point is, I'm willing to work with you. Shelby won't go without Jesse, and if—"

"It's a done deal, Kent." I threw in a tub of cream cheese and kept on walking. "You want to move to Denver, go ahead. You can drive up on weekends to see Shelby, if that's what you want. That's none of my business."

He cleared his throat, glancing around to see if anyone had overheard. "All right. I can tell you're not listening. We'll talk later, when heads are cooler."

I left him in the dairy aisle, but my blood kept simmering long after my exit.

My foul mood clung to me on my way to pick up Jesse, and I hated it. My boy was the brightest part of my life. Always had been. I'd gotten lucky with him, and I knew it. How he'd turned out had little to do with Shelby or me. He was…good, all the way through. Smarter, too, than any thirteen-year-old had a right to be.

I sat in the library parking lot, engine idling while he finished up inside. That place had been his after-school haunt for years. As soon as the final bell rang, he'd walk over and spend a couple hours getting his homework done before disappearing into some book.

According to him, I wasn't allowed inside. It was his place, and he didn't need his old man embarrassing him. Fine by me. I'd never been much of a reader anyway. I read the paper, kept up with what was going on in the world, but I'd never gotten lost in a book the way Jesse did.

A few minutes later, Jesse came jogging out of the library, a smile stretching across his face. All long, gangly limbs, he made it to my truck and threw open the door.

"Hey, Dad." He tossed his backpack in the back seat and yanked the door shut, still grinning.

"Hey, bud." I reached over, ruffling his shaggy hair, and made a mental note to get him into the barber, reminding me I needed to see to my own hair. He was getting as scraggly as I was.

"Good day?"

"Yep." He had a stack of papers clutched tight in his hand. "Ms. Clark told me about the coolest thing. I really want to do it, and I need you to keep an open mind."

I'd been about to pull out, but slid the truck back into park and turned to him. "I'm already not liking the sound of this, bud. Why don't you come out with it instead of trying to hype me up?"

"Okay, but listen before you react." He shoved the papers at me. "Ms. Clark found this robotics summer camp she thinks is perfect for me. It's for kids my age, and it's three weeks long. I'd stay in the dorms at U of Wyoming, which is really cool. Technically, I could come home on the weekends, but they do stuff like going to baseball games and amusement parks, so I might not want to. But I could if you miss me. And it's in August, so I'd be home all of June and July to help on the ranch. It's not even that expensive, Dad, and it sounds like I'd get to do a lot of hands-on work—"

I cut him off. "Ms. Clark told you all this?"

His mouth slammed closed, and he nodded. "Yeah. She found this camp for me. I missed the cutoff date to apply, but she spoke with the director—"

"She spoke with the director?" I ground out.

"Uh...yeah." He rubbed the back of his neck. "Dad, why are you getting all red? Did I say something wrong?"

I turned the truck off. "No. *You* didn't do a thing wrong. Stay here while I go speak with Ms. Clark."

"No—what?" He put his hand on his door. "Dad, you don't need to talk to her. It's okay. I won't—"

"Stay here, Jess."

Good as he was, he listened without argument, though he didn't want to. He had a special affinity for the librarian. Probably thought I was going to rip her head off or something. I was pissed, but he didn't have to worry about that. I was going to have a conversation with this woman who thought it was okay to talk to him about something that was never going to happen—to set him up for disappointment and make me the bad guy.

I slammed the truck door a little harder than I meant to and stalked across the parking lot, my boots crunching over gravel. The automatic doors slid open, letting out a waft of that dusty paper smell I'd always associated with school.

Inside, it was quiet as expected. A couple kids were bent over laptops, an older man was reading a newspaper, and a mom was trying to corral her toddler near the kids' section. I spotted the front desk and made a beeline, scanning for what I imagined would be a stern old librarian with a tight bun and even tighter mouth.

Instead, what I found stopped me short.

Standing at the counter, sliding a stack of books into a bin with smooth, practiced motions, was a woman I recognized instantly. Her long brown hair was pulled back in a loose ponytail, a soft lavender cardigan rested over her white T-shirt, and dark blue jeans hugged her legs.

Alice.

Alice *Clark*.

My brain short-circuited. *This* was Ms. Clark? The Ms. Clark Jesse had been talking about for years? The one who sent him home with stacks of books she knew he'd like, helped him with his homework, found websites and projects that would interest him? Alice had been all that for Jesse, and I'd had no idea.

She glanced up, and when she saw me, her eyes rounded. "Caleb?" she said, her voice quiet in the hush of the library. "Hi. I didn't expect to see you."

I blinked at her like an idiot. "You're…Ms. Clark?"

Her lips quirked, a hint of amusement in her eyes as she tugged on the end of her ponytail. "That's what they call me around here."

Of course they did. Because that was her name. I scrubbed a hand over my beard, trying to shake off the confusion, leftover anger simmering under my skin. Right. That was why I was here.

"We need to talk," I said gruffly.

Her brows lifted, and she tilted her head to the side, studying me. "About Jesse, I assume?"

"Yeah. About Jesse."

"Okay." She gestured toward a small side office off the front desk. "Let's step in here so we don't disturb anyone."

I followed, my eyes catching on the sway of her ponytail as that same spicy scent mixed with a hint of old books wrapped around me. I tried not to get swallowed up in how good she smelled. I didn't have time for those thoughts. I was here to put a stop to whatever idea she'd planted in my kid's head before he got his hopes up about something he couldn't have.

As soon as she closed her office door, I tossed the papers she'd given Jesse onto her desk.

"You shouldn't have told him about that camp. That wasn't your place."

She glanced down at the papers then back at me. For once, she didn't have any trouble holding my gaze.

"I would have brought it up to you or his mother, but neither of you ever comes inside." She tapped the stack with a well-manicured fingernail. Did she always have polish on her nails? I'd never noticed.

Christ, I was getting off track. Alice was talking, and I was looking at her nails.

"—told me about his robotics club, and I knew he'd love this camp. I've spoken with the program director. He graduated from MIT—"

"I don't doubt it's a great camp," I interjected before she got too far. "The fact of the matter is, you overstepped your bounds. You've got it in Jesse's head he's going to be going away for nearly a month. He's only thirteen. What thirteen-year-old leaves home for that long?"

She raised her chin, pulling her sweater tight around her. "Plenty, actually. Many kids go to camp for entire summers—at much younger ages and farther away. This program is only three weeks, and you could easily go see him, or he could come home for the weekends. If you would've read the information, you'd know that. It's not about taking Jesse away. This is about giving him an incredible opportunity to explore interests he, quite frankly, cannot do while hanging out on a ranch all summer."

I inhaled sharply. "Have you got something against ranch life, Ms. Clark?"

She didn't back down. Not even a little bit. "Absolutely not. I'm sure Jesse's learned a lot growing up on a ranch. But he needs *more*. Why would you not want him to have that?"

I crossed my arms over my chest. "Because he's thirteen, Alice. Thirteen. He doesn't need to be off living in dorms, surrounded by strangers. He's a kid. He should be at home."

"He *will* come home," she reminded me, like I needed it. Hell, maybe I did. "On weekends, if he wants to. And he'll call you every day. They have strict check-in policies. Did you read any of the packet Jesse gave you?"

"I don't need to read it," I bit out. "I know what's best for my son."

She flinched almost imperceptibly, and regret instantly twisted in my gut. I hadn't meant to be harsh with her. Sure didn't like making her flinch. Especially when she didn't deserve it. This was a sore spot Shelby and Kent had already danced all over. It was difficult not to lash out.

She didn't let it stop her.

"Do you?" Her voice was gentle, but her gaze was unflinching. "Seems to me you're thinking about yourself right now."

I bristled, heat creeping up the back of my neck. "Don't do that. Don't stand there and act like you know what's going on in my mind or house. Jesse's fine right where he is."

"Of course he is. He's a wonderful boy," she said, like she was stating a simple fact. I liked that. "He's also *more* than fine. He's brilliant, Caleb. He wants to build things and program things and understand how the world works. Don't you see that spark in him?"

"I couldn't miss it," I said gruffly. "But he's still a kid. He's got his whole life to be away from home. Why rush it now?"

"Because he *is* a kid. And kids grow. Their worlds get bigger. Their minds stretch to places we can't always follow. That's what's supposed to happen. We should encourage it."

I swallowed hard, my jaw tight. "I don't want him to go," I said lowly. "I just...don't want him gone."

She blinked, and for the first time, her expression gentled with understanding. "I know. But holding him back won't keep him close. It'll only teach him he has to shrink to stay loved."

That cut deep, sharp and clean. I didn't say anything. Couldn't. My tongue felt too heavy in my mouth.

She reached across her desk and laid her hand over the papers. "Take these home. Read them. Talk to Jesse. And...please think about it."

I did what she'd said: read the papers and questioned myself.

Would I have had the same knee-jerk reaction if I hadn't just come away from a confrontation with Kent?

The god's honest truth was probably not, and that pissed me off. Kent shouldn't have been in the equation at all.

I picked up the phone and called the most levelheaded person I knew. I would've walked over to his house if Jess weren't in the other room brooding, but a call would have to do.

My dad answered on the first ring. "Hey, Cay."

"Hey. Got a minute to let me bounce some thoughts off you?"

"Yep. Always. Hit me."

I pictured him sitting with his feet up on the coffee table, my mom either tucked up beside him or close by. They didn't stray far from each other. Never had.

"The librarian, Alice Clark, gave Jesse information about a summer camp in Laramie. It's three weeks long, and he'd stay in a dorm. Jesse wants to do it, but—"

"Three weeks is too long for you?"

"Way too long." Him gone a week at a time was my limit. I couldn't even wrap my head around more than that.

"What kind of camp is it?"

"STEM, focusing on robotics." I explained everything I'd read about the camp—the experts who'd be teaching, the activities, what the schedule would be like, what Jesse would learn.

He sucked in air through his teeth. "Ah. No wonder Jesse wants to go. Sounds like his idea of heaven."

"Yeah."

"Yeah," he echoed. "Your hesitation is it's too long to be away from home?"

"That, and the idea came from nowhere. The librarian found this camp for him. She contacted the guy who runs it to secure Jess a slot and told Jess about it. I may not have reacted well."

My dad went quiet for a beat. "Don't tell me you were a dick to her."

"I won't say it, but...yeah."

He hissed again. "Caleb Kelly, I don't like hearing that. That's not the man I know you to be."

It wasn't often I was scolded by my dad. Not when I was younger, and especially not now. When it happened, I felt it deep in my gut.

I stared at the paperwork spread across my kitchen table. "I know. I know I messed it up. But I can't get behind him going away for that long."

"What if you're stopping him from having the best time of his life? What if he comes home more confident, more curious, more himself than he's ever been?"

"That's what Alice said."

"She's a smart woman." I could hear the smile in his voice. "Listen, Cay. I get it. You're his dad. You don't want to let go. But part of raising a kid to become an independent adult is letting him learn he *can* be away from you and still be okay."

I rubbed the back of my neck, close to admitting defeat. "I know you're right. I do. I...just...he's my boy."

"Do you think he'll ever stop being your boy? Look at you, calling your dad for advice at your ripe old age." He chuckled. "Think about it this way: if you say no, will it be for him...or for you?"

That landed deep in my chest, heavy as a rock.

"For me," I choked out, hating the taste of it.

"Then you know what you need to do."

I nodded, even though he couldn't see me. "I do."

I'd put some thought into it, and no matter what, three weeks was a long time to be away. I couldn't agree without discussing it with Shelby and thorough research.

"Good man," he said. "Apologize to Alice as soon as you can. And don't forget to tell Jesse you're proud of him."

He was right on all counts. First, I'd make things right with Jesse, then I'd get to work on smoothing things over with Alice. "Thanks, Dad."

"Anytime. Love you."

"Love you too."

I hung up, staring at the kitchen wall for a long minute. Then I gathered the camp papers, squared the edges, and set them where I couldn't ignore them in the morning.

Chapter Nine

Alice

I WASN'T SURPRISED WHEN Jesse Kelly stopped by my desk two days later. First, he was a fixture at the library, and second, because of the conversation I'd had with his father.

The last two days, I'd mulled over my choice to give Jesse information about the camp, and finally decided I'd done nothing wrong. If either of his parents ever came inside the library, I would have spoken to them first. Maybe I should have made more of an effort there, but I'd been excited to tell Jesse about the opportunity I'd found for him.

Only to be ripped a new one, as much as I hated that expression.

I rose from my seat and smiled. "Hey, Jess."

The way he rubbed the back of his neck reminded me of his dad. "Hey, Ms. Clark. Can I talk to you for a minute?"

"Of course you can."

Jesse Kelly was something special. He'd been curious since the day I met him, never too shy to ask questions and learn about the world around him. The first couple years, his interests were varied, bouncing from one topic to the next. Lately, he'd homed in on robotics and history—two subjects I wouldn't say matched, but that was how his mind worked.

"Well, I wanted to tell you I'm sorry. I didn't know my dad was going to come in here, and I don't know what he said, but I hope—"

I raised my hand. "You have nothing to be sorry for. Your father had questions I hope I was able to answer. Don't worry even for a second."

His brows rose, crinkling his forehead. "Yeah? Are you sure?"

"Positive." I waved it away. "It's in the past. Now, tell me about your club meeting yesterday. Are you guys ready for the competition?"

His whole face lit up, his worries falling away. "Almost. We worked on adjusting the gripper arm because it wasn't rotating smoothly enough to grab the blocks off the ground. We figured maybe the motor was bad, but it turned out one of the wires was loose. So we fixed that, and now it's working way better."

"That sounds really awesome," I said, smiling at the way his hands moved as he explained. "Did you get to test it out?"

"Yep, ran a full practice match, and we killed it. Except"—he grimaced, shoulders hunching a little—"we realized it was too heavy on one side. Every time we turned it too fast, it tipped, so we had to take off part of the frame and replace it with a lighter panel. I think it'll work better now, but we won't know until we test it tomorrow."

I leaned my elbows on the desk. "That's how real engineers do it. They solve problems on the fly."

He grinned, ducking his head sheepishly. "I guess. I just hope it works. If it tips during competition, I might throw up right there on the mat."

I laughed. "Let's hope for everyone's sake it stays upright."

He laughed too, his shoulders relaxing as he rocked back on his heels. "Thanks for listening, Ms. Clark. It...helps. Talking about it."

"Anytime, Jess. You know where to find me."

He nodded and stepped back, but before he turned to go, he said quietly, "And thanks again for the camp thing. I still really wanna go."

My chest tightened, but I kept my smile, hoping against hope he wasn't disappointed. "Let's cross our fingers. No matter what happens, though, you should be really proud of yourself for all the work you've put into learning robotics. I couldn't be prouder."

His ears turned pink, and with a little wave, he hurried back toward his favorite table to study at, leaving me with a heart that ached in too many ways to count.

For the second time since I'd taken over as head librarian of Sugar Brush Community Library, Caleb Kelly strode up to my desk. I didn't even have to look up to know it was him. The wall of him blocked out the light for miles around, and his footsteps were rolls of thunder in a calm sky.

Even knowing it was him, I took my time looking up...and up...and up. Not as a power move—to brace myself for his next onslaught.

Finally, I stood, meeting his gaze head-on.

"Hey," he gruffed, rubbing the back of his neck like his son had a couple hours ago. "Am I interrupting?"

I flung my hand toward my computer. "Just...you know, work. It can wait a minute or two."

"Good." He nodded and dropped his hands to his sides. "I'm sorry for the way I spoke to you. It wasn't right. I could tell you I have a lot going on right now, but that's no excuse."

"No, it isn't. I have a lot going on as well, but I don't take it out on other people."

He jerked slightly, as if I'd surprised him with my rebuke.

Dang it, he deserved it.

He'd made me feel about two inches tall—on top of rejecting me a couple weeks ago.

He swallowed, glancing down at the floor before looking back at me. His eyes were like melted chocolate, so earnest, it made something inside me twist.

But I ignored it. Or tried to.

"I read the information," he said. "About that camp. Robotics and coding and engineering...sounds like a good opportunity."

I folded my hands in front of me, fighting the urge to fiddle with the hem of my sweater. "It is. It's one of the best STEM camps in the country for kids his age. I thought of him as soon as I heard about it."

"I believe that, and I understand why it'd be good for him." He nodded slowly, rubbing his jaw like he was working something out in his mind. "The thing is, I've got five years left with him. I know he's not staying in Wyoming for college, and if I'm honest with myself, he won't be back after he gets his education. At least, not to live. The thought of losing some of the little time I have left kills me—and I already have to split it in half with his mom."

"That makes sense," I said, and I meant it. No matter what I felt about Caleb, I didn't doubt he loved his son down to his bones. It was part of what made him so attractive to me.

Dang it.

"It's no excuse, though." He pinned me with more earnest staring. "I shouldn't have stormed in all half-cocked and gotten in your face. There was no call to do that, and I'm more than sorry I went there with you."

"I accept your apology."

He sighed, and it was a tired sound, like the weight of the ranch and his son and his entire life pressed down on his chest. "Appreciate you doing that. And for looking out for Jess. He loves coming here, talking to you. I'd hate to ruin that for him."

"You didn't." I tucked my hair behind my ear. "You couldn't."

"Thanks."

He looked so worn out, standing there in his dusty jeans and gray T-shirt, boots scuffed, hair tousled from his hat. A part of me wanted to reach out, smooth his hair, and tell him he was doing a good job. But I kept my arms tight against my sides.

The truth was, it would be easier to get over him now. After seeing this side of him—the rigid, defensive side that lashed out before thinking—I didn't want to hold on to the little hopes I'd carried for so long. He'd also shown me, while I'd been pining away for him, memorizing his tells and hanging on his every word, he hadn't even bothered to learn a single thing about me.

"Anyway," he said, shifting his weight. "I'm going to look into the camp. See if we can make it work."

"That's great. I think he'd thrive there."

His eyes flicked over my face, lingering for half a breath before he nodded and turned away. As he walked toward his son's table, I let out a slow, quiet sigh.

Maybe it would hurt a while longer. Eventually, I'd let go of what I'd once wanted with him.

What I wanted now was someone who saw me from the start—and didn't need to be convinced to treat me with care.

Joy waylaid me as soon as I ducked behind the bar. She'd been watching me like a hawk the past couple weeks, as if waiting for me to break down.

"Not ready to quit yet?" she asked.

I laughed as I took off my jacket and grabbed my apron. "No. I told you I like working here. It's not about the money."

She crossed her arms. "How're you ever going to build a life when you're either here or at the library every second of the day?"

I tied my apron in a neat bow. "That's a gross exaggeration, and you know it. You haven't let me work Saturdays in ages."

"'Cause you should be out there, enjoying your youth. I've never been one to think a woman needs a man—*you* don't—but everyone needs to let loose." She tugged on the ends of my hair. "You let your hair down, now what're you gonna do about it?"

I took her hand in mine and gave it a squeeze before dropping it. Joy wasn't the touchy-feely type, so I didn't push my luck.

"I went shopping last weekend—with other people."

Elena and Margot had swept me off to Cheyenne, just like they'd said. Now I had drawers and a closet filled with clothes they'd stamped their approval on. And they'd been right—purple was definitely my color. I may have gone overboard with it, but that was okay. I doubted anyone but me would notice what I was wearing anyway.

Joy nodded. "That's a step in the right direction, at least." Her mouth turned down as she peered at me. "You ever want to talk about her?"

My hand paused on its way to tucking my hair behind my ear. "Who?"

"Your sister. You haven't said a word since you got that letter. I've been waiting for you to bring her up."

I stuffed my hands in my apron pockets, sighing. "There's nothing to talk about. We weren't close. It's sad she's gone, but she didn't have an easy life. The last few years...I don't know how bad it got. She wouldn't allow it. She's not in pain anymore, though, and that's a relief."

"All that might be true, but that's all her. You didn't say anything about you—how you're feeling."

I should have known this was coming. Joy wasn't one to drop things, and despite our differences and her gruff, closed-off nature, I didn't doubt she cared about me.

"I think..." I bit down on my bottom lip, searching for the right words. "I think I did my grieving when Silla cut off contact with me. And...I guess I'm sad about what a waste her life was, and that there's no possibility of reconciliation. But for me, she's been gone for a long time."

Joy clamped her hand on my shoulder a little too hard, like she wasn't used to comforting someone.

"I hope that's how it stays, Alice. If it hits you out of the blue, you come to me. I'm not much of a hugger, but if you need it, my arms are open to you."

She left me quickly, avoiding my glassy eyes and the little sniffle I couldn't hold back. She shouldn't have said such lovely things if she didn't want to deal with the consequences.

Pulling myself together, I went to work, taking orders and delivering drinks and food with my brightest smile. After all this time, the movements were rote, so my mind drifted.

To Caleb and his too-late apology. To Jesse and the miracle of his curious mind. To Silla, who hadn't let me love her, no matter how many parts of myself I gave. To Joy, who had let me in despite herself.

I kept Joy's words closest. They were a reminder I wasn't as alone as I sometimes felt. I had at least one person in my corner without me having to ask.

The thought didn't take away the sting of rejection or the deep, hollow ache of loneliness, but it steadied me, giving me something to stand on when the floor felt shaky.

Exactly what I needed.

Chapter Ten

Alice

FOR THE SECOND DAY in a row, Caleb blocked out the light around him. He found me in the stacks, his massive shadow suddenly looming over me. I let out a yelp and jumped backward, hitting the book cart beside me.

His arm shot out, catching my elbow. Once I was steady, I removed my arm from his grasp.

"Sorry," he murmured, holding up his hands. "I thought you saw me coming."

I pressed my hand over my fluttering heart. "I didn't. I was concentrating on my task."

"Sorry," he repeated. "I'll give you a warning sign next time."

"That sounds like a good idea." I licked my lips, but it didn't do much good. "Jesse should be at his favorite table."

"He is. I spoke with him."

"Okay..." I took a step back, tucking my hair behind my ear. Caleb's eyes followed the movement.

"You changed your hair."

My mouth fell open, stunned. Not only had he noticed, but he'd remarked on it. Admittedly, it looked great. I'd perfected using the curling iron, only burning myself once. But why was he bringing it up? Why was he here, talking to me at all?

"I did. A couple weeks ago."

He nodded. "I noticed...that day at the diner. When you were on your date."

I wrinkled my nose. "I remember." That had been an incredibly awkward few hours. We'd had nothing in common, and I'd over-compensated by laughing too much. At least it had been a good lesson in what I didn't want in a future partner.

"Right." He rested his elbow on the shelf beside him. "It looks nice, but you didn't need to change it."

I stopped myself from smoothing a hand over my bouncy curls. "I *wanted* a change."

He cleared his throat. "Hope it wasn't because of me—of what I did."

I let out a quiet laugh, shaking my head. "No, Caleb. The changes I've made have nothing to do with you."

He nodded once, then harder a second time, like my answer had really mattered. "Good. That's good."

"Yeah." I exhaled slowly, unsure where to go from here. He wasn't clueing me in. "Is there something I can help you with, or was that it?"

A faint smile curved his lips, and his eyes flicked up to mine, warmer now. "Actually, I was wondering if I could get a library card."

That surprised me enough I almost lost my footing and stumbled into my cart again. Luckily, I caught myself on the shelf. "A library card? You don't have one?"

He shrugged one of his massive shoulders. "Never needed one before. Jesse always checks out his own books. But there's one I'm interested in reading, so I figure it's time."

"That's a very good reason." I smiled, and it wasn't even wobbly. This was my territory—where I was most confident. I could handle Caleb here. "I can definitely help with that."

I led him between the stacks and out to the main desk. Jesse watched warily as we passed, but Caleb waved, telling him everything was all right without breaking step with me.

I moved behind the desk, gesturing to the clipboard with the sign-up sheet. "Just fill out your name and address there. I'll get you all set up."

He picked up the pen, his big fingers dwarfing it, and bent over the paper. I tried not to watch him, but failed spectacularly. His handwriting was unexpectedly neat, almost blocklike.

"How long have you been a librarian, Alice?"

I jerked my eyes from the paper. His head was still bowed, the pen moving rapidly as he filled in the blanks.

"Since I finished my master's degree five years ago."

He nodded. "You need that kind of degree to do this job?"

"Not to work in a library, but to be a librarian, yes, you do."

He finally lifted his head to eye me with interest. "You have a master's degree and you're still waitressing."

"It fills my nights." My mouth curved into a half smile. "And I don't know if you know this, but being the head librarian in Sugar Brush isn't exactly going to make me a millionaire."

Though technically, I was one now. I only had to lose my entire family for that to happen.

"No, I guess not." He shook his head. "I should have guessed it."

"Guessed what?"

"That you were a librarian. The way you always snuck in reading a few pages between customers."

My heart flipped. He'd noticed that...yet, he'd missed a whole lot more.

"You didn't have to guess, Caleb." I lifted my chin, meeting his warm gaze. "Anytime in the last four years, you could have asked."

"Yeah." He put down the pen and laid his big hand across the application. "I should've. I'm seeing that now."

Too late. Too late. Too late.

Opening his eyes now, after all this time? It was almost insulting.

I swallowed past the lump forming in my throat and pulled the application toward me. "Why don't you go find the book you're interested in while I get your card ready?"

He hesitated, eyes holding mine like he wanted to say something more, then he gave a single nod. "Yeah. Okay."

As he turned and strode off between the stacks, I shook off the effects of being in close proximity to Caleb Kelly and went to work. My hands moved automatically, inputting his details into the system like I'd done dozens of times.

What book could Caleb possibly want to check out? He wasn't a reader. He'd admitted that.

The card printer whirred to life. I was focused on peeling the adhesive backing and slotting it into the protective sleeve when his boots sounded on the carpet again. I looked up, ready to ask what he'd chosen, and froze.

In his big hand was a hardcover copy of *The Shadow of the Isle.*

My favorite book. The one I reread at least once a year. It was on the tip of my tongue to tell him that. How it had gotten me through countless hospital waiting rooms, the weight of my sister's illness, lonely days and nights, and had transported me to another realm when everything was too heavy.

Instead, I clamped my mouth shut, took the book from him, and scanned it.

He rested his elbow on the counter. "I heard it was good."

"It is." I didn't quite meet his gaze when I smiled at him. "I hope you like it."

"You know, if you wouldn't mind, I'd like to talk to you about it as I read it." He took out his phone. "Could I have your number?"

It wasn't often I got angry. I'd never found much use for it. Now? Red flashed behind my eyes as a ball of fury filled my belly to the point of bursting.

Could he have my number?

Could he have my *number*?

Oh, this man. Whatever he was playing at was not happening. I was over him. I'd moved on. He didn't get to suddenly take an interest in me.

"No." I pushed the book and his new card toward him.

He went stock-still for a moment, then uttered, "No?"

"Right." I squared my shoulders. "No. You can't have my number."

He dropped his phone on top of the book and stared down at me, his brow furrowed in deep lines.

"Alice, I—"

I held up one hand. "After four years of liking you and being too"—I dropped my voice to a whisper—"chickenshit to do anything about it, I finally made a move, and you rejected me, which is your right. So—"

"You've liked me for four years?" he asked, incredulous, which showed how little he paid attention to me.

"I hate to admit it, but yes." I tucked my hair behind my ear and put on a brave face. "Then I decided to get over you, so I did."

"You did?" he echoed.

"Yes, I'm over you."

I sounded a lot more sure than I felt. Eventually, though, it would be true. Hopefully, sooner rather than later.

Before Caleb could say another word, Jesse appeared beside him. "Are you checking out a book?"

Caleb slid his gaze from me to his son. "I am. Thought on the nights you've got your nose stuck in one, I could join you."

"Really?" Jesse screwed his face up, skeptical. "I mean, I know you can read, but can you *read*?"

Caleb choked out a laugh. "Yeah, kid, I can read. It's been a while since I finished a book, but I'm pretty sure I can handle it. Besides, I hear this one is really good."

Jesse peered at the title, his eyes darting to mine. "He's reading your favorite book."

I shot a grin his way. "That's the rumor. You'll have to let me know if he actually does."

He crossed his arms, side-eyeing his dad. "Oh, believe me, I will."

Caleb ruffled his son's hair. "All right. Enough making me the butt of your joke. Are you ready to head home?"

"Yep." Jesse's brows shot up. "But first, I need to ask Ms. Clark a question."

I leaned forward, my hands on the desk. "What's that?"

He glanced at his dad then back at me. "If you're free Saturday, it would be cool if you came to my competition. It's in Lander, at the high school. You don't have to come or anything, but you know, you might like to watch."

I hesitated, but couldn't think of a reason why I shouldn't go. Jesse had been telling me about his team's robot for months. Seeing it in action would be incredible.

"Yes, I'd like that very much."

"Cool." He shrugged, a small smile tugging at the corners of his mouth. "It starts at ten. You might want to get there around then to get a good seat."

I tapped my temple. "I've got it in the schedule. I'll be there."

When he walked back to his table to grab his backpack, Caleb was still watching me, his eyes unreadable as he tucked his book under his arm.

"You don't have to go. He'll understand."

I frowned. "I want to. From what Jesse tells me, his robot's going to destroy all the others. How could I miss that?"

The corner of his mouth hitched. "When you put it that way, I guess you couldn't. And don't worry, I'll keep clear of you."

"It's no big deal if you don't."

"Right." He rocked back on his heels, his gaze sliding over my face and neck before returning to meet my eyes. Then his mouth formed the words I'd said before Jesse interrupted us. "*Over you.*"

"Yeah," I agreed softly. "Over you."

He saluted me with my favorite book, then turned to join Jesse, leaving me standing there, confused and a little pissed off. Why was he looking at me like that? Turning up at *my* library? Asking me questions? Showing more interest in a few days than he had in four years combined?

I'd never know why, and it didn't matter. I'd moved on.

You're over him. You're over him. You're over him.

I almost believed it.

When I arrived home, there was a potted plant on my porch that hadn't been there when I'd left. I bent down to examine it, finding a small, folded piece of paper tucked in the leaves. Opening it, I read the neatly scrawled note inside.

Alice,

Hope an apology plant is okay. My grandmother said this kind is easy to take care of and hard to kill. Don't know if you have a green thumb, so I thought it was a safe bet.

This is a thank-you plant too. I appreciate all you've done for Jesse, giving him a safe place to spend time, being a listening ear, encouraging him. Means a lot to me, and Jesse too.

Be good and take care.

• CK

I sank down on my porch step, thoroughly bowled over. Damn that man. He'd found a way around my flower ban and hastily constructed walls. Did he not understand how hard I was working to move on?

Probably not.

Well, I'd have to work harder.

I took out my phone, opened my dating app, and swiped to the conversation I'd been having with a guy the last few days. I'd been lukewarm about meeting him. Now I couldn't remember why.

It might have been his slightly off-color jokes or the fact that his profile picture was him holding up a fish half his size, but I knew better than to judge a book by its cover.

I needed to move on. Truly.

It had taken less than five minutes to arrange a date. That easy. He was looking forward to it. By Saturday night, I was sure I would be too.

I looked at the plant beside me, its bright-green leaves unfurling under the porch light.

"I'm done," I whispered to it. "Really. I'm done."

I stood, brushed off my skirt, and carried the plant inside.

Chapter Eleven

Caleb

Aside from a couple seasons of football, I hadn't been much of a joiner back in my school days. It was all I had been able to do to sit through class. Where I really wanted to be was on the ranch. I'd long ago accepted my son wasn't anything like me, though—not when it came to school and learning.

I sat in the bleachers, elbows resting on my knees, watching the semi-organized chaos happening on the gymnasium floor. Kids darted between tables and taped-off lanes, some crouched over laptops, others fiddled with little wheeled robots that reminded me of souped-up vacuums.

Jesse was with his team, all of them wearing matching forest-green T-shirts. He'd spent half of last night on a call with his team, going over strategy and last-minute adjustments. This morning, he'd had so much on his mind, he'd barely spared me a word. I hadn't taken it personally. This was his world. I was just here to support him as he made it spin.

I shifted on the hard wooden bench, rubbing at the back of my neck, my gaze wandering across the crowded gym. Coaches imparted reminders. Parents drank coffees bigger than their heads, trying to look alert. Kids tinkered with their robots.

Shelby was supposed to be here, but she'd texted Jesse early this morning, canceling. She'd given some excuse about Kent having an emergency. I wasn't buying it, but I'd decided to mentally cut her some slack. Overall, she'd shown up to more of Jesse's activities than she'd missed.

That didn't mean I wasn't pissed she'd disappointed our son. He'd tried to play it off, but there'd been no missing the slump in his shoulders.

I raked my hand over my beard, wincing at how overgrown it was. When was the last time I trimmed it? Cocking my head to the side, I racked my memories. Before I could pin down a date, Alice stepped through the door on the far side of the gym, pausing just inside, taking everything in.

Her pretty, fluffy curls spilled over her shoulders, covered in a faded denim jacket she wore over an eggplant-colored top and black pants. She looked a little lost, clutching her purse strap as she scanned the bleachers and floor like she wasn't sure where to go.

I wasn't sure either. Anyone else, I would've waved. Said hello. Done the polite small-talk thing.

"I'm over you."

I'd been mulling over her pronouncement since she'd made it. It wasn't something I'd ever been told, and while I supposed I should've viewed it as a good thing, it didn't sit right with me. Problem was, I couldn't sort out why.

Alice being over me was a good thing—for her sake. Being into me wouldn't lead her anywhere good. Except, I didn't know what Alice being over me looked like. Did I get ignored? Would she no longer serve my table at Joy's? Get treated like I was every other customer?

I didn't like the sound of any of that.

Alice crossed the gym floor, dodging kids and robots, until she reached the bleachers. As she climbed, she glanced around for a place to sit. The wooden rows had filled fast. If I didn't speak up, she'd have to wedge herself between strangers.

"Alice."

She turned, easily finding me on the edge of a row two steps up. I pointed to the empty space beside me.

"Come on. There's room for you right here."

She flashed me a small, tentative smile and made her way up. I scooted over for her, giving her the end seat. As she sat down beside me, I caught the faintest hint of cinnamon.

"Do you bake?"

Startled by my question, her head jerked. "I...oh, no, not really. Why?"

I took a long whiff of the air around her. "You always smell like cinnamon."

She brought her hand up to the side of her neck, a little furrow forming between her brows.

"It's my perfume." She crinkled her nose. "I like flowers, but I don't want to smell like one."

I let myself have another whiff. "You smell like Christmas."

Her laugh was light and breezy. "I hope that's a good thing."

I grunted. "My favorite time of year."

"Mine too," she said quietly. Then she shifted slightly away from me but slid her eyes back my way. "Thank you for the plant. You didn't have to do that."

"You're welcome." I lowered my chin and voice. "Felt it was the least I could do."

"It really wasn't necessary." She lifted her hand, her thumb extended. "It's brown, by the way. The plant's still alive, but I can't guarantee how long it will stay that way."

It was my turn to laugh. "My grandmother swore that kind of plant is impossible to kill."

She narrowed her eyes. "Sounds like a challenge if I ever heard one."

Before I could think of a comeback, the overhead speakers let out a loud squeal, putting an end to our conversation.

"Attention, teams and spectators," the announcer boomed, his voice echoing off the gym walls. "We're about to begin the first round of obstacle course runs. Team sign-ups one through five, please bring your robots to the starting lanes."

Down on the floor, Jesse and his teammates scrambled to gather their equipment. I sat forward, bracing my forearms on my knees, eyes locked on my boy as he carried their little robot to the starting line. His face was set with determination, his mouth moving as he spoke to his friend beside him.

"He looks so confident," Alice murmured, as if to herself.

I glanced at her. Her elbows were pressed together in her lap, hands clasped tight, eyes bright with excitement as she watched the kids prepare.

She hadn't shown up to humor Jesse. She was into this.

"Yeah," I said. "He is. He's always been that way."

She shook her head. "He's such a cool kid."

"He sure is," I agreed, pleased she'd said it. "The coolest."

The buzzer sounded, and Jesse's robot shot forward, weaving through the first set of cones like it was nothing. His team cheered from behind the taped-off lane, and I joined in, giving a short, sharp whistle.

Alice laughed. "That's some whistle. Is that how you get your cattle to follow you?"

"Sometimes. I have to use all the tricks I have up my sleeve." I couldn't tear my eyes away from Jesse's robot as it pivoted perfectly around a corner.

"Well, it certainly carries," she said. "He heard you. Look at that smile."

She was right. Jesse glanced up into the bleachers, his grin wide as he pumped his fist at his team. My heart thumped hard in my chest.

The robot reached the final stretch, and Alice practically bounced with excitement. I should've been watching my son cross the finish line, but my gaze kept flicking sideways, catching the glow on Alice's face, the way her curls swayed with every small movement. She looked so alive, eyes shining, cinnamon drifting around every time she shifted.

The robot crossed the line, and Jesse's team erupted in cheers. I whooped along with them, but my throat was tight. I couldn't explain it. I was happy for my kid, but something felt off.

Alice leaped to her feet, clapping and jumping up and down. I stood beside her, calling Jesse's name, and he turned, grinning like a madman. Then he noticed Alice, and his smile grew bigger than I'd ever seen.

Yeah, that felt good. Exactly as it should've been.

When the applause died and the teams geared up for the next round, I took my place beside Alice. She smoothed her hands over her lap and pressed her knees together, taking up as little room as possible.

I knocked my knee against hers. "Thanks for coming. Jess's mom couldn't make it. It's nice you came out to support him."

"Of course. This is a lot more fun than I thought it would be." She moved her leg away from mine. "I'm sure his mom wishes she were here."

"Eh, don't know about that. Six months ago, I would've agreed, but she hooked up with this guy who's got her wound up all wrong. Her priorities aren't straight. All Kent, all the time."

As soon as it was out of my mouth, I wondered why I'd said it. I didn't spill my personal life all over town. In fact, I wasn't much of a talker at all.

"They come into Joy's sometimes." She seemed to have more to say, but clamped down on her bottom lip to stop herself.

I cocked my head. "Yeah? What kind of tipper is Kent?"

Her eyes flitted downward, and I chuckled. She didn't have to say a single word.

"That bad, huh?"

Her gaze sprang back up to meet mine. Fresh and green. Bright and alive. Reminding me of those minutes in the bar bathroom, her in my arms, her lips swollen from kissing mine.

"I'm pretty sure that's confidential," she sputtered.

"Yeah? Like a lawyer?" I teased.

"Something like that. I'm assuming you've never waited tables?"

"Nope." I shook my head. "Only place I've worked is on the ranch."

"Then you wouldn't know about the oath we have to take before starting the job."

My brow dropped. "Oath? Joy made you take an oath?"

I believed her for exactly one second, then she started giggling, blowing her cover.

Her giggle faded into a grin as she tucked a curl behind her ear. "You looked like you were ready to spit nails."

I shook my head, chuckling. "You almost had me."

"Almost?" She raised an eyebrow.

"Okay, you got me for a second. Didn't know you had it in you to jerk me around like that." I nudged her lightly with my elbow. "I was about ready to head over there and give Joy a piece of my mind."

"Please don't," she said, still laughing. "Joy probably wouldn't give you that piece back."

"No doubt she'd grind it under her boot." I bumped her with my leg again. "I'm glad you came. There's normally a lot of waiting around at these things. It's nice to have another adult to talk to. Makes the time go faster."

Her cheeks flushed rosy pink as she turned to scan the action on the floor. "Yeah. I'm glad I came."

We settled back into watching the next group set up. Alice rested her chin on her fists, enthralled with everything going on.

"I wish I'd done stuff like this when I was their age," she murmured.

"What did you do instead?"

"Nothing like this. All the fun I had happened in books."

"So you've always been a bookworm?"

She shrugged and ducked her head. "I guess."

"Makes sense to me. I've always been a cowboy. My dad put me on a horse with him before I could walk, and the rest was history. Guess we both ended up where we were supposed to."

"That's a nice thought." She glanced at me. "I've never ridden a horse."

"And I've barely read a book."

A laugh burst out of her, like buds in the spring—full of life, promising something beautiful. "I don't believe you. After all, you're a certified library cardholder now."

"True. I'm a changed man." I tipped toward her. "You'll have to come out to the ranch sometime. Me and Jess will get you riding in no time."

"Maybe I will."

I was surprised at how easy our banter was. Like this was normal. Like we did it all the time. Maybe after all that had gone down, we'd end up being friends. Stranger things had happened.

When the next round ended, Jesse and his team ran back to their table to start prepping again. I watched him for a second, pride burning in my chest, then turned back to Alice.

"We're probably gonna go out for pizza after this," I said, trying to sound casual. "Would you like to join us? Jesse'd be pleased if you did."

Her smile faltered for a split second. "Oh. I...I can't."

I frowned. "Are you working tonight?"

She hesitated. "No. I don't work Saturday nights anymore. I have other plans."

"Plans?" I echoed. "What kind of plans?"

It was none of my business, but her evasiveness had me curious. What did Alice Clark get up to on her nights off?

"Just plans. It doesn't matter."

The way she wouldn't meet my eyes set off a warning bell in my head. I narrowed my gaze.

"Alice," I uttered lowly, "what plans?"

She sighed, finally telling me, "I'm going out to dinner."

I sat there staring at her, trying to make sense of what she'd just said. Then understanding dawned.

"A date," I said flatly. "From an app?"

She chewed on her bottom lip, nodding.

"Christ," I breathed. I didn't like that. Those apps couldn't be safe. Meeting up with strange men whose intentions were unknown... "You know that's not safe."

"We're meeting at a restaurant. It's perfectly safe."

I didn't say anything for a long moment. My jaw clenched. My chest tightened with a wave of dread too big for the situation. Alice wasn't mine. She could do what she wanted. But I did not like this idea. Not at all.

I faced the floor, watching Jesse work with his team, something sour churning in my gut. I had no say here. I couldn't tell her not to go. Even if I did, she'd probably laugh in my face.

Dating apps have been around for a long time. It wasn't something I'd ever do, but I was old-fashioned in a lot of ways. Alice wanted someone in her life, and when I thought about it, I couldn't name a single man in town I'd match her with. Maybe trying another method made sense for her. My approval had no bearing here.

"Well," I said finally, my voice gruffer than I intended. "Hope it works out for you."

"I hope it does too."

She fell silent beside me, and for the first time since she'd sat down, the narrow space between us felt wide and empty.

I didn't know what I felt exactly, but I knew I didn't like it. Not any of it.

Chapter Twelve

Alice

I'D STAYED TOO LONG at the robotics competition, and now I was late. I rushed into the restaurant—really, more of a bar than I'd been expecting—crossing my fingers my lip gloss wasn't smeared on my teeth and my mascara hadn't smudged in my haste to apply it.

I found my date at the bar, looking exactly like his pictures.

Tall and rangy, James looked good in Wranglers and a T-shirt. In the back of my mind, I noted he hadn't dressed up for the occasion, but I set those judgmental thoughts aside. He might've been in as big of a rush as I had.

He grinned when he saw me and slid off his stool to pull me into a hug. His shirt clung to his overly warm back, and the sharp scent of his cologne mixed with something musky—like he'd been working all day and had sprayed himself without showering first.

"Glad you made it, Alice." His arms stayed around me too long, pressing me against him. I leaned back to create space, and even then, he didn't let go right away.

"Yeah, sorry I'm late." I laughed lightly, trying to shift the awkwardness aside. "The day got away from me."

He finally let me go to pick up his drink and take a long pull. "Let's order you a drink. Mind if we sit at the bar? We can eat dinner and watch the game."

If I had an objection, it didn't matter. James pulled out the stool next to his and gave it a pat. I guessed we were eating dinner at the bar. At least if we ran out of things to talk about, the game was on to fill the void. I could be a good sport.

"What do you want to drink?" James tipped into my space.

"I think I'll just have a Coke." My stomach was already a mix of nerves and trepidation. Adding alcohol didn't seem like the best move.

James was having none of it. He flagged down the bartender and ordered my Coke with a generous serving of rum. When it arrived, I laughed it off and took a sip. One cocktail wouldn't hurt, I supposed.

There was nothing about this man I liked, but he seemed to like me just fine. Five minutes after meeting, he'd rested his hand on my knee, squeezing every so often like he needed to remind me he was there. When our food finally came, he slid his barstool closer, his thigh pressing firmly against mine.

"You're so pretty," he said, leaning in close enough I could smell the beer and onions on his breath. "Way prettier than your pictures."

"Thanks." I tried to scoot away without drawing attention, but my stool was stuck to the sticky floor, so I ended up tilting my upper body at a forty-five-degree angle.

Forcing a smile, I pushed a fry through a puddle of ketchup. Maybe he was a little drunk. Maybe my urge to flee was an overreaction.

"So, what do you do again?" he asked around a mouthful of food, his other hand brushing against my waist.

"I'm a librarian."

"That's sexy. I bet you know how to be nice and quiet." His eyes flicked up and down my body. "Until it's time to get loud."

I swallowed hard, setting my half-eaten burger back on the plate. "I'm going to run to the restroom."

He pouted, leaning back on his stool and spreading his legs. "Don't worry. I'll guard your dinner and drink with my life."

I muttered a thanks then rushed by him as fast as I could without making a scene.

The restroom wasn't the most sanitary, but I was grateful for the moment of solitude. I washed my hands, staring at my reflection under the harsh fluorescent lights. My cheeks were pale, my eyes tired. *I should leave.* The thought pulsed through me with every beat of my heart. I couldn't think of a single reason to stay. James wasn't concerned about my feelings, so why should I worry I might hurt his by cutting this date short?

I took a deep breath and walked back out, my purse clutched tight against my side, the half a hamburger I'd eaten sitting like lead in my stomach.

"There she is." James grinned happily when I reached him, patting my stool. "Sit, finish your dinner and Coke."

"Actually, I think I should head home. I'm not feeling great."

"Oh no. That's not good." His voice dropped low, almost gentle. "No more burger for you, but you should finish your drink. It might settle your stomach for the ride home."

His sincerity made me hesitate. That, and the eyes of the bartender and the other guys sitting at the bar. The last thing I wanted to do was cause a scene.

"Okay. I'll stay a few more minutes." I perched on my stool and sipped my soda to be polite.

Much to my relief, James didn't put his hand on me. He concentrated on eating the rest of his fries and downing his beer while peppering me with a few questions about my life, putting me at ease. He told me a few stories about himself too. If even half were true, he'd lived a wild life. He'd been a rodeo clown, to war, divorced three times, and had patented an invention. I was so entertained, I finished my whole drink and most of my french fries.

The longer I sat there, though, a strange fuzziness began to spread through me. My limbs felt heavier than normal, and I couldn't quite grasp a single thought. I wasn't drunk. I knew what that felt like, and it wasn't this. I was...almost outside my body.

"You're not looking so great, Alice. I think it's time to wrap this up and let you get home." His voice sounded far away, but his face was so close to mine, it blurred. He wrapped his hand around my wrist, his thumb rubbing circles into my skin. "I'll walk you to your car."

"I... yeah, I..." I couldn't finish the sentence. My tongue felt thick in my mouth.

He smiled and helped me off my stool. "Come on, babe. Let's get you home."

The floor wavered beneath me as he guided me into the cool spring night. The fresh air did nothing to clear the fogginess of my thoughts. I tried to focus on the gravel crunching under his boots, on the smell of diesel, the faint scent of alcohol drifting out of the bar—anything to keep me grounded so I didn't float away.

James's grip on my waist was firm and possessive as he led me through the parking lot. We kept walking and walking. I swore I'd asked him where he was taking me, but since he didn't answer, maybe I was wrong and had asked it in my head.

My vision swam, bright lights from the bar flickering like distant stars. I tried to pull away, but my feet didn't obey, sliding clumsily on the gravel. Even if he let me go, I wasn't sure I'd be able to stand on my own.

"Where...my car..." I couldn't get my thoughts and my tongue to match up.

James chuckled under his breath. "Don't worry, Alice. I've got you. I'm going to take good care of you."

Panic ignited in my gut, then flickered and died as quickly as it had sparked. "No...my car..."

He steered me sharply to the side, between two big trucks parked near the back of the lot. The shadows swallowed us, and his fingers dug into my waist.

"That hurts," I whispered, but my plea came out as little more than a sigh.

He pressed me back against the side of one of the trucks, the metal cold through my thin blouse. His hand fisted in my hair, pulling my head back, straining my neck.

"You're going to be coming home with me," he said, his voice low and rough, his breath hot against my cheek. "I've been nice all night. It's time you returned the favor, little bookworm."

His other hand went up under my shirt, gripping my side hard enough to bruise. I tried to push him away, but my arms were useless, flopping against his chest and falling down to dangle at my sides.

"Please don't…" Tears burned hot behind my lids. My knees buckled, and I slumped forward into him. He shoved me upright, the back of my head hitting the truck door with a dull *thunk*. Stars burst in my vision, nausea rolling through me.

"This doesn't have to be hard, Alice. We can have fun together, sweet thing," he murmured.

I tried to tell him no, to shove him away, but he shook my shoulders so hard, my teeth clacked together. The ground tilted, the gravel beneath my shoes shifting sideways.

He jerked me forward again, trying to drag me away from the truck, but my foot caught on the tire. I stumbled, my ankle rolling, and went down hard. My elbow hit first, a sharp shock of pain shooting up my arm, then the side of my head cracked against the gravel.

For a moment, the world spun in blurry circles. James's face loomed above me…the dark sky…the orange glow of the bar sign flickering in the distance…

Then everything went mercifully black.

Chapter Thirteen

Caleb

THE LAST PLACE I wanted to be at the crack of dawn on Sunday morning was the emergency room. But when one of my hands gashed himself up in the stables, it fell on me to make sure he got taken care of.

At least Jesse was with my grandparents until Shelby picked him up. I didn't have to worry about him while I sat through Emmett's stitches, X-rays, and discharge instructions. One of the boys was giving him a ride back to the bunkhouse, leaving me free to hunt for some coffee before heading home.

I was halfway down the hall toward the exit when a scream split the quiet morning.

"No! Get away from me! Please, I have to go. Let me go."

My whole body went cold. Every instinct honed from years of working cattle and raising my boy told me exactly what that scream was—pure terror.

I spun in the direction the sound came from. A nurse rushed past me toward one of the private rooms, a phone at her ear, her words sharp with urgency.

"She's waking up disoriented—watch her IV—someone get Dr. Tennison—Alice, the patient in room twelve—"

Alice?

It couldn't be. Not my Alice. She'd been fine when we parted ways yesterday. On her way to her—

Date.

The next scream shredded through me. It was her. I knew it. No idea how. Just did.

I hurried past a nurse to push into the room. Horror awaited me inside.

Alice thrashed on a bed, her hair plastered to her temples with sweat. Tears streaked her flushed cheeks. One arm cradled against her chest in a fresh cast as the other tore at the sheets.

"I have to leave. I can't stay here. Please." Her voice broke into a choking sob.

She didn't see me. Didn't see anyone. Her eyes were closed, like she wasn't quite awake yet.

My chest ached so deep, I thought it might split open. I stepped forward, to her side.

"Alice."

She didn't respond, but her eyes sprang open, darting wildly toward the nurses, the monitor, the bright light above her.

"Alice." I said her name louder, firmer, like I would to a spooked colt. "Alice, it's Caleb. I'm here."

I covered her clawed hand with mine.

Her frantic gaze shifted. Her eyes were glassy, unfocused, but for a split second, they locked on mine. She blinked, tears spilling over, her chest heaving with ragged breaths.

"Hey, Allie," I murmured as gently as I could. "I'm here with you now. I've got you. Anything you need, I'm here. I won't leave you."

Her lips trembled. "Caleb. Help me."

Crumpling against her pillow, she released a keening sob and clutched the blanket like a shield. There was a bandage on her forehead, swelling in her cheek and around her eye. It killed me to see her like that.

I looked up at the nurse on her other side. "What's going on? Help her. She's in pain."

The nurse adjusted her IV without looking at me. "Her doctor is on the way."

"That's not good enough," I snapped. "She's terrified. Someone needs to help her right now."

Before the nurse could respond, the door swung open and a tall woman in scrubs stepped in. She gave Alice a quick once-over, eyes narrowing in clinical assessment.

"Alice," she said. "I'm Dr. Tennison. You're in the hospital. Do you know why you're here?"

Alice's chest shook with another sob. Her lips moved, but no sound came out.

The doctor leaned over Alice, shining a small penlight into each eye. Alice flinched, whimpering.

"Easy," the doctor soothed. "You have a mild concussion, and your wrist is broken. Do you remember what happened?"

Alice turned her head toward me, refusing to look at the doctor. I cupped the side of her face, wiping tears away, only for more to replace them.

"All right. You don't have to talk right now," the doctor said, jotting something down on her tablet. "Your labs are still processing. Once we know what substance was in your system, we'll be able to monitor accordingly."

"Is she going to be okay?" I asked roughly, my throat tight.

Dr. Tennison finally looked at me, her brows lifting over her glasses. "Are you family?"

"I'm her friend. And I won't leave her, so please don't bring it up."

She studied me before giving a small nod. "She'll be monitored closely, but she'll need a friend when she goes home."

None of that eased the ache in my chest, but what could I do? Not much other than stand here, hoping I never heard a cry of terror like the one that had nearly ripped me in two again.

Especially not from Alice.

There was a substance in Alice's system. *A substance.* I wasn't stupid. I knew what that meant. And it took everything in me not to punch a hole in the nearest wall.

Dr. Tennison turned back to Alice. "Do you need anything right now, Alice? Are you in pain?"

Alice's hand tightened around mine, her knuckles bone white. She shook her head, tears dripping off her chin.

"Okay. That's good to hear." The doctor gave her a small nod then addressed the nurse. "Page me if anything changes."

The two women left the room, the door clicking shut behind them. I reached up and brushed a damp strand of hair from Alice's forehead, careful of the bandage there.

She closed her eyes at my touch, another tear sliding down her cheek. Her grip on my hand trembled.

"Don't go," she whispered so faintly, I almost didn't hear her. "Please stay with me."

I swallowed hard, the burn in my throat threatening to choke me. Pushing past it, I squeezed her hand gently.

"I'm not going anywhere, Allie," I promised gruffly. "You don't have to worry about that. If you want to close your eyes, you can. I'll be here when you wake up."

Like those were the exact words she needed to hear, she let out a shuddering breath and went limp, her eyes fluttering closed again. Even as sleep pulled her under, her fingers stayed tangled tight with mine.

An hour later, Alice woke with a gasp and knifed upright, her eyes rolling around in terror.

"I have to go," she mewled. "I can't stay here anymore."

I pushed to my feet and took her face in my hand. "You're in the hospital, Allie. You're safe."

She shook her head. "No. No, please take me home. If I stay here—I can't stay here, Caleb. I *can't*."

Her voice broke on a sob, and her whole body trembled under the thin hospital blanket. She clutched my wrist with her uninjured hand, her grip weak but frantic.

"Allie..." I said softly, brushing my thumb along her cheekbone, careful to avoid the swelling. "You need to let the doctors take care of you. You're hurt."

"I can't," she whispered, shaking her head, fresh tears streaming down her face. "Please, Caleb. Tell them I need to go *now*."

Something in my chest splintered at her quiet desperation. She was more lucid now and just as terrified. Maybe more so.

I looked over my shoulder at the empty doorway then back at her, feeling helpless. *What the hell do I do?* Keeping her here was the logical choice. The right choice. But I couldn't force her to stay. Not if she needed to go.

"All right," I said roughly, nodding once. "All right, darlin'. I'll get you out of here."

Relief rushed over her face, so fierce and bright, it almost knocked me backward. She let out a shaky breath and slumped against the pillows, still clutching my wrist like she was afraid I'd disappear.

I found the call button and pressed it. A nurse appeared a few minutes later, pumping sanitizer into her cupped hand at the doorway.

"She wants to go home," I said, trying to keep my voice level. "Discharge her."

The nurse's mouth tightened as she rubbed her hands together. "Sir, she's under observation for a concussion and has a fresh fracture. Besides, we're waiting for the police to—"

"She can rest at home," I interrupted, impatience prickling my skin. "You can send whatever paperwork she needs with us. The police can talk to her there."

The nurse hesitated, glancing between me and Alice.

"I'll get the doctor," she said finally, leaving the room.

Fifteen minutes later, after a brief, albeit tense, conversation with Dr. Tennison, they released her. They insisted on a wheelchair, and Alice kept her eyes clamped tightly shut as I guided it down the hall and out through the automatic doors into the early morning air.

At my truck, I lifted her easily into my arms. Her cheek pressed against my chest as she curled closer to me with a small, broken whimper.

"It's okay," I murmured against her hair, tightening my grip. "You're going home now."

"Thank you so much," she whispered. "Thank you, Caleb."

I set her gently in the passenger seat, buckling her in like I used to with Jesse when he was little. Right before I closed the door, she released a shuddering breath of relief.

Climbing behind the wheel, I started the truck and pulled out of the hospital parking lot. I glanced over at Alice. She was curled into a tight ball against the passenger seat, but more alert now that she was free.

I'd been questioning whether I was doing the right thing, but she was breathing easier. Steadier. Her tears had stopped. She was pulling herself together. If I'd forced her to spend another minute in that place...no, I couldn't have.

I reached over and took her hand in mine, squeezing gently as the ranch fences came into view in the distance.

"You're safe now, Allie," I whispered, not really sure if I was saying it for her sake or mine. "I promise. You're safe."

Chapter Fourteen

Alice

ONCE I WAS OUT of the hospital, I could breathe and think clearly. Well...sort of. My body held a whole host of aches, my head was throbbing, and I was more exhausted than I'd ever been in my life.

All those things were distracting. What was consuming me was being in Caleb's house.

The moment he'd carried me over the threshold and settled me on his couch, I'd felt like I'd been wrapped in one of his worn-in flannels. Rugged wood floors stretched under my feet, scuffed and sun-kissed in the paths he and Jesse had been making for years. The couch was a simple corduroy in mushroom brown and smelled faintly of leather, grass, and him. Tucked in the corners were a couple mismatched throw pillows, dented in the middle from the two heads that must have regularly lain on them. Everything else was neat and tidy, like he didn't own anything he didn't need.

Caleb was written into every surface and quiet corner. Practical. Steady. Rough around the edges but deeply comforting. A sweet place for a father and son to live their lovely, beautiful lives.

In the back of my mind, I wondered if I was concentrating on Caleb's decorating style so I didn't have to think about what had happened to me. An act of avoidance if I'd ever heard one.

Caleb brought me a glass of water then paced the length of the living room while I sipped it. It seemed like I should have been saying something.

"You were right."

He stopped in his tracks, his head swiveling in my direction. "I was right?"

"Yes." I put my empty glass down on the coffee table, wincing from the stretch. "You were right about dating apps."

His brow dropped low, a storm gathering behind his gaze. "You think I wanted to be right? Christ, Alice. I would have been glad to have been proven wrong."

He lowered himself to the couch, keeping a full cushion between us. I tipped my head back, studying him in the light of his home. Something I never imagined I'd get to see.

Oh, yes. I was definitely not focusing on the right things. But the way the sunlight streaming through the picture window glinted off Caleb's beard, turning the rough, tawny hairs into threads of gold, was so much more pleasant.

"That was a stupid thing to say." I rubbed my sweaty palms along my legs. I'd been given scrubs because the police had taken my clothes to test for—

Oh god.

I brought my trembling hand to my mouth. "This could have been so much worse," I rasped.

My memory was patchy, but I was certain James hadn't gotten me out of that parking lot. Someone had come in time. Someone had stopped him from doing what he'd intended. He'd hurt me, but not as badly as he could have—as he *wanted* to.

"There's not a single thing stupid about you," Caleb said. "Nothing about this is your fault."

I shook my head. "You don't know what happened."

"Don't have to, Allie. I know you didn't ask to be hurt. I know you were careful and smart. That's who you are."

"I don't feel very smart right now." I blew out a long breath, moving the topic away from last night. "I think I should explain my behavior at the hospital."

"You don't need to explain anything. I saw how scared you were, and I see you're better now." He leaned toward me, his brow rising. "Aren't you?"

"Yes." I gave him a wobbly smile. "So much better. Your house is so cozy. You didn't have to bring me here, but...thank you. I like being here."

His shoulders relaxed, just barely. "Good. Jesse is with his mother this week, so I want you to stay here. Let me see to you."

"You don't have to do that."

"I know. I want to. Your doctor said you'd need a friend, and I'm going to be that."

"Okay. I don't really have the energy to fight you on it." I tucked my feet up under me, feeling the pull of my sore muscles, and rested my cheek against the back of the couch. "I don't like hospitals."

Caleb frowned, a little crease forming between his brows. "I saw that."

My fingers worried the edge of a throw pillow seam. "I spent a lot of time in hospitals when I was younger. More than anyone ever should. I can't stand to be in them now. Even the smell makes me feel like I can't breathe."

I felt his gaze on me, like a hand pressed between my shoulder blades. I didn't look up, just kept tracing the frayed threads.

There was a long pause. I could tell he wanted to ask. What happened to you? Why so many hospitals? But he didn't. Caleb was many things—blunt, gruff, a little intimidating—but he wasn't intrusive. He only reached for what I was ready to give.

"Then I'm glad I could get you out of there. Hope you can breathe better here."

A thick knot formed in my throat, and I swallowed against it. "Thank you," I whispered. "I can breathe perfectly."

Before he could reply, a firm knock rattled the front door. Caleb's head snapped up, his body tensing. He rose in one fluid, powerful motion, and for a moment, stood there, shoulders squared, jaw ticcing, as if ready to throw himself between me and whoever was on the other side.

Then he exhaled and walked to the door.

When he opened it, two uniformed officers stood on the porch—a man and a woman.

"Good morning, Caleb," the man greeted. "Sorry to be out here on official business. We're here to speak with Ms. Clark about last night. Her doctor said she's here."

Caleb glanced at me, his eyes dark with worry and something fiercer I couldn't name. I nodded, telling him without words I was ready.

"Come in," he said quietly, stepping aside.

I pulled my knees tighter to my chest as the officers approached, bracing myself for what came next.

Caleb stayed the entire time. He sat beside me while the officers questioned me and I told them every detail I remembered. I winced when I recounted drinking my Coke after I returned from the restroom. They all tried to convince me I wasn't stupid, but I didn't agree. I went to college. I knew better than to leave my drink unattended. That kind of thing was drilled into girls' heads from an early age.

Yet...

My desire not to make a scene had overridden my common sense.

There was no way I would forgive myself for making that decision. No one could ever get me to believe anything different.

Once I'd given the officers every detail I could remember, they filled in the blanks.

The bartender had noticed something off when James had walked me out. She'd grabbed a couple regulars and followed us into the parking lot. When they got there, I was unconscious and bleeding, and James was half dragging me toward his truck.

They saved me.

If they'd been even a minute later...but they hadn't. Whether it was luck, the universe, or something more divine, they'd come in time. They'd stopped him.

And now, I was here. Alive. Safe. He had taken something from me, but not anything I couldn't get back with time.

James had been arrested on the spot. The tests confirmed what everyone had suspected—I'd been drugged. The officers couldn't promise anything, but they said it looked like an open-and-shut case.

When they left, I was so tired I could barely see straight. More than that, I needed to be alone. I couldn't bear to even look at Caleb, and he wouldn't turn away from me.

"I'd like to take a nap," I whispered.

He was so tuned in, he had no trouble hearing me. "Of course. I'll show you the guest room." He took my hand in his and pulled me up from the couch. "I've got you. Come on."

Any second, he would let go. There was no need for him to hold my hand all the way down the hall. I wouldn't get lost. Not when I was following him.

But he didn't. He cradled my hand in his until we reached the guest room, and at the door, he gave it a squeeze.

"If you'd let me give you flowers, they'd be a so-damn-sorry-this-happened-to-you bouquet," he said.

I sighed so heavily my shoulders rolled, and my chest felt hollow. "That would be a terrible first bouquet. I'm glad you're not giving them to me."

"Yeah." He ducked his head, scuffing his socked foot on the floor. "I hate everything those cops just told us. But I almost wish they hadn't caught him so I could take care of him myself."

"Then you'd be in jail." I laughed dryly. "I'm okay, Caleb. I feel like the dumbest person on the planet, but I'll survive."

"Allie," he breathed, cupping the side of my face. "You're not dumb. Nothing that man did was on you. You are right about one thing, though. You'll survive out here in the light, and he's gonna rot, locked away in the dark."

My nose tingled, and a huge lump formed in my throat. All I could do was nod.

He dipped down, pressing a quick kiss to the top of my head. "Sleep well. I won't go far. All you have to do is call for me, and I'll be here."

I didn't know why he was doing any of this for me, but I wasn't questioning it. Not now. Wordlessly, I stepped into the guest room. It smelled faintly of cedar and laundry soap. The quilt was plain but fluffy. Sunlight slipped in between the curtains in hazy golden bars across the bed. I sat down on the side and waited until his footsteps faded down the hall.

Then, safe and warm in Caleb Kelly's house, I pulled the covers over my shoulders and fell asleep.

Chapter Fifteen

Alice

I DIDN'T LET MYSELF sleep long. Just enough to take the unbearable edge off. When I woke, I washed my face in the bathroom, careful not to look too hard at my reflection. I wasn't quite ready to see what I looked like—especially not when I had to face Caleb.

Not that he cared what I looked like.

But I did.

I found him in the kitchen, and he wasn't alone. His mom was pouring coffee into a mug, looking as put together as always. Her pale-blonde hair was a silky sheet over her shoulder, and her casual athleisure seemed tailored to her body. She moved with easy confidence, tipping a splash of milk into the mug and humming softly as she stirred it.

Caleb was leaning against the counter, his arms folded across the vast expanse of his chest. He was scruffy and rumpled and beautiful.

Elena's only reaction to the sight of me—to the mess I knew I was—was a slight flare of her pretty blue eyes.

"Alice, darling, there you are. I brought you clothes." She patted the pile of folded cotton on the island. "I assumed you wouldn't want to stay in those scrubs any longer than necessary."

"Thank you so much." I practically fell on the new clothes. "I want to feel terrible you went out of your way for me, but you're right. I can't stand to be in these scrubs another minute."

"Don't you dare feel terrible." She rounded the island to stand in front of me, smoothed my hair away from my face, and dropped her voice to barely above a whisper. "Go change. When you're ready to face the day, I'll make you something to eat and we can get on with it."

"I can make Alice food," Caleb grumbled.

Elena's mouth quirked. "I'm aware you're capable, but I'm taking charge."

She shooed me back to the bedroom. As soon as I closed the door, I ripped the scrubs off and kicked them into a corner. They'd served their purpose. I wanted nothing more to do with them. Like paper carried history and stories, memories and beauty, those scrubs were more than fabric. They were a reminder of pain, boredom, feeling trapped and unseen. Recovery from procedures I didn't choose, looming faces and roaming hands.

The clothes Elena had brought were cloudlike. Lounge pants, a tank with a built-in bra, and a hoodie. Softer and finer than anything I'd ever bought myself, and they smelled like lavender caught in a breeze.

She'd included a toothbrush, lotion, and a hairbrush. By the time I emerged again, I felt almost human. Still groggy and achy, but much better.

Elena had made us sandwiches. She must have brought her own ingredients because I didn't imagine Caleb would buy croissants for himself. I ate my first sandwich so quickly, Elena made me another without a word. I went slower but downed it all.

Caleb's chuckle snapped my gaze from my plate to him. His eyes were on me, light dancing behind his gaze.

"You know, when I gave you that box full of pastries from Sugar Rush, I was thinking there was no way you'd be able to eat it all." He chuckled again. "I've been proven otherwise."

Elena reached across the table and swatted his hand. "You know better than to comment on someone's appetite, Cay."

My cheeks heated as he grinned at me. "I'm glad you're eating," he said. "Makes me happy to see it."

I wiped my mouth with my napkin. "I didn't eat *all* the sweets you gave me." Then I rushed out, "Not in one sitting."

His laugh was a resounding boom. I was fascinated by the way he tipped his head back, sending his good humor toward the sky like a spotlight, making everything above him brighter.

"Not in one sitting, huh?" His smile reached the corners of his eyes and burst outward in deep crinkles.

"At least two." My smile was a bit wobbly, but it wasn't forced. It was real.

He held both hands up in surrender. "I'm not one to judge. I know what my sister's baking does to people—me included."

Elena looked back and forth between us, curious, but refrained from asking what circumstance had led to Caleb giving me pastries. For that, I was grateful. In fact, I was grateful for everything this woman had done for me.

"Thank you for lunch," I said to her. "I didn't know I was as hungry as I turned out to be."

"It was my pleasure." She swiveled in her chair to face me. "I hope I'm not intruding too much. I saw the police and came over to check out what was going on."

I read between the lines. Caleb had told her what had happened to me. I didn't mind her knowing, and not only because I trusted her. After what I'd put him through today, Caleb might need someone to lean on too. I was glad he had his mom.

I shook my head, swallowing the lump in my throat. "No, you're not intruding at all."

Needing to move, do something other than feel like I might cry, I took my plate to the sink and washed it. It wasn't easy with one good hand, but I managed. Then I washed an empty mug and two forks. When I ran out of dishes, I looked around for something else to do, finding the kitchen sparkling clean.

Elena came to stand beside me. She put her hand on my shoulder and leaned close. "Can I give you a hug, darling?"

I turned my head, meeting her bright, concerned eyes, and all I could do was nod. Slowly, careful not to spook me, she brought me into her arms. I couldn't remember the last time anyone had hugged me. Years, for certain. I'd learned to do without.

Elena wrapped me up almost too tight. Her arms were long and willowy but stronger than they looked. She cupped the back of my head and pressed it against her shoulder, the other hand stroking the length of my back. It was so nice, so very, very lovely, I had to stop myself from melting against her.

She placed her mouth next to my ear. "I know, Alice. It happened to me too. It was a long time ago, and it's faded, but it left its mark." I held my breath as she went on, whispering her secrets. "The shame is his. Never, ever yours. It was hard for me not to take it on. I had a lot of therapy and the love of a few special people to get me right. Even now, forty years later, I still have an inkling of it."

I squeezed my eyes shut, hating this for her more than I'd ever hated anything in my life. "I'm so sorry."

"I know. I know, darling. I'm so sorry you have become part of this club. I need you to know, to listen to me when I tell you, none of this is your fault. No choices or mistakes you think you made led you to deserve what happened to you."

I shook my head against her shoulder. "He didn't—I mean, he was stopped before he..." My tongue was too thick. I couldn't say the word.

"I know. I'm so very glad someone stepped in before he could."

My fingers curled into the fine, feathery fabric of her shirt. "He would have. He almost—"

"But he didn't. He didn't, Alice." Her fingers moved through my hair in slow, gentle slides. So soothing, I could have fallen asleep standing up. But it was her firm, gentle words that slowed my heart and unknotted my gut. "You can't take this on, darling. You would never blame another woman for a man hurting her, would you?"

"Never," I whispered.

"Then give yourself that same grace."

"Okay. I'll try."

"Good." She cupped the back of my head again. "Lean on Cay. He can take it."

That was harder to agree to. "He doesn't want—"

She shifted back to meet my gaze. "He does. My son doesn't do anything he doesn't want to do. He's stubborn like that. He gets it from his mom."

I let out a wet laugh. "I can try."

"That's all you can do."

She held me for as long as I needed. Letting go was difficult, but I forced myself to pull back, and she squeezed my shoulders, smiling gently.

"You're going to be okay," she said. "Promise."

"Thank you. For everything." I yawned. "I might need another nap."

That made her laugh. "That sounds like a good idea. You need to rest so you can heal."

I turned to head toward the guest room, stopping short when I spotted Caleb in the doorway, his brow dipped low, his eyes pinned on me. A deep frown tugged at the corners of his mouth, and I imagined he'd been standing there a while. Maybe the whole time.

"I'm going to take another nap."

"Rest easy," he uttered, thick and raspy. "I'll be here when you wake up."

When I passed him, I looked up into his haunted eyes, and my stomach clenched. "Thank you for everything."

The lines on the side of his mouth were carved granite. "Don't need your thanks. Just need you safe and well."

"I am." I allowed myself one fleeting graze along his arm, and I didn't say it—he didn't want to hear it—but in my head, I added, "*Thanks to you.*"

Chapter Sixteen

Caleb

"There's something you're not telling me."

With Alice sleeping, the kitchen cleaned, and nothing left to do, my mother was on her way home to my dad. I thought I'd gotten off light—no major inquisition—but I should have known better. She stopped on my front porch, pinning me with a prodding stare.

"There's a lot I don't tell you," I said.

That earned me an eye roll. "Sure. About cattle and fences. You don't hold secrets. You've never been good at that." Resting her shoulder against a support beam, she regarded me with the kind of suspicion that had always made me crumble. "What's your connection with Alice?"

I pressed my lips together, considering how much I should say—how much Alice would want me to divulge.

Something told me she wouldn't mind if I told my mom—not after today and the way Alice had taken the comfort she'd offered.

I would never forget Alice's painful screams at the hospital, and now, the picture of her sinking into my mother's arms would be forever burned into my brain. I'd never witnessed anyone so in need of a hug. The things they'd said to one another had twisted in my gut, making me feel both violent and grateful for my mother.

"Alice expressed interest in me, and I—" I looked away, moving my jaw back and forth as I gazed out over my family's land. "I agreed to take her out, then thought better of it and turned her down gently."

"Why did you turn her down, Cay?"

Resting my hands on the railing, I exhaled slowly. "I'm good where I am, and I'm not looking to add any kind of relationship to the mix. I thought it was better to end things before they started. And at the time, I barely knew her. She'd been my server at Joy's, but I wasn't even aware she was Jesse's favorite librarian."

"How in the world did you miss that?" she asked, not hiding her incredulousness.

I lifted a shoulder. "Pheobe told me I have a habit of not seeing what's in front of me. I think she might be right." I rubbed at the tension in the center of my forehead. "I can't help thinking she wouldn't have been in this position if I'd gone out with her. It wouldn't have been a hardship. We would have had a good time, and she—"

"Cay..." My mom moved next to me, leaning her head on my bicep. "I'll tell you what I said to Alice: do not take this on. What that man did has nothing to do with you. You can bring up a million what-ifs, but who does that help? Not Alice, and not you." She gave my arm a sharp poke. "That's for not knowing Alice is our librarian. Your sister's right. You need to open your eyes more often. There's no telling what you're missing."

"You're not going to get after me for not going out with her?"

She straightened and tipped her head to meet my eyes. "I'm not. Today's not really the day to get into it. Though...I do question your entire premise."

"What do you mean?"

"Not getting into it, honey." Then she gave me one of her bone-crushing hugs. "I love you. Take care of Alice. Call me or Dad if you need anything."

"Love you too, Mom."

She waved on her way down the steps. "I know you do."

Alice came out of her room a few hours later. I'd spent the time doing chores I'd been putting off around the house—anything that could be completed quietly—trying like hell not to replay her screams. It was difficult, but knowing she was all right under my roof drowned some of it out.

She looked better after resting. Her hair was still a little wild, and her eyes were puffy, but there was color back in her cheeks, and the small smile she offered was a relief to see.

"Hey," she said, her voice raspy from sleep.

"Hey yourself. Hungry?"

"Yeah. I think I am. Can I help you cook?"

"Normally, if you're here, you help. But I'll make an exception this time." I pointed toward a stool at the island. "Sit down. Keep me company."

She waved her casted hand. "Is it because of this?"

I grinned at her. "You guessed it. The girl with the cast gets to take it easy."

I was no chef, but I'd been a single dad long enough I'd mastered a few meals. I whipped up some pasta, garlic bread, and roasted brussels sprouts. We sat at the kitchen table together, eating in near silence. It wasn't uncomfortable, though. Alice's company was mellow and easy.

After dinner, she helped me clear the table despite my protests. I ordered her to have a seat while I cleaned up the kitchen. She didn't give me much trouble, sitting at the island again, looking around my place with curiosity. I watched her while I dried my hands on a towel, trying to figure out if she needed anything from me.

Maybe more of this. A quiet night, with nothing to do, no questions to answer. More *easy*.

"Do you want to read with me?" I asked.

Her head popped up, her eyes wide. "Read with you?"

I nodded to her phone. "Do you have books on there? I'd offer to lend you one of mine, but I don't think you'd be interested in one of Jesse's comics or robot manuals. His biographies, on the other hand..." I raised a brow.

She laughed. "I'm not much of a nonfiction reader, no matter how hard Jesse tries to convince me. But yes, I do have books on my phone." She chewed on her bottom lip for a beat. "The doctors told me to give my brain a break. Sadly, that includes reading."

I should've known that. A woman with a fresh concussion needed to take it easy. But just because she couldn't read didn't mean...

"How about I read to you?"

Her spine straightened as she perked at the idea. "Really? I'd love that, but you don't have to."

"I offered." I gestured toward the living room. "Come on. Let's sit in here."

Alice took one corner of the couch, and I took the other, tossing her a throw blanket. She spread it over her lap, and it satisfied me in a deep, surprising way to see how comfortable she was here, with me, after what she'd been through.

I cracked open the hardback I'd checked out from the library. "Do you want me to start from the beginning?"

She shook her head. "No. You don't need to do that. I won't be lost if you start where you left off."

Mindful of her head injury, I tried to keep my volume low, not wanting to do more harm than good. Given the circumstances, I wasn't able to really get lost in the story like I had the first time I'd sat down to read it. My eyes kept sliding over to her, making sure she was awake and okay. Seeing if she needed anything. Too aware of her presence to concentrate.

"Do you like it?" she asked when I came to the end of a chapter.

I looked up. "Like what?"

"The book." Her mouth tipped at the corners. "I can't tell if you're enjoying it."

I glanced down at the book beneath my hand then back at her and sighed. "I like it more than I thought I would. Just having trouble concentrating tonight."

She nodded, her eyes going soft with understanding. "Do you want to talk about it?"

My brow creased until I realized she meant the book. I rubbed a finger over the words on the paper. I had been wondering something, and I couldn't read fast enough to get to the answer. There were two more books after this one, and I was worried I'd have to get through them both before I did. Maybe Alice could end my suspense.

"I have a question."

Her eyes lit as she turned her body toward me. "Hit me with it."

"Why is Fathaniel able to walk under Glavspor's eighth moon when Binboa can't? Aren't they both Dorfits?"

The clock hanging on my wall ticked, ticked, ticked, then a laugh burst out of her, light and breezy.

She shook her head. "I can't tell you that, Caleb. You're going to have to keep reading."

I scratched behind my ear. "Figured you'd say that." I jabbed at the pages. "Just tell me, will I find out in this book or the next one?"

She pressed her lips into a flat line, shaking her head again. "No way."

"You're mean," I grunted. "I could flip to the end, see for myself."

She gasped. "No! Don't do it. You'll ruin the magic!"

"Yeah." I ducked my head, hiding my grin. It was cute how serious she was about this, but it made sense. Books were a big part of her life and who she was. "I'll keep reading."

"Good." She curled her legs to the side and rested her head on her arm. "Thank you for tonight, Caleb. I'm starting to feel almost normal."

More satisfaction filled me. "That's the goal."

She gave me a sleepy smile then turned her eyes to peer out the window. I watched her for another second before forcing myself to focus on my book again. It was a good story. Action, friendship, a side of romance. I could see why she liked it. If she hadn't been sitting a cushion away with a black eye and concussion, I'd probably be enjoying it.

When I came to the end of the next chapter, I looked at Alice to ask her if she wanted me to keep going, only to find her asleep. It did me good to see her so peaceful, covered in the same blanket my boy liked to snuggle under.

I tipped my head back, letting my mind wander over my last couple days. It was always peaceful at night on the ranch, but tonight was a little sweeter.

Most evenings when Jesse was at his mom's, I either hung out with family or had dinner at Joy's. Then I'd come home, finish my chores, shower, and go straight to bed. Being alone in the house never bothered me much before.

With Alice curled up on my couch, her quiet breaths and tiny reactions filling the space, I realized this was nice too. Having *her* here was nice, even if the circumstances were shitty.

I'd better not get used to it, though.

The last thing I needed was to start wanting something I couldn't keep.

Chapter Seventeen

Alice

CALEB SCOWLED AT ME when I brought up going home the next morning. Really, he'd gone above and beyond for me—*way* above and beyond. I wasn't in imminent danger of falling into a coma. And I had a library to run.

But Caleb wouldn't even entertain the idea of me leaving. Nor did he think I should be on my own yet. That was how I ended up shadowing him while he worked the ranch.

The sun was peeking over the hills when we headed out to the barn. I was wearing Jesse's boots and sweats, and one of Caleb's flannels. I looked absolutely ridiculous. When Caleb saw me in my outfit, he'd patted my head like a child.

"Stay close." The muscles in his back flexed as he pushed open the barn doors. "Don't need you getting trampled."

I laughed, careful not to jostle my sore ribs too much. "No. Getting trampled is the last thing I need."

He shot me a smirk, then guided me to sit on an overturned bucket before he got to work alongside a few other men. Despite their curious looks my way, he hadn't introduced me to them. And that was fine. I wasn't much in the mood to talk to strangers anyway.

I watched him check feed bins, heft bales of hay like they weighed nothing, and swing saddles over horses' backs in one smooth motion. He brushed down a palomino mare, his hands firm and sure on her sleek flank, and I wondered if he'd let me ride her. Not today, obviously, but one day.

At one point, he turned and caught me staring. "Are you bored yet?"

"Not at all. Actually...it's kind of fascinating."

His brow furrowed, like he didn't believe me. "It's just work, Alice. Nothing special."

I grinned. "Well, to me it is. I've only read about ranchers. This is my first time experiencing one in real life."

He put his dirty hands on his hips and stared for a long beat before nodding. "Then we'll have to give you the full experience."

He took me out in a UTV, driving at a snail's pace over bumps and bends. When he continuously slid his gaze over to me, I suspected his low speed was for my sake, but I didn't complain. Not when I was still so achy all over and there was a low throb in my temples. The fresh air was doing me good, though, and I couldn't take in my surroundings quickly enough.

The Kelly ranch was something out of the old Westerns I used to read. This land was rugged and raw. Yellowed grass stretched for miles, brittle under the summer sun, dotted with clumps of sagebrush and the occasional wiry bush clinging to life. Rocks jutted up from the earth, their edges worn smooth by wind and time.

We drove past herds of cattle spread out across the plains, their dark bodies stark against the pale grass. Some picked their way carefully around the rocks, others stood huddled under the scant shade offered by a lone tree, its leaves fluttering in the late spring breeze.

Dust billowed behind us as Caleb steered around a rut, the UTV bouncing over the uneven terrain. It was harsh country. Unforgiving, sunbaked, and vast. It was beautiful, too, in a way that made my chest ache. This land made me feel small, in the best way possible.

I glanced at Caleb as he navigated the rough terrain, one hand loose on the wheel, the other resting on his thigh. He made sense here, like he'd been born from this rugged land. As he slowed to check a broken fence post, I couldn't stop the bloom of heat that unfurled in my chest.

"I'm going to put you to work," he stated.

"Oh yeah?" I held up my cast. "Are you sure I can handle it?"

"Think you can hold a nail?"

I grinned. "Yeah. I'm pretty sure I can manage that."

He motioned me over to him. "Then get over here. The day's wasting."

With surprising eagerness in my belly, I climbed out of the UTV and went to where he was standing by a sagging section of fence. He gave me a bundle of nails to hold, the calloused pads of his fingers brushing my palm. Every time I passed him one, his fingers slid along mine, making my breath stutter.

I decided not to think about my feelings today. My brain was supposed to be resting, after all. Instead, I let the steady motion of pass, hammer, pass, hammer soothe me. I didn't think I was cut out to be a rancher full time, but there was something to be said for spending the day outdoors, working with your hands, and seeing the results of your labor immediately.

Caleb paused often, checking on me with quiet glances, handing me his water bottle before I could ask. The air was still cool, but the sun was high. Sweat beaded at his temples and ran down the column of his neck, disappearing under the collar of his shirt.

I tried not to stare, but...wow. Caleb, in his natural environment, was the most compelling thing I had ever seen. The breeze whipped his brown hair into streamers. His massive boots were planted in the soil like he'd grown out of this ground—like *he* was one of the sandstone outcroppings.

I turned away, swallowing hard. *Enough of that.*

After checking the rest of the fence line, we headed back toward the barn. When he stopped the vehicle, he turned to me, one hand draped over the wheel. "You hungry, Allie?"

No one had ever called me Allie. I guessed this was going to be Caleb's thing. And I...didn't mind it. Not even a little bit.

"I'm getting there."

"Come on." He jerked his chin in the direction of his house in the distance. "We'll grab something then I need to check the north pasture."

He fed me sandwiches—two, just like I'd eaten yesterday—then took a long look at me. Whatever he saw made him nod a few times.

"You're staying here the rest of the day."

I raised a brow. "I am?"

"Yep. The terrain is rougher up north. I can't have your brain getting jostled around."

That made me laugh a little. "Can't get trampled, can't get jostled, what *can* I do?"

Caleb guffawed, low and rumbly. "You can take it easy, that's what." He gave my head another pat. "I'll be back in a few hours. You give me a call if you need me before then, and I'll head right back."

"I'll be fine." Then I decided to tease him again, since I liked hearing him laugh. "But I don't know what you'll do without your nail holder."

He gave me exactly what I'd been hoping for—another roll of thunderous laughter. "I'll have to make do as best I can." His smile softened. "See you in a while, Allie. Be good."

"See you, Caleb."

That night went much like the one before, except Caleb took a call from Jesse. I listened in as they talked about his day at school. He mentioned I'd been absent from the library, which was a rarity, and told his dad my assistant, Roberta, had said I was sick. Caleb assured him I was probably fine.

I'd never been close with my dad. He'd worked a lot, and when he hadn't been at the office, he'd only had enough bandwidth for one of his daughters. Silla's illness had been like a black hole, sucking up our parents' time, attention, and affection. I couldn't blame her for that. None of it had been her fault. I couldn't really blame my parents either. Having a sick child...well, I couldn't imagine. I hadn't needed them with the same urgency, so they hadn't looked my way.

I couldn't picture Caleb ever turning away from Jesse. Not with how zeroed in he was during their conversation. The questions he asked, the way he nodded along with the stories Jesse was telling on the other end of the line.

After he hung up, Caleb set his phone aside and turned to me. "Are you feeling up for a little reading tonight?"

"I'd really love that." *Such an understatement.*

We settled in our corners of the couch, and he grabbed the book from where he'd set it on the side table. He flicked on the lamp, casting the room in a golden glow, and started reading where we'd left off. His gravelly baritone drew me in. Outside, the wind rattled against the windowpanes, but in here, it was warm and still.

I watched him more than I listened to the words. The way his mouth moved as he read. The crease between his brows when he concentrated. Every once in a while, he glanced at me, like he was checking to see if I was following along. I always was. Just...not the story.

I was following him.

I tucked my knees under the blanket he'd given me and leaned my head against the back cushion. I could get used to nights like this.

And that was the problem.

This wasn't my home. This wasn't my life. Caleb was being kind because that was who he was. Soon, this house, with Caleb reading to me, dinner dishes drying in the sink, the sound of the horses in the distance, would be nothing more than a really good memory.

I'd leave tomorrow even if Caleb fought me on it. If I stayed any longer, if I let myself slip any deeper into this cozy cocoon, it would hurt to claw myself back out of it.

I closed my eyes, letting his voice roll over me. Tomorrow, I'd go home and get back to my life. I would let myself have this one more night.

Chapter Eighteen

Caleb

ALICE HAD BEEN GONE for a week when Jesse and I showed up at my parents' for dinner. We were greeted by Silas, who rammed his big toddler head into Jesse's knees, squealing like a conquering Viking. Jesse played along, collapsing in the entry, letting his cousin use him like a jungle gym. I would have been worried for my boy, since Silas didn't know the definition of taking it easy, but Remi was leaning against the wall, watching his son with a careful eye and a big grin.

I patted his shoulder in greeting. "Kid of yours needs to come with a warning."

He chuckled. "He's got energy to spare, that's for damn sure. If I'd known I was going to have a Hannah 2.0, I would have gotten started younger so I could keep up with him."

That got me laughing. "Our parents survived Hurricane Hannah. You'll make it through Silas. Now, if you have another one like him…"

Remi palmed his face, but he was still grinning. "Yeah, I definitely should have started younger."

Rem and I were the same age and had been friends most of our lives. I didn't like to think of myself as old yet, but my kid was more than halfway grown. Could I start over again?

I shook off the thought. It didn't matter. I wasn't going there.

Eventually, Silas let Jesse up off the ground, but only if Jesse carried him. My boy loved his cousin, so Silas didn't have to twist his arm much. He scooped him up, and Silas roared in victory before snuggling into Jesse's hold.

Remi and I exchanged a long look, and my heart gave a hard kick inside my chest. It was cool as hell to share this with him. After all the years we'd been friends, we were now brothers, and our kids were cousins. Never would have seen it coming, but I was happy it had.

My sister could do a better job not sucking the life out of his neck, but that was Hannah. No one could tell her what to do. If we tried, she'd go even harder. Thankfully, Remi rarely showed up with hickies anymore, but it still happened on occasion.

Hannah was in the kitchen with our mom and grandmother. Grandma was supervising while Mom and Hannah finished cooking dinner. Remi joined them, shadowing Hannah like he was wont to do. My father and grandad were at the long kitchen table, which never seemed to run out of space, no matter how many family members we added.

Once they'd greeted everyone, Jesse and Silas sat on the other side of the table where Silas had abandoned his plastic trains, which had once belonged to Jesse. My heart gave yet another kick at them together. Jesse would have been a great big brother. At least he now had a cousin to play with. Hopefully, Phoebe and Deke would give him another one soon. Maybe one day, we'd have a whole brood. The table could hold it.

"Caleb." My grandad's deep voice drew my attention. His hair was pure white now, but his shoulders were still broad, his back still straight. The man had been born a rancher, and he'd die one. "Did you get the herd moved over to the south meadow this week?"

I pulled out a chair next to him and sat down. "Yeah, we moved them Tuesday. They'll have good graze there for a couple weeks."

Dad rubbed his scruffy chin. "Did you see how that lower slope's filling in? Might be worth giving it another week before we put anything back on it."

"That's what I was thinking too." I leaned back, threading my fingers together on my stomach. "If we push it too soon, we'll end up with bare patches again. That's not gonna do us any favors next year."

Grandad grunted in approval. "It's always better to be patient. Cattle can't eat what isn't there."

I didn't mind them questioning me. Grandad had been technically retired for a couple decades, but he lived on this ranch. It was in his blood. He and my dad had taught me everything they knew. I still had Dad out there with me part time, and I'd take it as long as he wanted to give it.

"Enough of this shop talk at the dinner table," Grandma cut in, her crisp voice softened only by the smile in her eyes. She might've been stern, but she loved all her boys. She wiped her hands on a linen towel and turned toward us, diamond earrings glinting beneath her silvery-blonde hair, swept back in a tortoiseshell clip. "You can discuss cows and grass during work hours. Right now, we're going to sit down as a family and talk about absolutely anything else."

"Yes, Lily, my love," Grandad said with a wink.

Dad straightened, giving his mom a grin. "You heard her, Caleb. Ranch talk's banned until dessert."

"Fine by me," I said, letting my shoulders relax as I looked around the kitchen. Hannah was plating up rolls, Mom was stirring gravy on the stove, and Grandma was directing Remi as he folded napkins to her specifications. Jesse and Silas were crashing trains and cracking each other up.

Yeah. This was what it was all about. The long days, the hard work, the never-ending worry about grass and cattle and business—it all led back here. To family. To this table.

As I was about to ask where Cormac was, the front door opened, and my brother's voice called out, "On your best behavior, everybody. We've got a guest."

Guest? Huh. As far as I knew, Cormac wasn't seeing anyone. He dated here and there, but his heart had taken a licking back in college, and he'd never quite moved on.

Curiosity had me shifting in my chair to look toward the entryway.

Cormac appeared a moment later, tall and broad in his work clothes, the collar of his button-down open, sleeves rolled to his elbows. But it wasn't him who had snagged all the attention in the room.

It was the woman walking beside him.

Alice was here—in my parents' home.

Her hair was pulled back in a loose braid over one shoulder, and she wore a pale-purple dress that skimmed her knees. She clutched the strap of her purse, and her eyes were wide, like she was shocked she'd ended up here.

"Look who I found out front," Cormac said, his voice filled with amusement as he guided her into the kitchen, a hand on her back.

Mom turned from the stove, her face lighting up. "Alice darling, I was worried you might not come."

Alice's wide gaze swept over me before locking on my mother. "I didn't realize the whole family would be here. If I'm intruding…"

Would she not have come if she'd known? Was it that unpleasant to spend time with me? I'd done her wrong, but I'd thought we'd moved past that. Maybe not. Maybe I hadn't done enough to convince her I'd done an asshole thing, but wasn't a jackass at heart.

"Nonsense," Grandma said, striding over to take her purse and set it on the counter. "You're not intruding. We always have room for one more. Or two. Or ten. Come sit down. Dinner's almost ready."

Alice gave her a tremulous smile and turned toward the table. There were a lot of empty seats. She had her pick.

I stood automatically, my chair scraping against the floor. "Hey, Alice."

She flicked her gaze up to me, but only for a flicker before she dropped it again. "Hi," she whispered.

"How are you?"

She waved her cast around. "Banged up, but pretty good. You?"

My gut had been tied up in knots since she'd left. I'd only been able to convince her to stay with me for two days before she'd insisted she needed to get back to her own life to start feeling normal. Since I didn't want to be another man to take what she didn't want to give, I'd had to let her go. I hadn't liked it, and it didn't sit right, but it was what it was.

When she'd left, though, my house had never been more quiet. I'd found every reason I could to be out of it until Jesse had returned. Only then had *I* started to feel normal.

I guessed seeing Alice hurt the way she was had affected me more than I'd thought. Seeing her now, out and about, most of her bruises faded, did me a world of good.

Of course, I wouldn't be telling her any of that.

"Pretty good too," was all I said.

Fortunately, Jesse took over, excited to see his favorite librarian in his grandparents' house. He insisted she sit beside him and play trains with him and Silas.

Once she was seated, I sank back down into my chair, trying to swallow the hard knot in my throat as she crashed her train into Silas's, making him squeal with delight.

I hadn't expected to see her here tonight. But damn if I wasn't glad about it.

Chapter Nineteen

Alice

IF I'D KNOWN I would be walking into a Kelly family dinner, I never would have come. Of course, they acted like my being here was the most normal thing in the world.

Well, most of them, anyway. Caleb kept looking at me, like he was trying to figure out why I was here. I hoped he didn't think I was stalking him or some obsessed fan. Elena had invited me, and after she'd taken care of me last week and checked on me every day since, I couldn't have possibly said no.

I regretted that decision now. This family was lovely and welcoming, exactly as I thought they'd be, but the last thing I wanted was to make Caleb uncomfortable. He'd shown me a lot of kindness last week, but I hadn't misinterpreted that as anything more than him being a wonderfully protective human being.

Elena ordered everyone to take a seat at the long farmhouse table. Chairs scraped against the hardwood as everyone grabbed a spot. Caleb was already directly across from me, and it was difficult not to sneak glances at him, especially when I felt him staring.

"Now, Alice, tell me," Lily said from her spot beside Caleb, her blue eyes bright with curiosity. "How's our little library doing? Are they still cutting your funding every other year?"

I swallowed a mouthful of lemonade, trying to gather my thoughts. "Not enough funding is a fact of life as a librarian, but we're managing. Yes, we could use some new computers, and the roof leaks in the back office whenever it rains hard, but we'll find our way through."

Lily clucked her tongue in disapproval. "You shouldn't have to find a way through. I don't know if you're aware, but I spent my career in politics. I know how to convince people to donate to a worthy cause. Leave this to me. I'll find the funds for you."

In my career, I'd met a myriad of people, but the Kellys stood apart. They were something else. "That is so kind, Lily. Thank you. But please don't think you have to and don't go out of your wa—"

"Don't be silly," Lily cut in. "At my age, I only do what I want to do, and I want to do this."

Her husband patted her hand and shot me a wink. "Let her have it, Alice. My Lily loves a project."

She leaned into him. "That's right. I do."

"Then, thank you." I stacked my hands on the table. "Let me know what help you need. I have a few volunteers who also love projects. I'm sure I could lend them to you."

Jesse lifted a forkful of mashed potatoes. "Did you guys know Alice wrote a book?"

Everyone's head swiveled toward me, including the man across from me. His gaze was like sitting too close to a campfire. Enticing, but so hot, I could barely stand it for more than a minute.

"What kind of book?" Elena asked from down the table, her elbows propped up as she leaned forward.

I almost dismissed it. It was on the tip of my tongue to tell her it was nothing worth speaking about, but I stopped myself. No one would ever know me unless I let them. And wasn't that what I wanted—to be seen and known?

"I'm writing a middle grade fantasy series. I'm working on the final book now. Then...well, I don't know. I suppose I'll actually have to let people read it."

Jesse waved his fork at me. "I've already volunteered as tribute. I mean, I'm the target audience, right?"

I snorted. "You are. You've let me pick your brain so much, if this thing ever gets published, you're going in the credits."

He twisted his mouth as he considered this. "That'd be cool, but only if I get to be the first reader."

"Jess," Caleb grumbled, "lay off."

"It's all right. I don't mind," I assured him. To Jesse, I added, "I'm not sure if I'll ever let anyone read it, but if I do, you'll be at the top of the list."

"Not just a book, a whole series." Caleb's dad, Lock, shook his head like he was amazed. "That's a big deal, Alice. I hope you know that."

"Right?" Cormac shook his head like his father had. "Along with Remi, you're the second author I've met."

I laughed softly. Remington Town had spent over a decade as a conflict photographer and documented his experience in a book. There was no comparison.

"I'm not an author," I argued.

Lock's brow crinkled. "Have you written multiple books?"

Biting my lip, I nodded.

"Then you're an author." He pinned his chocolate eyes on me, and I felt like I was seeing Caleb in the future. "If you won't be proud of yourself, we'll handle it."

Jesse puffed his chest. "Yep. I'm the proudest here since I helped. Did you guys know I helped Charlie with his book too? He needed a robotics expert, so I stepped in."

"Remind me who Charlie is," Remi said as he handed his son another roll.

"The guy who loiters at Sugar Rush," Caleb said flatly. "Taking up a table so other customers can't sit."

Elena tsked at her son. "I'm sure Phoebe doesn't mind."

Hannah speared a green bean with her fork. "If she minded, she'd sic me on him, and I'd get rid of him. I'm not saying I haven't had to tell Charlie to skedaddle at closing time, but he's harmless."

I risked a glance at Caleb. His jaw was tight, eyes focused on his plate. He'd barely said a word since I'd arrived. I was becoming more and more convinced I was making him uncomfortable.

"Anyway," I said quickly, trying to end the attention on me, "for now, writing is a hobby. The library is my real job."

Lily waved her hand dismissively. "Sometimes the things we think are hobbies end up being the most important work we do."

Hannah nudged her husband. "When Alice is ready, you'll introduce her to your agent, right?"

Remi nodded then turned to me. "If that's what you want, I'd be glad to make the connection. My agent might not be the right fit for you, but she has a lot of contacts."

"That's..." I didn't quite know how to respond, so I said, "Thank you, guys. That would be incredible."

"It's no trouble," Remi replied.

It might not have been any trouble, but it was a big deal to me. A kindness I would have never asked for and hadn't been expecting. I guessed that was just the Kellys.

Dinner wound down with the clinking of forks against empty plates and Hannah telling a wild story about one of her farrier clients. She mostly took care of horses, but one of her clients owned goats who thought they were lap dogs. On her last visit, she thought one of them was snuggling with her and ended up with a hole in the seat of her jeans from the sneaky little goat's teeth.

"That's what I get for trusting a goat," she said. "I know better."

I laughed so hard, I snorted. "I'm sorry, but if you'd told me when I was living in San Francisco five years ago I'd one day be sitting on a ranch, listening to a story about ornery goats, I never would have believed it."

Hannah grinned at me, her lively eyes twinkling. "Aren't you glad you moved here?"

I nodded without hesitation. "I haven't regretted it even once."

When everyone was finished, I gathered my plate and began stacking others nearby to help.

"Oh, don't worry about that, Alice," Elena said, reaching out to take the plate from my hands. "We'll let the boys handle cleanup."

"Are you sure?"

She gave a small, elegant shrug. "They eat enough for three people each. They can wash the dishes."

Jesse took my plate and his, dropped them in the sink, then returned. "Do you want to go outside with me, Ms. Clark? You've never seen stars until you see them out here."

"I'd love that," I said. "And you know you can call me Alice when we're not at the library. It feels weird to be formal at your family's house."

"Okay." He shuffled his feet, a grin twitching on his lips. "Okay, Alice. Let's go."

Outside, the sky spread out in a velvet-black expanse, thick with pinpricks of silver light. The air was cool, carrying the scent of cut grass and a faint whiff of horses. Silas toddled out behind us in his little cowboy boots and pajama pants, Hannah holding his hand.

"Look, Alice," Jesse whispered, tilting his face up. "See it? That dusty line across the sky? That's the Milky Way."

I tipped my head back and sucked in a breath. "Wow..."

Stars sprayed across the sky like glitter, so dense it was dizzying. Hannah helped Silas plop down on the grass, and he started pointing up with chubby fingers, babbling, "Moon, moon, moon."

"It's beautiful," I agreed, wrapping my arms around myself as a breeze sifted through my hair. "There's nothing like this where I'm from. We're lucky to see a singular star in the city."

I would never get over Wyoming skies. Daytime or night, there was nothing like the endless expanse above. It didn't make sense the sky could be bigger here, but it was.

"Yeah." Jesse flopped onto his back in the grass. "My great-grandad taught me all the constellations when I was little. He has a sick telescope. Maybe if we ask him, he'll bring it out when you're here next time."

Hannah lowered herself to sit cross-legged beside her son and leaned back on her hands. "Your great-grandad taught me about the stars too. Do you know what else he told me? If I ever feel disconnected, I should think about how many people before us looked up at the same stars and how many people are looking up at the same sky as me."

I nodded, feeling my throat tighten. A night like tonight made me feel small but deeply connected at the same time. Like my roots were finally planted, and I was part of something bigger than me.

Suddenly, the front door banged open behind us, making me jump. Cormac stormed out, his shoes hitting the steps hard and fast. His face was dark, jaw clenched so tight, the muscles in his cheek ticced.

"Maccie?" Hannah called. "Everything okay?"

Not answering, he stalked past us across the gravel driveway, climbed into his truck, and slammed the door. The engine roared to life, headlights sweeping over us as he peeled out, tires crunching on the road until his taillights disappeared into the dark.

Silence fell heavy over the yard. Silas blinked up at me, unbothered, then went back to poking at the grass.

"What was that about?" Jesse asked.

Hannah shook her head, worry pinching her brows. "I don't know. Maccie doesn't get mad like that. Something must be wrong." She scooped Silas off the ground and glanced at Jesse. "Come on, guys. Let's go find out what happened."

Jesse pushed himself up with a sigh, brushing dirt from his jeans. "Wonder if Dad knows."

"Probably," Hannah murmured, already heading toward the house.

I didn't follow them. It wasn't my place, and whatever was going on with Cormac was none of my business. I'd already intruded enough for one night.

I slipped around the side of the house to where my car was parked. For a moment, I sat inside it, gripping the steering wheel, something like dread curdling my gut. This night had been so perfect. I wish it wasn't ending this way, but everything ended—one way or another.

I finally pulled away, letting myself have one more glance at the house in my rearview mirror. The windows glowed bright against the long, dark night.

Then I turned onto the dark road, leaving the Kelly family behind me.

Chapter Twenty

Caleb

I WASN'T A BIG talker in person, even less on the phone. I'd been holding mine for the last fifteen minutes, going back and forth on whether to make the call. Now was the time to do it. Jesse was in his room for the night, and if I waited any longer, it'd be too late. This hesitation wasn't like me. Once I made up my mind to do something, I got it done.

Finding no real reason to stop myself, I sighed, punched in Alice's number, and tucked my phone against my ear. She answered on the third ring.

"Caleb?" Surprise and wariness threaded through my name, which I thoroughly deserved.

"Hey, Allie." I did as best I could to blanket *her* name in assurance. "You left without saying goodbye."

There was a pause then almost a strangled sound. "I know. I feel bad about that. I texted your mom, but—"

"You didn't have to go." I sat on the edge of my bed, facing a window. There wasn't much to see unless I looked up. At night on the ranch, the endless sky was where the magic happened.

"Hannah was worried about Cormac," she explained. "I thought it was better to give everyone privacy, but I do feel terrible for not saying goodbye."

My brow dipped at her regretful tone. "You don't need to feel bad. No one was offended, I promise you." I cleared my throat. "Cormac was upset."

"I did gather that."

I chuffed at how prim she sounded as she sassed me. "Yeah. Figured you did. You're probably wondering what's going on."

"Sure. I'm human, so I'm curious, but it isn't my business. You don't have to explain."

"It's not a deep, dark secret or anything, and I don't think my brother would mind if I explained." I shoved my fingers through my hair. "My parents got a wedding invitation in the mail for their college friends' daughter. Cormac spotted it on the coffee table, and he—well, you saw how he reacted."

"Oh," she whispered, tickling my ear. "Through context clues, I'm guessing he isn't happy about the marriage."

My mouth hitched. The way she spoke was different from anyone I knew, and I liked it. "Cormac is as easygoing as they come, but when it comes to Zara Vasquez, he's a closed book. No, don't think he's happy she's getting married. He doesn't like the guy. That's part of why he and Zara fell out years ago. It's sad, but I'm hoping this is what it'll take for him to move on."

Killed me to see my brother down. He had always been a happy kid and had grown into an affable man, but on this subject, he was weighed down by a darkness he couldn't seem to navigate himself out of. He also refused to share the burden, even though he had to know any of us would have helped him take it on.

"Sometimes it takes a swift kick in the pants for moving on to happen," she said, and I easily read between the lines. I'd been the kicker, and she'd moved on from me. "I'm sorry for Cormac, though. That can't be easy."

"No, but he's got us to lean on. If only he'd take anyone up on it." I rubbed my leg and dug my fingers into my knee. "Anyway, that's what was going on tonight. I thought you should know."

"Thanks for telling me, Caleb."

"Yeah." For once, I wasn't ready to hurry off the phone. Alice's voice was nice to listen to, and I had a few questions about what I'd learned tonight. "So you've written two books, huh?"

"Well, yes. But they're middle grade, so they're shorter—"

I frowned. "Don't downplay your accomplishment. Remember what my dad said?"

There was a long pause before she murmured, "I'm an author."

"Hell yes, you are." I balled my fist on my knee. "And I'd love to read your books, Alice."

She hmphed. "You have another book you need to finish first."

Ah, deflection. I'd let her have it. As curious as I was, it wasn't like I deserved to have a first look.

"You're right about that." I eyed the hardback on my nightstand. "I'm halfway through. Reading it on my own isn't the same as reading it to you."

"Well..." Something rustled on her end. I imagined it was her shifting around, curling her legs beneath her like she had when she'd spent time on my couch with me. I hoped her living room was comfortable. That she had lots of fluffy pillows to lean on, and a warm, fuzzy blanket to cover her. "I have a little time before I need to get to bed. Would you like to read a chapter or two to me?"

I got stuck swallowing, so it took me a beat to respond. When I did, it came out choked. "You wouldn't mind?"

"Mind listening to you read my favorite book?" Her laugh was a gentle breeze through the line. "No, Caleb. It wouldn't be a hardship. That is…if you want to…"

"I want to," I hurried. "I'd like it a lot."

Picking up the book, I settled against the headboard and flipped to where I'd left off the night before. Alice was quiet, but I heard her soft breathing in my ear, waiting for me to get started.

So I did.

I read to her for a long time, past when I usually turned off the lights. The book was good—compelling even—but it was the little noises she made that kept me going. She'd read these words on her own dozens of times, but she reacted like it was the first. Gasps and hums pushed me to turn the page again and again, just to hear more.

When Alice yawned, I finally put my bookmark in the crack.

"Tired, Allie?"

"Mmmhmm. You must be too. Don't you wake up at the crack of dawn?"

My mouth hitched. "I do, and I am. But it seems you've got me hooked."

I could almost hear her smile. "I told you you'd love this story."

"Yeah, the story…" I replaced the book on my nightstand and rubbed the grit out of my eyes. "Same time tomorrow night?"

"I can't possibly turn that down."

"Good. I'll talk to you then. Night, Allie."

"Good night, Caleb."

We had a repeat the following few nights. Spent time talking about our days, then I read to her.

I didn't dread picking up the phone to call her. It was kind of funny how quickly it became part of my nighttime ritual. A month ago, cracking open a book wasn't even on my radar. Now, I looked forward to diving into the story with Alice on the other end of the line.

"I'm gonna need book two pretty soon," I said.

"I'll save it for you behind the desk," she replied. "Will you want to read that one to me as well?"

"Probably." I slid my hand over the protective plastic covering the book in my lap. "Maybe this is why I never got into reading. I needed a captive audience to read to."

She laughed. "You know, that could be it. Personally, I love being quiet with a book, but I can see how some people aren't meant for that. Some aren't solitary creatures."

"You think you're a solitary creature?"

"I'm happy in my own company. I spend most of my days around a lot of people, so I enjoy having time to just be quiet."

"I get that." It brought up a few questions, but only one was safe to ask. "Do you think you'll go back to work at Joy's?"

"Of course. Why wouldn't I?" she asked, genuinely puzzled.

"I don't know...you've got a broken wrist. The last thing you need to deal with is drunk assholes in a bar."

"Fortunately for me, Joy's doesn't attract too many of that kind. And when customers get out of line, Joy nips it in the bud pretty quickly. If she'd let me, I'd be back at work now. She's making me wait until next week."

I sat up straight, my brows rising. "Next week? You still have a cast. That's too soon."

"I'll be fine. You know Joy. She'll make sure of it."

That didn't reassure me like it should have. Joy was tough as nails. She'd do right by Alice. Still, I didn't like the idea of her waitressing. Not when she was hurt—and not after what she'd been through.

"If it's about money, I—"

She cut me off in a hurry. "Believe me, money isn't a problem. I *like* working at Joy's. If not for that job, I'd spend *too* much time on my own. It would be easy for me to become a shut-in." Her voice gentled. "I appreciate your concern, Caleb. Really, I do. But I promise I'll be okay."

I rubbed a hand over my jaw, trying to dislodge the tight feeling. "It's not that I don't believe you. I just..." Just what? I didn't know how to explain myself without sounding like a damn lunatic. Like some overbearing jackass who didn't trust her to make her own choices. That wasn't it. I did trust her. I didn't like the thought of her being back in that bar, where anything could happen. Joy was there, but she'd been there the night Bart had grabbed her, and she'd ended up bloody too.

She must've heard something in my silence, because she spoke again, softer this time. Like she was trying to comfort me. "You don't have to worry so much. I'm not fragile."

I wanted to argue she'd been through enough—that her bones were still mending along with the parts of her I couldn't see. But I bit down on the urge. Hard.

Before I could say something I'd regret—or worse, something I meant—she changed the subject.

"Do you still want to read tonight?" she asked. "I could use a little escape."

I exhaled, deciding to let her take the wheel. "Yeah. I definitely want to."

We settled into it the way we had every night this week. I cracked open the book and started where we'd left off, my voice filling the quiet space between us. She hummed once, then again, and the tension in my shoulders began to ease.

Little by little, her sounds stopped, and her breathing slowed. She'd fallen asleep, but I was still wide awake. Wondering if she was in bed—if she was comfortable so she didn't wake up with a crick in her neck tomorrow.

I closed the book, but I didn't hang up right away.

Just sat there with the phone to my ear, listening to the rhythm of her breathing like it was some kind of lullaby I didn't know I needed. I told myself I was giving her time to wake up, in case she'd dozed off for a minute. I was being polite.

The truth was, I stayed on the line longer than I'd ever admit to anyone.

Because for some reason, the sound of her sleeping calmed something in me I hadn't even realized was restless.

I didn't know what that meant. Didn't try to name it.

I just listened.

Chapter Twenty-one

Alice

Mrs. Taylor was a faithful patron of Sugar Brush Community Library, but she did not trust me. Every time she checked out a book, she gave me a serious stink-eye—and I was almost certain I'd never steered her wrong.

This afternoon, she peered at me over the top of her reading glasses, the library's copy of *Wild Like a Cowboy's Heart* clutched tightly to her chest, like it was in danger of being stolen.

"I need to know," she whispered, as if the other patrons might eavesdrop. "Is it...*spicy*?"

I glanced at the cover—shirtless cowboy leaning against a fence post at sunset—and fought the smile tugging at my lips. I might've been a devout fantasy reader, but that didn't mean I never ventured onto the wilder side. I liked a good, steamy cowboy romance as much as the next person.

"I think it's pretty spicy, but I suppose that would depend on your personal definition."

"You know." She wiggled her stark white eyebrows. "Not just kissing. I don't have time for all that slow-burn malarkey."

Biting back a laugh, I flipped the book open and scanned a few pages I found pretty dang delightful. "I'd say it's a medium burn.

There's a barn scene about halfway through, and…well, I won't spoil it for you. You'll know when you get there."

The blush that suffused her cheeks made her look fifty years younger and not nearly as cantankerous as I knew her to be. "Perfect. My blood pressure's been low lately. The doctor says I need excitement."

"I think you'll find plenty in those pages," I assured her.

She questioned me for a few more minutes and requested I order a book by one of her favorite romance authors, then she promised I'd be hearing from her if the cowboy spice wasn't up to snuff. I told her I'd be ready to face the music if that happened.

When she finally toddled toward the exit, I was grinning to myself, but I froze when I spotted the mountain planted beside the front door.

Caleb Kelly sauntered over to my desk, one hand tucked in his jeans, the other holding a miniature potted plant. I held my breath until he reached me, the crooked grin blooming under his scruffy beard entrancing me.

Dang it all to hell.

Our nightly reading sessions were doing nothing to help me move on from this damn man. Yet I always picked up when he called.

I liked to think I was a smart woman, but when it came to Caleb, I was a drooling, simpering dolt.

"Hey." He leaned his elbow on my desk and grinned down at me. "Seems like your last customer was giving you a hard time."

"Nothing I can't handle." I stood up. It didn't put us on an even playing field, but we were closer. "Mrs. Taylor takes her steamy romance very seriously. She doesn't want to waste any time on books where the author closes the door when things start to heat up."

His brows popped. "You have that kind of book here?"

"Oh yeah." I propped my hip beside my keyboard and smirked. "Why do you think the library's so popular?"

"Well, hell…" He raked his fingers through the side of his hair. "I think I've been looking in the wrong section."

A laugh spilled out of me. "Are you regretting reading *Shadow of the Isle*?"

"Not at all." He rapped his knuckles on my desk. "In fact, that's part of the reason I'm here. I'm ready for book two. Do you have it for me?"

"I do." I reached down and grabbed the hardback I'd set aside for him. "Here it is. *Wing of the Sea.*"

He put the little plant he'd brought on the counter. "Let's trade. I'll take the book, you take this."

The plant was a succulent, with adorable, round, plump leaves, tucked in a very small pot that looked hand painted. But I…didn't know why he'd brought it here.

I blinked at it. "What's this for?"

"Your desk," he said simply, like that explained everything. It absolutely did not. "I thought it could use some color and life. And when I saw this little guy, I thought of you."

My fingers hovered near the pot, not quite touching it. I'd been given gifts plenty of times. In my position, I was on many Christmas cookie lists, and children loved to draw me special pictures. But I'd never been given something like this. Something small and charming Caleb had seen and thought, *"That's Alice."*

I didn't know what to do with the warmth that pooled in my chest, or the unbearable ache that came right after.

"Caleb, you didn't have to—"

"I know." His eyes softened, and I had to glance down at the succulent before I drowned in them. "I wanted to. You spend a lot of time here. You deserve something pretty to look at."

"Well, thank you. I hope I can keep it alive."

He chuckled. "Is the last one I gave you still green?"

"So far, so good. But it's only been a couple weeks."

The corners of his eyes crinkled. "I have faith in you, Allie. You can do it."

"That makes one of us. I guess time will tell." I busied myself with shuffling the papers on my desk, giving it my fullest attention.

He took the book from the counter, tucking it under his arm. "When are you starting back at Joy's?"

"Wednesday night," I stated, making the neatest stack of papers in the history of stacks.

"You're sure you're ready?"

I finally looked up. "I am, Caleb."

"Good." He nodded once. "I'm glad you're feeling confident. That's good."

"Yeah," I whispered, though confident was the last thing I felt. I would have said discombobulated. Confused. A little angry. Not confident.

He cocked his head, oblivious to the storm brewing within me. "I hope you'll have time to read with me. Does tonight look good?"

I truly couldn't keep carrying on like this. Clearly, it wasn't good for me. One day, if Caleb wanted to be friends, I might've been able to, but not now. I hadn't been able to shake these feelings off, and I wouldn't, not with him around every corner and in my ear each night.

"Actually…" I rubbed my palms over my thighs, wishing Mrs. Taylor would march back in, demanding to know about another barn scene, "I'm not going to be available to read this week. I've got a lot going on."

It wasn't a complete lie. My to-do list at the library was endless, and Lily had hopped right on the fundraising idea, so I had tasks to complete for her as well. But mostly, I needed distance. As much as I could get.

His brow creased, but he only nodded. "All right. I'll get started on my own. Let me know when you have time for me."

"Okay," I replied. "I will."

Once he was gone and I could breathe normally again, I picked up the little pot and smiled at the brightly painted design. It really was a sweet gift, and I already knew I'd like looking at it.

Then a folded piece of paper that had been beneath the pot caught my eye. My mouth went desert dry as I picked it up and unfolded it, revealing Caleb's familiar scrawl.

Allie,

Hope you like this little guy. My grandmother says it only needs watered once a week, and it'll do fine with minimal sunlight.

This is a thank you for humoring me *plant. My evenings have been a lot more fulfilling since you picked up the phone. Consider this a bribe in case you're getting tired of me.*

I'll talk to you soon (hopefully tonight).

Yours,

CK

I slowly refolded the note and let it rest in my palm. It felt heavier than a scrap torn from a spiral-bound notebook should have. The paper was ridged where his pen had pressed into it, the blue ink pooling in the curves of each letter, like he'd gone over them at least twice, giving the words he'd left more meaning. Caleb wasn't a reader, and I doubted he was much of a writer, but I could almost see him in my mind, hunched over one of his son's notebooks at the kitchen table, considering each word he committed with ink.

The last time I'd held paper that felt this heavy, it had been the letter from a lawyer telling me my sister was dead.

Now in my hand was something just as unexpected. Not news that could break me, but if I wasn't careful, I might end up that way anyway.

This man...did he really have no idea what he was doing? Could a person be so oblivious?

Considering it seemed the entire town had been aware of my feelings, while Caleb had remained in the dark, I'd venture to say the answer was yes.

I groaned again, tucking the note in my pocket, already knowing I'd water that little plant every week without fail.

While cursing Caleb Kelly every single time.

Chapter Twenty-two

Caleb

THE DOOR TO JOY's swung shut behind me and Remi, letting the cool air of the late spring night slip away. Inside, the place was as busy as I expected for a Friday. A couple guys parked at the bar, the jukebox humming low beneath the clack of pool balls from the back corner where a half dozen ranch hands were leaning over their cues.

It wasn't hard to spot Alice. She was at the ranch hands' table, balancing a tray against her hip, the cast on her left wrist making her movements slower but no less sure. She set down a fresh round of beers, her smile catching in the bright glow of the pool table lights. One of the men said something that made the others laugh, and she tipped her head politely and stepped back, tucking a loose piece of hair behind her ear.

Remi jerked his chin toward our usual table. Tearing my eyes from Alice, I followed him, parking myself in my seat. It'd been a long, strange week. Quiet without my boy and the phone calls with Alice I'd gotten used to quicker than I expected. Not that I'd had time for reading.

Remi shook his head. "You look worn out."

"I am. Seems everything that can go wrong is happening all at once. A water line broke, we had a downed fence, and last night, a heifer had trouble giving birth. We had to call out the vet and"—I expelled a heavy breath—"well, needless to say, when it rains, it pours."

"That's a lot." He put his phone on the table in case my sister called. He didn't have to explain that to me. That was simply who he was. A good husband and father. Exactly who I wanted for her. "If you want more than a couple drinks, I'll do the driving tonight. You can spend the night at our place."

Remi was a good friend too.

I grinned at him. "Remember the wake-up call I got last time I crashed with you?"

He groaned. "Yeah. I'm still sorry about that. I don't know how Silas bypassed the gate to get to you. He's as wily as a fox."

I chuckled in agreement. I'd been sprawled out in their downstairs bedroom after a rare night of tying one on, and next thing I knew, my nephew was prying my eyelids open with his little fingers. Once he'd had my attention, he'd decided to entertain me by singing gibberish at the top of his lungs.

Not the wake-up I'd been expecting, but it was impossible to be mad when he'd climbed out of his crib and over the gate at the top of their stairs in order to get to me. That, and he was cute as hell.

"You don't need to be sorry. I grew up with Hannah. You think that was the first time I'd had my eyeballs pried open?"

Remi's grin widened. "I am absolutely sure it wasn't."

"Nope. Not even the second time." I gave my shoulder a shrug. "We'll see where the night goes. Maybe I'll take you up on it."

Alice showed up at the table, catching me off guard. I hadn't been paying attention and turned at her quiet greeting, taking her in up close.

She'd pinned the front of her hair back out of her face, and the rest fell in loose waves over her shoulders. It looked pretty that way. I was glad she was no longer hiding behind it.

What she was wearing, though?

Her plum-colored tank top had thin straps and a low neckline, revealing the tops of her small, high breasts. It was tucked into dark jeans that fit her thighs like they were made for her. I'd never seen her reveal so much skin.

Nice skin.

Lovely, smooth, velvety skin.

Aw, damn.

If Hannah were here, she'd have told me I sounded like a serial killer. That was how thrown off my game the sight of this woman had made me. Had she always been this pretty? She must've been. I couldn't understand how I'd missed it for so long.

Alice's smile was quick, polite, containing none of the warmth she'd been shining on me recently.

"Good evening, guys. What can I get you?" Her voice was steady and professional but distant. Hearing it, you wouldn't have known we'd spent hours talking to each other on the phone.

I opened my mouth to say something casual, maybe ask how she was doing, but it was clear she was here on business. Still, I eyed the cast on her wrist, wondering if it was hindering her. If she was in pain. If she should have been working here at all after everything. But I didn't ask. She'd already brushed aside my concerns once this week.

Remi grinned at her. "I'll take a beer. Something cold and quick."

I glanced back at Alice, searching for a sign of...well, I didn't know. *Something.* I didn't find it. "I'll have the same."

She jotted it down as carefully as ever, even though I was sure she didn't need the notepad. It gave her a reason not to have to look at her customers.

At me.

A flicker of frustration hit me. Where had the easy connection gone? I'd thought we'd been on the road to becoming friends. That must have been wishful thinking. After all, she was *over me*. Maybe that extended to the very end of the definition, meaning she wanted nothing to do with me except *this*: taking my order and walking away.

"Everything all right?" I finally asked, unable to stop myself.

She paused, then gave a small, polite nod. "I'm fine, thank you. It's busy, and the cast makes things slower."

I wanted to press her, find out what else was going on, but she was already stepping back toward the bar.

"I'm surprised she's back to work so soon," Remi remarked once we were alone. "Joy runs a tight ship, I guess."

"Nah, Alice wanted to come back. Joy tried to get her to take more time off, but she wasn't hearing it."

Remi paused, his gaze finding mine. "Huh. I know your mom is friends with Alice. I didn't realize you were too."

"We've talked a few times," I hedged.

What could I say to explain what had happened over the last month? When it came down to it, not much. Mostly to preserve Alice's privacy, and a little because the rest made me look like a jackass. Remi might've been my brother-in-law and closest friend, but I didn't need him knowing all the ways I'd screwed up.

"Yeah? Does she have a lot to say?" Remi asked. "I haven't ever seen her being chatty."

"Chatty isn't a word I'd use to describe her," I grunted and picked up my napkin, twisting it with my fingers. "No one would describe me that way either, I suspect."

"Truer words, buddy." He tipped forward. "You didn't answer my question, though."

I cocked my head. "Does she have a lot to say?"

Remi nodded, and I considered my reply. "Alice is...interesting. I think what I know of her barely scratches the surface."

"Hmmm." He scratched at the scruff on his chin. "Well, if your mom has her way, Alice'll be over weekly for dinner. Maybe you'll get a chance to dive beyond the surface."

"Maybe." If she let me. The way things had gone this past week, I wasn't sure.

Alice came back with our drinks a few minutes later, setting them down with her usual careful efficiency. "You guys know what you want for dinner?"

Remi didn't even open the menu. "I sure do. A cheeseburger with fries and extra pickles."

"Never too many pickles, right?" she teased.

He shot her a grin. "You've got that right."

Alice turned to me. "How about you, Caleb? What would you like?"

"How about the steak sandwich?"

Her pen was poised above her notepad. "Are you asking my opinion?"

I lowered my chin, my brow crinkled. "If you're inclined to give it."

She brought her pen to her mouth, nibbling on the end. "If you get onion rings to go with it, I think you'll be very pleased."

I took my time answering as I tried to figure out what was going on in her head. All she was giving me was her polite little smile.

"I trust you, Allie. You know what I like."

"Got it," she said quickly, jotting it down before heading off again. No lingering, no teasing, no asking about my week like she used to. Just...gone.

Remi gave me a long, pointed stare. "What was that?"

I paused, my beer halfway to my mouth. "What?"

His eyes narrowed. "I could be wrong, but it looked a hell of a lot like you were trying to flirt with Alice." He blew out a puff of air. "I can't say I've ever seen you flirt with a woman, but I'm pretty sure that's what that was."

My chuckle sounded closer to choking than laughter. "I was being friendly."

There was no mistaking his laugh for anything else. "Since when are you friendly?"

"I'm capable of it." I sat back in my chair and crossed my arms. "I'll remember not to do it again in your presence. Wouldn't want Hannah to get jealous if she thinks I'm flirting with *you*."

He rolled his eyes and grinned. "I know deflecting when I hear it." Then he sobered slightly, resting his elbows on the table. "I'll lay off, man. Just saying, if you want to share, I'm all ears, and I promise not to give you a hard time."

He wouldn't, and I knew it. Trouble was, I didn't know what *to* share. I had a lot on my mind, but none of it was clear enough to try to get out.

"I'm good," I stated, and it was mostly true. "Thanks for the offer."

Alice kept up the same routine all night. She flitted back and forth to our table to drop food, refill our drinks, and clear plates, each time staying long enough to do her job before disappearing. The rest of the time, I caught glimpses of her smiling at other tables, leaning in to hear a joke, laughing with people I'd never seen her speak to before.

I picked at my sandwich, more interested in tracking her than eating, which was a first for me. Not much got in the way of my appetite, especially when it came to Joy's cooking. But every time she laughed with someone else, I felt it, that new, unfamiliar restlessness in my gut. There was no room for anything else. I didn't understand it, just that it'd been happening more and more often when she was around.

She'd just taken our orders for another beer when it happened.

A song started up on the jukebox. Something older and lively. I tapped my toe under the table, and more than a few customers hummed or quietly sang along.

When Alice reached the bar, Bryan, one of the old-timers who parked himself on his favorite stool most nights, hopped up and snagged her tray, putting it on the bar top. Then he held out his hand. After a beat, she slipped hers into it, and he yanked her into his chest.

Alert, my muscles tensed.

Alice threw her head back and laughed as Bryan pushed her away and spun her in dizzying circles. Her hair slid from her shoulders and cascaded down her back as she twirled like a ballerina in a music box. Just when I thought she'd never stop spinning, Bryan brought her into his arms and led her into a bouncy two-step. Alice's cheeks were rosy, her eyes alight, and her mouth was poised in a grin wider than I'd ever seen.

Boom.

I was still in my chair, but I'd hit the ground without even realizing I'd been falling. I knew I'd missed a lot, but there was no missing this sudden, bone-deep awareness that I wanted to be the one making her laugh like that—be the reason her eyes shone and cheeks flushed pink.

I sat frozen, watching her spin under Bryan's hand, every turn unraveling something in my chest. I wasn't jealous, not of Bryan, who was old enough to be my grandfather. But I was feeling mighty stupid. If I'd been smart, that might've been me twirling her.

Now? She looked happier and more alive than I'd ever seen her, and I hadn't been the one to make her so.

The song wound down, and Bryan gave her a playful bow. She clapped, still beaming like the brightest star in the sky, then slipped back behind the bar like nothing had changed.

But something had.

For me at least.

Chapter Twenty-three

Caleb

I SHOWED UP AT my parents' house the next morning as early as I dared, but I didn't walk in. My siblings and I had learned the hard way our parents were living it up as empty nesters. Their age hadn't slowed their passion for one another, and as happy as I was to have a mom and dad madly in love, I didn't want to witness it. Once was more than enough for ten lifetimes, dammit.

My dad opened the door to me in under a minute. My timing had been all right after all. He ushered me into the kitchen, where my mom was sipping coffee and reading the paper. She tilted her chin, and I bent down to kiss her cheek.

"This is a surprise," she said.

"Yeah." I lowered myself into the same chair I'd sat on since I was a small child. "I didn't do a lot of sleeping last night."

My dad sat beside her, his arm stretched across the back of her chair, curling his fingers around her thick braid. "Something on your mind, son?"

I was under no illusions my mother didn't share everything with him, so there was no doubt he was up to speed on the Alice situation. Meaning I could dive right in.

Glancing back and forth between them, I simply stated, "Alice."

My mother nodded. "I assumed this conversation would happen sooner rather than later."

The corners of my dad's eyes crinkled as he turned to her. "Are you going to explain to our son how to get his head out of his ass?"

She brushed her fingertips over his beard. "Am I ever." Then she gave me a pointed look. "That is, if that's why you're here."

"That's why I'm here. And I've braced myself, so please, don't pull any punches."

That got my dad laughing. "I don't think she knows how, Cay."

The corner of my mouth hitched. "Yeah. You're right. I'm ready for it."

She folded her hands under her chin, her icy blue gaze sweeping over me. "I told you I questioned your whole premise for turning Alice away, and I stand by that. You say you don't need a relationship to be happy, and while that is true, I know you, Cay. You don't like to be alone. Family and friends are your lifeblood. When Jesse's not home, you find every excuse to not be either. You're here or with your brother or sisters, or at Joy's. You're the opposite of a loner. You thrive on being in a pack. And I absolutely believe you'd be more fulfilled if you had a partner to share your life with."

I was taking in what she was saying, but she wasn't finished with me. "You've been doing the single father thing for a long time. I can understand why you wouldn't want to rock the boat. But what about adding someone who would bring a balance you didn't even know you were missing? Why would you deprive yourself of that? Why would you settle for what you have when you could have even more?"

"I have a lot," I argued feebly.

"You do, and you could continue living the rest of your life the same way." Her eyes narrowed. "But, the next few years, I think you'll see everyone moving forward while you're still standing still. Before you know it, Jesse will be off to college, your siblings will get busy with little ones, and you...well, you'll have more time on your hands than you want or know what to do with. Maybe you'll be ready for a partner then...but it might be too late. The right one might have moved on."

I'm over you.

I shoved my hands through my hair as my stomach twisted. "If she already has?"

Her spine straightened as she stared me down in the way only my mother could. "Then hopefully you've learned a valuable lesson."

For the second time, I felt like my ass had hit the ground, knocking the wind out of me. There was every chance Alice would not give two damns about me coming around. She'd told me as much, and last night, I saw for myself how *over me* she was.

"How'd I miss her?" I asked, more to myself than either of them.

My father answered anyway. "One of your best attributes is how focused you are. It's also one of your worst. You're single-minded to the point of being stubborn."

"I can't deny that."

My mom dropped her hand on top of mine. "I've spoken to Alice every day since she was attacked. She's been through a lot—possibly more than you know. She's doing really well, but I don't know if she's ready to begin anything with you."

I shook my head. "My timing couldn't be worse."

Her fingers squeezed around mine. "You came for advice, so here's mine: be clear. If you would like a relationship with her, don't pussyfoot around the topic. She put herself out there once. Now it's your turn. Give her the knowledge and power and let her decide what she wants to do with it."

As oblivious as I could be, I wasn't a coward. Now that I knew what I wanted, I would have no trouble saying it. But I didn't want to do the wrong thing and hurt Alice any more than I had.

I glanced between my parents. "Like you said, she's been through a lot. Is it even right for me to add to that?"

"I'd like to think she'd view it as a good thing," my mother said. "Besides needing a haircut and beard trim, you're quite a catch, Caleb Kelly."

I chuffed. "Isn't it your job as my mom to say that?"

She lifted a shoulder. "It was my job to raise you into the man you are. Now I get to be proud of my creation."

My dad tugged on her braid. "I married a mad scientist."

"Just a mom." She leaned into him. "You know your father dumped me in college."

It'd been decades since he'd made that mistake, but his eyes flared with panic, and he clutched her even tighter against him.

"And I quickly realized the grievous error of my ways," he stated firmly.

She patted his cheek. "Maybe the Kelly men have to be stupid before they wise up. Fortunately for us all, you've been perfect ever since." Then she turned her gaze back to me. "My point in dredging up ancient history is, once your dad realized what he'd given up, he worked hard to win me back. He showed me I could trust him and he would be steady for me. It was what I needed."

I understood what she was telling me. "I've got to be that steady presence for Alice."

"Always," my father agreed. "I've seen you weather storms. I know you're a good man. You have what it takes to be the kind of partner a woman like Alice needs. Show her that."

"But don't push," my mother added. "Don't pressure her."

"I would never," I replied with vehemence.

She patted my hand. "I know you wouldn't, sweetheart. But I feel it's imperative to remind you to allow her to take the lead."

"That's what I'll do," I said firmly. "I'll be there for her, as long as it takes."

My dad's mouth curved into the faintest smile. "I have a good feeling about this."

I wasn't quite so optimistic, but I was determined. And if I became doubtful, I'd think back to last night, at the feeling of Alice shining her light on everyone but me. I wanted that light, and dammit, I wanted her to lean on me the way my mother did my father. How had I not seen that? How had I never wanted all that goodness for myself?

Maybe it was Alice I'd been waiting for all along.

I wasn't going to make the same mistake again. This time, she'd set the pace, and I'd match every step.

No matter how long the road was, I'd walk it.

Chapter Twenty-four

Alice

MY THUMB WAS SO darn black, I was ready to rip up my whole yard and replace it with pebbles. I wanted bright, pretty flowers growing everywhere. Instead, I had dandelions and clover. Not to mention the hundreds of dollars I'd spent on perennials that had bloomed once then never again.

On my knees in the dirt, I sighed, swiping my sweat-beaded forehead. This was hopeless. It was probably better to give up on my front yard for the day and expend the rest of my energy on something else.

As soon as the thought had entered my mind, the distinct rumble of a pickup truck approached down my quiet street. As it slowed, I turned, surprised to recognize the oversized white vehicle then momentarily panicked.

Caleb was parking his truck at my curb, and I was a sweaty mess. I also didn't have a drop of makeup on, and I had thrown my hair on top of my head in a messy bun. Not to mention, I was only wearing cutoff jean shorts, a worn-out college tee, and no bra. And I was almost certain I'd just smeared dirt across my forehead.

He climbed out of his truck, circled it, then grinned at me on the ground. My heart did a painful twist, rattling the bars of its cage, and I couldn't seem to get my limbs to cooperate to stand up.

"Hey, Allie," he called as he made his way down my walk. "Doing some gardening?"

"Hey." I waved my spade at him. "Yes, I'm trying, but I think I'm failing."

When he reached me, he offered a hand. I let him pull me to my feet then quickly took my hand back, retreating a couple steps.

Caleb didn't miss any of this. His mouth flattened into a thin, hard line.

"How are you?" he asked. "How was it being back at Joy's?"

I tried to stuff my hands in my back pockets, but the casted one got stuck, so I let them fall to my sides.

"I'm really good, actually. I think getting back into my routine has done me well. I feel almost normal. Your mom's been a big support. So, that's..." There weren't really words for Elena. She was like an extra backbone and beacon, guiding me through. I kept waiting for nightmares and panic attacks—both of which I'd had plenty growing up—but they hadn't come. If I'd had Elena around back then, I felt I would've fared a whole lot better. "Well, you know what she's like."

"I do. There's no one like her."

He nodded a few times, and that was when I noticed he'd gotten a haircut. His long hair was tidy, skimming his collar, but still long enough in the front to tuck neatly behind his ears. His beard had been shaped up too. I could see his lips when he spoke and his straight, white teeth when he smiled.

He noticed me checking him out, and his big hand brushed along the back of his head.

"I made a stop at the barber this morning. Long overdue."

"It looks great, Caleb. I liked the long hair too, but like this…I can see your smile."

"Yeah?" He cocked his head. "I'll be sure to keep up the trims."

"Okay." What was happening right now? "Did you need something else?"

He glanced toward his truck then back to me, almost like he was debating with himself. Finally, he reached into his back pocket and pulled out something flat, neatly wrapped in brown paper and tied with a thin piece of twine.

"This is for you. I found it in the ranch's resort store and thought of you." He held it out, palm open.

I hesitated before taking it. The last thing I needed was another gift from this man. It was bad enough I was reminded of him every time I looked at the little pot on my desk at work. But I couldn't help my curiosity. The paper crackled as I untied the string and peeled it away, revealing a slim bookmark made of clear acrylic with a pink tassel on top. Pressed inside were tiny wildflowers—purple, white, and yellow—arranged like a miniature bouquet frozen in time.

"It was made by a local artisan," he said quietly. "The flowers grow up on the ridge trail this time of year."

I traced a fingertip over the cool acrylic, the little petals still vivid despite their stillness. "This is…I mean, I don't even…" I shook my head. "Why?"

His jaw worked, like he wasn't sure how to answer. "I wanted you to have flowers."

"Caleb…"

He held up his hands. "It's not a bouquet. Not yet. But I saw it and thought you'd like looking at it when you're reading."

My confusion only deepened. He was standing in front of my house, checking in on me, finding a work-around on my previous declaration to give me flowers that would never wilt. Not only that, he was looking at me in a way I could only interpret as tender.

It didn't make sense.

"Can we talk for a minute?"

I nodded, following him to the porch, hoping he'd clear things up so I wasn't in a constant state of whiplash.

We sat on the steps, side by side, the wood creaking under us. Caleb put his back to the support post and twisted his body toward me. His long legs stretched down the steps, heavy boots resting on the bottom one.

He got started, saying the last thing I expected. "I've really missed our calls. Reading without you isn't the same."

I didn't know how to answer that, but that was okay, because he didn't wait for me to speak. He leaned forward, his elbows on his knees, eyes on me.

"I have a problem with not seeing the world in front of me and sometimes overlook important things. Beautiful, wonderful things. Like you. You have become such an intrinsic part of the fabric of my life, I only noticed your threads were some of the brightest and most vibrant when you unraveled yourself." He blew out a heavy breath. "It was your absence after I screwed up that made me wake up to what I was missing."

My mouth had gone dry. My nose twitched. And I couldn't summon a single word. I was half convinced I was dreaming, but even in my dreams, Caleb had never said anything like this. Still, I pinched myself to be sure. A girl couldn't be too careful.

Of course, he saw it, and his smile was so endearingly crooked, I might've laughed if I didn't half feel like crying.

He reached across the narrow space between us and brushed his rough fingertips over the top of my hand. "You told me you're over me, but I'm hoping maybe there's a small part of you that isn't. That maybe you'd allow me to prove myself to you and grow that tiny seed until it blooms again." He curled his thick fingers around mine, squeezing ever so gently. "My timing couldn't be worse, but I need you to know I have more patience than sense. I will wait as long as you need."

I licked my lips, trying to formulate a coherent response. Weeks ago, sitting here like this would have been everything I'd ever wanted. Now, I didn't know how to trust this was real.

"What do you want from me, Caleb?" I asked.

"I'd like our phone calls back." He turned my hand over, resting it on his, and traced his fingers over the lines on my palm. "I want to hear about your day and tell you about mine. I'd like to take you out for a meal. I don't know if you like to dance, but if you do, I'd love to spin you around a dance floor."

All I could say was: "I've never really danced."

His thumb stilled on my palm, the faintest smile tugging at his mouth. "Then I'll teach you. I'm no expert, but I think we could have fun together. I *know* we could."

I shook my head quickly, trying to clear the cobwebs. "I don't understand where this is coming from. Is this some kind of misguided guilt thing? Because of what happened to me?" My voice came out sharper than I meant, but I couldn't stop it. "You don't have to—pity-date me or whatever this is. The attack wasn't your fault. You have to know that."

His brows drew together, and the hurt in his eyes was immediate, unguarded. "No. God, Allie, no." He leaned closer, his voice low but fierce. "This isn't about that. Not even a little bit. This is about me finally getting my head out of my ass and seeing the beautiful woman who gave me the best damn kiss of my life in a bar bathroom."

My cheeks burned, and my heart gave a wild, traitorous kick. "The best kiss?"

"The absolute best, no question," he confirmed. "I think we could add a lot to each other's lives. Not just kissing. Though I'm on board for a lot more of that too."

The laugh that bubbled out of me bordered on hysterical. This was too much. "I'm sorry I don't have a better response. I simply don't know what to say."

"You have nothing to be sorry for." He curled his fingers around mine again, and my hand was lost within his. It was brand new and immediately became one of my favorite feelings. I suspected hugging him would be even better. "I don't expect you to give me any kind of answer today or anytime soon."

"That's good, because I'm so very confused."

His smile was warm, dosed with even more tenderness. "That's my fault, and I'm sorry as hell. From here on out, I intend to be as clear and honest as I can. That is, if you want that."

"Honesty? Of course I want it."

"I meant from me. Here I am, showing up at your house, and I don't even know if you want to see me." His eyes darted between mine, searching for something. "I never want to put you in a position where you feel like you don't have a choice."

And this was why I'd always be a goner for him. Despite everything, he really was a good, solid man. But I was still shaken up, and he was right—the timing was all wrong. As much as I wanted to, rushing headlong into something so intense was probably a bad idea.

"I just..." My throat worked, and I looked away toward the half-dead petunias by my steps. "I need time to think about everything you said."

"Of course." No hesitation. No flash of disappointment. Just an easy nod, like he'd anticipated that answer. "I'll leave you to your gardening."

He stood, his shadow falling over me for a moment before he started down the steps. I sat there, the bookmark beside me, watching him cross the walk. His gait was slow. Not like he was hoping I'd beg him back, but maybe he was in no hurry to leave me.

He'd opened the truck door, one boot already inside, when the words tumbled out of me before I could think. "Caleb...wait."

He turned, hand braced on the doorframe, eyebrows raised.

I stood, heart hammering, and crossed the short stretch of yard to him. "There's something I'd like...well, I guess *need* is the better word for it. Will you give me one thing?"

"Anything you want or need—it's yours," he vowed.

I sucked in a shaky breath. "Would you give me a hug?"

For a second, something in his expression softened so much, it made me ache all over. Then he stepped down from the truck and wrapped those big arms around me, pulling me flush against him.

Heaven help me, the second my chest hit his, I melted. He was tall and strong, but there was nothing hard about the way he held me, just solid warmth and a slow, steady heartbeat under my ear. His beard brushed the top of my head, his hand splayed broad and protective against my back. It was everything I'd imagined...and so much worse, because now I knew exactly how it felt.

"Is this good?" he murmured.

"So good," I answered, barely resisting the urge to rub my face against the well-worn flannel of his shirt.

"Yeah," he rumbled. "It is."

I might have stayed there forever if the sound of a car in desperate need of a new muffler hadn't brought me back to earth. With a sigh, I took a step back. Caleb looked down at me, his thumb brushing a stray hair from my cheek.

"Thank you for giving me that."

"Anything you ask for, Allie," he murmured. "Take all the time you need. I'm not going anywhere."

Chapter Twenty-five

Alice

THE TIME I NEEDED turned out to be approximately twenty-nine hours and thirty-seven minutes. I'd done nothing but think about what Caleb had said, how he'd said it, and that hug. Oh, that hug.

His phantom arms had stayed around me for hours after he left. I'd been so fortified from less than a minute in his embrace, I'd gardened the hell out of my yard, the whole time thinking about what it would be like to give Caleb a chance.

I bet I'd get a lot more of those hugs. And more. So much more.

I really wanted more, especially with him. I'd never wanted it with anyone else.

I managed to hold off until nine that night. The usual time of our phone calls. My hands only shook slightly as I dialed his number.

I'd almost lost my nerve by the time he answered on the fourth ring.

"Allie? You okay?"

"Hey, I'm fine," I replied, though that was an exaggeration. I was somewhat freaking out. "I've been thinking."

"Give me a second, I want to hear everything you've been think-ing." I heard movement then a door closing. "Sorry. I got Jesse back this afternoon. He's in his room, doing his thing, but I doubt he wants to hear his old man on the phone with his favorite librarian."

I laughed. "Did he have a good week with his mom?"

"Sure. They get along pretty well. I appreciate you asking, but I suspect Jesse wasn't what was on your mind."

"You want me to cut to the chase?" I teased.

"To tell you the truth, I'm so glad to have your voice in my ear again, you could read me a receipt, and I'd listen."

A gush of air rushed out of me so fast, I fell heavily onto my couch cushions. "That was sweet."

"I told you I missed our calls, and I meant it."

"I have too." I nodded to myself, rubbing my hand along my thigh. "And I'd like to maybe start them again, if you want."

"You know I do," he cooed roughly, sending goose bumps flooding down my arms.

"Okay. Then we should. There are a few things you should know—to know what you're getting into with me."

"I'm all ears. Eager to know as much of you as you'd like to share."

There was a loose thread on my cutoffs, longer than the others. I curled it around my finger and gathered my thoughts. They stacked and stacked on the tip of my tongue until spilling out all at once.

"You were right, Caleb. I think I'm a lover girl at heart, and I do want something serious. I'm not in a rush, but I would like to be married and have at least one child. If that isn't something you could see yourself having with me, we should—"

"It is," he rushed out, cutting me off. "If I couldn't see myself possibly going there with you, I wouldn't have approached you."

Relief settled me, but only slightly. I had a lot more to get through.

"Good. You should also know I don't have any family to speak of. I was estranged from my parents when they died. My sister too. And that night I kissed you, I had received a letter from her lawyer telling me she'd passed."

I braced for his reaction, but all he said was: "Christ, Allie, I'm sorry for your loss."

"Thank you. We had a very complicated relationship and were never close. It's a strange feeling, knowing I'm alone in the world. She also left me all her money, which was a lot."

He released a long, heavy breath. "Complicated or not, I'm still sorry. But you're not alone in the world. You've got Joy, and my mom is not giving you up, and me—you've got me, no matter how this phone call goes."

That was true. I did have Joy. She'd become more of a mother to me than my own had been, and she'd only known me four years. She'd probably cringe and shoo me away if she heard me thinking of her as a mother figure, but deep beneath her hard, rough exterior, I knew she loved me.

I wasn't ready to consider Elena and Caleb yet. It was much too soon for that.

"Thank you. There's more, though."

"Hit me with it. I'm ready."

"Okay. Here goes." I took a deep breath and let the rest of it spill. "I only have one kidney. I donated the other to my sister, then she never spoke to me again. I have all this money, and the only thing I can think to spend it on is more books—for me and the library. I don't really want to go on an exotic vacation or buy a fancy car. I might become the old woman who lives in a shoe, only I'd live in a book."

When I paused, he asked, "Is there more?"

"Yes."

"Let's hear it," he gruffed.

"You should also know I'm a virgin—not for any religious reasons or personal convictions. It just hasn't happened, then I moved here and seemed to have developed a thing for you I couldn't shake...and...well, that was probably more information than you signed up for."

I clamped down on my bottom lip to keep myself from saying anything else. If I hadn't ruined things yet, that stream of consciousness surely would have done it.

Then Caleb asked, "You can't shake it, huh?" and he didn't sound the least bit turned off. In fact, I was pretty certain he was teasing me.

"I can't. It's the damnedest thing," I teased back. "Try as I might, I'm hooked on you."

"Good, because I'm hooked on you too, Alice."

My heart tumbled off a cliff and flew right back up. "You are? Even after I dumped all that baggage on you?"

"More," he rumbled. "I like you telling me about yourself. I want to know it all."

"Are you sure that wasn't too much information? I'm cringing over here."

"I wish I could see you. I bet you're cute when you cringe."

That made me laugh. "I doubt it. I wish I could see you too."

He took a long beat before answering. "If I were to ask you out on a date, would you say yes?"

"I would."

He hummed. "As much as I love my boy, I wish this was the week he was with his mother. We're gonna have to wait until next week."

"That will give you a whole week to work up the nerve to ask me."

He chuckled, low and deep. "I like this side of you. You're getting comfortable with me, aren't you?"

"Am I? I don't know." Then I whispered, "I think maybe I am. You're not running for the hills after I shared all...that."

"No, nothing you said changed my feelings for you. Actually, that's not true. I'm even more curious and eager to know everything about you. I want to know about your sister, and if she's why you're scared of hospitals. I'd like to know what kind of books you want to fill your house with, and if you need more bookshelves for all of them. And yeah, I'd like to talk to you about being a virgin, and where you want to go with me."

"Oh, that last one's easy. I want to go all the way with you. Over and over."

His groan was so deep and immediate, I didn't have the chance to regret my blunt honesty. He *liked* it. And me.

I was truly beginning to believe it.

"I guess we should put a pin in that." I was kicking my feet and grinning wide. "You know, until you actually ask me out on our first date."

"Didn't I do that?"

"No, I don't think you did."

"Hmmm. I should rectify that. The problem is, I'm not sure I can wait a week to see you."

"That is a problem," I agreed, tapping my thumbnail against my teeth.

"I'm having a thought...you wouldn't happen to be planning to eat at the diner tomorrow night, would you?"

I caught on to where he was going and let out a mock gasp. "Funny you should mention it. I was thinking I might like to go out to dinner."

"That *is* pretty damn funny." I could practically hear the smile stretching across his face. "If you were to show up there—purely by chance, of course—it would be downright rude of me not to ask you to join Jesse and me."

"It would be. Dreadfully rude," I said solemnly, the corners of my mouth twitching. "It would probably be a serious breach of etiquette if we didn't sit together."

"I was thinking the same thing."

"So...hypothetically speaking...what time are you and Jesse coincidentally going to be there?"

"Oh, I'm not sure." I could picture him leaning against his headboard, getting a kick out of teasing me. "If I had to guess, I'd say around six thirty."

"It would be wild if I were to feel a sudden craving for a cheeseburger at six thirty tomorrow night."

"Funny," he said, his voice dipping low, "I'm craving one right now. Mostly though, I'm craving the company."

That was it. My toes curled into the couch cushion, my face was warm, and my chest felt like it had been stuffed full of champagne bubbles. I was giddy, ridiculous, and maybe a little in over my head.

I loved it.

"So tomorrow?"

"Yeah," he agreed. "You're not trying to rush off the phone, are you?"

"Seems like I should quit while I'm ahead."

"I disagree. I think you owe me."

My brows shot up. "I do?"

"You do. Since you decided to ditch me, I've been reading on my own. You didn't tell me book two was going to put me through the wringer."

My smile grew so wide my cheeks ached. "I'm pretty sure I warned you it would be emotional."

"Did you? I don't recall that," he shot back. "Now, you've got to let me read to you. Fair's fair."

My heart kicked. "You want to read to me?"

"I do. If I have to go through Fathaniel's fuckups, I'm bringing you along with me."

I laughed, settling deeper into the couch, and tugged a blanket over my lap. "All right then. I'm ready to get back on this journey with you and our bumbling hero."

There was the rustle of pages, a low clearing of his throat, then his voice slid through the phone like molasses. I closed my eyes and let him take me through the story, his deep rumble filling every quiet space in my living room.

Somewhere in the middle of a paragraph, I realized I was happy. Genuinely, truly happy. And hopeful. I wanted this with him every night.

When he finished the chapter, there was a pause. "Are you still with me?"

"I am," I said, tired but nowhere near ready for this to end. "I could listen to you all night."

"If you're not careful, I might take you up on that."

Some time later, after Fathaniel had fallen for another one of Tarkarian the wizard's tricks, I went to sleep with Caleb's voice still in my ears and near certainty this wouldn't be the last time.

Chapter Twenty-six

Caleb

JESSE TRAILED AFTER ME into Gray's Diner. Usually, my patience with him was close to infinite, but he'd dragged his feet getting out of the truck then moved across the parking lot at a snail's pace for no good reason. I was at the end of my rope.

"You forgot to check in with the hostess," he said from behind me.

"Don't worry about it," I gruffed over my shoulder. "I see Alice over there. Let's go say hi."

"Ms. Clark?" Suddenly, he was right beside me, craning his neck. "She's here?"

She was. We were now seven minutes late, and she was sitting by herself in a booth, a hardback book open in front of her, a glass of water sweating beside her cast.

As we approached, she looked up as if surprised, though the corner of her mouth was already lifting.

"Caleb," she said with a teasing lilt. "And Jesse. What are the odds?"

Jesse grinned. "Pretty high, I think. There aren't a lot of places to eat around here."

"You have me there," she conceded.

I stepped closer, resting a hand on the back of her booth. "Are you here alone?"

"I was," she said, sliding the bookmark I'd given her between the pages before closing the book. "But I'd much rather have company. Would you two like to have dinner with me?"

I didn't even have to look at Jesse. He'd already started toward the empty side of the booth, and I followed, lowering myself across from her. The light from the overhead fixture fell across her face, making her eyes sparkle.

She met my gaze for a second then glanced away, fingers brushing the edge of the bookmark like she couldn't help herself.

"How's the hand?"

"Still attached." She waved it in front of herself.

Sitting this close but not being able to reach across the table and drag my finger along the rose in her cheeks was a true test of endurance. It was what I deserved. If I'd made a move sooner, she might've already been in my arms.

But we were here now. This was no place for regret, not when we were moving forward, exploring what had been building between us. A time would come when I wouldn't have to think twice about pulling her into my arms or taking her hand in mine. I was confident we'd get there.

I leaned back, letting Jesse launch into a story about his day, but I didn't stop watching her. I took my time, cataloging every detail. The way her lashes fluttered when she laughed, the pink high on her cheeks, that bookmark poking out of her book. I hoped when she looked at it, she thought of me. I damn sure had been doing a lot of thinking about her.

"How much longer do you have to wear that cast?" Jesse asked.

Alice gave it a poke, scrunching her nose. "It should be two more weeks. I can't wait to get it off. The downside is I have to go back to the hospital to get it removed."

Jesse cocked his head. "You don't like hospitals?"

"I don't," she replied. "I spent a lot of time in them as a kid, and I'd do just about anything not to go back. But getting this thing off my wrist will be worth it."

"It won't hurt, will it?"

"Nope." Her eyes rolled to the side then returned to him, filled with mischief. "Unless the saw slips. But I'm sure they'll be able to reattach my hand."

My boy looked alarmed for all of two seconds before Alice's snicker gave her away.

From there, the two fell into a flowing conversation, and I sat back, listening, liking the hell out of what I heard. She asked him about school, and not just general questions. She knew some of his teachers' names and projects he was working on. And it was obvious every answer he gave mattered to her.

When he told her about the robot his team was planning to build in the fall, she leaned in like it was the most fascinating thing she'd heard all week.

"An arm attachment?" she asked, her pretty eyes wide. "What does it do?"

Jesse's hands flew into motion as he explained, sketching shapes in the air, picking up speed with every word. She shifted to summer camp, wanting to know what activities he was most excited for, if he was nervous about living in the dorms, what he thought about being away for three weeks.

"I'm certain they're going to keep you so busy, you won't have time to get homesick. But I hope you have time to write back to me. I'm warning you now, I love writing letters. There's no way I'm not going to write at least two. Maybe three."

Jesse grinned. "People still write real letters?"

"I do, and I'm pretty sure I count as a person," she quipped.

He sighed, like he was the most put-upon teenager on the planet. "I mean, if you really want to write me, I guess I can probably find the time to write back."

"That would be incredibly kind of you, Jess," she said, amusement lacing her words.

The two of them didn't really need me here, but I didn't mind. I ate my dinner, letting their conversation ride. There was nothing forced about their interaction, and it was clear Jesse liked the addition of her to our table.

By the time the plates were cleared and the check was paid, there was a warmth in my chest that had nothing to do with the coffee I was sipping.

Jesse glanced across the diner, spotting a friend from school at the counter in the front. He was out of the booth before I could say a word, tossing over his shoulder, "Be right back."

Then it was just the two of us, the space between us suddenly feeling smaller, charged in a way it hadn't been a moment ago.

I put my hand on the table, palm up, and Alice did not hesitate to slip hers in mine. When I closed my fingers around hers, her much smaller hand got lost.

"It's not easy."

"What's not?" She shifted forward on her side of the booth.

"Sitting across from you and not doing this."

"Holding my hand?" she asked.

"Yeah. Seeing the way you are with my boy, it was hard not to pick up your hand—or better yet, lean across the table and put my mouth on yours."

She bit down on her bottom lip, peering at me from beneath her fluttery lashes. "Well, now you have me."

"You're so damn pretty," I said. I couldn't not.

"Thank you." She swallowed hard. "I really like the way you're looking at me right now. How you've been looking at me this whole evening. It makes me feel like...this is real."

"It is."

Her nod was slight but decisive. "I know, Cay."

I glanced at her cast. "What day is your appointment?"

She looked down then back at me. "Oh, it's the Tuesday after next, in the morning."

"All right. I'll meet you there."

She startled, her fingers flexing in mine. "Really, it's not—it will be a short appointment. I can handle it."

"I know you can, but I want to be there. I don't want you going it alone, and you don't have to. I'm in your corner now, so let me be with you."

"You're busy on the ranch," she tried.

"I am, but I have time for you. Didn't you say it won't take long?"

She sighed and squeezed my hand. "I did say that."

"So are you going to let me be there?"

"It won't be particularly exciting," she warned.

"I'll be with you."

She sucked in a little breath. "Okay. You've convinced me."

My mouth hitched. "That wasn't too hard."

"You're pretty good at hitting the exact right argument." Her fingers wiggled. "I didn't really want to go alone."

"And you won't have to."

Jesse reappeared a minute later. If he noticed Alice slipping her hand from mine, he didn't show it.

"Ready?" he asked.

"Ready," I said, even though I could have sat there a few more hours.

We slid out of the booth and left the diner together. Alice's car was parked a few spots down from my truck, and Jesse fell in step beside her, telling her about some game he and his friend were planning for the weekend. When we reached her car, he surprised both of us by giving her a quick, awkward, teenage hug.

"It was nice having dinner with you, Alice," he said, shoving his hands in his pockets.

Her smile warmed. "I really liked it too, Jess. Maybe we can do it again sometime soon."

"Yeah. That'd be all right with me," he replied.

When he stepped back, I didn't waste the opportunity to hug her too. I pulled her into my arms, my hands splaying on the center of her back, and just like that, she melted into me the same way she had in front of her house.

I lingered for as long as I could, breathing her in, feeling the soft give of her against me, the wispy little breaths she took. The part of me that knew I should step back kept losing the argument.

Finally, I forced myself to ease my hold, staying close enough her spicy scent clung to me as we parted. Her eyes found mine, practically glowing like pieces of sea glass in the sun.

"Drive safe, Allie," I said, my voice rougher than I meant it to be.

"You too, Cay." Her smile, aimed at Jess and me, wobbled. "See you guys soon."

"You will," I promised as she climbed into her car.

I watched her taillights disappear before I turned toward my truck, finding Jesse staring at me with a smirk. I ignored that look until we were both in the truck.

"Say it," I grumbled.

He shrugged. "Nothing. Just...you have a thing for Alice, don't you?"

I shifted my gaze his way. "What makes you say that?"

"I'm not stupid or blind. I saw you holding her hand, and you basically attached yourself to her before she got in her car."

My jaw dropped. "I didn't...*attach* myself." I shook my head, trying to decide if I had. I didn't think so, but it really had been hard to let go.

Jesse snickered, and I glared at him. "Dammit, kid. Are you trying to give me a complex?"

He patted my shoulder. "If you were attempting to be smooth, you failed. But if you were trying to show her you like her, I think she got the message. I bet everyone in the diner did."

I took a second to consider if I cared who knew Alice and I were becoming...something, quickly deciding I did not. I *did* care what Jesse thought, though.

"Are you good with me taking her out?" I nudged him with my elbow. "Maybe without a chaperone?"

He twisted in his seat, facing me head-on. "I'm good with it, Dad."

"You're not going to tell me to treat her right?"

He tilted his head. "If I thought I had to tell you that, I wouldn't be so okay with you taking her out."

"You have a good point," I conceded.

He scratched behind his ear as he eyed me. "Actually, I was getting concerned about you. You know, I'm going to college in a few years and you're going to be all alone. It's about time you found a girlfriend."

"You were concerned about me?" That was news to me, and I didn't know if I particularly liked it.

"It wasn't constantly on my mind or anything, but yeah. I was a little concerned. Now I don't have to be. You have Alice, which means I get to have her more, and that's cool."

"That would be cool, but let's not get ahead of ourselves. First, I need to take her out and not screw things up."

He reached across the cab and patted my shoulder. "I know you speak to cattle and horses more than women, but I have faith in you."

"Thanks, kid. I appreciate the confidence."

"No prob." He faced forward again. "I'm all talked out. Can we go home now?"

"Sure. And since you're all talked out, you're going to go directly to your room and knock out your homework instead of getting on a call with your buddies, right?"

His groan told me exactly what his plan had been.

I shook my head as I started the engine. The boy could talk circles around me when he wanted, but he'd given me more tonight than he realized.

Jesse was good with the direction Alice and I were heading. I glanced at him, his head against the window, and promised myself I would get this right.

Then I spent the rest of the drive planning my first real date with Alice.

Chapter Twenty-seven

Alice

THE LAST WEEK CRAWLED and flew at the same time. I marked time by my interactions with Caleb. Our near-nightly calls where we talked and read together for hours. Him lingering at my desk when he picked up Jesse from the library, giving me little presents that did nothing to help me straighten my head.

He'd given me a book on gardening in Wyoming. A pair of floral gardening gloves. And I couldn't fail to mention the pressed-flower journal and packet of wildflower seeds for my yard. I was honestly impressed at how many ways he'd found to give me flowers that didn't include a bouquet.

And I was terribly, irrevocably smitten with Caleb Kelly, just like always. Only now, I was beginning to believe he returned my feelings.

I glanced at the clock and groaned. I was running late, and it was entirely my fault. I'd gotten caught up in a book and lost track of time. And I *needed* as much of it as I could get.

Tonight was important. Monumental. *Our official first date.* Caleb was on his way to pick me up, and I wasn't ready.

Mentally, I was—beyond ready. But my hair was only half curled, and he'd be here any minute.

When my hair was finished, I swapped the curling iron for my lipstick and smoothed my dress over my hips. My pulse raced in anticipation, every beat whispering, *He's coming. He's coming.*

My doorbell rang, followed by a firm knock. I froze, suddenly more nervous than I had been all day.

He knocked again, and I forced my feet to carry me to the front door. One more breath, then I swung it open.

Caleb filled the frame, broad and towering. So solid, he blocked out the street behind him. Dark jeans and a pale-blue button-down stretched across his chest and shoulders, the fabric pulling a little where it met the convex curve of his stomach. His hair brushed his collar, and his neatly trimmed beard revealed the crooked curve of his pink lips. But what nearly undid me was the way his chocolate eyes swept over me, slow and intentional, lingering like he wanted to memorize every detail.

"Hey, Allie," he crooned.

"Hello, Cay," I whispered back.

In his hands was a bundle of wildflowers wrapped in brown paper and tied with twine.

"Oh." My throat tightened, and I had to blink fast against the heat stinging my eyes. "They're beautiful."

His mouth canted, a little sheepish but full of pride. "These are an I'm-so-damn-excited-to-have-you-on-my-arm bouquet."

I touched my fingertips to my burning cheeks. "How did you know? That's my favorite kind."

He stepped forward, one foot into my house, slipped his arm around my waist, and dipped his head. I stopped breathing as his face came closer to mine.

"It's not traditional, but I'm hoping we can start this date with a kiss," he murmured to my lips.

I nodded. "I'd like that very much. As long as we end it with one too."

His lips grazed mine. "There might be some in the middle too."

Our smiles touched. "I've always thought it was a waste to only kiss goodbye."

"Agreed." He kissed me so softly, it was barely there. "What do you think about inviting me inside for a minute?"

I brought my hand up to his chest, gripped his shirt in my fist, and pulled him the rest of the way in. He kicked the door shut behind him, placed the flowers on my entry table, and took me into his arms.

I tipped my head back, he tilted his forward, and still, we were too far apart. Carefully, gently, Caleb lifted me, pressing me against my door. By instinct, my legs circled his hips, and my arms laced behind his neck.

"That's better." He ran his nose along mine. "I've been thinking about how tonight would go all week."

"You have?" Heat bloomed in my belly. "Did you think it would start this way?"

He smiled as he pressed a light kiss to my jaw. "Can't say I did, but I'm not the least bit upset about it."

"Neither am I." I touched his cheek, turning his mouth back to mine. Then I kissed him, our lips slotting perfectly together.

His mouth was certain on mine, a slow press that deepened when I parted for him. The scrape of his beard brushed my skin, sending sparks racing across my nerves. He tasted like mint and something distinctly him, and the low sound he made in his chest when I tugged him closer went straight to my core.

I kissed him harder, greedy for more. Just when I thought I might dissolve completely into him, Caleb groaned and pulled back. His forehead rested against mine, his breath coming rough and uneven.

"I could stay here and kiss you all night," he said, his voice strained with regret. "But then we wouldn't get to have our first official date, and I'll be damned if I miss that."

I let my head fall against the door and cupped his bearded cheeks. "You're right. If we don't stop now, those flowers might become a made-out-at-your-front-door bouquet."

He chuffed, lowering me to my feet. "Can't have that." He kissed my forehead. "Let's get those flowers in water then hit the road."

"That sounds perfect."

Caleb took me to dinner in Laramie, which was nice. Then he took me to a bar to listen to live music, which was even nicer. Especially our seating arrangement. We were side by side on a padded bench, facing the small stage. Far enough away we could hear each other speak, but with a perfect view of the band.

Caleb's arm was resting on the back of the bench, and his fingers trailed along my arm. Our thighs were pressed together, and when he turned his head to talk to me, his mouth grazed my ear. Being tucked in the cave of his body was so cozy, I never wanted to leave. But it also made me wonder how it would feel to sleep curled up with him, or what it would be like to have him on top of me, or behind me, or—

He brushed my hair behind my ear. "You look like you're deep in thought."

I smiled at him. If he only knew. "I'm thinking how much I like being close to you like this."

"I like it too, Allie." He grazed his knuckles along my bicep. "Feels like I'm exactly where I'm supposed to be."

"Me too," I agreed.

"You know," he brushed his nose against my hair, taking time to inhale deeply, "I was jealous as hell when I saw you out on a date. I didn't realize it, but yeah, that's what I was."

I blinked at him. "Really?"

"Mmmhmm. I wanted it to be me making you laugh."

"Those were fake laughs," I admitted. "That was the most awkward two hours of my life."

"I'm sorry you had to sit through that, but not sorry at all it didn't work out." His lips touched my temple, making me sigh. "Have you done a lot of dating? Back in college or...?"

"Not a lot by any standards, but I've been on dates." I shifted so I could look at him better. "Enough to know this one is the best I've ever been on. Though I'm not sure we can count this as our first date."

"No?" One brow raised. "Why's that?"

"I'd call dinner last week our first date."

"But I didn't bring you flowers. And my kid was there."

"I think it still counts. And if we're being precise, I'd also count when you brought me coffee on Tuesday and sat with me while I drank it. Oh, and when we both ate ice cream while we were on the phone Friday night."

He cocked his head. "Those were all dates?"

"Yes." His beard was slightly rough under my palm as I smoothed it over his jaw. "What about you, Caleb? How does this date rank for you?"

He pressed his face into my hand, his eyes closing for a moment. "I don't know. I don't remember ever going out with anyone else."

I narrowed my eyes at him. "I know that's not true."

He lifted his big shoulder. "I'm not thinking about anyone else when I'm with you. But if I was, nothing would compare, so why bother expending the energy?"

"Well—" I had to take a moment to catch my breath and think of what I could possibly say to that. "Um...I guess you shouldn't. That would be a waste of time."

His eyes crinkled in the corners. "Glad you agree, Allie-girl."

And just like that, I melted into him, as I had a habit of doing when I was in his arms. That I'd been in his arms enough to have developed a habit was pretty crazy.

He took my chin between two of his fingers, angling my face where he wanted it, and kissed me. His lips were soft but confident as they moved over mine. He tasted like the mint he'd had after dinner and...Caleb. I opened my mouth to sip from his lips and swallow his flavor, moaning as his fingers tangled in my hair, tipping my head back even more.

We kissed until my lips tingled and my toes curled inside my shoes. Until I was boneless and Caleb had almost hauled me into his lap. With no regard to the public—but blessedly dark—venue, we kissed like time meant nothing. His hands were in my hair, on my neck, down my spine. Mine were fisting his shirt, stroking the skin above his collar, tracing the curve of his ear.

I hadn't made out with a man since college, and that had been nothing like *this*. Unhurried and curious, learning each other, swallowing the sounds we elicited, petting and stroking the slips of bare skin we could reach.

We only broke apart when the audience exploded into applause at the end of the band's set. My eyes fluttered open, meeting his heavy-lidded gaze, and I laughed.

"I forgot where we were."

His swollen lips curled into a smile. "Can't say I much care where we are."

I dragged my fingers along his jaw. "We should probably go now that we've scandalized everyone here."

That earned me a low laugh. "I don't much care what anyone else thinks either, but I hear you. I don't want the night to end, but we both have to get up early."

"We do. You earlier than me. I still have time to stare at the ceiling, replaying every single second of the night before I have to go to sleep."

He dropped his forehead to mine and groaned. "You are so damn sweet."

"Should I be a little coy? Maybe keep my cards closer to my vest?"

"Absolutely not," he gruffed, like the idea made him mad. "Don't change a thing about yourself. Besides, I'm going to be replaying tonight too. All of it."

Oh, I'd have those words on repeat for a long time to come. They felt so good, they almost hurt. I'd waited a long time for this man, and he was proving he had been worth every second.

Chapter Twenty-eight

Caleb

Normally, I had all the time in the world for my boy. But I was sitting outside Alice's house, where she was making dinner for us, and he wouldn't stop talking so I could hang up and get in there.

Still, I didn't rush him. I missed him when he was with his mom, and I would never take for granted that he was thirteen and still liked talking to me, even when we were apart.

"What are you eating for dinner tonight?" he asked.

"Don't know. Alice is whipping something up for us."

"Wow. You didn't screw things up and she agreed to a second date?"

I snorted a laugh. "That's right. Maybe I'm a little more charming than you thought."

"Yeah, maybe. I mean, I've never seen it, but anything's possible."

"Thanks, kid. This is exactly the pep talk I needed right before walking into her house."

He gasped. "You're at her house and didn't say anything? Get in there. You can't be late. She might not let you in. Well...Alice is nice and would probably let you in anyway, but she could turn down another date because of your time management issues. So—"

"Jess," I interjected. "Do you think your speech is helping my timeliness or confidence?"

Laughing, he stopped. "No, I guess not. Quit talking to me and get in there."

Alice was waiting at her open door by the time I made it up her porch. Her feet were bare and stacked on top of one another. Her dress skimmed her curves, stopping midcalf. She looked casual and beautiful, even with her arms crossed and the little crease between her brows.

"Is Jesse okay?"

"Yeah, he's fine." I glanced back at my truck then at her. "How'd you know I was talking to him?"

"I was guessing. You get this look on your face when you're together, like you're simultaneously perplexed and so proud you could burst. You had that face in your truck, so I put two and two together."

I liked that she'd noticed that. And she was dead-on about how my kid made me feel.

My hand on her stomach, I pushed her out of the doorway and stepped inside, kicking the door closed behind me. She bit her bottom lip, and I slid my arm around her waist before slipping it lower, beneath her bottom, and lifting her.

When we were face to face, she grinned. I leaned in and kissed her curved lips.

"You're right. I was talking to Jesse. He was surprised you had said yes to another date with me. According to him, I hide my charm really well. So well, he's never seen it."

Laughing, she cupped my face and wrapped her legs around my waist, her heat seeping through the fabric between us. "He might not have seen it, but I have." She touched her lips to mine, lingering long enough to give me a heady dose of her sweetness. "How's Jesse doing, by the way?"

"Too smart for his own good. Mine too. Otherwise, he's fine. Ready for school to be out, but that'll be here soon enough." I put her back on her feet and followed her into her kitchen. "It smells incredible in here."

She smiled over her shoulder. "Yeah? I can't say I'm a gourmet cook, but I have a few dishes I've perfected. I figured you're a meat guy, so I made my world-renowned pot roast."

Laughing, I patted my stomach. "What gave you that impression?"

Her smile was wistful. "Caleb, I've been serving you dinner for four years."

"You got me there." I looked around her kitchen to see if there was something I could do. The timer on her oven was counting down. There was a bowl of salad on the counter and a basket covered with a cloth napkin. "I'd eat anything you make. If you don't usually eat—"

She held up her hand. "I've only perfected meals I enjoy. Otherwise, it would have been a waste."

I nodded. "You got me again. Now tell me what I can do to help."

She closed the space between us, leaning her full weight against my front. "Grab yourself a drink, then sit down and talk to me while I get our food plated."

"I think I can manage that without too much difficulty."

Alice had grossly undersold her cooking skills. She claimed to have made nothing more than basic meat and potatoes, but that was like calling the ocean a pond.

I caught her grinning as I shoved my last bite of pot roast into my mouth and cocked my head. "What's that look for?"

"Nothing." She waved me off. "It's just the way you eat. I like that you don't hide how much you're enjoying yourself."

I wipe my mouth roughly with my napkin. "Why would I? You made a hell of a meal."

"Thank you. I don't cook for other people often. Sometimes I bring leftovers to Joy, and on occasion, I can twist her arm and convince her to come over for a meal, but that's pretty much it. I like having you at my table."

I reached for her hand, taking it in mine. "I like being at your table. And if my siblings hear about the meal you made me, I guarantee they'll be angling for an invitation."

Her eyes lit. "I'd love that, but I don't think I'm quite ready to entertain the whole Kelly clan. Maybe next week, you and Jesse could come over."

I chuckled. "Absolutely. Count on Jess being a snoop, though. He can't help himself."

"I'll be sure to pack away anything incriminating."

Placing her hand on my knee, I leaned closer. "I find it hard to believe you have anything incriminating. What are you hiding?"

The pink in her cheeks deepened. "Well, nothing really..."

My brows shot up. "That blush has got me intrigued. Am I gonna have to go hunting and uncover your secrets myself?"

Her eyes gave her away, sliding in the direction of the hall leading to her bedroom.

"Caleb," she whispered, a little desperate.

I shook my head. "I'm teasing you, darlin'. You don't have to reveal your secrets to me unless you want to."

Her fingers flexed inside mine. "I was just joking, for the most part. I'm as boring as they come."

"I wholeheartedly disagree with you there."

She blew out a light breath. "Thank you. I mean, I don't have any secrets, unless you count the contents of my nightstand—and I doubt Jesse is *that* nosy."

"He might not be, but I am."

That made her laugh. "Maybe I'll show you."

I tugged her hand, pulling her from her chair. She gave a startled yelp before settling on my lap, like she'd always belonged there. My palm found the back of her head, her hair spilling through my fingers, and I met the bright green of her gaze.

"When you're comfortable enough with me to do that, I'd be honored," I murmured. "But we've got time. There's no need to rush into anything. I'm happy learning you piece by piece."

She rubbed her lips together and pulled in a shaky breath. "I love that, Caleb. I do. But if I'm being honest..." Her voice dropped, low and husky. "Slow is the last thing I want with you."

That hit me like a jolt. "Yeah?" I sounded rougher than intended. "I'll follow your lead. I'm ready for whatever you want with me, but I need you to be sure."

Her lashes lowered, her fingers finding the button of my shirt, toying with it. "Do you think I'm damaged?"

"No way in hell." My brow knit tight. "Why would I think that?"

Her eyes didn't lift. "After I was attacked, I felt stupid. Afraid. Like I'd been walking around with blinders on. But in some ways,

I'm lucky I don't really remember what happened. The drugs left a blank spot in my mind. I know I was hurt, and he would have done worse if no one had intervened. I'm luckier than so many women."

She swallowed hard. "But that night has nothing to do with what I want with you. When we're kissing, when you touch me—it's not connected to him in any way. Not even close. I'm not scared with you. I want you. I want this. More than anything, I know I'm safe with you."

"Good. You'll always be safe with me. Wherever this leads, that won't change," I promised, my throat thick with emotion I did my damnedest to tamp down. Now wasn't the time to get angry. I had Alice here, in my arms. No one was going to hurt her. I'd make certain of that.

She cupped my face with both hands and skimmed her lips along mine. "I would love to sit here in your lap and talk to you all night, but I won't be able to relax until I clean up the kitchen."

I rolled my forehead on the side of her head. "I hear you. But you cooked me one of the best meals I've ever had. There's not a chance you're cleaning up."

"We'll do it together."

I patted her hip. "You got a deal, darlin'."

Even scrubbing dishes with Alice sounded far better than anything else I could think of.

At the sink, she bumped her hip against mine, handing me a soapy plate. "If you're not careful, I'm going to get used to this."

I grinned, flicking a drop of water at her. "That's the plan, Allie-girl."

Chapter Twenty-nine

Alice

IF I WERE MORE levelheaded when it came to Caleb Kelly, I would have said three dates in one week was too many. I would have been worried we were rushing—burnout from too much, too soon. But then he'd asked me over to his place Saturday for dinner, and I hadn't hesitated to accept.

Now, we were on his deck, drinking beer and eating the chicken he'd grilled. His flannel hung loose on me, the sleeves rolled three times still swallowing my wrists, but it smelled like him. The night was cool enough I burrowed into it, grateful for the excuse to wear something of his.

Overhead, the sky stretched wide and endless, pinpricked with stars so bright they seemed almost close enough to touch. We weren't far removed from town, but it felt like we were in a different world.

I leaned my head back and sighed. "I love it out here."

"Me too," he agreed. "Don't think I could live anywhere else. Not long term."

"I don't blame you. I love cities, and I'm glad I got to live in San Francisco, but this is a lot more my speed." I crinkled my nose. "I prefer not to be so close to other people."

His mouth quirked under his beard. "I'm sorry. Should I move back some?"

I reached out and snatched his hand, cradling it between mine. "Don't even think about it. In fact, you could be closer."

He nodded toward my plate. "Are you finished?"

"I am, but—"

Before I could get the rest of my words out, he pulled me from my chair into his lap. This was quickly becoming my favorite place to sit. Caleb's thighs were long and thick. His lap was practically a throne for me. His arms wrapped around me, strong enough to make me feel safe but never trapped. I leaned into his chest, trailing my fingers along his well-worn flannel, smiling at the solid warmth of him. He was broad and powerful, almost all hard lines and muscle. But with a soft belly pressed against me—which I completely adored—it made him feel even more human, a little tenderness in the middle of all that strength.

"Oh, okay, I'll sit here," I quipped.

"Seems to me you fit just right." He picked up my casted wrist, humming as he examined it. "Are you ready to get this off?"

"Past ready." I kept forgetting it was there and bumping it against everything. It made it harder to do both my jobs—and just about everything else. And it was a constant reminder of the attack. I'd never forget it, but it would be nice not to have the evidence staring me in the face.

His eyes flicked between mine. "You're dreading it."

My heart leaped into my throat. "The hospital. I'm dreading that part."

"Can you tell me about it?" His big hand splayed over my abdomen. "About donating your kidney? What made you hate hospitals the way you do?"

I'd known this would be coming, and it was best to get it all out in the open, but I wished I could put it off a little bit longer. I couldn't deny this to Caleb, though. He'd made it abundantly clear he was interested in everything about me, and Silla's illness had shaped me into who I was.

"It's a long story. Maybe I should move back to my own seat," I said, though that was the last thing I wanted.

Caleb's hand pressed more firmly on my abdomen. "There's no reason for that. I'd rather you stay right where you are." He kissed my temple. "Tell me."

"Okay. If you really want to know." He confirmed he did, so I drew in a steadying breath, ordered my thoughts, and began. "My sister, Silla, was born with a rare genetic anemia. Without treatment, she wouldn't have survived childhood. Even then, her life expectancy was far too short. I came along when she was five, and they used my cord blood stem cells to help her. My parents never explicitly said it, but when I got older, I understood that was why they'd had me. I was born to be her donor."

Caleb hissed, his arms tightening around me, but he stayed silent, giving me all his attention.

"She had to have transfusions, endless appointments, long hospital stays. I was dragged along because I couldn't be left at home. I didn't have playdates or friends outside of school. My whole world revolved around hers."

"That's when you started reading," he filled in.

"Yes." I smiled faintly. "We didn't take vacations or go on adventures. Silla couldn't, so we didn't. And I didn't mind so much, but I needed...something of my own. I needed an escape from staring at hospital walls and feeling invisible. Books became that for me. My love for reading came out of those years, and I don't regret it."

I shook my head, only pausing to take a breath. "When I was seven, I donated bone marrow to Silla. The procedure itself wasn't terrible. I'd been asleep, and when I woke up, I was sore, but it was fine. The worst part was waking up alone. I *hated* that so much. I can still remember how scared I was, and no one was there. They were with Silla. I guess she needed them more."

I plucked Caleb's button, my head and heart thick with memories. "I don't think I ever begrudged her the attention she got. I didn't know any better. Even now, I think I understand. My parents didn't mean to overlook me, but they had only so much bandwidth, and all of it was used up on my sister."

"No excuse," Caleb muttered fiercely. "None."

"I know." I sighed. "They weren't malicious, but they did neglect me. As an adult, I can see that. Back then, it was my life. They gave their all to Silla, and there was nothing left for me. I kept waiting for the day I could leave home and finally be seen."

His eyes swept over me in a tender exam. "They took your kidney before you left home."

I nodded. "Silla's kidneys were failing. I was willing—of course, I was. But my parents thought they had to bargain, so they promised to pay for any college, anywhere I wanted to go, if I did it. I chose California. I had the surgery, gave her my kidney, and...that was it."

"Did you wake up alone that time too?" he asked, and I didn't miss how pissed he sounded.

"I did. They were with Silla." I touched my lower abdomen, where my scar was. "That was the last piece I'd had to spare. Once I left, I hardly heard from any of them. Silla had always kept her distance, so that was no surprise. I guess my parents hadn't really been a surprise either."

Caleb blinked at me like he couldn't quite process what I'd said. "You gave her parts of your own body, and she kept you at arm's length?"

My chest tightened with that old, familiar ache that always came when I thought of Silla. "I never needed her gratitude. I only wanted us to be on the same side. I loved her...but I can't say I ever truly knew her." My breath wavered. "She knew from a very young age she wouldn't have a long life. Maybe keeping her distance was the only way she knew how to cope. Maybe she hated needing me, the healthy one, when she had to be the sick one. It wasn't fair to either of us. I'll never understand all her choices, but I know this: her life was hard. And I'm glad she's not suffering anymore."

A low sound rumbled from Caleb's chest. His hand skimmed down my arm, over my thigh. His eyes locked on mine, a deep line furrowing his brow.

"Your life wasn't easy either."

I gave a weary smile. "But I'm alive. I'm here. I might be missing a few parts, but I'm still whole. I'm healthy. That's more than enough to be grateful for."

"You're too good," he muttered, almost angrily. "Too forgiving."

"I haven't said I forgive them, Caleb." I flattened my palm on his chest, right over his thumping heart. "I understand my parents, but they made me feel like I was a pane of glass. When I left, they'd let me go without a fight. But what good does being angry with them do?

They're not here. Even if they were, we couldn't repair something that had never been right to begin with. All I can do is let it go and try to make myself be seen."

He took my face in his hands. "I was another person who didn't see you, and I'll have to live with that. But I promise you, Alice, that'll never happen again. You're in my line of sight, you're important to me, and I will always see you."

My eyes fluttered closed as I leaned into his touch, his palms warm against my skin. "You did make me feel invisible once. But I let it happen because I expected it. I don't anymore."

"Good," he rasped. His thumb brushed across my mouth, slow and tender. "Because I couldn't look away from you now if I tried."

My mouth curved into a smile, and he traced the shape of it. "That's a relief. We both know I haven't been able to look away from *you* since I set my eyes on you."

That earned me a light scoff, and the furrow in his brow deepened. "I'm still trying to understand that. I'm just a scruffy rancher, and you're...*Alice.*"

I touched his trimmed beard. "Not so scruffy anymore."

"I'm trying to impress my girl."

My girl...

Sigh.

"You don't have to try." I bit my bottom lip and wiggled closer, my arms looping around his neck. "It happened my first night working at Joy's. You were there with Hannah, and I was a bumbling mess. Hannah gave me her order quick as lightning, and I was so nervous, it went in one ear and out the other. You smiled at me the way you do—"

"The way I do?"

I nodded. "Yes. You have an incredible smile. It takes over your whole face. Your eyes get crinkly in the corners, your cheeks get a little rosy, and your mouth turns into this perfect *U*. It's a really good smile."

A rumble vibrated his chest. "That smile must be reserved for you. No one else has ever told me that."

If I hadn't fallen for him ages ago, I would have hit the ground right then and there. Jesse might not have seen his dad's charm, but it was alive and well and aimed directly at me.

"I wasn't finished with my story," I protested.

He gifted me my own personal smile. "By all means, darlin'. I want to hear the rest."

"It's not especially exciting, but here goes. You smiled at me and repeated her order nice and slow. Didn't make a big deal of it, you just did it. Then later, I dropped your drink on the ground, and you laughed it off and said you didn't want another beer anyway."

"I'm sorry, I don't remember that. Now that I've got you in my arms, I wish like hell I did."

"Now that I'm in your arms, it doesn't really matter. I'm here."

"You are." He rolled his forehead along mine. "Are you going to be able to go inside and relax with me if we leave the dishes until later?"

I huffed. "Not a chance."

Chapter Thirty

Alice

ONCE THE KITCHEN WAS cleaned up and I could fully relax, Caleb and I settled on his couch to watch a movie. If asked, I wouldn't have been able to tell anyone what the movie was about, though. Not with Caleb's arms wrapped around me, and his mouth constantly seeking mine. Every time I thought he might settle in and pay attention to the screen, his lips brushed over mine again.

Slowly, we sank into the cushions, me half on his chest. His broad frame was an addictive mix of steel and comfort beneath me, and I melted further with every kiss. His hand traced lazy paths along my back, up to my shoulder blades, then down to my waist, as if he was drawing his own map of me. Each pass sent a shiver through me.

He sighed into my hair, his breath warm against my crown. Fingers curved around my hip, then spread wide, pulling me up his torso to bring our faces level. He slipped lower, gathering the hem of the flannel I'd stolen from him, making my pulse jump. With his eyes locked on mine, he eased it upward until his knuckles brushed bare skin.

Then he stilled, his forehead tipped to mine, his breathing uneven. "Is this all right?" he murmured, gruff and gentle at once.

"It is." I pushed up on his chest, despite his grumbling protest at the sudden space between us, and began unbuttoning the front of my flannel. "I want you to touch me. You don't have to treat me like I'm glass."

"I'd never do that." He reached for my shirt, undoing the last button for me and slipping it down my shoulders. One at a time, he freed me from the sleeves and tossed the shirt away. Still too covered in my long-sleeved T-shirt, I tugged it over my head, leaving me in my bra.

Caleb's brow dropped, and a growl vibrated his throat. "Allie..."

My lips curved with satisfaction. It was a good bra. White and lacy, pushing my small breasts up like an offering. "Caleb...touch me, honey."

He moved slowly, giving me every chance to change my mind. With a low sound in his chest, he shifted, rolling us so I was flat on my back, and braced himself on one elbow beside me. His free hand skimmed over the curve of my waist, calloused fingertips stroking my belly, a frown of concentration tugging at the corners of his mouth.

I carved my fingers through his hair, tugging gently until he bent for a kiss. The scrape of his jaw against my cheek made my toes curl. I hooked my feet along his long legs, restless for more of him pressed against me.

Caleb was in no hurry. After kissing me until I was breathless, he left my mouth to trail lower, brushing slow, open kisses over my collarbone and the slope of my shoulder. I arched into him as his lips grazed the swell of my chest, heat pooling low in my core.

His hand came up and covered my ribs before sliding to my breast. With excruciating patience, he eased down one cup of my bra then the other, watching me the whole time, making sure I was with him. My breath caught. When I nodded, his thumb swept across my bare skin.

"You're so damn beautiful," he murmured. "I could look at you all night and not get enough."

I tugged on his hair again, whispering against his temple, "Look at me, but don't stop touching me."

He dragged his thumb over my pebbled nipple then dipped to follow the same path with his mouth, wetting the sensitive flesh. I gasped and arched, my body asking for more.

"Like that?" he asked roughly.

"I really do."

"See if you like this too."

Lips closing around my nipple, he sucked. I clung to his silky hair and moaned, so distracted by what he was doing to my breasts, I didn't notice him opening my jeans until his hand slipped inside. His thick fingers stroked along my lower belly then slid down, through my tuft of hair, until he found my cleft.

To my disappointment, he lifted his head from my chest to peer down at me. "There's a lot more I'd like to do with you, but I need more room to do it. What do you think about moving to my bed?"

My heart climbed up my throat, my answer barely squeezing out past it. "I think that's a really good idea." I was nervous, but I meant every word. Not because this was unexplored territory. This was *Caleb*. Everything with him felt important.

Caleb stole my nerves by kissing me so deeply I lost my thoughts as well as my breath. Once I was limp and clinging to him, he climbed to his feet, lifted me into his arms, and carried me down the hall into his room, setting me on his king-size bed. Standing over me, he dragged his eyes along my body like we had all the time in the world—like looking at me this way was as mandatory as touching me.

I reached for him, needing his hands on me again. "Cay, come here."

His eyes slid up to mine. "Can I take your jeans off?"

Biting down on my bottom lip to stop it from quivering, I nodded. "You can."

He peeled my jeans down my legs, his knuckles grazing my calves, my ankles, my inner thighs, until the denim was gone, leaving me in nothing but lace and goose bumps. His gaze swept over me again. There was hunger there, but also something so tender, I felt it deep in my chest.

Maybe this was just as important to him.

He lay beside me, his palm tracing the line of my panties, following the delicate waistband across my hip, down the dip of my stomach, and back again, teasing but never rushing.

"You're so sexy. I can't get enough of you," he whispered. "Can I take these off too?"

"Please." I lifted my hips to make it easier.

He slipped off the satin and lace in one slow, smooth motion. Heat flared in my cheeks, but the look in his eyes rid me of any thoughts to hide. Propping himself on one elbow, his other hand splayed on my thigh, he bent low until his lips brushed the inside of my knee.

"Allie," he murmured, his voice husky with restraint, "I need to taste you. Can I put my mouth on you?"

Oh god did I want that. But I couldn't have lain there for another second without feeling him too. He was still wearing all his clothes, and my fingers twitched to touch him.

I tugged on his shirt. "Take this off first. I want your skin on mine."

He cocked his head. "Yeah?"

"Yes." I gave his shirt another tug, lifting it upward. "Take this off, Cay."

His mouth hitched at my demand. "Sexy and bossy. You're showing me all sides of yourself tonight. I like it."

Reaching back, he yanked his Henley over his head, and I nearly swallowed my tongue at the sight of him shirtless. The breadth of his chest, smattered with fine hair, led to his thick midsection and disappeared in the waistband of his jeans. Leaning forward, I nuzzled the center of his chest, the light hair tickling my lips. He held the back of my head as I slid my lips over his small, dark nipples and dragged my teeth along the bottom of his pec.

Raising my eyes to meet his, I undid the top button of his jeans and dropped my hand to graze over the thick bulge behind his zipper.

"More," I rasped. "I want to see all of you."

He caught my wrist, holding it firmly. "You sure?"

"I've never been more sure. I want to see you and put my mouth on you."

His jaw flexed, warring with himself. With a sigh of defeat and a low curse, he unzipped his jeans and shoved them down, kicking them off along with his briefs. My breath caught at the sight of all of him stretched out before me. He was a big man, and his cock was in proportion to the rest of him. Thick and heavy, it strained against the air between us.

Caleb stilled, letting me look, letting me touch. His eyes stayed locked on mine as I wrapped my fingers around him, tentative at first, then bolder as I grew used to his heat and weight. His chest rose and fell unevenly, a tremor running through him as I stroked his length, testing, exploring.

"Allie," he ground out. "You're going to undo me before I can give you what I need to."

I licked my lips, emboldened at the way his breath hitched under my touch. "Maybe that's what I want."

He groaned, cupping my face for a rough kiss that left me dazed. Then he pulled back, shaking his head sharply. "No, darlin'. Not yet. I need you on me."

Before I could ask what he meant, he rolled, lifting me with that same surprising ease, and positioned me so I was straddling his chest. Taking me by the hips, he guided me higher until I was hovering over his face.

"Hold on to the headboard for me," he ordered in a voice smooth as velvet. "I'm going to make you feel so good. But you need to tell me if there's something you don't like."

"I will," I promised, already knowing there wasn't anything this man could do to me I wouldn't like.

I curled my fingers around the thick wood of his headboard, clutching so tightly my knuckles went white. He took me by the thighs, wrapping his big hands around them, and held me right where he wanted me. The first hot stroke of his tongue shattered every single nerve I had left. My head tipped back, a cry breaking free as pleasure arced through me.

"Caleb—" This was nothing like I'd ever imagined, and I'd thought about this, with him, a lot. It was better, miles and miles above all my fantasies.

He groaned into me and dragged his tongue deeper, tasting me like I was dripping the sweetest nectar. My thighs trembled against his shoulders, my fingers digging into the headboard for dear life, while his mouth worked me open with slow, devastating skill.

My pleasure was a burning pyre, built so tall, it became an out-of-control inferno before I knew it. I couldn't stop the high, keening sounds spilling out of me. My thighs tightened around his head, my hips rocking helplessly against his mouth. Caleb groaned, the vibration shooting through me, and spread me wider with his strong hands.

"Cay—I can't—" My warning broke into a cry as heat detonated low in my belly, racing outward in wave after wave, until I was completely lost to it. I scrambled to hold on to the headboard so I didn't fall into a boneless, quivering heap.

It wasn't enough for Caleb. He didn't stop. If anything, he grew hungrier, coaxing every last tremor from me, licking me through the aftershocks until I was gasping and babbling nonsense. My legs shook against his shoulders, my body oversensitive, and he held me steady, groaning like I was the best thing he'd ever tasted.

Another crest rose, impossible but real, building on top of the first. I was shuddering all over again, sobbing his name as a second climax tore through me, hotter and longer than the last.

As it ebbed, I slumped forward, my forehead pressed to the headboard, my breath coming in ragged pulls. Caleb eased me down, kissing the inside of my thigh with tenderness that didn't match the way he'd wrecked me to my core.

He looked up at me, his mouth wet, his eyes molten. "Allie-girl," he rasped, "I could keep you right here all night."

"But I want to do that to you." I scooted back as much as he would allow and tapped his swollen lips with my fingertips. "Let me taste you."

"If you want…"

"Oh, I do." My legs wiggled with impatience, making him huff a wrecked laugh.

He gave in, letting me slide next to him on the bed. We lay in opposite directions, his body stretched long, his cock straining thick and weeping on his stomach. I trailed my fingers over him, watching goose bumps sprout along his flesh. When I made it to his cock, I reached beneath it to take his heavy balls in my hand, giving them an experimental squeeze.

"Christ," he groaned, his hips jerking. "What are you doing?"

"Learning your body." I traced the seam all the way to the underside, wishing I had all the time in the world to find out what my touch did to every inch of his skin.

Maybe another night. I was too impatient to feel him on my tongue.

I bent and licked, tentative at first. When his chest rattled like he was close to death, I became bolder. His taste drove me harder. Before I knew it, I had him between my lips, sliding deeper, sucking with more desperation than skill.

Caleb's hand caught my thigh, lifting it high and open, then his mouth was on me again. I gasped around him, nearly choking. The shock of his tongue against my swollen flesh made me moan instead, the vibration pulling a curse out of him.

It was wild, clumsy, neither of us utilizing any finesse. My jaw ached, my head spun, but the more I sucked him, the wetter and hotter I became. Pleasure and dizziness tangled until I couldn't tell what was making me tremble more: his tongue or the stretch of my lips around him.

"Allie—fuck—you need to pull off."

I shook my head and sucked harder. There was no way I wasn't getting the full experience.

His hips arched, and he moaned helplessly, giving in to me. A few more passes was all it took for him to spill into my mouth. So much, some seeped past my lips, and I liked it. Maybe because it was him, I didn't know, but I wanted more of it.

When I'd sucked him dry, he gave my hair a tug, and I lifted my head, wiping my lips with the back of my hand, giddy and breathless. "Oh my god, Caleb."

He stared at me like he didn't know whether to apologize or worship me. "You're...you're giggling?"

"Yes." I pressed my forehead against his chest, my whole body humming with joy and pleasure and satisfaction. "I'm so happy right now, I can't even stop."

He snagged me under the arms and pulled me onto him, taking my laughing face in his hands. "You are something else." He shook his head, smiling at me. "I'm happy too. Don't have the energy to laugh, but I feel the same way."

I brushed my lips over his then tucked myself against him, listening to the steady beat of his heart. I'd been attached to him before, but right now, if I could have crawled beneath his skin, I might have. I wanted to be close to him.

"Are you feeling okay?" he asked, trailing his fingers down my back.

"Better than okay." I toyed with the hair on his chest, loving how it felt against my cheek. "I know that blow job wasn't the most expert, but I think you enjoyed it."

His chuckle shook me. "Understatement of the year. I don't need expert. Your mouth is all it takes."

"We're lucky, then, since I have one of those."

He reached down, pushing my chin up with his thumb, and touched his lips to mine. "A gorgeous mouth."

"I don't want to leave tonight," I whispered. "Can I stay?"

Caleb's arms tightened around me instantly, and his voice rumbled low in my ear. "If you tried to walk out that door, I'd hunt you down and bring you right back here."

A startled laugh escaped me, muffled against his chest. "Why does that sound kind of fun?"

"Don't get any ideas. You're not going anywhere." His mouth pressed to the top of my head, leaving kiss after kiss. "I want you here—with me."

I tilted up to look at him. His messy hair. Sleepy eyes. The sweet little smile that sent another burst of giddiness through me. I grinned right back, unable to help myself.

We didn't say anything else. We didn't need to. I was pretty sure we both knew we'd found something special that was all ours. We just curled tighter into each other, trading lazy kisses and dopey smiles until sleep pulled us under.

Chapter Thirty-one

Caleb

I WOKE WITH ALICE draped over me like a blanket. I never slept naked, but I couldn't say I regretted being able to feel all her smooth skin on mine. Her cheek was pressed against my chest, her hand balled in a fist beside my neck. Every few breaths, she made these humming noises—sleepy, content sounds that went straight to my ribs, cracking them wide open.

I should've been thinking about chores, Jesse, the day ahead. Instead, I lay there, greedy as hell, soaking up every second of her weight on me, every rise and fall of her body against mine. We'd never have another first morning together, and I wanted to memorize every detail of this one.

The trouble was, I was missing her, even though she was on top of me. It loathed me to disturb her, but I was tempted to wake her up anyway. Her smile when she was wide awake knocked me to my knees. I had a feeling her sleepy smile would flatten me.

"Mmm." She shifted on my chest, her fist opening and splaying on my shoulder. "Are you looking at me?"

"Yeah. Can't deny it." I stuck my nose in her hair and took a deep whiff. She'd be on my sheets and pillow when she was gone, but it wouldn't be the same as having her in my arms. "Wanna give me your eyes?"

Slowly, she pushed up on my chest, and her eyes fluttered open. It took a long beat for her to focus on me, but when she did, I was rewarded with a smile that held sunshine. "It wasn't a dream."

I took a piece of her hair between my fingers and tucked it behind her ear. "As real as it gets, darlin'."

"Oh good." She slid all the way up, bringing us nose to nose. "How do you feel about morning kisses?"

I threaded my fingers through her hair, holding the back. "With you? I feel good about any kind of kiss I can get."

"All right. I've heard some people are afraid of morning breath—"

My fingers tightened in her hair. "Allie," I laughed, "that means I want your mouth on mine."

"Oh." Her brows popped. "Okay then."

She dove in, first with a brush of her lips, then more, her tongue teasing the seam of my mouth, making me groan. Whatever air I'd been holding in my lungs slipped right out of me.

The kiss went from sweet to hungry in no time, her tongue sliding against mine, her hands clutching at my shoulders like she couldn't get close enough. I rolled, taking her with me, until she was flat on her back and I was braced over her, careful not to crush her. Gasping, she reached for me, her legs hiked around my hips, arms winding tight around my neck.

I lost myself in her. In the taste of her lips. In the little sounds she made when my mouth trailed down her jaw, her throat, her collarbone. She arched into me, offering more, and I couldn't help but take—kissing, nipping, memorizing the feel of her bare skin under my palms.

Her hand slid lower, her fingers brushing over my hip then slipping between us to wrap around my erection. My whole body went hot and tight with a need so powerful, it was a punch to the chest, but I caught her wrist and lifted my head so I could see her.

"I didn't mean to start this."

Her legs tightened around me. "Why not?"

I exhaled, my control teetering. She felt so good beneath me, and the way she stared up at me, her green eyes almost glowing with desire, made it nearly impossible to stop.

"I don't know. I want to make sure I do right by you." My brow furrowed. "Tell me how far you want to take this."

"I told you, Cay." Her tongue darted out to wet her bottom lip. "I want you. If you're worried about me being a virgin, don't. I have toys...they're not as big as you, but I don't have a sacred hymen you need to protect or anything."

I slammed my eyes closed, unable to stop a laugh from shaking my shoulders. "Sacred hymen? You're too damn much. Christ..."

She wiggled free from my loose hold and slowly pumped my length. "I know I want you. But...are you ready?"

My eyes opened. "My virginity ship sailed almost two decades ago."

She grinned. "I figured, since you have a kid and all. I mean, are you ready to take this step with me?"

She might as well have reached into my chest and cradled my heart in her palm. She wasn't just asking if I wanted sex—she was asking if I was ready for *her*. For *us*.

My chest was so tight, it was damn near bursting. That she cared about me so much she'd stopped to check on *me* made me want to hold her tighter—made me realize, all over again, how different she was.

I'd been in this position before, but it had never felt this important. Nothing between us was routine or casual. This was *Alice*, and I had to get this right—for us both.

But heaven help me, I wanted her so bad, my whole body ached.

I kissed her as my answer, pouring everything I couldn't say into her mouth. My hand slid down, cupping between her thighs, finding her already slick with wanting. Her breath caught, her hips rising to meet me as I stroked her swollen little bud.

She mumbled my name, holding on to me with every fiber of her strength. I teased her entrance, and she spread her legs wider, trembling as I slipped a thick finger inside her, crying from pleasure, not pain, when I added another.

She began to shake, her insides clenching around me, and I pulled back to watch her fall. Rosy lips parted, she arched her neck, sighing. It was a beautiful sight, and I couldn't remember ever being so utterly turned on in my life.

When her shudders eased and her eyes landed on mine, she reached for me, dragging me back to her lips, kissing me with a fierceness that stole my breath. Her feet slid up and down the outside of my hips, antsy, still needy, even moments after I'd made her come.

"Caleb, I want you," she said against my mouth. "Are you ready?"

I had to laugh. I was harder than steel and dripping with need for her. "Yeah, I'm ready. Long as you're sure."

She lifted her legs higher, rubbing her wet heat against me. "If I have to keep trying to convince you, I might change *my* mind. Actually, let's just be friends."

Oh, she had jokes. Her little teasing grin as she continued to grind herself against me was almost too much.

But she'd made me laugh. My head fell forward as my shoulder shook. "We can be friends, all right—but that's not all we're going to be." I pushed up on my knees and slid my palms along the backs of her thighs, holding them open.

She licked her lips, staring up at me with wide, bright eyes. "I'm on birth control. If you want..."

"I want," I grunted, eyeing her glistening flesh. She thought she was ready to take me, and maybe she was, but the fact remained, she was a hell of a lot smaller than me, and I had to get this right. Rushing wasn't the way. "You need to let me take my time. Can you be patient? If I hurt you, I'll never forgive myself."

"I'm good at being patient."

"You are." Bending forward, I moved my hands to hold on to her hips, bringing her to me. Then I took myself in hand and angled the head of my cock toward her entrance. "Keep breathing, darlin'. If it's uncomfortable, don't hide it. We're gonna go slow."

Even if it killed me.

She wrapped her fingers around my forearm, her gaze unwavering. "Come inside, Cay."

I pressed forward, barely breaching her, and she gasped, her nails digging into my arm. I froze instantly.

"Allie?" My voice was rough from the strain of not sinking all the way inside her. Because damn, did she feel amazing. "Talk to me. Too much?"

Her chest rose and fell fast, then she gave me that brave little grin that always got me. "You're a lot. But not too much. Don't you dare stop. I'll be so mad if you do."

"Can't have you getting mad at me." I pushed forward, watching her face as I did. "I need you to take some deep breaths for me."

Nodding, she did as I told her. "You're really big."

I huffed a laugh, kissing the corner of her mouth. "You're not surprised, are you?"

"Bigger than my vibrator," she mumbled, rubbing her face against my arm. "I want more."

Slow, steady, I fed myself into her, stopping when her breathing stuttered or her muscles fluttered too tight, giving her time to stretch around me. Every second was torture, but seeing her take me, feeling her body welcome me in, was almost better than any release I'd ever known.

"I need you to open up for me." I nudged deeper. She was still so tight, I was afraid I'd hurt her unless she relaxed.

Tipping her head back, eyes shining up at me, she let out a long breath. "More, Cay."

Her body gave way, inch by inch, as I reminded her to breathe and kissed her—not to distract her, but because kissing her was better than breathing. "You're doing such a good job, darlin','" I panted against her lips. "Taking me like you are. We're almost there."

She nodded, squeezing her legs around me, tugging me closer. "Keep going."

Wet heat eased the rest of the way inside her, until finally, *finally,* I was home. My hips nudged into hers, deep as I could get, and it was all I could do not to pull out and slide right back in again.

"There we go," I gritted out. "That's my girl."

She whimpered, her head falling back, and I kissed her throat, murmuring what a good job she'd done and how beautiful she was against her skin.

"Caleb," she whispered, her voice trembling but sure. "You feel...god, you feel perfect."

I braced my forehead against hers, swallowing hard. "You're killing me. You really are." After a few seconds, I lifted my head, searching her face. "Are you okay?"

"Better than okay. But if you keep holding still like this, I *am* going to change my mind about being friends."

A laugh burst out of me, ragged and desperate, and I kissed her again. Hard this time, giving in to the pull of her body. I moved inside her, each stroke dragging fire through my veins. Her hands and mouth trailed over me, kissing and sucking every inch of flesh she could reach as she moved with me. Every shift of her hips drew me deeper. Every sound she made burrowed under my skin.

It'd been a long time for me, but that had nothing to do with why it was so hard to keep hold of my control. It was all Alice. Her cinnamon scent, how enthusiastic she was, the sounds she made, the way she did nothing to hide how much she was enjoying herself. And Christ, was she gorgeous. Her little breasts bouncing under me. Chestnut hair spread on my pillow. Shining, glazed eyes latching onto mine. Swollen cherry lips seeking me out again and again. Smooth legs squeezing my hips, urging me deeper.

"Alice," I ground out, jaw tight. "If I don't slow down, I'm not gonna last."

She took my face in her hands, giving me a fierce, adorable, sexy frown. "Don't hold back. Please, Caleb. I want to *feel* you when I'm not with you. I'm begging you to give me that."

She lassoed my control right out of my hands, her words being all it had taken. Pulling out, I pushed back in harder, my hips finding a rhythm I couldn't deny. She cried out, wrapping her legs higher around me, taking everything I gave.

"Yes," she gasped, the word breaking on a moan. "Just like that. Don't stop."

Her hand slipped between us, fingers finding her clit. The sight alone—her working herself while I drove into her—nearly ended me. She was wild and beautiful beneath me, her body straining toward mine, her lips parted in desperate need.

"Come with me," I panted, thrusting harder, deeper, until we were both shaking with the effort to hold on. "That's it, darlin'. Let go for me."

She cried out as her body tightened around me. The moment she came apart, I lost it too, burying myself deep as a bone-rattling release tore through me. We shook together, tangled and gasping, clinging to each other as the waves ebbed.

I rolled to my back, taking her with me. She was limp on my chest, sprawled in a boneless heap. We lay that way for a long time, coming back to ourselves.

When I managed to open my eyes, she'd propped herself on my chest and was staring right back. Her cheeks were flushed, hair a wild halo around her head, lips swollen from having the daylights kissed out of them.

Gorgeous.

Then, out of nowhere, she started giggling.

I blinked in surprise, then barked out a laugh of my own and wrapped her right in my arms. I couldn't quite figure out why we were laughing, only that I was enjoying myself.

Eventually, our laughter petered out, leaving us grinning at each other like a pair of fools.

"I liked that," she whispered, as sweet and sincere as could be.

Boom went my heart.

"Me too. Liking it would be an understatement."

Her eyes pinched. "Well, I thought I'd undersell it a little so you wouldn't know how desperately into you I am."

Boom went the rest of me. I hit the ground all over again.

"I'm not hiding anything." I took her chin between my fingers. "I'm all the way gone for you."

She let loose one of her spring-breeze laughs. "*Finally*."

Boom.

Boom.

I hit the ground so hard, I'm never getting up again.

Chapter Thirty-two

Caleb

AFTER I DROPPED JESSE off with his mom, I drove to Alice's house. My stomach did an unfamiliar but not unwelcome free fall when I spotted her waiting for me on her porch steps, looking pretty as a picture. From the look of her cutoffs and discarded gloves, she'd been attempting to garden again.

Alice could do a lot of things, but keeping plants alive wasn't one of them. It was almost a relief to find out she wasn't completely perfect. I would've thought I'd dreamed her up otherwise.

"Hey, darlin'," I called as I made my way up her walk.

"Hi." She put her hand on the box beside her. "I got a delivery."

That was when I noticed something wasn't right. Her words were flat. Her eyes were a little too big. What the hell was in that box?

I crouched in front of her, cupping her knees. "What'd you get?"

She sucked in a short breath. "It's from Silla...from her apartment."

"Yeah?"

"Yes. I paid a company to pack everything up and donate what they could. They sent me the things Silla had set aside for me." Her eyes slid to the box like it was haunted. "I don't know what's in there."

"You gonna open it?"

Rubbing her lips together, she returned her gaze to me. "I've been thinking about it but decided to wait for you."

"That was a good idea. No reason for you to do it alone." I squeezed her knees then took her hands in mine. "Give me a kiss, then we'll take it inside and see what's in there."

A small smile curved her lips as she leaned forward and gave me my kiss. Firm and lingering. Not long enough for me, but we'd get to that after facing down what we needed to.

I pulled her to her feet and picked up the box, which was lighter than I'd expected. Guess Alice's sister hadn't had much in the way of personal items. Being sick all her too-short life, maybe Silla hadn't had the chance to collect a lot.

I took the box to her living room and placed it on the coffee table. Alice wrung her hands as I unfolded my pocketknife and poised it over the tape.

"Ready for me to open it?"

Her forehead crinkled, but she nodded. "I don't know. Let's get it over with anyway."

I sliced through the tape and spread the cardboard flaps. Tucking my knife away, I stood behind Alice, my hands on her waist. She let her back rest against my front for a drawn-out moment then took a deep breath.

"Okay. Here goes," she whispered, reaching into the box.

The first thing she pulled out was a well-worn gray hoodie with "UCLA" printed on the front. Alice clutched it to her chest then pressed her nose into the fabric.

"This was her favorite sweatshirt. Silla desperately wanted to go to college there." She pulled in another deep breath. "That wasn't going to happen, so she told me I had to apply there. I did, for her, and when I was accepted, I lied and said I wasn't."

"To protect her?"

She nodded. "I didn't want to go there, and I knew it would gut her that I had the opportunity to go to her dream school and turned it down. It was better she didn't know."

"You were a good sister."

"I don't know about that."

The next few items were shirts and a hat from Alice's alma mater, Savage University. A San Francisco snow globe Alice had sent Silla when she'd moved there for grad school. The eye mask and slippers Alice had given her for one of her birthdays. Copies of the academic publications featuring research papers Alice had written in college. A binder filled with short stories Alice had written for Silla when she was a child. A Playbill from a musical the whole family attended during one of Silla's good spells. The programs from their parents' funerals. Alice's high school diploma. A scrapbook of movie tickets, most Alice and Silla had seen together.

By the time she got to the bottom of the box, she was sitting on the ground, surrounded by the things her sister had deemed important enough to save. Pieces of their life together—and Alice's after she'd moved on.

Alice shook her head as she reached for the final item—a photo album. "I don't understand her," she rasped. "How did she...why would she care about any of this?"

I sat behind her on the couch, peering at the album over her shoulder as she flipped through it. She dragged her fingers along each page, over the younger version of herself and the girl who looked so much like her. Even though their resemblance was uncanny, it was clear who the healthy one was and who was sick.

As Alice turned the pages, the girls got older, and the space between them widened. Silla became more haunted with shadows as she leaned away from her younger sister. And Alice's smiles became smaller, her gaze distant, until the final picture, where she wasn't looking at the camera at all.

Alice closed the album, her shoulders slumping as she released a long exhale. "That's it."

I leaned forward and kissed her crown, letting her know I was there but allowing her the space to work through it.

She drummed her fingertips on the album. "I hoped maybe she'd written me a letter. I don't know why. Just...why would she keep all these things and only let me know after she was gone? Why couldn't she have shown she cared when she was here—"

A sob broke free like an escaped prisoner. Once the wall had been breached, more followed, each more frantic and desperate than the next.

"I don't get it," she cried. "I don't understand her."

This woman was tearing my heart to shreds. Unable to take it or let her go through this alone a second longer, I lifted her into my arms. She came easily, pressing her face against my chest. Holding her close, I rocked her as she let her feelings flow. Her sadness and grief fell like rain, and her body shook like panes of glass in a storm.

I'd been waiting for this. She'd been too calm telling me about her sister. Too removed, like she hadn't been speaking about her own life. That wasn't Alice. She felt things. She was sensitive with a tender heart. I'd known she had to be hurting, but she'd been hiding it, maybe even from herself.

There was only so long a person could hide from their own feelings; Alice's had finally caught up to her. As much as it killed me to see her this way, I was glad she was facing it with me. I'd be here to hold her up and help her heal in any way she needed, even if that meant holding her while she cried.

"Maybe this was her letter," I said. "This box was her showing you what you meant to her."

A heart-wrenching keening sound came from her, and she fisted my shirt in her hand. "It's too late. Why couldn't she have shown me years ago? It's too late now."

"I know, darlin'. I know," I crooned, stroking her back, her hair, anywhere I could to soothe her. "Something kept her away. I wish I could explain it, but I can't. All I know is, I see a big sister who was proud of her little sister, and she wanted you to know it. That's what I see in that box."

"She should have told me. Why couldn't she have said it?" She squirmed, like she was trying to get closer, like she wanted to crawl under my skin. "This isn't fair—sending me this box when I can't scream at her for ignoring me all these years. I want her here so I can tell her how messed up this is. Why isn't she here? She needs to be here so I can tell her—"

Another racking sob stole the rest of her words. She cried and cried, years' worth of tears, anger, and sadness rising to the surface and bubbling over. I held her through it, letting her tear at my shirt, pressing her wet cheek to my throat. And I looked at the pile of mementos Alice's sister had saved. Wondering about the woman who'd sent them, if she'd had any idea how badly Alice had needed a connection with her. Or had she been too caught up in her own turmoil to notice?

We'd never know what she was thinking, but it was clear to me how she felt. She might've been jealous of Alice's life, but she was also proud. Watching from afar, seeing her sister's accomplishments, keeping track. And one of her last acts was to make sure Alice knew Silla hadn't been able to live out her own dreams but watched while Alice had gone after hers.

It was terribly, incomprehensibly sad. I didn't know the right words to say or how to make any of it better.

All I could do was be here.

After a while, Alice's tears stopped flowing, and she got so quiet, I thought she might've fallen asleep. Then she lifted her head and blinked at me.

"I got your shirt wet."

Despite everything, I laughed. "I'm honored to be the one to soak up your tears." I swiped her cheek with my thumb. "Though I'm hoping you don't cry a lot of them with me. If you do, I'll make sure they're happy ones."

That earned me a groan as her forehead fell to my chin. "Dang it, Caleb, stop being so...so...lovely. I'm already far too attached to you."

"Is that so?" I gave her hair a gentle tug, pulling her face back so I could look at her. "I disagree with that. You're the right amount attached, but I'm thinking you could be a little more."

Her eyes darted between mine. "Keep this up, and it's going to happen." She brought her hands up to my jaw, sliding them along my beard. "Thank you. I'm really glad I didn't have to go through that box alone. I don't know if I feel better or worse, but I'm glad you were here with me."

"You get it, right? That's what I'm here for. You have something heavy, I want you to share it with me."

"Okay. It might take me some time to get used to that, but okay," she said softly. "The same goes for you, you know."

I dragged my palm along her back, splaying wide at her waist. "Are you okay, darlin'?"

"Yes, I think I am." She rolled her lips over her teeth. "I'm sad, and kind of angry, but I'm okay. I have to accept I'll never understand what she was thinking."

"You won't. But now you know you were always on her mind."

"Right." Fresh tears welled in her eyes, and she blinked them back. "I'm pissed she didn't tell me that...but what can I do about it?"

"Nothing except grieve what could have been and move on from it." I touched my lips to hers. "You don't have your sister anymore, but you have a whole lot, Allie. You're not alone, and you won't ever be."

She groaned again and whispered, "Attached," making me chuckle. What was with this woman—breaking my heart in two then making me laugh out of nowhere?

If anyone was attached, it was me. I was completely gone for her.

So I told her, because she deserved to know. "I like the hell out of you, Alice Clark."

She traced the bottom of my lip with her thumb and smiled. "I think you know I feel the same, Caleb Kelly." She tugged at my shirt. "This is all wet. Why don't you take it off and come to my room?"

"You have another shirt for me?" I was trying to remember if I'd left one here. There was no way I'd fit more than an arm in one of Alice's.

She shook her head. "I don't. No shirts at all."

It took me far too long to catch on, but what was new?

I raised my brows. "Are you flirting with me, darlin'?"

Her grin turned teasing. "I was trying. I'm not well practiced, but—"

She squealed as I swooped her up with me, carrying her to her bedroom. I tossed her onto her bed, making her yelp and giggle.

"Is this where you wanted to be?" I asked as she scrambled back on the mattress, making room for me.

"You still have that wet shirt on." She bit down on her lip, raking her eyes over me, looking at me like she'd never seen anything better. It was a heady experience, something I couldn't remember ever having. "You should probably take it off before you get sick."

I reached behind my head and yanked my shirt right off, tossing it on the floor. Alice's swollen eyes lit from within, and she reached for me. Unable to deny her anything, I climbed over her, fitting my hips between her spread legs. She fell back on the mattress, her hair spreading around her.

Her palms flattened on my chest, sliding down my flanks and around my back. I let her explore as I took my time looking at her. Her cheeks stained from her tears, her nose a little red at the tip, she was still as gorgeous as ever.

She looked up at me. "This isn't to distract myself. I want to be close to you. I want *you*."

"You've got me." I dipped down to skim my lips along her throat. "I always want you."

"Yeah?"

"Mmmhmm." I gathered the hem of her T-shirt, slowly revealing her creamy, smooth skin. Her stomach flexed as I slid my knuckles over it, and her breath snagged when the cool air kissed her bare breasts. "So damn pretty."

We got lost in one another. It was easy to do. Her lips slotted with mine like corresponding pieces, and her skin was nothing I'd ever felt. We shed our clothes quickly, then took our time with everything else. Touching, tasting, feeling.

Slipping between her spread thighs, I laved at her slick flesh. She pressed her feet to my back and tangled her fingers in my hair, holding me against her, asking for more, directing me where she needed me, riding my tongue until she was crying for nothing but pleasure.

I kept going, and she got impatient, writhing and demanding. I loved her like this; it was cute and sexy, and I couldn't get enough of her taste. I took her over the edge one more time before she pulled me on top of her.

Taking me in her hand, she gave me a slow pump while watching my reaction. "I'm still not sure how this fits inside me."

I laughed, but she twisted her hand around my head and gave another firm pump, making it short-lived. I rocked with her, watching her watching me. Biting her lip. Staring down between us, where she had complete control of me.

"Are you trying to get me to make a fool of myself, Allie-girl?" I groaned as she did another evil twist. "That's where we're headed."

Her lively green eyes found mine again. "I really like playing with you."

"I like it too. That's the problem." I cupped her between her legs and dragged a finger to tease her entrance. "If you want me in here—"

"I do." She shifted her hold and arched her hips, lining me up where she wanted me. "I want you, Cay. Make it fit."

I took over, guiding myself inside her little by little. She was right—we shouldn't have worked together. From the outside, we were mismatched. But her body wanted mine, and lord knew mine wanted hers. It took every ounce of dwindling patience I had to work myself inside her. When I was fully seated, she fit around me like a custom-made glove.

Perfect.

We got lost in each other again, finding our rhythm and holding on to one another, laughing, panting, groaning. Alice was fun and eager, and so incredibly sexy beneath me, it was nearly impossible to hang on. But I didn't want it to end. Not when she felt so good and was right here with me, not in the dark place I'd found her earlier. We were in the light, only making it brighter and brighter.

I reared back onto my knees and brought her with me so she was straddling my legs, hers wrapped around my waist. She let me move her, sliding her up and down my length while she kissed and nipped and sucked my shoulders and neck.

"Always want you," I gritted out. "Never stop thinking about you."

Her fingers dug into my shoulders as she tossed her head back. "Caleb, oh god. Keep saying sweet things like that."

"I mean it. You're on my mind all the time." I cupped her breast, rolling her nipple with my fingers. "These pretty tits. Love them bouncing when you ride me."

"What else?"

I grinned and slid a finger down her stomach to the subtle curve under her navel. "Love this part of you, how it's a little soft right here." Then I gave the patch of hair over her cleft a tug. "This is so sexy. Love the feel of it in my mouth. I want your cunt on my tongue morning, noon, and night."

She gasped, her inner walls clenching around me like a vise, cutting off my ability to speak or do anything other than thrust into her, seeking the relief only she could provide.

We found it together. Falling, falling, tumbling head over heels, until we hit the ground at the same time, shattering the air around us with our frantic cries.

I took her with me to the mattress, her body sprawling over mine. She tucked her face into my neck, her breath hot on my skin. I held her close enough to feel her skittering heartbeat. Closing my eyes, I inhaled her scent, which I would forever associate with Christmas and her. Two of my favorite things, but Alice was number one.

I told her that too. "You're better than Christmas."

Her head popped up. "I am?"

"Mmmhmm. To me, you are."

"Even though I cried all over you?"

"Yep." I took her face in my hands. "I love that you trusted me enough to break down with me. Makes me feel like I'm in there."

She tapped her chest. "In here?"

"Am I?"

"Undeniably." Her nose scrunched. "I can't shake you."

I raised a brow. "Are you still trying?"

"No." She scooted up my body to bring us face to face then ran her nose along mine. "I've learned to give up on exercises in futility."

With a growl, I rolled her to her back and rubbed my scruff all over her chest and neck, making her shriek and giggle. Laughing, I raised my head and planted a kiss on her lips.

"Don't you forget it, darlin'."

Chapter Thirty-three

Caleb

THERE WERE ONLY A few people I welcomed visits from outside of my family, and the man standing on my porch wasn't one of them. If he hadn't caught me outside, awaiting Alice's arrival, I wouldn't have welcomed him at all. It was either my unlucky day or Kent's lucky one.

Then again, the last few weeks with Alice had been some of the best of my life, so maybe I was due for some upheaval.

On the weeks Jesse was with me, Alice and I took things slow, but we still saw each other, and she fit in seamlessly. She'd cooked with Jesse and me at my house. Met us in town for a meal or two. Went fishing with us one weekend and held her own at a few Kelly family dinners. Jesse had always liked her as his favorite librarian. Now that he'd gotten to know her as his dad's girlfriend, his affection had only grown. I couldn't have been happier about the way things were going.

When Jesse was with his mom, though, Alice and I made up for lost time. Whole stretches of days blurred together with her laughter in my kitchen, her socks tucked into the corner of my couch, her hair spread across my pillow. I'd laughed more in a few weeks with her than I had in the last year. Never could have predicted how funny and playful my shy little librarian would turn out to be once she trusted me enough to let it show.

And it was *everything*.

I'd been afraid of change, certain shaking up my careful balance would end in regret. But she'd proven me wrong just by being herself. Life didn't have to stay the same to be good. With her, it was better. Richer. Brighter. She'd brought light to corners I hadn't even noticed were dark.

Maybe I'd had it too good for too long and Kent showing up now was the world's way of balancing the scales. Still didn't change the fact that his presence on my porch pissed me off, and he hadn't even said a word.

He raised a hand as I got up from my rocking chair. "Hey, Caleb. How are you?"

I folded my arms over my chest. "Where's Jesse?"

After a week with him, I'd dropped him back with Shelby a few days ago. As far as I knew, that was where he was, but Kent driving all the way out to the ranch had my alarm bells ringing.

"Oh." He scratched the back of his head. "He's with his mom. I'm not here about him."

Relief swept through me, quickly replaced by trepidation. "Then I can't think of any reason for us to be talking. We have no business with each other."

"Well, we might. I was hoping we could have a conversation, man-to-man." He plopped himself on my porch railing, his legs stretched out and crossed at the ankle, making himself at home.

"A call would have sufficed."

He spread his hands in front of him. "Some conversations need to happen face to face. This is one of them."

I let out a heavy sigh. "You're not gonna leave until you've said your piece, are you?"

He gave me what I imagined he thought was a congenial smile, but it mostly gave me the creeps.

"This won't take long, and I appreciate you taking the time to listen," he started. "I'm sure you know I've been having trouble finding a job."

"I don't keep track of your employment status."

He chuckled, but it didn't quite ring true to my ears. Maybe it was the sweat beading his forehead or the way he kept tugging at the collar of his plaid button-down. Seemed to me Kent was nervous.

"All right. Of course. My point is, with Shelby and me unable to move to Denver for work—"

"No one's stopping you from moving," I reminded him.

"Well, I can't leave Shelby...and Jesse. I get where you're coming from, not letting us take him. You don't want to be without him, and that's completely understandable." He shot me another tight smile. "I've got some things in the pipeline around here. It's looking good. The thing is, I have some bills coming due, and I'm not sure I'll be employed in time to pay them. Shelby's helped me as much as she can, but I need a little more to see me through."

My jaw rippled as I clenched it tight. I could not believe this man was about to ask me for money. There was no way...was there?

I didn't give him any help getting to his point, just stared him down as he floundered.

He sighed. "I'm here asking for a loan. I'd need a month, two max, then I can pay you back. It's not a lot, not for a man who has all this." He gestured broadly. "Like I said, I'll be working by the end of the summer, but I have some bills that need to be paid back immediately.

I'm in a bind here. I'm hoping you can find it in your heart to help me out."

I raised my brows. "How much?" I had no intention of lending him a dime, but I was curious what he'd come here seeking.

Hesitating, he gripped the rail on either side of him. "Five—no, ten thousand would do it. That would alleviate a lot of stress and give me some breathing room to find the right job. And of course, I would pay you back by the end of summer. You'd definitely have your money before Halloween."

I couldn't stop myself from guffawing. *Ten thousand dollars?* He wanted me to loan him ten grand? He had to be truly desperate and out of his mind.

"Since when is Halloween the end of summer?"

He didn't blink for a beat then he broke into a high-pitched laugh. "Who remembers when summer ends? I'm not a calendar." His grin was wide and strained. "The date isn't important. Let's discuss the loan."

I shook my head, my humor gone as fast as it had come. "I have to give it to you. You've got a lot of nerve, Kent. Marching onto my porch, asking me for ten thousand dollars like I owe you something. What reason do I have to want to help you out? I'm racking my brain and can't think of a single one."

His grin faltered, and his shoulders hunched like he was trying to make himself smaller. "Caleb, come on, man. Please consider rethinking your position here. I'm not asking for charity, just a hand up. You know I'm here for Jesse. I care about him too."

My blood instantly heated, and my arms came down from my chest, fists curling at my sides. "Using Jesse to try to get to me is not a smart move. You've got nothing to do with my boy's well-being, and dragging his name into this to grease the wheels? That's about as low as you can get."

Kent flinched, then recovered with another shaky laugh, his eyes darting toward the road like he wished he hadn't shown up here.

That was when Alice's little car turned down my drive, kicking up dust as she pulled to a stop. She climbed out, sunlight catching her hair, and my whole body eased before I remembered my unwelcome visitor. Kent's sharp inhale told me he recognized her.

"Well, look at this." He turned back to me, his head tilted. "I know her. I wasn't aware librarians made house calls," he said, laughing at his own joke.

I stepped off the porch, putting myself square between him and Alice, my voice low and sharp. "You've overstayed your welcome. Get off my property and don't come back."

Alice, catching the tail end of things, slowed her steps, her eyes flicking between us. But I didn't look away from Kent until he pushed off my railing and slunk down the steps, muttering under his breath.

I watched him the whole way to his car, ready to step in if needed, but all he did was nod at Alice before climbing in and driving away.

As soon as the dust from his tires settled, I turned back to Alice. She stood there with her keys in her hand, her brow furrowed, uncertainty clouding those pretty green eyes. I closed the space between us, sliding my hands around her waist and pulling her in until her cheek pressed against my chest.

"Hello, you," I murmured into her hair. "That was Kent. Shelby's boyfriend."

She tipped her head back to look at me, her gaze sweeping over me with concern. "You don't look like you had a good visit."

"It wasn't." My jaw worked as I tried to keep the bitterness out of my tone, though I wasn't sure I succeeded. "From what I understand, he's been living off Shelby for a while, racking up debt, and now he's got it in his head I should float him too. We've barely exchanged pleasantries, but he came here asking for ten grand, like that was ever going to happen."

Alice's nose wrinkled, her distaste plain as day. "Ten thousand? Caleb..."

"I know. I give him credit for his nerve, but that's it." I shook my head. "Something tells me this isn't the last time he'll try to stick his hand out."

Even though his taillights were long gone, unease lingered. This wasn't the first time someone had come to me for a loan. I'd helped a few people over the years, but they were men who worked for me, who I knew and trusted and had reason to believe would make good on their word. Kent wasn't one of them. I didn't know him from Adam, except that he spent a hell of a lot of time around my boy.

Up until now, I'd been neutral, figuring Shelby was smart enough to keep her eyes open and protect our son. After today, I'd bet money she'd had no damn clue about Kent showing up here. If he was sneaking around asking me for ten grand, it made me wonder what else he was getting up to right under her nose.

Alice slid her hand up to my chest, toying with the buttons on my shirt. "So what are you going to do?"

"I told him not to come back. And I meant it." I bent, brushing my lips against her temple. "I also promised you a ride this afternoon, and that's what we're going to do. No sense letting Kent ruin our day."

Her frown faded, replaced by the kind of smile that made all the weight on my shoulders lift. She gave a little nod, squeezing my shirt in her fist. "Okay. Horses."

"That's right, darlin'"—I stepped back enough to lace my fingers through hers—"let's head out to the stables. I'll get them saddled up. We're going to have some real fun."

"As long as I don't fall off."

I squeezed her hand, and it did more to settle me than anything. "I'd never let that happen. Nothing will hurt you as long as I'm around."

Chapter Thirty-four

Alice

I HAD ALWAYS UNDERSTOOD horses were large, but until I sat perched on top of *Hellion*, I hadn't quite grasped how large. From up here, the ground looked much farther away than I'd ever imagined, and the animal under me shifted like she had her own opinions about my being there.

"Hellion?" I gave Caleb a sharp look, tightening my grip on the reins. "I have to say, I don't find her name reassuring. Is this a prank?"

He chuckled as he stood at my knee, one broad hand stroking the horse's neck. This was all second nature to him. He'd been riding horses since he could walk, and they lived in what was essentially his backyard. I had to remind myself he was the expert, and in his hands, I was safe.

"Not a prank, darlin'. Her mama was a wild one. We expected Hells to take after her, but she's as gentle as they come." He squeezed my calf and slid his hand up to my hip, stroking me the same way he had the horse. "I wouldn't let you up there if I thought for a second you weren't safe."

"I know," I whispered. Because I did. I trusted Caleb completely, and Hellion seemed like she didn't mind me being on her back too much. "I'm farther off the ground than I'd been anticipating."

That made him laugh again. "And you're going to stay up there until you're ready to get down."

Then he swung up onto his own horse, Brick—short for Brick House. A mountain of muscle and dark hide that made Hellion look like a pony. My nerves scattered, forgotten. All I could see was Caleb in the saddle, the brim of his hat low, thighs gripping leather, shoulders straight. Pure cowboy. *My* cowboy. As natural as could be. Like he'd been born to sit in that saddle.

"Wow," I breathed.

He cocked his head. "Why're you looking at me that way?"

My cheeks were hot, and it had nothing to do with the afternoon sun. "You look like you belong on the cover of one of Mrs. Taylor's favorite cowboy romances."

He chuffed and patted his middle. "I think this disqualifies me. Don't those guys have at least an eight-pack? I'm a few short."

I bit my bottom lip, taking all of him in. "Believe me, Cay, you're not missing anything."

His gaze swept over me. "As long as I'm the right fit for you, nothing else matters to me. Besides, I think I can live without being one of Mrs. Taylor's fantasies."

I giggled. "I think I can live without that too. You'll just be mine."

He groaned. "Are you trying to get out of this ride by making me want to take you in the barn and sort you out?"

"Well, I wasn't, but if you'd rather..."

"Not a chance, Allie-girl. We're taking our ride." His eyes never left mine as he lifted his reins. "We'll see about sorting you out afterward."

Caleb led Hells and me down a path designed for children. It was smooth and level, no jutting rocks to climb over, no hills to traverse. Eventually, I was able to relax and enjoy the smooth ride atop my horse, due in part to Hellion's calm nature, but also because I was distracted by my view of Caleb in front of me.

There might have come a day when the sheer breadth of his shoulders didn't take my breath away, but today wasn't it. Especially not while watching him control the horse under him, who, to my untrained eye, was easily double Hellion's size.

We followed the trail until it opened to a narrow stretch of river. Sunlight glittered off the surface of the water, drawing me closer. Caleb swung down first, tying his horse to a nearby branch. Then he came to my side, steadying me with both hands as I slid awkwardly to the ground.

The moment my boots hit dirt, my legs wobbled, tingling and half-dead from gripping the saddle. "Oops," I muttered, trying to shake them back to life.

Caleb didn't laugh or tease. Right there in front of me, he crouched down, his big hands smoothing over my thighs and cupping the curve of my butt as he tipped his head back to examine my face.

"Are you sore?" he asked. Serious. As if this were a medical exam and not him being unbearably sweet and distracting.

"A little," I whispered, heat flooding my cheeks. "I think I'll survive."

He gave my backside a squeeze. "You will. The more you ride, the more you'll get used to using these muscles."

"I guess I'll have to, having a cowboy for a boyfriend."

"That's right," he chuckled. Leaning forward, he placed a kiss on my belly button. "My pretty little darlin's going to be a cowgirl yet."

Satisfied I wasn't broken, he rose and guided me to a wide, flat boulder overlooking the water. We sat together, so close my leg was almost on top of his. That was where he'd put me, where he wanted me, and I had no objections.

After a while of listening to the river's quiet flow, Caleb reached for my hand and brought it to rest on his thigh. My heart stuttered, and warmth pooled low in my stomach. I leaned into him and laid my head on his shoulder.

The last few weeks with Caleb had been the sweetest stretch of my life. He'd made me laugh until my stomach hurt, touched me with a possessiveness that never left me doubting, and proved over and over the reticent man who'd once turned me away was long gone. Caleb Kelly was all in with me—unapologetically, wholeheartedly—and he showed it in every word, every look, every action.

He'd folded me into his little world with Jesse like it was no big deal. They'd taught me to fish but never made me bait my own hooks. We'd cooked dinner together, sharing the prep and cleanup duties. We'd had quiet moments, but mostly silly, happy, laughing times.

For a woman who had lived most of her life feeling invisible, being seen by this man was a revelation. To him, I wasn't glass, but he still treated me like I was something valuable and delicate. He checked on me on the days we didn't see each other and thoroughly scoured me with his eyes when I was in his arms.

Things were changing, but I wasn't afraid anymore.

"Before I headed here, I stopped at Joy's to pick up my paycheck and we had a talk." I traced little patterns on the back of Caleb's hand where it still covered mine.

He made a low sound of acknowledgment. "Oh yeah?"

"She fired me."

That got him. Caleb's shoulder shook under my cheek as he barked out a laugh. He angled his head down at me, eyebrows raised in disbelief. "Come again?"

"I'm not kidding. She fired me. I'm no longer her employee." I turned my face toward him, the corners of my mouth twitching. "She hired a new waitress to replace me this week and told me it was time I had a life of my own. She also said I'm not allowed in the bar unless I'm a paying customer."

He shook his head. "Wow. I gotta say, I didn't see that coming."

"Can't say I did either. Then again, this is classic Joy. She's not one for heart-to-hearts. She shows her affection through blunt force."

That got him to chuckle. "Have to admit, I'm not real sorry about this. You worked too much, and I'd like to claim as many of your free evenings as I can." His amusement transitioned into concern. "I know you liked your job, though. How do you feel about not working there anymore?"

I thought about my answer for a while, watching the river glisten as it ambled by. Then I leaned closer, pressing into the solid wall of his body, and tilted my face up to catch his gaze. "I think she's right. It's time." My lips curved before I added, "I will miss spending my evenings there, though."

"You don't have to worry about that." He swept my hair off my face and cupped my jaw. "Any time you want to go, I'll take you. It'll be a nice change to have you sitting at the table with me instead of scribbling on your little notepad and running away."

I gasped. "I haven't run away from you in a long time."

"You haven't." He took my chin between two fingers. "And you're not going to ever again."

After we finished our ride, we made dinner together then curled up on Caleb's couch. He was reading to me, but he kept stumbling over his words, to the point I wasn't certain he knew what he was saying.

I placed my hand on his arm, bringing him to a stop. "What's up, Cay? Seems like you're not into the story tonight."

With a sigh, he put the book down in his lap and scratched behind his ear—a sure sign something was on his mind.

"Yeah. I guess I'm not. I'm loathe to admit it, but Kent's visit got under my skin." He took my hand in his and toyed with my fingers as he frowned. "A while back, Shelby told me she wants to move her and Jesse to Denver with Kent."

I hissed a breath. "I hope you shut that down."

"Of course I did." His troubled gaze swept to mine. "I don't want him leaving. *Ever*, if it were up to me. I'm smart enough to get that's not a possibility. But in the back of my mind, there's some niggling doubt. Should I have allowed it? He'd have a lot more resources available to him in Denver—"

"Caleb, no. Jesse is thriving here, and you know that. His education is important, sure, but what he gets living with his family, on this land, is just as valuable, if not more. You're letting him spread his wings this summer, and he's safe to do that, knowing he can come back to his nest when it's over."

He laid his head back on the cushions and groaned. "I know you're right. I've been telling myself the same thing. So why am I still questioning it? Why is parenting such a mindfuck all the time?"

Pushing up on my knees, I climbed onto his lap and slid my fingers through his hair. "I've never been a parent, so I don't know. But I think it's a good sign you're regularly tortured with uncertainty. That means you care deeply about your son, and you're willing to drive yourself crazy getting it right."

"Tortured is right." He wrapped his arms around me, pulling me against his chest and running his nose along the side of my head. "What else can I do for him? If he wanted to play football or join the 4-H, I'd have no problem, but I don't know the first thing about robots or science."

I almost laughed, but held it in. Now wasn't the time. "He gets robots and science at school and the library, honey. With you, he gets all your knowledge of running a large ranch, land as far as the eye can see, animals and fishing any time he wants, and a family who sees him as someone important and vital. You're sending him out into the world with all that, and I have to say, he's better off than most kids. Even those who go to science academies and take college courses starting in middle school."

He let out a long sigh but kept his eyes narrowed on me. "You'll tell me if I miss something, right? If I get too myopic and don't see an opportunity I should be giving him?"

My chest swelled with emotion. Him asking me to do that when he'd been angry at me for the same thing a couple months ago only highlighted how drastically things between us had changed. We were in this together. He trusted me and my judgment. I was part of his life, and that included his son.

"I don't think that'll happen, but yes, I promise to tell you when you're screwing up."

He chuffed. "Appreciate it, darlin'. I need my girl to keep me humble and on my toes." Then he pressed a kiss to the side of my head. "Thank you for reminding me of what I'm giving him. Means a lot to me you see that."

"It's true. And I'll keep reminding you. As many times as it takes."

He gave a low hum, his arms tightening around me until I could feel the steady beat of his heart against my cheek. We stayed like that for a while, his big hands sliding up and down my back, mine tracing lazy circles along his shoulders and chest.

After a long silence, he murmured into my hair, "You're going to be a great mom when you're ready, Alice."

The words and certainty behind them hit deep. My throat tightened as I tilted my head to meet his eyes. "I want that," I whispered back, the admission catching on my breath.

His gaze was as soft as a feather brushing over my skin, but his voice was firm. "Then I'll make sure you get it."

I sank against him again, letting the weight of his promise settle in my bones. It was too soon for us to be making commitments like that, but right now, in his arms, it didn't feel that way. Not even a little bit.

Chapter Thirty-five

Alice

PHOEBE WAS A BLUR of pink sundress, long, pretty hair, and easy laughter as Deke spun her across the little square of worn wood Joy's generously called a dance floor. The jukebox warbled out an old country tune, and the two moved in a way that spoke of lots of nights like this, not a single misstep between them.

I was still smiling at the sight when Caleb's big hand slid over mine. "Come on," he said, pulling me out of my seat.

"Caleb—" I dug my heels in halfway, but he didn't even break stride.

"I want to dance with my girl, darlin'. Don't deprive me of that," he rumbled, pulling me against his chest.

How could I argue with that? Besides, I had known this was where tonight had been leading. We'd shared dinner and drinks with Phoebe and Deke—our first real double date—and they'd told us all about the dance club they liked to frequent with their friends, Chris and Tilly. Deke hadn't been a dancer until he met Phoebe, but she'd converted him. And dang it, they were sweet together.

Phoebe's laughter rang like church bells as Deke whirled her past us. I looked up at Caleb, panic fluttering in my stomach. "I can't dance like that. I've only ever danced alone, in my kitchen, when I'm cooking."

"I've seen you do that. I know you've got moves." His mouth curved at the memory of walking in on me shimmying my hips and singing into my spoon a few nights ago. "All you have to do is let me lead you. I'm no expert, but I've got a few moves of my own."

Before I knew it, he bent, nudging my shoes onto his boots until I was standing on his feet. I yelped, grabbing for his shoulders, but he only tightened his arms around me and straightened to his full height.

"Hold on," he said, as if I'd ever let go.

We were off, gliding in a wide circle while Phoebe and Deke twirled like professionals in the middle of it all. I clung to Caleb, laughing helplessly as the bar tilted around us. For once, I wasn't worried about who might be looking at me or what I was doing right or wrong. How could I have thought about anything other than balancing on my cowboy's boots and letting him carry me around the dance floor?

"I'm going to be so dizzy," I cried into his chest.

"Good. I'll have an excuse to carry you."

My fingers curled harder into his shirt. "Like you've ever needed an excuse."

He dipped his head to put his mouth beside my ear. "Why should you have to walk when I've got two arms and you fit perfectly in them?"

I rubbed my cheek against his. "You have a point."

"Glad you finally see it, darlin'."

After a while, the four of us took a breather at the table. Caleb and Deke got us fresh drinks, and Phoebe held hers up for a toast.

"What are we toasting?" Caleb asked, holding his glass against his sister's.

"Lots of things," Phoebe started. "To my brother having the best girlfriend ever."

"Damn right." He clinked his glass against hers and mine. "What else?"

Phoebe's eyes lit on mine. "To Alice, who fits right in with all the crazy."

I laughed. "I don't know about that, but I'll drink to it anyway."

She winked. "It's bad luck if you don't." Then she leaned toward her husband, who hadn't taken his eyes off her since we'd sat down. "And cheers to us and the little cinnamon bun growing in my oven."

It took a solid five seconds for Caleb to get it. When he did, he shot to his feet, circled the table, bent down, and wrapped his arms around both Deke and Phoebe. They were laughing, grabbing his arms as he kissed his sister's head, congratulating them, telling them how happy he was for them and that he couldn't wait to meet his new niece or nephew.

My heart swelled, and my eyes burned as I watched them. When Caleb finally let go, I got up and hugged Phoebe too.

"I'm so happy for you," I whispered in her ear. "What a lucky kid you're going to have."

And when she let go, I went to Deke. We were still getting to know one another, but I couldn't stop myself from throwing my arms around him too.

"You're going to be such a great dad," I told him, meaning it with all my heart.

"I hope so," he mumbled.

"You will. Phoebe wouldn't have chosen you otherwise."

He jerked slightly, then said, "Means a lot. Thanks, Alice."

Caleb was still standing, waiting for me, so I walked right into his arms. He squeezed me tight and buried his face in my hair, breathing heavily. When he finally loosened his hold, I looked up. The tears in his eyes matched my own, and I wondered how I ever thought I could get over this man.

Joy approached the table, going straight to Deke. "Were you ever going to tell me?"

He got up from his seat, started to lift his arms, then dropped them. "Yeah. Of course we were, Aunt Joy. You were next."

She nodded toward his arms, loose at his sides. "Well, get those around me." She sniffed, and I swore I saw a little wetness at the corner of one eye. "This kind of news deserves a hug."

Phoebe let out a strangled sob as the two of them embraced. It was awkward—like two people who'd only ever seen other people hug but had never put it into practice—but they held each other hard and tight. Joy was saying something quiet, for only Deke to hear, and he nodded, his eyes slammed shut.

I had to wipe my own tears. There'd been no holding them back anymore—not with my stoic, tough Joy getting emotional.

It didn't last long, of course. Joy had a reputation to uphold, and I imagined, between comforting me and now this, she'd reached her capacity for tenderness for the year. She pulled back from Deke, gave Phoebe a pat on her shoulder and well wishes, then returned to her spot behind the bar like it had never happened.

I caught Joy watching us a little while later. Our eyes met, and an unspoken understanding passed between us. If she hadn't pushed me to seek my own life, I would have still been a waitress with my trusty notepad, watching this scene from across the bar.

I mouthed, "Thank you," to her, even though it wasn't nearly enough. I knew she got it, though. She always had.

Chapter Thirty-six

Alice

CALEB OPENED THE PASSENGER door of his truck, slipped his arm under me, and lifted me out. He carried me into my house, closing the door behind us and flipping the lock. Then he pressed me against the door, cupped my jaw, and stared down at me.

We hadn't planned on coming to my house after Joy's, but I'd gotten the sense he wasn't in the mood for the long drive back to the ranch. That was fine with me. After spinning in his arms all night, I didn't want to spend more time than I had to out of them.

His nostrils flared as he sucked in a deep breath. "I'm feeling a whole hell of a lot."

"Do you want to talk about it?"

"I don't." He leaned in, dragging his mouth along my neck then nipping my ear. "I need to keep feelin' it with you. Can I do that?"

"Of course you can." I dug my fingers into his hair, tugging on the ends. "Give it to me, Caleb. I want to feel it too."

His answering growl vibrated against my skin, then his mouth claimed mine, hot and insistent. My legs locked around him as his hands skimmed down my sides, charting my body. I gasped against his lips when he palmed my hip and hauled me into him, my heated core flush with his middle.

"Caleb—" Whatever I'd meant to say burned away the second his tongue slid against mine. He lashed at my mouth, battering it down with an onslaught of emotion he couldn't express with words but wanted to share with me, nonetheless. I understood exactly what he was communicating, answering with my own kisses and caresses, arching my hips into him, on an endless mission to get closer and closer.

When he finally tore his mouth from mine, his breathing was ragged, his forehead resting against mine. "Bedroom," he breathed. "Gotta get you into the bedroom."

I nodded my consent, though we both knew I was going wherever he was. I didn't plan on unwrapping myself from him until it was necessary. He stumbled down the hall with me in his arms, knocking into furniture and walls, stopping every few steps to kiss me before continuing.

My bedroom was barely lit, the glow of the lamp I'd left on casting everything in muted gold. Caleb fumbled with the hem of my dress, gathering it at my waist in one hand. I leaned back enough for him to yank the fabric free from where it was stuck between us, and he pulled it the rest of the way over my head, leaving me in nothing but my bra and panties.

I slid my palms beneath his T-shirt, feeling the dichotomy of hard and soft. There was no part of him I liked best. Made of iron strength and pillowy comfort, I could have studied his body and face for the rest of my life and still not have had enough. I always wanted him over me, inside me, around me. If it were possible, I would have curled up inside him too. Instead, I worked on melding myself to his skin, kissing and touching him with every ounce of impatience and reverence he stirred within me.

When I pressed my mouth to his chest, he shuddered. His hand threaded into my hair and held me there, above his thudding heart.

"Christ, do I need you." He walked to my bed and lowered me onto the mattress. "Get naked for me, darlin'. I want to look at you for a minute—see what's mine."

He stood there, his broad shoulders rising and falling with each labored breath he took, eyes dark and intent on me. I reached behind me, unclasping my bra, then slid the straps down my arms. The cool air kissed my skin as the fabric fell away, and Caleb's chest heaved like he'd been punched.

He always looked at me that way. No matter how many times I bared myself to him, he reacted like I was the most beautiful thing he'd ever seen and couldn't quite believe his eyes. Under his gaze, I gained confidence. I *wanted* him to see me, to show me how much he wanted me, and he never failed to deliver.

His gaze tracked every movement as I hooked my thumbs into the waistband of my underwear and slipped them down my thighs, kicking them free at the end of the bed. I leaned back on my elbows, bare and open, the heat of his stare burning hotter than anything else.

Caleb dragged a rough palm down his face then dropped it to press against the heavy bulge in his jeans. Rubbed once, hard, like he couldn't help it. Then he stared at me, unmoving, as if the sight of me had ripped him raw.

He shook his head, still pressing on his erection. "This is it. You're going to kill me, Allie-girl."

Without warning, he dropped to his knees, gripped my thighs, and dragged me forward until my hips perched at the edge of the mattress. Before I could draw in a full breath, his mouth was on me.

Hot, hungry, unrelenting. He buried his face between my thighs, tongue sliding against me in long, devastating strokes that had my fingers tangling in his hair so I didn't hit the roof.

He held me open, devouring me like I was the only thing he'd ever wanted—the only thing he *would* ever want.

He licked and sucked in a rhythm that made my hips buck helplessly, each stroke dragging me higher, closer, until I was trembling against his mouth.

"Caleb...you...I..." My fingers fisted in his hair, pulling, but he only growled and doubled down, sliding one thick finger inside me as his tongue circled and pressed. The stretch of him, the steady rhythm, the heat of his mouth—it was too much. I couldn't stand it for another second.

The world went white hot as I broke apart, gasping his name, my thighs clamping around his head as pleasure tore through me. He didn't stop. He licked me through it, swallowing every tremor, holding my thighs wide while my body shook and shook.

When I finally started to come down, he kissed the inside of one thigh then the other. I opened my eyes in time to see him reach for my nightstand drawer and pull it open.

My breath stuttered. "What are you doing?"

He held up the slim, familiar shape of my vibrator. "I told you I was nosy," he rumbled, flicking the switch with his thumb until it buzzed to life. The sound alone made me whimper, but him holding it over me, like a threat and promise, had my legs shaking and my hips rising off the bed.

"Caleb," I sighed, reaching for him.

He pressed on my abdomen, holding me down. "Do you like how this feels? Do you slip it inside yourself or rub it on your clit?"

"Both." I licked my parched lips. "I like to do both."

He dipped his head to bite the inside of my knee. "Both, hmmm? You like to play with yourself?"

"Sometimes," I rasped.

He dragged the vibrator along my inner thigh, never taking his eyes off my face. "Do you think of me?"

"Yes." There was no use trying to deny it. This man was the center of all my fantasies. "Real life is so much better."

"I believe you." His thumb stretched to rub the top of my cleft. "I'd like to see anyway. Wanna know what you look like when you come against this and think of me."

He rose, scooped me up, and placed me at the top of the mattress. Then he kicked off his pants and climbed onto the bed beside me, his cock thick and angry. He paid it no mind. His attention was locked on me.

It was a heady, devastating feeling.

He lay on his back and patted his thighs. "Sit on me. Let me see you."

As boneless as I was, I managed to crawl over him and straddle his legs. When I reached for his length, he caught my wrist and lowered my hand to my side.

"Not yet." He slipped the vibrator along my folds, back and forth, back and forth. "Should I turn it back on?"

"Yes." I rocked against the hard silicone, wishing it was him. "Please, Caleb."

He flicked the switch and slid the toy up to my clit. All it took was one touch for me to rocket forward, catching myself on his chest.

He chuckled. "You like that, don't you?"

"I like it better with you controlling it."

"Everything's better when we're doing it together," he murmured, pressing the vibrator more firmly against me. He watched me react, listened to my breathing, moved when I shifted, circled when I mewled, giving me what I needed without my having to ask.

My body went tight, hips rocking against the steady pressure he had absolute control over. He held me in place with one big hand on my hip, not allowing me to escape the rhythm or chase it faster, giving me exactly what he wanted me to have.

"Right here, Allie-girl," he coaxed. "Let me see you fall apart for me."

I did.

I shattered with a high, keening cry, my body quaking as another release burst out of me. I collapsed on his chest, and he flicked the toy off, tossing it aside. Then his hands were on me, cupping my face. His mouth claimed mine, and he kissed me like he was trying to breathe me in. I clung to his shoulders, frantic even though I'd just broken into a million little pieces.

"Please," I panted against his lips. "I need you. Inside me. Now."

He guided me forward, directly above his thick, dripping cock. Together, we lined him up, then he pressed inside, stretching me slowly, until I was fully seated, our bodies locked tight.

I gasped from how full I was, blindly reaching for his hands, and they were there, wrapping around mine. Neither of us moved, not really. His chest rose and fell beneath me, his eyes locked on mine with a heat so fierce, it was almost unbearable.

The air went still.

The whole world went still.

Gone was the panicked desperation that had driven us together moments ago. We just *stared*, connected in every way that mattered, neither daring to move. Something inside me became rewritten. Thoughts and memories shifted aside to make room for this one. Instinct told me this was important. The tenderness in his gaze, his hands around mine, his body planted in me so deep I could barely breathe...it went beyond the physical. It was a story committed to paper in ink.

In my mind, I whispered, *"It's a love story."*

"Mine," he rasped, his voice breaking on the word. "You're my girl, Alice. You mean the world to me. You know that?"

I slipped my hands free of his to slide them along his chest. "Yes, Caleb. I do know that. You've shown me."

His throat worked, like he wanted to say more. Instead, he gripped my hips, holding me steady. "Let me keep showing you." He guided me, lifting me slowly before easing me back down, letting me feel every deliberate inch of him.

I gasped, bracing my palms against his chest. The motion was unhurried, almost achingly so, but it let me savor the stretch, the slide, the way my body molded around his. Caleb's thumbs stroked slow circles against my skin, his gaze never breaking from mine as he set the pace.

"That's it," he whispered, moving me into another rise, another fall. "Just like that, darlin'. Love the way you take me. Can't get enough of it—of you."

Our rhythm synced like we'd been doing this for decades. Each roll of my hips drew a low groan from his throat. Each shift of his hands tightened the connection between us. I was drunk on him, on this moment, on the way we were together.

He'd already made me come twice, but pressure began to mount in my center. He lifted his hips to meet me, the friction driving me closer and closer to the jagged edge. His fingers dug into my waist, and a line formed between his brows as he struggled not to lose it.

"Caleb, honey, I'm getting there." I cupped the sides of his neck, tendons rippling beneath my palm. "Take me there."

His grip tightened, his jaw flexing as he drove into me in long, deliberate strokes. "Come with me," he ordered, desperate and tender all at once. "I want to feel you when I let go."

I wanted that too. I moved faster, chasing it, until my pleasure broke free, splitting me apart. My cry echoed into his chest, my body clenching around him. Caleb's low roar followed, his hips surging, burying himself deep as he spilled inside me, holding me to him like he'd never let me go.

When it was over, we stayed where we were, me draped over his chest, his arms banded tight around me, keeping me right there, his heart pounding against my ear.

Neither of us moved. Neither of us wanted to.

"I've got you," he whispered finally, his lips brushing my hair. "Always."

"You do."

I hummed against his chest, still trembling in the aftershocks, tracing lazy circles on his sweat-damp skin. "You know," I said, smiling to myself, "I don't think I'll ever be able to look at that vibrator the same again."

Caleb's chuckle shook me. "You've no real cause to look at it anymore. You want to use it, I'll be the one holding it."

"Oh? What if the mood strikes when you aren't around?" I grinned.

"It might. But the fact is, even if you have the thing in your hand, it'll be me holding it, won't it?"

"Yes." I reached up to touch his scruffy chin. From now on, I'd be able to picture nothing else but Caleb bringing me over, even if I was alone. "I'm glad you didn't get weird about it. I've heard some men don't like their women having toys. They feel like they're competing with them."

"Competing? Nah..." He arched a brow, deadly serious in that way only Caleb could be. "Darlin', I know damn well I'm the winner in this situation. I've got you, don't I?"

My heart kicked, making me breathless and giddy. "You do."

His arms tightened, and he dipped his head to nuzzle my hair. "Besides, that piece of silicone can't hold you like I can. It can't tell you you're gorgeous and my favorite sexy little librarian."

I laughed as I tried to dig my face beneath his breastbone. Since that didn't work, I settled on pressing my cheek over his thumping heart.

"You're comfortable."

"And you're mine," he said simply.

I was.

It was written in ink on the paper of my soul, and there was no erasing it.

Chapter Thirty-seven

Caleb

I woke with a start, disoriented at first. Then the sweet woman next to me moved, and I came back to myself.

Alice was sound asleep, her head tucked on my shoulder, breathing even. I looked around the room in the dark, remembering we were at her house. We didn't spend a lot of time here. We both preferred the ranch, but her house was a lot more convenient to town.

Plans were coming together in my mind. How I wanted us to be. A timeline of when that would happen. Jesse'd be on board. I knew that, but we'd have a discussion anyway. By the end of the summer, Alice would be a permanent fixture at my house. No more missing nights together. I'd wasted enough time. She belonged with me, and I was better when she was at my side.

I lay there, staring up at the ceiling, wondering why I was awake when it was pitch dark outside and Alice had worn me out. By any stretch, I should have been as fast asleep as she was.

Turning, I grabbed my phone from the nightstand to check the time. Just as I registered it was a few minutes past midnight, it vibrated with an incoming call from Jesse.

I knifed upright, bringing the phone to my ear. "Jesse? You okay?"

"Dad?" The tremble in his voice put me on red alert. "Uh...sorry, I don't know if I should have called you..."

I did my level best to stay calm, even though my insides were screaming. "What's going on, bud?"

"Something weird is happening. Kent's here, and I think something's wrong."

I shot to my feet, my fingers shoved in my hair. "What's wrong?"

"I don't know." I could almost hear him shaking his head. Probably pacing around his room too. "He...I was sleeping, and something loud outside woke me up. Then I heard him and Mom talking. I think she was crying. I went to check, and Kent was kind of all...bloody."

Shit. What the hell was going on?

"Okay. Stay in your room. I'm in town at Alice's. I'll be there in a few minutes."

He made a choked sound, and it was a shot to my gut. "You don't have to come," he whispered.

I had to clear the panic from my throat before I could speak again. "You need me?"

After a short pause, he answered, "Yeah."

"I'm coming. Hold tight, bud."

I threw down my phone and searched for my clothes in the dark. I was coming up empty, about ready to head over in my briefs, when a light flicked on. Alice was already skirting the bed, a bundle of clothes in her arms.

"Here." She thrust my jeans and T-shirt at me. "Give me two minutes, and I'll be ready."

"No, darlin', go back to sleep." I yanked my shirt over my head. "I can handle this."

She shook her head as she darted around the room, slipping on her discarded sundress and shoving her feet into a pair of flip-flops. She was fully dressed, her phone in her hand, before I'd gotten my jeans zipped up.

"Is Jesse okay?"

"Think so, but something's going on in that house he doesn't need to be a part of." I took her by the waist and rolled my forehead along hers. "I'm going to pick him up and take him home."

"Okay. I'm coming too." She said it so firmly there was no room for argument. There was no time either. I needed to get to my boy and see with my own two eyes he was okay.

"All right." I held the back of her head, making sure she was hearing me. "But no matter what, you're staying in the truck."

"I'll do what you need me to."

It wasn't an agreement, but it was as good as I was going to get right now.

It took exactly three minutes to drive from Alice's house to Shelby's. As much as I liked living out on the ranch, I was thanking my lucky stars I'd been in town. I didn't know if I could have handled a thirty-minute drive to get to Jesse. As it was, my heart was damn near ready to explode.

I had my phone to my ear as I strode up the walk to the front door. Jesse answered on the first ring.

"Dad?"

"I'm here, buddy. If it's safe to come out of your room, open the front door for me."

"Okay," he whispered. "I'm coming right now. But...I think Mom's pretty upset. Be prepared."

My shoulders locked tight around my ears, but I did my best to keep the tension out of my voice. The last thing he needed was both his parents going haywire. I'd be his rock, even if it killed me.

"I'm good, bud. Now come let me in. I'll take care of the rest."

It was a point in Shelby's favor I couldn't hear any yelling or crashing coming from inside. As I peered through the sidelights beside the door, all I could see was her neat-as-a-pin living room, illuminated only by a hall and kitchen light.

Jesse opened the door slowly, peeking his head out. "Dad?"

"I'm here." I pressed the door the rest of the way open and grabbed the side of his face, checking him over in the moonlight. "You okay?"

He nodded, his mouth flattened into a thin line. "Kinda freaked out, but I'm not hurt or anything. Mom wouldn't let that happen."

There were different kinds of hurt. And I already knew Jesse would carry tonight with him. Shelby should never have allowed him to be exposed to Kent's problems. There was no excuse I'd ever accept.

I slid my hand down to his shoulder, not missing the slight tremble in his tight muscles. "All right. Here's what we're going to do. I want you to go to your room and grab what you need for the week. I'm going to go talk to your mom and Kent."

He sniffled and wiped the back of his hand across his cheek. "But your week doesn't start until tomorrow."

"Let me worry about that, bud. You go grab your stuff."

He gave me another doubtful look before letting out a shuddering breath and trudging toward his room. I stepped into the house, following the low voices coming from the kitchen.

"Shelby, Kent, I'm coming in," I warned right before stepping into the room.

They both whipped around to face me, competing looks of horror and confusion on their faces. Shelby was in her nightgown, a spot of blood on the front. Her mouth hung open as her eyes darted over me, like she couldn't believe I was standing there. Kent, on the other hand, flinched dramatically. From the bruise blooming on his cheek, two swollen eyelids, and cut lip, I understood why. The man had been through the wringer tonight, but I felt no sympathy.

Not when he'd brought it home to Jesse.

"Cay? What are you doing here?" Shelby smoothed her hand over her hair, but it didn't do anything to right the situation. "It's the middle of the night."

I folded my arms over my chest. "Exactly. When our *son* calls me *in the middle of the night*, telling me he's scared because his mother's boyfriend showed up at *his house*, covered in blood, there's not a chance I'm not going to be here."

All the color drained from her face. "Jesse called you? But..." She turned toward the hallway leading to his room. "He's asleep. I didn't think he'd se—"

"Did you think about him at all?" Fury edged my vision with black, but I didn't let it show. I swallowed it down like a ball of barbed wire, feeling every jagged inch as it made its way to my gut. "When you *allowed* this man into your house, where *our son* was sleeping, did you think of him at all?" I swung my gaze to Kent. "What kind of danger did you bring here?"

He held up his hands. One of his fingers had been broken. It was angry and turning black, twisted at a forty-five-degree angle. A sick kind of satisfaction pumped through my veins. I hoped like hell he was in a lot of pain and that finger never healed quite right.

"There's no danger," Kent claimed unconvincingly. "I had an accident, and Shelby's helping me clean up. Jesse is fine. He doesn't need to worry about anything."

"Where's Jesse? I have to explain..." Shelby took a step toward his room, and I shifted in front of her. She frowned up at me, bringing a shaky hand to her chest. "What are you doing?"

I inhaled a steadying breath. More anger wasn't needed in this situation. "Jesse's coming home with me tonight. He's in his room packing his things."

Her jaw dropped once again. "What? No." She shook her head hard. "It's still my week. You can't take him."

"He called me," I intoned. "Do you get that? He saw your boyfriend covered in blood, and he called me, Shelby. He didn't go to you. He called his dad—because he knew I would provide him a safe place."

She started to defend herself. "Safe...? I'd never do anything to harm him—"

I jerked my chin toward the bloody man sitting at her table. "You let that in here. There are no words that will convince me he got that way from an accident—not when he was at my house a couple weeks ago begging for a loan. I'm not stupid, Shel. I can put two and two together."

She whipped around to face Kent. "You begged him for a loan? Why in the world would you do that?"

She had no idea. Just as I'd suspected. That didn't make it better, though. She still brought this piece of shit into our son's life when anyone with half a brain could see he was less than pond scum. He might not have been violent, and he may have cared about Shelby and Jesse, but that was the bare minimum.

Kent tried to explain, but I wasn't listening. His excuses didn't matter to me. Nothing he could say would be good enough.

Jesse emerged with a backpack and his duffel bag. Shelby tried to go to him again, but I stood in her way. Taking the duffel from Jesse, I put a hand on his nape and steered him toward the door, Shelby on my heels.

"Wait, Caleb...please—*wait*," she pleaded, following us out on the porch. "Let me talk to Jesse."

I gave Jesse's shoulder a pat. "Go get in the truck. Alice is waiting for you. I'm going to talk to your mom for a second."

He peered around me, sadness tugging at his mouth as he looked at Shelby. "I'm sorry, Mom. I was scared. Don't be mad at me."

Shelby sucked in a ragged gasp. "I'm not mad, baby. Never. You don't have to leave—"

I gave Jesse a gentle push. "Go, bud. I'll take care of this."

He hurried to the truck, where Alice was standing beside the open door. She tried to give him the front seat, but he shook his head and threw himself into the back. *Good boy*. He remembered his manners, even stressed and exhausted. We'd done a whole lot right with him, tonight notwithstanding.

"Who's that?"

I swiveled back to face Shelby, my chest cracking from the pressure of holding in a nuclear explosion.

"My girlfriend." I lifted my chin, daring her to say something about Alice.

"Isn't that the librarian?" She took a step, like she was heading to the truck to check, but I shook my head, stopping her in her tracks. "I need to know if you're bringing Jesse around someone."

I let out a dry laugh. "Okay, Shel. We're not going to talk about Alice. When you take care of what's going on inside your own house, we can have a conversation." I jabbed my finger toward the open door. "You need to handle that. I know you care about our son, but you're not doing a good job of showing it. Getting a call like that from my boy is unacceptable."

"I told you..." she whispered, clutching her hands to her chest, "I wanted to move so Kent could find work, but you wouldn't allow it. He stayed for us, because he loves us. But he's gotten himself into a bind—"

"Nope." I took a retreating step, fed up. "I'm not interested in Kent. He's a done deal. Jesse will not be in that man's presence again."

"You can't decide that." She reached for me. I gave her outstretched hand a scathing look, and she dropped it to her side. "You're going against our custody agreement. I'll let you take Jesse tonight, but you don't get to decide when he comes back or who he sees when I have him."

I cocked my head. "Don't I? Is that loser in your kitchen worth losing your son over? If you fight me on this, I will take you to court. You'll break Jesse's heart, but I will handle that if I have to."

"Caleb." A wet sob shook her shoulders. "This isn't fair. You can't do this. I love Jesse. You know I do. But I deserve to have a life, and Kent—"

"Kent is dog shit," I bit out. "What kind of trouble is he mixed up in that he comes home with a broken finger and two black eyes? And from the way he was moving, I suspect a few broken ribs too. Who'd he borrow money from? Are you even asking him those questions? Do you care?"

She collapsed into herself like she'd been shot, her arms banding around her middle. "I don't know," she rasped.

"You don't need to know. Get him out of this house—and your life. Jesse's not safe around him, and neither are you. Don't make my boy lose his mother. Don't do that to him, Shel."

I left her with that. What else was there to say?

I had to hope this would be the wake-up call Shelby needed. I didn't want to keep Jesse from her, but I would do what I had to do to protect him.

Even if it was from his own mother.

Jesse was barely awake by the time we got home. Once he hit his room, he crawled into his bed like a mindless zombie. When I went to sit down, though, he scooted over, giving me plenty of room.

I put my hand on top of his head, the same way I'd done since he was born. And he blinked at me with guileless eyes that never failed to make me feel like I had to mold the world into a better place for him.

"You doing all right?"

"Tired." He rubbed his eye, then let his hand fall heavily onto his comforter. "Do you think Alice is okay? In the truck, when we were waiting for you, she told me she was, but I'm kind of embarrassed she had to see all that. She's going to think Mom isn't a good mom, and yeah, I get that, but I don't want her to think that because it isn't true."

I clenched my hand into a fist, biting back my anger. This wasn't something Jesse should have been concerned about, but at the same time, I was proud of him for thinking beyond himself and caring for Alice.

"I'll talk to her, but you know Alice." I took my hand from the top of his head to nudge his chin with my knuckle. "She's one of the smartest, kindest people I know. I can't think of anyone smarter or more kind, can you?"

He solemnly shook his head. "No. I don't think so."

"I'm sure she's worried about you, bud, but she's not judging your mom. Everyone makes mistakes." The words tasted bitter coming out, but he needed me to say them. As furious as I was with Shelby for putting all of us in this position, my kid loved his mom, and there was no way I was going to come between that. Not unless I absolutely had to.

Jesse licked his lips, his eyes drifting to the dim light of his lamp. "What if I'm judging? I mean, a little bit. What if I'm thinking Mom really screwed up?"

"You can think what you want. Tonight was a pretty big shit show, huh?"

He whipped his head back toward me, his eyes bugging. "Yeah. It was a massive shit show."

Chuckling despite myself, I ruffled his hair. "I'll give you a pass on the cussing for one night."

He narrowed his eyes at me. "I was just repeating what you said. Anyway, I'm traumatized. I don't even know what's coming out of my mouth. I can't be held accountable."

I knew he was joking, but there was some truth behind it. Jesse had led a pretty idyllic life. Seeing Kent in that state would have been jarring to anyone, but especially for him.

"Kent will be okay. Once he gets his act together, he'll be all right." I held on to his chin until he gave me his eyes. "You hear me? He's not our responsibility, and you don't need to worry about him. He's out of your life for good."

He swallowed hard, nodding. "I'm glad," he whispered. "Tonight was enough for me."

"Me too." I jerked my head toward the door. "You're drooping fast. Do you want me to get outta here, or would you rather I stay?"

He mulled it over, chewing on his bottom lip. "You're going to be down the hall, right? Alice too?"

"Right," I confirmed. "We'll be close."

"Then I'm fine." He slid his arms under his blanket and sighed. "As long as you and Alice are okay too."

"We are," I lied, leaning forward to kiss his forehead. "Night, Jess. Love you a lot."

"Love you a lot too, Dad."

Alice was waiting for me, but I couldn't bring myself to go to her after I left Jesse. Not feeling the way I was. My blood was filled with fire and regret. Guilt was etched in my bones. My gut was leaden, so heavy, it was all I could do to make it to the couch and fall on my ass.

I wasn't a perfect father, far from a perfect man. But until now, I'd never felt so utterly useless. Doubting every word I'd said to my son. Wondering how I hadn't seen the warning signs and intervened before Jesse witnessed his mother cleaning up her badly beaten boyfriend in her kitchen. And Alice...I'd dragged her into all this along with me.

It killed me.

I raked both hands down my face and let my head fall back against the couch. The silence in the house was deafening. All it did was give room for the voices in my head to get louder.

I shouldn't have let any of this happen. Should've paid closer attention instead of laughing Kent off. Jesse deserved a father who saw trouble coming before it walked through the door, and Alice deserved a man who could keep her out of this mess instead of pulling her into it.

I leaned forward, bracing my elbows on my knees, gripping the back of my neck until my vision swam. Until my lungs ached, and I tasted bile from my roiling gut. This was useless. Wallowing in all the what-ifs was a waste of time.

I shut it all down. Dammed up the flood of thoughts and voices until there was nothing but silence in my head. Because the alternative was breaking open right there on the couch.

Then I'd be no good for anyone.

Chapter Thirty-eight

Alice

CALEB SAT WITH JESSE in his room for a long while. He told me to go to sleep, but that wasn't happening. Not until he was in bed with me, and I could make sure he was okay.

Just when I began to wonder if he'd fallen asleep in Jesse's room, I heard his heavy tread in the hallway, but it was headed in the opposite direction. Toward the living room. Probably checking that the doors were locked and everything was shut down.

But the minutes kept ticking by, and he didn't come back. I sat cross-legged on the edge of his bed, staring at the door, willing it to creak open.

But...

Nothing.

Finally tired of waiting, I padded out to the living room. Caleb sat hunched on the couch, elbows on his knees, staring at nothing. His phone was on the coffee table, his hands hanging loose between his legs. He didn't even flinch when I approached him.

"Caleb?"

His eyes lifted. They were so shadowed looking at him made my chest ache.

I crossed the room and sank down beside him, sliding my hand along his leg. "How's Jesse? Is he okay?"

For a long moment, he didn't answer. When he finally did, his voice was flat, scraped thin. "He'll be fine, but I'm all talked out."

I reached for his hand anyway, lacing my fingers through his, and leaned into him. "Then we don't have to talk. Not right now. Come to bed with me."

He didn't give me a response, only stared past me again. It stung, but I swallowed it down. This wasn't about me. I pressed a kiss to his shoulder, then slipped my hand free and stood. "Okay. I'll be in bed if you change your mind."

I turned toward the hallway, bracing myself for the wrongness of going to bed without him, when I heard him shift behind me. His footsteps followed, slow and plodding. By the time I reached the bedroom, he was with me, stripping off his shirt before sliding beneath the covers without a word.

He let out a long breath and flung his arm over his eyes. "You shouldn't have waited up. I know you're tired."

I slipped into bed with him, rolling to my side and touching his arm. "We're all tired. Let's try to get some sleep. Things always look different in the light of day."

He found my hand under the blankets, brought it to his chest, and sighed. "Then it's good the morning will be here before we know it."

I scooted closer, and he opened his arm so I could rest my head on his shoulder. His skin was warm, his chest rising and falling beneath my cheek in a rhythm I let myself match.

For a long moment, neither of us spoke. The air between us was quiet, the kind that came after a storm, when the dust was still settling and no one quite knew what the daylight would show.

Caleb pressed his lips to my hair and whispered, almost too low to hear, "Stay close to me tonight, Alice."

"I wasn't planning on moving at all," I murmured back, curling tighter into his side.

His grip around me tightened, and finally, with his heartbeat slowing under my ear, I let my eyes close.

Jesse was far more resilient than either of us. By morning, he'd bounced back like nothing ever happened. We had breakfast together, then he was off to go fishing with his grandfather, barely looking back as he ran out the door.

It was plain as day what had happened was weighing heavily on Caleb. He was quiet, even for him, moving around his house like he was underwater. The show he put on for Jesse was almost convincing, but as soon as Jesse was gone, the light behind Caleb's eyes snuffed out.

"When you're ready, I'll drive you home," he said as I finished washing the breakfast dishes.

I put down the last plate I'd been drying and turned to him, my back against the counter. "I'm in no hurry to leave. I still have the clothes your mom let me borrow here. I don't need anything from my house."

He shuffled his socked foot and gazed toward the window behind the sink. "I've got a lot to do around the ranch. Chores I've been putting off. If you stay, you'll be sitting here by yourself. It's better you go home."

My stomach sank like a thousand-pound stone, but I tried one more time. "You don't need a nail holder? You put me to work before. I think I did a pretty good job."

He turned to face me, a trace of a smile curving his lips. "Not today, darlin'."

"Well, I'll hang out here. I don't mind."

"I'll feel bad, thinking about you here by yourself." He cocked his head toward the door. "I'm gonna put my boots on and head outside. Meet me out there when you're ready to go."

He walked right out of the house without another word, and I was utterly breathless. What was happening? He had never once sent me home, and when he left my house, it was only after coming back two or three times for another kiss and promise to see me soon.

Still, I knew he was upset, and he might've needed time to work through it. The ranch was in his blood and bones, so maybe sinking his fingers into the dirt would bring him some solace. This didn't have to mean things were going awry between us. I could give him space.

I just wished walking out to his truck in last night's dress and a pair of flip-flops didn't feel so final.

But logic gave me a nudge, whispering that was my history telling me stories that weren't true. I reminded myself of that when Caleb closed the passenger door without kissing me first, and again when he pulled away from the ranch without checking that I was buckled up like he always did. He had a lot on his mind. None of these jarring changes had to mean something bad.

But the silence filled every corner of the cab until it pressed against my ribs. Caleb kept his eyes on the road, one hand on the wheel, the other resting loose on his thigh. Normally, he would've threaded his fingers through mine, but today, my hand lay empty in my lap.

The miles between the ranch and my house had never felt longer. With each one, the knot in my stomach cinched tighter, an old familiar ache blooming around it. That terrible fear of only being visible when I was useful, forgettable when I wasn't.

When he pulled up to my curb, the engine ticked as it idled. Caleb didn't kick me out of the truck, but he also didn't yank me across the cab to kiss me stupid like he'd done the last time we were in this position.

Give him space. Make it simple for him.

"What if I come back when you're done with your chores, and I cook dinner for you and Jesse?" I asked. "He really liked the pasta I made last time. I think I have all the ingredients. It would be easy to whip up."

Caleb's jaw worked as if the words were stones he had to grind down before he could speak. Finally, he said, "I can't give you an answer right now. I'll call you if we're up for company."

It shouldn't have felt like a door slamming in my face, but it did. When it came to this man, I was tender all the way to my core. Lately, he'd been taking care of my soft places, but it seemed he had too much on his mind to do that today.

"Okay," I whispered. "Let me know when you want to see me again."

With a great sigh, Caleb turned the truck off and hopped out, circling around to my side. He opened my door and held his hand out to me. "Come on, Allie-girl, let's get you inside."

I slipped my hand in his, allowing him to help me out of the truck and walk me to my porch. He took my keys from me, unlocking my door. I held my breath as I waited to see what he'd do next.

Finally, he wrapped his hand around the back of my head and placed a firm kiss on my mouth. It wasn't sweet and gentle. It wasn't passionate and needy either. It was a kiss he'd never given to me before, one I couldn't identify as his.

"I'll talk to you later," he murmured, taking a step away from me.

I almost let him go. My worries and fears nearly won. It would be easier to lock my door and fade away in the shadows of my home until Caleb decided to give me some of his light back. But I didn't want easy. I wanted the life I'd begun to build with this man. Sitting in the dark waiting for him wasn't an option anymore.

"When?"

He jerked, his eyebrows shooting up. "When what?"

"When will you talk to me?"

He dragged a hand through his hair, exhaling hard. "I don't know. I've got work to do, and I need to clear my head. I can't give you a timeline right now. I'm sorry."

So was I. Sorry he couldn't find it in himself to deal with stress without pushing me away. I'd had a lifetime of being shut out when the going got tough. I never thought Caleb would do it to me.

I lifted my chin. "If your intention is to shut me out any time things go wrong, I need you to understand I can't accept that. If you need space, then please take it. Sometimes, I need that too. But it feels like you're pushing me away, and I don't like it."

He started to speak, but I held my hand up. I wasn't finished. If I didn't say what was on my mind, I would let it swallow me up and never find a way to get it out. "You don't have to say anything.

Really, Cay. Go back to the ranch, get your head on right. But please understand, I am not a fish on a hook who will hang out indefinitely. I care for you very much, but how you're acting is making me sad in a way that reminds me far too much of my family."

I patted the center of his chest. "I care for you, Caleb," I repeated. "Take your space, but please don't go so far I can't reach you. I'll miss you."

His hand came up, closing over mine. He brought my fingers to his mouth and kissed them. "I won't go far." He sighed, softer now. "I'll call you tonight, darlin'. Promise."

"Okay." I slipped my hand from his and tucked it behind my back. "I'll see you."

He lingered a second longer, like he might have said more, but the words never came.

I stepped inside, the familiarity of my cozy house wrapping around me. I stood with my hand on the door, but I couldn't bring myself to watch him walk away, so I slowly shut it.

I touched the fingers he'd kissed to my lips, squeezing my eyes closed.

Caleb Kelly was the strongest man I knew. He'd deal with what he needed to, then he'd come around. I just hoped he didn't make me wait too long.

Chapter Thirty-nine

Caleb

I HAD EVERY INTENTION of going back to the ranch and spending the day working hard enough to shut everything else out—to sweat out my worries and bleed my anger. But as I sat in my truck in front of Alice's house, I couldn't bring myself to leave.

I looked down at the book in my hands. The third in the *Shadow of the Isle* series, *Crown of the Sky*. We were almost finished. Fathaniel and Balboa were on the cusp of solving the riddle of the dragon and the stars. Their happy ending was within reach. They'd harnessed the sky and learned how to rewrite the stars. But Fathaniel was still screwing things up, as always. He couldn't stop going off on his own, trying to carry the entire universe on his shoulders, even when he had Balboa right there, ready to be his partner.

I banged my head on my steering wheel, frustration pounding behind my eyes. The parallels between me and the bumbling hero were so on the nose, it wasn't funny. Hell, nothing was funny about the last look Alice had given me. Nearly defeated while still holding out hope I'd get my act together.

I dropped the book onto the passenger seat and sat there for another long minute, gripping the wheel so hard I was surprised it didn't crack. I wasn't going to be a fool like Fathaniel, stumbling alone until it was too late. Not when Alice was willing to walk beside me.

She was delicate on the outside, sure. Small hands that disappeared in mine, a dulcet voice I had to carefully listen to so I didn't miss a word, an easy disposition that made it impossible not to like her. But underneath all that, she was steel. She'd faced challenges that would break someone weaker. But she was still standing, still lovely and curious and brave.

With a muttered curse, I shoved the truck door open and climbed out, rocks crunching beneath my boots. Determination burned hot in my gut as I crossed her yard.

By the time I reached her porch, my heart was thundering in my chest, not from nerves, but the simple, bone-deep truth of what I wanted. A real life with her. One that meant she got the good and the bad, the sunshine and the storms.

I lifted my hand and knocked once. Then again, louder.

The door cracked open, and Alice's wary eyes met mine.

I didn't wait for her to ask why I was there. "I didn't go far," I said, voice rougher than I meant. "I couldn't even start the truck. Let me inside, Alice, so you can put your arms around me while I tell you how sorry I am."

She opened the door wider, revealing her wet hair and a long T-shirt sticking to her skin. What she didn't do was welcome me into her house.

"I have to put my arms around you to get an apology?"

"No. You don't have to do anything. I was hoping you might want to, though."

Her eyes darted between mine, sweeping over my face and down my arms to my hands, before coming back to meet my gaze. Water dripped from her hair onto her shoulders. A cricket chirped somewhere in the grass. A cool breeze broke through some of the early summer heat.

Alice took a breath, stepped back, and opened her arms. My knees nearly buckled with relief when she closed them around me. I curled over her, burying my face in her wet hair, and breathed in the scent of her shampoo.

"Christmas," I rumbled.

"Your favorite."

"Damn right."

I lifted her off her feet and walked into her house, carrying her all the way to the couch. I sat down, Alice tucked in my lap, questioning myself for thinking I needed to go it alone. I already felt a lot better with her in my arms and hers wrapped tight around me.

"I'm sorry, Alice." I laid my forehead on hers. "You were right. Things got heavy, and instead of sharing that, I balked. It was the exact wrong thing to do. I knew it, but I did it anyway. Thank you for calling me out on it. Otherwise, I'd be out on the ranch, by myself and miserable, instead of here with you."

She swatted my shoulder, but there was no force behind it. "You can't do that to me, Cay. Don't do that again."

"I won't. I can't promise I won't screw up in other ways, but not this."

She toyed with the hair at the base of my neck then slid her fingers through the back, cupping my head. "I don't expect or need perfection, honey. I just have to know you need me the way I need you. I can't stand to be made to feel expendable."

"You aren't. There's no world I'm in where I don't require you to be with me. I always want you beside me. *Always.*"

"Except today," she whispered.

"I'm sorry I screwed up and put doubt in your mind, Alice, but I absolutely need you today." I pulled back so she could see me and really hear me. "When I got in my truck, I was looking at our book. Remembering how pissed off I got when I read about Fathaniel making the decision to go off without Balboa to protect her."

She huffed a little laugh. "You said it was bullshit because Balboa is equally as powerful as Fathaniel." Her fingertips grazed my chin. "You were really pissed off."

"Yeah...well, he's an idiot." I shook my head. "Never thought I'd get steamed up about a book, but you gave me that, Alice. You've changed me for the better in a lot of ways, but I'm still me. I'm stubborn to a fault. I get in my head, too internal for my own good. I forget having a conversation would solve a lot of problems."

"I know you're not always going to be in the mood to talk, honey. You don't have to change who you are for me." She trailed her fingers along my jaw, up to my ear. "But please know you can be quiet with me. I want more than anything to be the person you can lean on. It hurt me that you didn't think you could do that. Or that you didn't want to."

"I want to. I want *everything* with you." My next breath was shaky. The one after was a lot more even. "I have this...backbreaking guilt for allowing the Kent situation to carry on as long as it did. Feel like I failed Jesse in a lot of ways. I hate that he saw what he did last night. Hate you saw it too. I'm pissed I had to take him from Shelby, because despite these circumstances, she's been a good mom, and our boy loves the hell out of her. But I don't know if she'll do the right thing, and I'm fearful of what that'll mean for Jesse. I don't want to have to fight her, but I will."

"I hope you don't have to do that, but if it comes down to a fight, I'm in your corner." She cupped the side of my neck and brought her forehead to mine. "Are you in my corner too? I want to be on your team, Cay. We have to be in this together or not at all."

"Don't say that," I growled. "There's no 'not at all' when it comes to us."

"Then don't make me feel that way," she admonished, gentle as a lamb. "It isn't your fault I've been hurt before, and I don't blame you for me being extra sensitive to rejection. But please be aware I am. When I'm pushed away, I'm immediately taken back to a lifetime of being ignored and cast aside unless I had a use, and I don't want to go to that place ever again, especially not with you. I've begun to think of you as my safe place—"

"I am, Alice. You can think of me that way, because I will be that for you. I'm sorry I let you doubt that for even a second."

"I forgive you," she murmured against my temple as she stroked my beard—comforting me when I was the one who'd hurt her. That was who Alice was. It was why I was here, and why I'd never make the mistake of leaving her again. "I know how much you love Jesse, and last night really wrecked you."

"It did," I agreed.

"We'll get him through it." Her lips were a whisper on my cheekbone. "You'll support him, and I'll be your rock, holding you up. Let me be that for you, honey."

I clamped my eyes shut, overwhelmed by wonder. How had I gotten so damn lucky to be able to call this woman mine? I'd never know the answer to that, but I wouldn't forget how fortunate I was that Alice's light was shining upon me when, by all rights, it should have dimmed years ago.

Now that I had it, it was my duty to keep it bright, to huddle around it and shield it from the elements and all the ugliness in the world. To protect it, even from myself if I had to.

I pulled back, so she could see me when I laid out the plans I'd been making for us in my head—so she could look into my eyes and see for herself how completely in I was.

"Allie-girl," I rasped, my throat thick with my feelings for her and all the words I wanted to say rushing to get out at once. I took my time, making sure I explained myself as clearly as possible. She needed to understand what she meant to me.

"Caleb." Her eyes glinted like dew on a leaf catching the morning sun.

"You can't see inside my head."

She let out a breezy laugh. "No, I can't. That's true."

"My meaning is you can't see how I feel about you. I am going to do a better job of telling you. Beginning now."

Her hand found mine on her waist, and she threaded our fingers together. "I'm listening." She tilted her head to give me her ear, and I chuckled. She was so adorable and sweet, I couldn't help it.

"It happened when you were dancing with Bryan at Joy's. This...*implosion* inside me. I hit the ground, on my ass, without ever realizing I'd been falling for a long time." I squeezed her fingers. "To be clear, I mean falling for you, Alice."

She tried to bite back a smile, but it was no use. "I figured, but thank you for clarifying."

"That's the least I can do after mucking about for so damn long."

"Not too long, though." She touched her lips to mine. "It seems to me you were right on time."

"I don't know about that," I muttered, less willing to give myself a pass. "But I do know I keep having that same feeling when I'm with you. I see your smile, or you share an insight about Fathaniel and Balboa, or you make my kid laugh, and I hit the ground again. I didn't know it was possible to fall for someone over and over, but here I am, head over heels for you and still tumbling."

She gasped a sharp breath and shook her head. "Caleb, I—"

"I'm not done yet, so hold on." I slipped my hand from hers to take hold of her chin, tipping it back. "I thought I had a pretty damn perfect life with my boy and my family nearby. You know all too well I didn't see a need to add to it. But I was wrong. The time I've spent with you has only proven how closed off I was. Having you in my house, in my life...you fit. We fit together. You're a piece I wasn't aware I was missing until I had you and everything became so much better. You took my heart in your soft little hands and cracked it wide open."

She blinked at me, catching tiny teardrops in her lashes. Her rosy lips parted, but no words came out. That was all right. I wasn't ready for her to speak yet.

"In my head, I've been planning a future with you. I'm picturing you moving to the ranch by the end of summer. I've got an idea of where we can put your books, and I've looked up plans for shelves I want to build you." Her whimper almost stopped me, but my tongue was loose, and my feelings were a raging river, flowing out of me without any constraints. "I've been thinking of things down the line—not too far—like where we'll have our wedding, and if the kids you and I have will be like Jesse or completely different. When you came to me all those months ago, I couldn't see myself going there, but now that I know you and what it's like to truly have you, it's impossible for me not to want all that with you."

There was more, a lot more, but only one thing needed to be said now. It was the most important part, and since I had her rapt attention, now was the time to tell her.

Holding her chin, I unfurled our hands to stroke along her throat, finding her fluttering pulse. I leaned forward to kiss her there, once then twice. She sucked in a breath, and her pulse jumped. Still, she stayed quiet, giving me the floor.

"The fact is, my sweet Alice, I'm in love with you, and everything I learn about you has me falling deeper. I'm going to do my best to show you that through actions and words. You've always been the brave one, and it's my turn to be that for you."

A whimper was the only warning I got before she dove for my neck, tucking her head beneath my jaw. Her shoulders trembled as she burrowed into me, getting herself as close as she could without finding her way under my skin. I wrapped my arms around her, letting my head fall back on the cushions from the relief of finally freeing the thoughts that had been whipping around inside me like a brewing storm. My mind was calm now, content with Alice knowing exactly how I felt for her, needing nothing from her in return. Not now. Not today.

This was all I needed.

Peace with my girl in my arms.

Chapter Forty

Alice

My mind was a battleground, fighting to accept Caleb was in love with me. Logic knew, understood, and embraced every word he'd shared, but the dark corners of self-doubt tried to shove it away—cloak his love in impossibility, denying it could be true.

He hugged me through it. As my thoughts rushed and clashed within my skull, his embrace never wavered. He didn't demand a response or seem to be put off by my silence. Caleb was patient as ever, relaxed with me tucked in his lap, circled by arms so strong, they were close to breaking through to me.

If he hugged me a little longer...

If his heart stayed steady for a few more beats...

If his chest warmed me enough to melt...

I said the only three words I could: "I'm so tired."

His hum vibrated my cheek. "Didn't sleep well?"

"No, not really."

"I didn't either."

He shifted us on the cushions, never letting me go as he laid us on our sides, his big body spooning around mine. I pressed my cheek against the cradle of his arm and sighed.

"Are you comfortable?"

"Yeah. I'm just right." He smoothed my hair from my face and pulled me closer. "Let's get a little rest, then we'll head back to the ranch."

The tiny ball of tension in my stomach unfurled a little bit more from knowing exactly where we were headed next. "I like the sound of that."

"I do too." He kissed the back of my head. "Close your pretty eyes. I'll be right here when you wake up."

I woke to Caleb's even breathing next to my ear and the deeply comforting rise and fall of his chest against my back. Sometime during my sleep, my shirt had ridden up. His roughened hand rested against the bare skin of my stomach, his thumb drawing slow circles that kept me floating in that hazy place between dreaming and fully waking.

I didn't open my eyes right away. Just let myself soak in the feeling of being cradled in his arms, the heat of his body at my back, the gentle weight of his palm on my stomach.

Turning my head, I found him watching me, his gaze hazy but intent, and wondered if he'd slept at all. "Hi," he mouthed. My lips curved, and I leaned back, brushing a kiss against his mouth. Sleepy, unhurried, giving myself a taste.

He answered with the same slow sweetness, fingers gliding over the curve of my hip, tracing the line of my ribs, trailing along the underside of my breasts. Like maybe he was soaking me up too.

His hand drifted lower, toying with the waistband of my panties before sliding beneath. I sighed into his mouth, our lips brushing more than kissing. But every time we parted, we rushed back together to continue the connection.

His fingers slipped between my thighs, and I draped my leg over his to welcome his touch. He knew me, had learned my body through careful study, and easily found the spot that made me tremble with a slight roll of the pad of his finger.

We kissed in fragments—delicate presses, breaths mingling, the scrape of his jaw against my cheek as he nuzzled close. His fingertips moved without haste, exploring, stroking, circling until pleasure tightened in my belly.

When my release came, it spread through me like winding rivers of heat, my body shaking against his, breath caught in my throat as he held me through every quiver. Caleb kissed my temple, my jaw, the corners of my lips—everywhere he could reach without moving away from me.

Before the shivers faded, he shifted, his hand leaving me only long enough to tug at the barriers of fabric between us. When he returned, his heated skin pressed against mine. I lifted my leg higher, allowing his thick length to slide between my soaked folds. His broad head nudged at my entrance, and I gasped, arching into him. He entered me slowly, filling me until there was no space left between us.

A low groan rumbled from his chest, and he buried his face in my hair. He took his time, holding me close as he slid into me. Stroking my skin. Kissing me everywhere. I let him set the rhythm and gave my body over to him. Because I trusted him and knew he would take us where we both wanted to be.

I reached back to touch his face, our cheeks rubbing together, our mouths finding each other again and again. The world shrank until it was just the two of us, making love on a couch on a sunny afternoon. And what a perfect world it was. I couldn't think of a book or dream that could compare to this.

Caleb began to deepen his thrusts, still unhurried but powerful, every stroke stealing the breath from my lungs. His arm banded across my stomach, holding me snug against him, and I pressed my hand over his as pleasure built and built, until it unraveled.

I trembled around him, shudders rippling through me as he groaned my name into my hair. He thrust once more, twice, then stilled, burying himself deep as his release broke through him in a long, raw sound that seemed torn straight from his chest.

We stayed like that, locked together, as time slid by and our breathing evened out. His lips brushed the back of my neck, light kisses trailing over damp skin, while his hand never left mine.

When he softened and slipped free, I turned in his arms, needing to see him, needing his eyes on me. He looked beautiful. Ruddy cheeks, heavy-lidded eyes, kiss-bitten lips smiling back at me. But it was the way he was looking at me that undid me. If he'd had walls, they'd been demolished, bringing any part he'd been holding back out into the open.

He was mine.

Really mine.

His mouth curved into a smile so sweet it made me ache. Then he said it again. The words I wanted him to write down on a piece of paper so I could feel the infinite weight in my hands.

"I love you."

This time, giving it back to him was as easy as breathing. "I love you too, Caleb." My chin trembled, but my heart was sure. "I wish I could tell you the one moment I knew I had fallen for you, but for me, it would be a list of a thousand little seconds. It'd started that first night, with Hannah, then there were small things you did without a thought, like saying my name when you gave me your order, and bigger things, like the way you love your son and family. Then there were the moments that were only ours. Laughing in bed with you, reading my favorite books and debating the story. You never letting me sit in a chair when your lap is available."

He chuckled. "Doesn't make sense to waste a chair when you fit just right on my lap."

"Yeah. That's a good point." I grinned, the war in my mind finally, mercifully over. "Would you write it down for me?"

"Write what down?"

"The words. That you love me. I want them on paper." I bit down on my lip, wondering if I sounded as foolish as I felt.

"So you can feel them," he supplied.

"Yes." My heart kicked, and my soul rested easy at being understood. "That's it exactly."

"I can do that for you, darlin'. Besides that, I have my mission now: I'm gonna keep adding to your list so it never runs out."

"You just have to exist for that to happen." I slid my fingers through the side of his hair. "You might not have noticed, but I've got a thing for you I can't seem to shake."

"I noticed. I notice everything about you." He dragged his nose along mine. "I've got a thing for you too, and I have no interest in shaking it."

For a while, we stayed there, kissing, grinning, lazing the afternoon away. Eventually, he gave a little groan and nudged his forehead against mine.

"As much as I'd like to keep you here all day, we need to get back to the ranch." He stood and pulled me to my feet, bending to steal one more kiss, then gave my backside a pat. "Pack enough for a few nights. I don't want you out of my sight more than you need to be."

It didn't take long to gather a small bag of clothes and toiletries—everything I needed for the upcoming week. Caleb waited by the door. When I stepped out with my bag, he immediately reached for it, slung it over his shoulder, then his free hand found mine.

I squeezed his fingers as we headed out the door. "Let's go home."

His hand tightened around mine, the barest hitch in his stride as he stopped and stared down at me.

A slow, pleased smile spread across his face.

"Home," he echoed, like he was tasting it. "Yeah, darlin'. Let's go home."

Chapter Forty-one

Caleb

THE THUNDERSTORM HAD TORN through in the early morning hours, hard and fast, leaving behind a sky scraped clean and the ranch in chaos. I bounced along the pasture in the UTV, mud flying from the tires, the smell of damp earth and ozone hanging in the air.

My radio hadn't shut up for hours. Cows were scattered along the ridge, a fence line had flattened on the north side, a yearling bogged down knee deep in mud. Everywhere I looked, my men were spread wide, some on horseback, others on rigs, hollering and whistling as they tried to push the herds back where they belonged.

"Keep pressure on their left flank. Don't let them break again," I directed into my radio, spotting a cluster of steers trying to flee for freedom. Slamming the UTV into gear, I tore across the pasture, cutting them off before they could scatter any more than they already had. A group of hands surrounded them on horseback, driving the cattle back toward the corral.

We'd been at this since daybreak, but there was still nothing but trampled fences, restless animals shifting in the heat, and thick mud as far as the eye could see. Hours of work lay ahead, maybe days before the ranch was fully set to rights.

Sweat burned my eyes. My shirt was plastered to my skin. I swiped my forehead with the back of my hand, taking a moment to sip some water and check the time.

Dammit. I hadn't even noticed how far the morning had slipped away.

I'd had plans that weren't looking like they were going to happen. Jesse was out of school for the summer and spending the day at his buddy's house then the library. I'd been thinking I'd head into town after work, grab Alice and Jesse, and take them out to dinner to celebrate Alice finishing the first draft of her series. At this rate, I wouldn't be back home before dark, only to turn around and start all over again at first light.

I pulled my phone from my pocket and dialed Alice. I hated interrupting her workday, but I was hoping she wouldn't mind hearing from me too much.

"Hey, Cay," she answered.

"Hello, darlin'. Are you having a good day?"

"It's fine. Quiet right now. I was looking up new recipes I might make for dinner. I'm going to run them by Jesse when he gets here."

Despite my exhaustion, I grinned. "Not by me?"

"Nope. We both know you'll eat anything I cook."

I chuckled. "That's because you're so good at it. Hope you know I appreciate you."

"I do know that. Now tell me what's going on there. I can hear the tension in your voice."

For a second, I let my eyes close so I could picture my Alice sitting in her small office, her hair swept up, held in place by a couple pens. I'd been gone before she'd gotten dressed this morning, but in my head, she was wearing her lavender sundress, a cream cardigan covering her shoulders and arms. Her desk was neat as a pin except for the stack of books she'd pulled aside to bring home. They'd be on my nightstand this evening, then replaced with a fresh stack by the end of next week when she read them all.

Just picturing her did a world of good to ease the knots in my neck and the pounding in my skull. Knowing I'd be coming home to her this evening would get me through the rest of the backbreaking work ahead.

"We've been going nonstop. A couple miles of fence got knocked out by the storm and the herd got spooked. We're moving as quickly as we can, but it feels like I've put out ten fires and there's still twenty more waiting."

Alice's concern was as sweet as honey. "I'm sorry, Cay. That sounds brutal."

"It is," I admitted, dragging my hand across my jaw. "But it's the job. I just hate it landed today, of all days."

"Why's today so bad?"

I took another swig of water, letting it soothe a path down my throat. "I wanted to take you out to celebrate, darlin'. It's not every day you finish writing three books." My voice dropped, rough with fatigue and guilt.

"That is very sweet of you. What if Jesse and I pick one of the recipes I bookmarked and buy the groceries we need to make it? We'll still celebrate, just in a different way than you were expecting. You can take us out when things settle."

I let out a long breath, some of the pressure easing from my chest. "Thank you, love. I don't know what I'd do without you."

"You won't ever find out. I can't shake you, remember?"

The corners of my mouth tugged into a tired smile. "I'd never forget. You know I'd be lost without you."

"Love you, honey."

I closed my eyes, letting that sink in. I was still getting used to hearing her say it, and it was never not a gift. "I love you too. See you tonight."

As soon as I hung up, my radio crackled to life again.

Break over. It was time to get back to work. At least I could do it with a clear head, knowing Alice and Jesse would take care of each other while I couldn't be there.

Chapter Forty-two

Alice

THE SECOND JESSE BUCKLED into the passenger seat of my car, he hit me with a request. "Can we stop by my mom's house? I need a couple things from my room I forgot to pack."

My hands froze midair on their way to the steering wheel. I hadn't expected that, and I didn't quite know how to respond. Since Caleb had picked him up in the middle of the night more than a week ago, Jesse had only seen Shelby once for dinner. The rest of their contact had been short phone calls. He wasn't ready to stay overnight at her place, and thankfully, she hadn't pushed.

"I should run that by your dad," I finally replied. "One second."

I pulled out my phone and called Caleb. It rang and rang, but he didn't pick up. I knew he was busy, and sometimes his phone was out of range at far corners of the ranch, but I tried one more time before giving up.

"I think he's still really busy from the storm," I told Jesse.

He pressed his hands together under his chin. "Please, Alice? I have to have my robotics binder. Sunny and I need to do some planning for next year, and I can't unless I have my binder. I swear, it'll only take a second."

Unease prickled the back of my neck, but it was difficult to turn him down. I didn't think Caleb would have a problem with Jesse stopping by his mom's house, but I wasn't sure I should have been making those kinds of decisions without running them by him first.

If it was only for a second, though, what could be the harm?

"Okay." I sighed, still unsure I was making the right move. "Let's make it quick. We still have to stop by the Grocery Barn."

"*Yes.*" He pumped his fist. "Thank you, thank you, thank you. You're the best, and I promise to be fast."

Jesse seemed as jittery as I was on the drive to his mom's house. His knees were bouncing, and he chattered nonstop.

"Hey, do you know what I heard?"

I glanced at him. "Tell me."

"There's a professor at Savage U who teaches a class on *Shadow of the Isle*. Did you take it when you went there?"

"No, sadly I didn't." I flipped on my blinker before turning down Shelby's road. "That's the one thing I regret about college. Professor Astor's class filled up so fast I was never able to sign up for it."

"If I go there, I'm definitely taking that class." He crinkled his nose. "I mean, if he's still alive. He's got to be pretty old."

I laughed. "I don't think he's *that* old. I'm pretty sure he's younger than your grandparents."

"Yeah...well, they're kind of old." He perked up when his house came into view. "We're here."

"We are." I pulled up to the curb, my gut churning. "In and out, right?"

"Right." He put his hand on the door handle but didn't get out. "Hey...um, do you think you could come in with me? I know it might be weird, but—"

I squeezed his shoulder. "Of course I will." I was almost certain Caleb would prefer it, even though he would never ask it of me. I was more than willing to be uncomfortable if it meant making sure Jesse was okay.

Jesse led the way to the front door, which swung open before we got there. Shelby stood in the doorway, drinking in the sight of her son like she had been parched for ages.

"Hi, Mom."

She reached out and ruffled his hair. "Hey, Jess. This is unexpected."

He shuffled his feet on the porch, his hands deep in his pockets. "I need some stuff from my room. Alice drove me here from the library."

Shelby's gaze jerked toward me, and she smiled stiffly. "That was nice of her." Then she moved to the side. "Go ahead and grab what you need."

Jesse darted by her, leaving us standing there in tense silence. I searched for something to say, but I didn't really know Shelby, and I couldn't think of anything besides commenting on the weather.

Thankfully, Shelby swept her arm out. "Well, come in. I know my son. He's never been fast in his life."

I stepped into her house and immediately got tangled up in a pile of bags inside the door. As I braced myself to eat the floor, Shelby caught my arms, keeping me upright.

"Oh shoot, I'm so sorry." She made sure I was steady before letting go. "My house isn't usually such a mess. This is the last of *his* shit. He's supposed to be picking it up soon, but I don't know when 'soon' is."

Shelby glared at the bags, like they'd personally affronted her. I guessed in a way they had. Kent's stuff lingering meant he still had a connection to her, and Jesse wouldn't feel comfortable returning.

I didn't know what I would have done in her shoes, so I certainly couldn't blame her. At least she was trying to set things right.

When she looked up at me, I offered her a tight smile.

"Your house is really cute." I looked around her tidy living room. Everything was cream or brown, but her walls exploded with color. "Your art is fantastic. The piece above your sofa is gorgeous."

"Isn't it? Would you believe I found it at a yard sale?"

I gasped. "Wow. The most luck I've had at yard sales is my collection of vintage Harlequin Romances."

She barked a laugh. "Oh man. My mother used to read those. The covers, *shoo*." She fanned her face with her hand.

"They don't make them like they used to, that's for sure." I tucked my hands in the pockets of my cardigan. "Though we do have a pretty nice selection at the library."

"Yeah?" Shelby ran her hand over her ponytail. "I should stop in. It's been a while since I've read a good romance."

"You should," I agreed.

Silence beat down on us again. Shelby yelled for Jesse to hurry it up, and he hollered he was almost done. Then she turned back to me, offering a smile that didn't quite ring true—especially not when she was wringing her hands and shifting back and forth on her feet.

"I'm really embarrassed," she said, barely above a whisper. "You must think I'm a terrible mother."

"I don't think that at all."

She huffed and looked away. "Well, I do. If Caleb hadn't shown up here that night and knocked some sense into me, I can't honestly tell you I would have kicked Kent out. I'm just...tired of being alone, and I guess having *him* seemed like a better option than no one. What kind of mother thinks that?"

I shook my head. "I don't know. I've never been a mother. But Jesse is wonderful, and he didn't get that way by accident."

She swiped the back of her hand across her eyes. "He's got the Kellys, you know? I mean, I think he's happy when he's here, but he can't wait to get back to the ranch. Who wouldn't want that? All that land, the big house, the family. I can't compete." She held up her hand to stop me from speaking, though I wasn't sure what to say anyway. "I know it's not a competition. I *know* that. But sometimes it's hard not to feel that way."

Thank goodness for Jesse. He came skidding down the hallway, a big duffel bag flung over his shoulder.

"Okay, I'm ready. I think I have everything."

Shelby held out her arms. "Come here, baby. I haven't gotten enough hugs from you lately. It sucks."

The corners of his mouth trembled as he went to his mom, dropping his bag at their feet. She reeled him in, and he let her, his cheek on her shoulder. Her sigh of relief when he was in her arms made my chest ache, and Jesse's expression of contentment sent me on a Tilt-A-Whirl. If I ever doubted Shelby, it had been laid to rest. She'd made a mistake, but she loved her son. I had faith she'd do all she could to get him back.

He pulled away first, his hands going to his hips. "I almost forgot. Tomorrow's trash day. I have to take the can out to the curb."

Shelby raked her hand down the back of his head. "You don't need to do that. I can handle it."

He shook his head firmly. "No way. That's my job. I'll take care of it." Then he disappeared into the kitchen. A moment later, he was heading out to the garage, the bag of trash over his shoulder.

I raised a brow at Shelby. "That's a boy who adores his mother."

"Yeah." She exhaled slowly, some of the tightness in her shoulders easing. "Thanks for being cool, Alice. I should have known you would be. Caleb's been single for most of Jesse's life. *He* wouldn't bring in anyone who'd make a mess of things."

Once again, I was stumped for a response. But Shelby was a talker, so she continued without me needing to say a word.

"I guess Caleb finding you gives me hope. I mean, you've been in town for years, right under his nose. Maybe there's some decent guy around here I've never noticed." Then she groaned. "Well, I'm not going to think about that now. My most recent ex's things are still by my door. Let me get done with one mess before I dive into another."

I let out an uncomfortable laugh. "That's probably a good idea."

A loud bang, quickly followed by the shriek of tires, made us both jump. Shelby and I froze for a beat, eyes darting to each other, then we ran for the front window.

A dark car fishtailed down the street, its engine roaring, smoke curling up from the tires. I didn't quite understand what I was seeing, but my stomach dropped to the floor.

"Jesse," Shelby cried.

I craned my neck, desperate for a glimpse of him. The overturned trash can lay on its side in the driveway, its contents spilling into the street. But Jesse wasn't there.

Oh god.

"Kent!" Shelby's voice cracked then rose into a furious snarl. "That son of a bitch." She spun on her heel and tore for the door, her face twisted in rage.

"Shelby, wait. Was that Kent's car? Did he take Jesse?" I scrambled after her. "We have to call the police...Caleb..."

She wasn't listening. She was already fumbling her keys from her pocket, throwing herself into the driver's seat of her car.

Panic clutched me. I didn't know what the right move was. If I let her leave alone, who knew what she'd do? She was in such a state, she might drive right off the road, and I'd never be able to live with myself.

I yanked open the passenger door and slid in beside her. "I'm coming with you."

The engine roared to life. Shelby's knuckles were white on the steering wheel, her jaw set like iron.

"Hang on tight," she growled.

This time, the squealing tires were hers as she peeled out after Kent.

Chapter Forty-three

Alice

THE WORLD BLURRED PAST in streaks of asphalt and dust. Shelby had both hands welded to the wheel, her jaw clenched, eyes locked on the empty stretch of road ahead. The dial on the speedometer spun all the way to the left and shook as she pressed the pedal to the metal.

My hands were slick around my phone. I pressed redial again, holding my breath through every ring. Straight to voicemail. Caleb still wasn't picking up.

"Come on, come on," I muttered, hanging up and trying again. Nothing. He must've been on some far corner of the ranch without reception. That was the only reason he wouldn't answer his phone, especially when he knew I was with Jesse.

Between attempts, I shot Shelby a look, hoping by talking to her, I could calm her enough so we didn't end up in a ditch. "Do you know where he's taking Jesse?"

Her knuckles whitened further on the steering wheel. "It has to be the damn fishing cabin." Her voice trembled, but it wasn't fear. Shelby was *angry*. Furious. "He's been crashing there since I threw him out. He has nowhere else to go."

"Where exactly is it?"

"On Elkhorn Lake. It's a rotted-out piece of shit." Shelby leaned forward over the wheel like sheer willpower could make the car go faster. "If he lays a hand on my boy—" Her voice broke. "I'll kill him, Alice. I swear to God I'll kill him."

"He won't. We're not far behind him. We'll get to him." I was telling myself this as much as I was her. It had to be true. Kent was nowhere in sight, but there was no way we were more than two minutes behind him. We'd get there in time. Jesse would be fine, and I'd bring him home to Caleb.

I hit redial again, but there was no answer. With shaking fingers, I switched to the keypad and dialed 911.

When the dispatcher answered, I gave them every detail I had, which wasn't much. We were told to pull over and wait for the police, but I didn't relay that message to Shelby. There was no way she would take it well or comply.

"They're sending someone," I told Shelby, my voice thin.

"That's good." Her jaw went rigid as she glared at the road in front of us. "Don't ask me to stop. One day, when you have kids, you'll understand why I can't do that. I have to get him back."

"I'm not going to ask you to stop," I said as calmly as I could. "Please just be careful. You won't be any good to Jesse if you crash this car, okay?"

Her hands tightened on the steering wheel as she sucked in a ragged breath. Then she let it out slowly and nodded. "I'm fine, Alice. Just hang on."

That was all I could do. Hang on and keep dialing Caleb.

Shelby's nostrils flared. "He's not picking up?"

"No. I think he's out of pocket. Some cattle escaped because of the storm—"

"Right. Call Bill. He'll get on the radio, let Caleb know what's going on."

"Bill?" I hadn't thought of Caleb's right-hand man. Even if I had, I had no way of contacting him.

"His number's in my phone." She picked it up from the center console and tossed it to me. "Bill will find Caleb."

She was right. As soon as I spoke to Bill, he promised he'd track Caleb down. He didn't ask many questions, and that was good, because my jaw was shaking so hard, it was difficult for me to speak. My heart was lodged in my throat, and my teeth wouldn't stop chattering.

I was a little bit of a mess, but Shelby was like steel. Her anger at Kent drove her forward and love for Jesse kept her steady.

We turned down a narrow road, and the blacktop gave way to gravel, then dirt, the car fishtailing as Shelby jerked the wheel hard. Dust billowed in our wake, sunlight flashing through the trees until the road opened to a small lake covered in scum.

A few shacks sat slumped along the shoreline, their tin roofs rusted and sagging. Kent's car was parked crooked in the dirt, and he was standing at the trunk.

Shelby slammed to a stop right behind him, and he spun around, eyes wide in surprise.

Shelby was already out of the car. She yanked open the back door, grabbed a rusted tire iron from the floorboard, and charged forward with a guttural sound more animal than human.

"Shelby!" I cried, scrambling after her, but my voice was nothing against her rage.

Her first swing crashed into the side of the trunk with a metallic clang. Kent stumbled back, throwing his arms over his face.

"Where's my son?" Shelby's demand ripped through the hot, heavy air. The tire iron came down again, splintering his brake light.

"I'm sorry." Kent's voice cracked, his back hitting the car as he cowered, hands trembling in front of him. "Shelby, I'm sorry. I wasn't gonna hurt him, I—"

"Don't say my name!" She swung again, and her aim was true. Kent screeched as the iron slammed into his bicep, and Shelby's whole body shook. "Give me my boy back!"

"I just needed some money," he tried. "Then I was going to bring him back. I swear it."

I stood a few feet away, my phone limp in my hand. Maybe I should have tried to stop Shelby when she raised the tire iron to hit him again, but...I didn't want to. This man had taken Jesse. When he fell onto the ground, yowling in pain, I could only think he deserved exactly what he was getting.

And still, my pulse thundered with the only words I couldn't let myself speak out loud.

Where is Jesse?

The thought hadn't even finished forming when a faint, muffled thump came from the car.

My breath caught. I shouldn't have even been able to hear it. Not between Shelby yelling and Kent's begging, but I had. There was no denying the second thump.

I darted around Shelby, past Kent's pathetic whimpering, and yanked open the driver's door. My fingers fumbled across the dash until they found the trunk release. With a sharp click, the lid popped.

"Jesse," I cried, rushing to the back.

Shelby froze midswing, her eyes snapping to me then the open trunk. She dropped the tire iron with a clatter and lunged forward.

There he was. Our sweet boy, curled up in the dark, his face streaked with tears.

"Mom!" Jesse's scared, broken sob cut me in two.

Shelby had him out of the trunk and in her arms in the blink of an eye. Her fury melted into raw, desperate love. Jesse was almost as tall as her, but she held him to her chest and rocked him like a baby as he clung to her, her own tears pouring down.

"I've got you, baby. I've got you. I'm here." Between comforting murmurs, she kissed his hair and promised he was safe.

Kent was a sniveling heap in the dirt, clutching his arm, muttering apologies no one wanted to hear. If I'd had it in me, I would have kicked him for good measure, but all I could do was stagger back until my shoulder hit the hot metal of his car. My legs were close to giving out as adrenaline fled my body. Leaning there, I let my own tears spill, quiet and unstoppable, my chest heaving as the terror drained out of me.

Jesse was safe. That was all that mattered.

Then, faint at first, the wail of sirens drifting over the lake got louder as they drew near.

Help was coming, but my chest was still achy and hollow. There was only one thing that would make it better.

I needed Caleb.

Chapter Forty-four

Caleb

I WIPED SWEAT FROM my brow, urging my UTV through the far pasture, scanning the fence line for stragglers. Cattle still wandered loose, and every second I was out here felt like chasing shadows. It was an exercise in frustration, and I was about ready to throw in the towel for the day.

From nowhere, Bill's truck came barreling over the ridge in a plume of dust, sending me on high alert. He never drove like that unless something was wrong.

I braked hard as he slid to a stop beside me and jumped down before the engine cut off, his face ashen under the brim of his hat. "Caleb...I don't know how to tell you this. Jesse's been taken. Seems Shelby's man, Kent, has him."

The world tilted sideways. For a second, I couldn't breathe. "What? Explain."

More information rolled out of him in short, frantic bursts. "Alice called me when she couldn't get in touch with you. She's with Shelby. They're following Kent. Shelby thinks he's headed toward Elkhorn Lake. Sheriff's on the way—"

I didn't hear the rest. My hands were already on the wheel, my boot slamming the pedal to the floor. The UTV lurched forward, engine growling, tires spitting dirt.

My boy. My son. Jesse.

The words pounded through my skull in rhythm with my heartbeat. All I could see was his face. All I could feel was the terror clawing at my chest. I pushed harder, faster, the machine bucking beneath me as I tore across the fields, cutting every corner I could.

Hang on, Jess. Just hang on. Your dad's coming, kid.

I was halfway across the last pasture when a mare bolted out of the tree line, wild-eyed and spooked.

"Shit—" I jerked the wheel hard. Too hard.

I skidded sideways, caught the edge of a rut, and tipped. The world snapped into chaos, the sky and earth flipping in a blur. My shoulder slammed against the roll bar, air punched from my lungs, then nothing but the violent tumble and the roar in my ears.

When the UTV finally crashed to a stop, silence rushed in, broken only by the ringing in my skull and distant rumble of Bill's engine. I tried to move, but white-hot pain lanced through my chest. Black danced at the edges of my vision, and hot copper filled my mouth.

Jesse.

That was my last thought before it all dimmed then faded to nothing.

Chapter Forty-five

Caleb

"Jesse!"

I tried to knife upright, but my body betrayed me. Muscles seized, fire streaked through my chest, and I collapsed back onto something too soft to make sense.

Where the hell—?

A hand pressed down on my shoulder, gentle but firm. Cool fingers skimmed my temple, comforting in my confusion.

What was happening?

I fought to push up again, but something sharp and tight tugged at my chest, and the hand on my shoulder pushed me back down. I struggled against it, but only for a moment.

"Jesse's safe."

Her voice in my ear.

My sweet Alice.

She was here beside me.

My boy was safe.

The fight bled out of me. I let go, sinking into the dark warmth of her nearness.

For now, I could rest.

Jesse.

My eyes snapped open as my heart thundered in my ears. Darkness pressed in on all sides. A lone green light blinked somewhere above me. A thin bar of yellow glowed near the floor.

"Where..." My throat was made of sandpaper, so raw, pushing out words was an exercise in pain. "Where am I?"

Shadows moved beside me, delicate taps on the floor. Then light, too bright for my tired eyes. I flinched, blinking against the glare, until a shape leaned over me, blocking it out.

"Caleb?" Her face came into focus, piece by piece. Her worried eyes. Her flushed cheeks. Her bitten lips. "Are you awake, honey?"

"Alice." I reached up, my arm traveling through thick mud to get to her. "You're here."

"Of course I am." She caught my hand, bringing it down to my side. "Let's get you something to drink."

She put a straw to my lips, and I drank like it'd been years since I'd had a drop of water. Hell, maybe it had. I couldn't say I knew the day or where I was. Just that Alice was here with me and my boy was safe, which meant all was right in my world.

"There you go," she murmured. "Do you want more?"

I let go of the straw and shook my head. "I feel like shit."

"Yeah." She put down the cup and brushed my hair off my forehead. "You had an accident. Do you remember?"

"I don't know." There was something on the edge of my memory, but I couldn't quite grab it. "Everything's fuzzy."

"That's the pain medication." She dragged her fingers through my hair, slow and drugging, lulling me into a state between awake and asleep. "It'll wear off once you get some sleep."

"You're going to stay."

It wasn't a question. I didn't want to give her a choice. I needed Alice here. If she left, I'd surely be lost.

"I'm staying, Cay. Always. I'll be here when you wake up."

"Come lie with me." I patted the bed next to me. There wasn't a lot of room, but she could lie on me. I'd prefer it.

"Are you sure?"

I gave her hand a tug. "Come're, darlin'. Give me a cuddle."

Soon, her familiar weight settled beside me. Feeling so right against me, I couldn't fight the pull of sleep.

I woke to my father's lined face hovering over mine. "What the hell?"

"You're awake," he gruffed, his frown deepening.

"Seems like it." I blinked a few times, clearing the sleep out of my eyes. "I'm in the hospital."

"You sure are. Banged yourself up good. Your meds have probably worn off. Are you hurting?"

It took me all of a second to assess my condition. "My chest...my ribs. Christ, did I break one?"

"Try three. Scraped the hell out of your chest too." He gave my shoulder a gentle pat. "You're gonna have to take it easy for a while, bud."

I couldn't argue that. Getting up out of this bed sounded like the last thing I wanted to do. As my head cleared and I fully woke up, memories of how I'd gotten here came flooding back.

I jerked, my eyes going wide with panic. "Jesse? Where is he?"

"He's fine. Shelby's with him at your house. That was where he wanted to be." He shook his head, the line between his brows a bolt of lightning. "He got scared, but he's not hurt. Can't say the same for Kent."

The door swung open before he could elaborate, and in walked one of the most beautiful sights I'd ever seen. My mother and Alice, arm in arm, their heads together. Alice was smiling, my mother laughing. And like she knew I was watching her, Alice's eyes found mine.

Without a beat of hesitation, she broke off and ran to my bed. Her hands flew to my face, holding it as she looked me over. I let her examine me for as long as she needed to. When her eyes finally met mine again, they were filled with tears,

"You only look a little worse for wear," she rasped.

I curled my fingers around her wrist. "What are you doing here, darlin'? You hate hospitals."

Bending over me, she brushed her lips across my cheek. "I still hate them, but I couldn't let you wake up alone, honey."

It hurt, the way my heart swelled inside my chest. This woman—*my* woman—who'd woken up screaming in terror in this very building a few months ago, had set it all aside to be with me. Because she couldn't stand the thought of me being by myself like she'd been too many times. I'd never been loved so damn well.

I'd already been a goner for her, but this? Oh, I was never letting her go. She was stuck with me for life.

My mother wrapped her arm around Alice's waist. "She's been with you all night, Cay. I'd only just convinced her to take a walk with me to get a bite to eat. It makes sense your stubborn self would decide to wake up when she was out of the room."

I closed my eyes as I bit back a laugh. "Jesus, don't make me laugh when I have three broken ribs."

My dad rumbled from my other side. "Maybe that'll teach you not to drive like a maniac. You scared the hell out of us."

I turned my head to look at him. "Then you know why I was driving that way."

We exchanged a long, loaded look. I had a feeling he'd probably driven much the same way to get to me when he'd been alerted to my accident. There wasn't anything that would keep me from trying to get to my boy, and he understood that all too well. After all, he'd been the one to shape me into the kind of father I was.

Finally, he nodded with understanding. "I get it. Doesn't mean I approve."

"Well, like you said, I'll be taking it easy for a while."

Alice's cool fingers stroked my jaw. "And I'll make sure you do."

I turned my head to kiss her hand. "Darlin'...I'm so damn sorry I didn't answer your call."

"I know you would have if you could've."

My mother gave Alice's waist a shake. "She and Shelby took care of business. Not that I condone them chasing Kent down, but...well, the result was glorious."

I blinked at her then Alice. "You...chased him down?"

Alice's cheeks went rosy. "Shelby did. I was just the passenger. And when we caught up with them, she sort of...beat the living daylights out of Kent with a tire iron."

I blinked even harder. "A tire iron?"

My dad took over. "I suspect he's in even more pain than you. Shel managed to fracture several ribs, his arm and hand."

"Mmmhmm," my mother agreed. "I'm certain he's in a world of regret right now. He should have just handed himself over to his loan sharks."

"Shelby was really mad," Alice added. "*Really* mad."

I stared at Alice, at the blush creeping up her cheeks, then at my mom, who looked downright smug. For a man laid up in a hospital bed with three busted ribs, I'd never felt more like laughing.

A tire iron. Damn. Leave it to Shelby.

"Never get between a boy and his mom," I rasped, the corner of my mouth tugging upward despite the ache.

"You're not wrong," Dad said, his lips twitching.

Alice smoothed my hair back from my forehead and eyed my expression. "Don't you dare laugh, Cay. You'll tear something."

I caught her fingers in mine, holding tight. "I'm trying not to, darlin'. I'm just...I guess I'm feeling grateful. My boy's safe. Shelby handled Kent. And you—" My voice went rough as I pulled her hand to my lips. "You're here."

She dipped down, her hair brushing my face, her lips grazing my temple. "Where else would I be?"

I shut my eyes, sinking into her touch. "Nowhere but here with me."

Chapter Forty-six

Alice

DRAGGING A MAN CALEB'S size wasn't easy, but I somehow managed. Jesse would have died of mortification if I hadn't. As it was, we were the last parents to leave. Even Shelby had driven away before us.

I understood why he was having a hard time leaving Jesse after everything. He'd spent the last few weeks watching him like a hawk, searching for signs of trauma.

As always, Jesse was resilient. He had three sessions with a therapist, but when it came time for the fourth, he'd asked if he could skip it. Through it all, the one thing he'd been most concerned about was his mom. Once assured she wasn't going to get in trouble for injuring Kent, he was ready to move on.

It was taking Caleb a little longer. I wasn't sure he'd ever get over not being there when Jesse was taken, even though it had been out of his control. It didn't help that he hadn't been able to work the way he was used to. He hadn't been on horseback since his accident, and his dad and Bill were keeping a close eye on him, ensuring he took it easy. That left him with far too much time to ruminate over how things *could* have turned out.

Two weeks ago, I'd gently shoved him toward setting up a therapy appointment. He'd agreed more easily than I'd thought, but I suspected he'd been struggling even more than I'd seen. It was hard for Caleb not to be the strongest person in the room. Fortunately, he was learning to lean on me.

When we reached Caleb's truck, he looked back at the dorm, a frown tugging heavily on his mouth. "I think he might've forgotten toothpaste. I better go back and check—"

"Caleb"—I squeezed his hand—"he has toothpaste. And if he needs anything, he can borrow from a friend or call us and let us know."

His mouth flattened into a hard line, but I could read the conflict warring behind his gaze like an open book.

I pushed up on my toes and looped my arms around his neck, finally gaining his attention. "Remember how excited he was this morning?"

He seemed like he wanted to argue with me, but he let out a heavy exhale and nodded. "Kid woke up at six without prompting. He couldn't wait to get here."

"That's right." I kissed his chin since his lips were out of my reach. "Did you see the look on his face when he met his roommate?"

That earned me a chuckle as he tugged me against his chest. "They started speaking technology the minute Jess walked into the room." He quickly sobered. "He's happy today, but I'm not convinced letting him come was the right decision."

"You'd have broken his heart if you'd denied him this. You know that, honey."

His brow dropped low. "I know. I do. But I'm worried about him, Allie. How do I get on with my life for the next four weeks when I can't kick this gnawing anxiety? Hell, I'm not sure how I'm going to get in my truck and drive us back to Sugar Brush."

"Well, you might like my surprise."

"Surprise?"

I kissed his chin again, then he dipped his head so I could lay another on his lips. "We're staying in Laramie for the weekend. I booked us a room close to campus, so if Jesse happens to need anything or changes his mind about staying, we can come right back and get him."

Jesse wasn't going to need us. That much I knew. We were staying close strictly for Caleb. Maybe a little for me too. I still hadn't been able to wipe away the sight of him curled up in that trunk. And I would miss having him close by like crazy.

"Alice." My name left Caleb like a great gust of wind, and his forehead fell to mine. "Did you really?"

"Mmmhmm. I did. Is that okay?"

"More than." He reached around me to open the passenger door, then lifted me up and placed me sideways on the seat. He stood between my knees, looking down at me with a mystified expression. "I wish I was better with words. There's gotta be something more beautiful than saying 'I love you' over and over. If I were Fathaniel, I'd rewrite the stars to make the world better for you. I'd hatch you your very own dragon so you'd never be alone and have a protector always. But I'm just me, so I'll tell you I love the hell out of you, Alice. You make every day better and brighter, and I never want to be without you."

A wet little laugh burst out of me. "I don't know, Cay, I think you're pretty good with words. But just so you know, I will never get tired of you telling me you love me, no matter how many times you say it."

"I do love you, darlin'." He reached into his pocket, pulled out a scrap of paper, and put it in my hand. "Add that to your collection."

I already knew what it said, but I looked at it anyway. In blue pen, in Caleb's neat writing, were the words, "I love you." It was heavier than a piece of paper ripped from the corner of a bill should have been, like the depth of Caleb's feelings for me had been imbued in the ink.

Looking up, I grinned at him, even as my heart did somersaults. "You know, I only asked you for one of these."

He'd already given me at least a hundred. I kept them in a wooden box on my dresser. It was so heavy from all the tiny pieces of paper inside, I feared it might fall through the floor.

"Want me to stop?"

"Never, ever." I took his hand in mine and clutched it to my chest. "I love you too, Caleb."

His chest rumbled with satisfaction. "Can't shake me, darlin'."

That was a fact. I would never get over Caleb Kelly.

And I'd never try.

Epilogue
Caleb

One Year Later

I RAN MY THUMB over Alice's ring as I held her left hand in mine. It was a habit I'd picked up the moment I'd slipped it on her finger last fall. When I'd added another ring to it at our wedding in the spring, I liked it even better.

"You could tell me where you're taking me any time now," she said, without even a hint of impatience.

But that was who Alice was. Her well of patience was bottomless—lucky for me. If she'd given up on me, we wouldn't be here, married and finally having our honeymoon in California three months later. There were reasons for the delay, like ranch business and Phoebe giving birth to our first niece, and the other reasons...well, she'd be finding out soon.

I sat down on the end of the hotel bed, took her by the hips, and pressed my face to her stomach. "Then it wouldn't be a surprise, would it?"

"You do have a point." She stood between my legs, her arms around my shoulders, stroking a path down my back.

I kissed the bump below her belly button before resting my cheek against her. "I like the feel of you, darlin'."

"He's getting big already. I'm a little nervous you'll have to roll me everywhere by the end."

I tipped my head back to look at my wife. She didn't look nervous at all, not with the dreamy smile on her lips.

"I think I have a wheelbarrow you'll fit in," I teased.

My favorite breezy laugh burst out of her. "If this guy is as big as Shelby said Jesse was, it might come down to that."

I gave her belly another kiss. "If it does, I'll toss in a few pillows for you. You'll ride in style."

We'd gotten a little bit of a head start at growing our family. Seeing Phoebe and Deacon welcome their daughter, Abigail Joy Slater, and Hannah and Remi, pregnant with their second, had spurred us on. Alice had tossed out her birth control pills a couple months before our wedding, and *boom*, she fell pregnant. Four months along with our son, she was more gorgeous than ever.

We'd taken our time to begin our journey, but now we were full steam ahead. Married, growing our family, taking our life by the horns and living the hell out of it. We'd had a lot to move on from, but we'd done it.

The piece of shit who'd hurt Alice was in jail. It wouldn't be nearly long enough, but that was the way of things. There wasn't any amount of time that would satisfy me. The same went for Kent. He'd be in prison a whole lot longer, and I imagined a guy like him wouldn't have an easy go of it. Whatever he got was nothing less than he deserved.

But those things were in the past. I'd done some time in therapy to help me deal with the anger and anxiety almost losing my boy had caused me. Talking it out had done me a world of good. Time and Alice's steady, supportive presence had done the most to bring me back to myself, though.

Christ, there was no one better than Alice. She was...*everything*.

A part of me would always regret not noticing her earlier, but it was getting easier to push those thoughts to the background now that we were headed in the direction we were supposed to. I'd never know if we would have worked out had I paid attention to her when she'd first come to town. I just knew we were right for the versions of who we were now. Exactly right.

I rose to my feet and touched my lips to her temple. "Think it's about time to get out of here. Are you ready?"

She practically bounced on her toes. "You know I am. I can barely stand still."

Chuckling, I pulled her into my arms. "Love you a lot, darlin'."

She nuzzled against my chest. "I love you too, honey." Then she gave me a kitten shove. "Now stop delaying and show me my surprise."

Alice didn't ask questions, even as our driver meandered through the campus of Savage University. But I could feel her vibrating beside me. I wasn't sure she'd figured out where I was taking her, but she was excited, nonetheless.

The car stopped in front of Whitlock Hall. I opened the door and slid out, then helped Alice out behind me. Her eyes were bright as she looked around, taking everything in.

"This was one of the reasons we had to delay our honeymoon," I said as I led her into the building.

"What do you mean?" Her head swiveled around as she took it all in. The students milling around, open classrooms, antique books inside display cases.

"We had to wait for classes to be back in session." I stopped in front of room 210, our destination. "We're here."

Her eyes widened, and she whispered, "Where are we?"

"We're being college students for the day. I thought you might like this class. It's called *Beyond the Isle: Themes and Worlds in Epic Fantasy*."

She gasped. "No. It's not..."

I nodded. "It is. And we better get in there, or we're going to miss the beginning."

She tugged on my hand. "Caleb, we can't just go in there. We...I..."

"We can, darlin'. It's all been arranged. Turns out, Professor Astor is something of a romantic."

The minute Jesse had mentioned Rhys Astor, the foremost expert on the *Shadow of the Isle* trilogy, who taught a class analyzing it at Savage U, an idea had sparked. It had taken a few emails and a phone call, then we were in.

"Professor Astor," she breathed. "He's teaching this class?"

"Of course." I took her chin between my fingers. "You ready?"

"Oh my goodness, *yes*."

We sat at the back of the room, behind students young enough to be my kids. I held Alice's shaking hand in mine as the professor strode into class. In his late fifties, his once-red hair was mostly white. He wore a crisp button-down, a waistcoat, and pressed slacks. Wire-rim glasses sat on his nose. I'd skipped going to college, but this guy was who I would have pictured as a literature professor.

As much as I'd enjoyed reading the trilogy, I'd come here for Alice, who'd been so inspired by these books, she'd written her own. They weren't published yet, but she'd finally let me read them, and like everything she did, they were incredible. Now she needed a push to share them with a wider audience. Maybe today would do it.

When Professor Astor got talking, I was on the edge of my seat as much as Alice. She was hanging on his every word, and I was right there with her. My thoughts were provoked as he discussed the symbolism in the story, making me want to read it all over again.

At the end, he waited for us in the front. Alice held my hand with both of hers as I led her to him. She was trembling, and I knew her well enough to recognize it was from both nerves and excitement.

I held my free hand out to him. "Professor Astor."

"And you have to be Caleb." He shook my hand. "Call me Rhys, please."

"Nice to meet you, Rhys." I pulled Alice in front of me. "This is my wife, Alice Kelly. She's the one who introduced me to this world."

Rhys's eyes crinkled as he smiled at her. "I hear you're a librarian. I have a special fondness for libraries. It's where my relationship with my wife, Delilah, began."

"Books can be very romantic." Her voice quivered, but she held herself straight and as tall as she could.

Rhys's smile was kind. "That I agree with. The written word is capable of evoking all manner of strong emotion, and romance is undoubtedly one of them. Now tell me, Alice, how did you enjoy my class?"

"Well, I wish I'd been able to sign up for it when I was actually a student here. As you know, it always fills up as soon as it opens."

He chuckled. "Yes, I'm quite popular, aren't I?"

That made Alice laugh. "You are, and for good reason. I've read your book, of course, but there's nothing like getting to listen to your analysis in person."

It was my absolute pleasure to watch them volley back and forth about their theories and interpretations of the story. My Alice was a book girl, and right about now, she was in heaven. Knowing I'd been the one to give her this—to put that smile on her face and light the flame in her eyes—was more than enough for me.

Too soon, Rhys checked the time on the watch he had tucked in the pocket of his waistcoat.

"As much as I'd like to keep this discussion going, I have office hours I need to get to," he announced.

We walked out of the classroom together, Alice and Rhys chatting all the way to his office. There, we stopped outside his door. He shook my hand again and gave Alice a hug.

"I heard from Caleb the two of you read the trilogy together," he said.

Alice nodded. "Caleb read it to me. It was kind of how we really started..."

Rhys rubbed his chin. "Another thing we have in common. I wooed my wife by reading to her too." He circled the air near Alice's bump. "It seems you're expecting."

"We are," she confirmed.

He hummed. "You didn't ask for my advice, but I'll offer it anyway. Delilah and I have six children. They're all adults now, and it's just us again at home, though we have a constantly revolving door of children and grandchildren coming through." He waved his hand. "That isn't the point. What I'm saying is, I never stopped reading to her. Even in the thick of parenting our brood, we found time for the thing that helped us fall in love with each other."

"Appreciate the advice," I said, intending to take it.

After we said our goodbyes to Rhys and made our way out of the building, I tugged Alice against me, holding her close. She tipped her head back, smiling.

"This was one of the best days of my life."

I bent to kiss her happy lips and murmured, "I knew you'd love it."

"That's because you really see me," she replied, her fingers curling into my shirt.

"Always. I see you so damn clearly, Alice Kelly." I rubbed my nose along hers. "You pick our next story, and I'll read it to you."

Her eyebrows rose. "Even if it's a spicy cowboy romance?"

"Even then." I gave her hair a light tug. "As long as you don't mind me pointing out all the inaccuracies."

She giggled. "Maybe we'll stick to fantasy."

She got going, listing all the books she wanted us to read together, telling me titles, debating which one we should start with. I just...held her and listened.

Knowing this was going to be my life.

A gorgeous woman in my arms. Our child between us and one back in Wyoming waiting for us. The home we shared. A town wrapped around us. Never-ending stories to read together.

Yeah, that sounded like a fantasy to me. Only this one was real, and it was all mine.

Stay In Touch

WANT TO HANG OUT? Join my reader group:
https://www.facebook.com/groups/JuliaWolfReaders

Acknowledgements

Before you ask, no, *Shadow of the Isle* isn't a real book. In my mind it is, but not in real life. I came up with it when I was writing *These Two Wrongs*. Can you guess who the MMC was in that book?

Yes, Rhys Astor AKA Professor Astor. How could a librarian not love Rhys's favorite book?

With each book I write in this world, I fall more in love with the Kelly family. There isn't another fictional place I'd like to go to more than the Kelly ranch. Who wouldn't love to sit down to dinner with the whole fam, then go stargazing with Silas?

I have to thank a few people who helped bring this book to life. First, thank you to Wander Aguiar for taking the perfect picture for the cover. They couldn't be any more Alice and Caleb if they tried.

Thank you to Kate for making this pretty cover, and Monica and Rose for editing the hell out of my words.

Without Amber, I'd be lost. Thank you for running my socials and my life.

And of course, thank *you*, reader. Your enthusiasm for my words keeps me going and inspires me to continue writing. I appreciate the hell out of you!

About Julia

Julia Wolf is a bestselling contemporary romance author. She writes bad boys with big hearts and strong, independent heroines. Julia enjoys reading romance just as much as she loves writing it. Whether reading or writing, she likes the emotions to run high and the heat to be scorching.

Julia lives in Maryland with her three crazy, beautiful kids and her patient husband who she's slowly converting to a romance reader, one book at a time.

Visit my website:
juliawolfwrites.com